Intelligent Para
Thrillers

By Dominic Buffery

# The Odyssey of Daniel Bonner

www.dominicbuffery.co.uk

Copy Editing by FCM Editing

Cover Design by FCM Media
www.fcmmedia.co.uk

IBSN 978 0 9926889 0 5

Published by

FCM PUBLISHING
www.fcmpublishing.co.uk

First printed in the UK - November 2013

FOR GEORGE AND LILLY

# CONTENTS



## Rags to riches

'Razor-wire,' groaned Daniel Bonner, as a flash of lightening danced across the steel butterfly blades, the final barrier to freedom. Behind him stood the Young Offenders' Correction Facility, in which he and his cell mate, Mark Cole had been incarcerated, and had lived a long year in an inhospitable atmosphere of cunning and survival.

Like a slumbering giant the prison had awoken, suddenly aware of their vacated cell, and the mournful wail of an alarm caxton, which spread news of their escape across the fifty metre band of cropped grass that was no-mans-land. Caught in the penetrating glare of rooftop searchlights, the two terrified boys kept running, and behind them, three prison dogs strained at their leashes, ready to bring down their quarry in the brutal way they had been trained. The handlers unleashed the German Shepherds, and once free from their chains, they sprang forward, quickly reaching the slash in the inner perimeter fence, through which Daniel and Mark had squeezed just moments before. Two of the pursuit dogs attempted to leap the twenty-foot high mesh fencing, but fell back in a snarling tangle. However, the third and largest animal used logic, running along the line until it found the gap. It forced its way through as the two boys had done.

Despair threatened to overwhelm Daniel and Mark, as they watched over their shoulders the single animal race towards them across the open ground, with the other dogs quickly following suit, sleek and deadly apparitions in the wind-driven rain, at twice the speed that any human could run.

The boys' legs felt suddenly leaden, and horribly inadequate, against the fleet-footed hunters, and without mercy, the lead dog slammed into the small of Mark Cole's back. He tumbled forward, hopelessly off balance, before sliding face down in the wet grass, like a landed fish on the slippery deck of an ocean-going trawler. Within seconds, the other two dogs were on him, tearing at his face and limbs, driven to a frenzy by his screams. Daniel glanced back. The dogs were tearing Mark apart, and not even the bellowed commands from the handlers could stop them. His screams became sickly squeals against the noise of the snarling animals and the storm that raged overhead. With a hopeless sense of loyalty, Daniel wrestled momentarily with the idea of going back to help his cell-mate, but the warders were now crowding around Mark's foetal form, making any attempt at rescue futile. The handlers tore the dogs from their victim, urging further pursuit, and in rapid response, Daniel spun on his heels and ran.

Mark's fate had inadvertently bought him valuable moments, and as scant protection, Daniel pulled his institution sweatshirt over his head, and plunged headlong into the baseline of the razor-wire. Frantically he clawed his way forward, but within seconds, the blades had cut relentlessly into his clothing and exposed flesh. He was hopelessly ensnared, and the more he struggled the greater the agony, until the dark hand of despair reached into his stomach and overwhelmed him. It was over. He had failed at the final hurdle, and the lacerations about his fifteen-year old face, stung beneath a flow of salty tears, and he heard his voice above the baying dogs and turmoil of the storm. It was a reckless plea for survival, and in those fateful moments of unthinking desperation, Daniel Bonner naïvely sold his soul to the Devil in exchange for freedom.

Ignorant of the enormity of his words, or that they now echoed along the corridors of the damned, he looked fearfully over his shoulder to the clear and present danger in the here and now. The dogs were almost upon him. And yet, in grateful irony, the razor-coils held firm between their snapping jaws and his young bleeding limbs.

More lightning split apart the broiling sky, and in the stark flash, Daniel detected movement on the free side of the perimeter. A lone figure had suddenly appeared in the driving rain, doing nothing, saying nothing, simply watching events unfold in the piercing glare of the searchlight, as the dogs wolf-like forms, haloed in the dazzle, hunted for an opening in the wire. Daniel cried out, and in turn, the stranger aimed a finger like the traversing muzzle of a machine gun, and incredulously the heavens calmed, and the dogs became still and silent. Placing his other arm under the razor-wire, the stranger began to lift the coils. Anchor fittings tore from the concrete placements, with a high tensile snap, like a pistol report, creating a tunnel just large enough for a body to pass under, and without hesitation, Daniel scrambled beneath the arch to the other side.

He stood dumbly before his liberator, listening to the other's simple instruction. The stranger's face was shrouded in darkness by the wide brimmed hat that he wore, and the long black hair that tumbled from his temples. His eyes glittered through the shadows like polished jet, and his voice cracked like a bull-whip that should have carried a hundred paces. Yet it was only Daniel with an ear to its sound.

'Follow each lightening strike. Do not deviate from the direction in which they point, and you shall find sanctuary, Daniel Bonner'. 'What are you waiting for boy, go now, and I shall hold your tormentors back, for as long as necessary.'

The boom and crackle of his voice was unnatural and frightening, but despite the shock of its volume, Daniel understood the instruction implicitly. He stared into the rain-laden clouds, as a vivid blade of lightening returned, and ripped open the belly of the clouds, slicing northward above the inhospitable moor. Without further prompting, he followed the order, and crashed into the night through the stubborn rows of wet gorse, that clung around his torn and laboured legs in a frustrating embrace. Thunder rolled against the hills of the moor, like a cannonade of heavy guns, and the stranger continued to stand alone to face the dogs and their masters. Against all odds, the animals sat placidly watching his every move, until the handlers eventually reached the razor-wire, accompanied with breathless threats of arrest by the senior officer. In reply the stranger stood his ground, staring into the glare, a chuckle resonating from his chest with such extraordinary volume, that any discerning baritone would have given his very life for.

'This ain't funny laughing boy,' bellowed the rather bewildered handler, soaked to the skin with sweat and rain, his fellow officers alike. 'I'll have you laughing on the other side of your bloody face when I get you this side of the wire, then your ass is mine.'

Already two security Land Rovers, laden with personnel, tore along the outside of the perimeter fence from both directions, headlamps on full beam, with electric blue strobe lights flashing the hallmark of their authority through the customised grilles. Above the roar of engines, the senior handler gave orders to initiate the stranger's arrest through the wire, unaware of the prison dogs' sudden change in attitude. The crescendo of the storm had returned, and without warning, the big male dog sank its canines into the warder's groin, with the impact of an attacking shark. All Hell broke loose; the attack dogs were out of control, lunging for their masters. The handlers thrashed the brutes, with a maelstrom of blows from heavy chain leads, but against such savage determination, they stood little chance against the animals. Bone and sinew collapsed in human flesh; the jaw of an unfortunate warder snapped in a crushing bite, as the second dog hung from its handler's face, before he was dragged screaming to the ground. The third circled relentlessly about its victim, before rushing in to lock its teeth into the fleshy part of the upper thigh, just below the buttock. It was a monstrous scene of frenzied primal aggression, the men fighting for their very survival, strangling, punching, kicking, in a vain attempt to once more become the masters they had long ago been conditioned to be. And as they began to weaken, the search-lights suddenly failed. The filaments dimmed then died, the vehicles headlight bulbs exploded in their reflectors, and their engines ground to a halt. The snarling of dogs, and the crying of men, faded into another disturbing calm, apart from the rain that continued to fall, heavy as bird-shot, and the stranger disappeared like a phantom into the night.

Deep in a vast circular subterranean chamber, the Devil's Chancellor sat on a forty foot high rock dais, surveying his army of grotesque minions, from the elevated position of his granite throne. Fifty well-trodden steps led down from the plateaux, to a hundred metre ring of flat bedrock, forming an encompassing auditorium. At the far perimeter of the bedrock, ran interspersed walls of intricately laid twenty-four carat gold brick gabions, stacked to one metre in height. They stretched away in gigantic segments, like that of a grapefruit when sliced in half across its girth. These were then interspersed by flagstone causeways, leading to the outer walls of the chamber, hazy with distance. Most of the one hundred segments were brimming with every conceivable treasure known to man, countless millions of uncut diamonds larger than a man's fist; emeralds, rubies, sapphires, and other stones more precious, yet to be discovered by the human world. In others stood the refinements of man; marble and stone sculptures, jewellery of unquestionable quality, gold chalices, crafted precious metal artefacts, priceless art, scriptures and writings, undocumented drawings and charts from the likes of Galileo and Da Vinci, others dating back from the invention of the wheel and beyond, a living testament to the ingenuity and progress of humankind. However, there were half the number again, that sat strangely empty, standing in readiness to house the artefacts that had yet to catalogue the fascinating evolution of homo-sapiens, and their hitherto unknown discoveries. The Chancellor had gloated all his day, at the precious rocks and metals, but over the millennia had tired of the priceless works of yesteryear. He longed for the new generation of probabilities, with which to manipulate and cajole man's basic instincts and weaknesses… invention, profit, greed and exploitation, to name but a few. Such was the existence and meaning of his office.

Set in the breathtaking span of the domed ceiling two hundred metres above, were embedded a million Sonantine Crystals, an element of infinite light and power, found only in selected pockets of the near-molten mantel, twenty miles beneath the earth's crust. It had been decreed by the Underworld, that it should remain undiscovered, until such time when mankind was ready for its use. If released too soon it would culminate in Armageddon, and if mankind should die, it would also herald the end of the dark and light angels. One day, far in the distant future, the time would be right for its discovery; but not yet. The supporting circular wall, a kilometre distant, was clad with towering treasures of architecture, wall-art and carvings, both ancient and modern, from around the world. Mayan, Inca, Egyptian, Greek, Roman, African, Aboriginal, Native American, and many others, that continued along two-thirds of the outer circumference, to end with the modern styles of the twenty-first century. The rest lay empty, as a blank canvass, in readiness for humanity's changing world. At the end of each causeway were circular apertures, like colossal storm-drains, the archways dressed in red-veined marble blocks, that accentuated the ominous darkness that lay beyond, deeper than sound could travel. It was from these gateways, that the Chancellor's brood had appeared, to travel the causeways and gather before their master at the centre. They looked up expectantly at the throne, silent and domicile.

Their wait was soon rewarded, as the Chancellor relinquished his throne for the one and only superior force in his existence, his Lord and master, the Devil himself. He had risen up through the living rock, to take his seat in silence, and an audible sigh of fear, awe and anticipation saturated the air around the heads of the waiting ranks. The Chancellor took his rightful place at his side, his rugged, almost handsome features, unmoving and expressionless, but never without an attentive ear.

'So we have a new and special candidate?' smiled the Devil, as he lounged in a pair of casual faded denim jeans, short-sleeved polo shirt and scuffed leather loafers. Locks of coiled golden hair folded back over his shoulders, seemingly with a life of their own. His face and body was a symmetrical sculpture, an unquestionable perfection of the human form, capable of winning or destroying the hearts of all that laid eyes on him, man or woman, bird or beast.

The exposed skin on the under part of his forearm, crackled and seared like pork rind beneath the shimmering heat of the near molten armrests of the throne, and he quivered ecstatically. Overjoyed at his master's obvious delightful burning, the Chancellor nodded sagely.

'You think we should treat this one with care?' the Devil suggested, inhaling the rancid smoke of his own burning flesh with something of a blissful sigh. The Chancellor's circle of disgusting creatures watched, in love and awe, from the stinking lower bedrock, as the wounds of their lord healed, then disappeared without trace.

'Enlighten me,' ordered the Devil.

He truly need not have asked. He was the font of all knowledge, but knew the necessity of empowering his Chancellor with such importance. It had been the way for thousands of years, and would continue to be so, providing his Chancellor remained useful.

'He is a fugitive from earth's law, my Lord... incarcerated for a murder. of which, believe it or not, he is actually innocent. He has suffered imprisonment for the sake of Stephen Bonner, his drug-addled sibling. Daniel was in the wrong place at the wrong time, later misguided into thinking his brother would come to right the wrong, and save him with a confession of guilt. Unable to betray Stephen, Daniel Bonner waited alone, and at the mercy of the court, was sentenced to immediate detention at the Queen's pleasure, until his eighteenth birthday, whereupon his case would then be heard for final sentencing. His brother never appeared, nor indeed was ever likely to, and our protégée, has clung to an idiotic sense of family honour and loyalty ever since, silent with the truth.'

'Then he's hardly a likely candidate for this world. Not exactly a wanton soul. Wouldn't you agree?' said the Dark Angel, comparing Daniel with the writhing sea of alcove dwellers below him. 'Surely this is not the reason for this meeting?'

'At this point I would agree, his soul is indeed untouched, my Lord.'

'Then perhaps you plan to instigate a crossroads of attitude in his life, maybe to cast a number of soul-changing deviations before him, as we have done with so many others.' The Devil made an expansive gesture with an outstretched arm, over the uncountable power and wealth of his exchequer. 'Avarice, my dear Chancellor, never fails, and yet I fail to understand the reason for this hastened council.' His question was utterly convincing, even though he knew the answer in the writings.

'Perhaps I can explain my Lord.'

The Devil prompted the other with a slight inclination of his golden curls, which danced like gossamer strands of spring steel, to the movement of his head.

'Daniel Bonner is young and we have his lifetime to work on this particular individual's weaknesses. However, from the moment I saved him from the razor- wire, I had a feeling about this young man, a very strong feeling my Lord. He's different to the others we harvest in droves on a daily basis. Something tells me he shall figure strongly in the future. He could very well be the one chosen to test the sea of filth at our feet. My Lord, as you have pointed out to me so often, there shall come a mortal in this very millennium, to play the great game like no other has done for thousands of years, as is indeed written in the scriptures.'

'Interesting,' mused the Overlord. 'If this is the one, then we must guard him closely. We must maintain the advantage. Keep him hidden for now, and when he has been given up for lost or dead by the authorities, I shall then decide what to do with him. As it is with every mortal, his pathway through life is written in the books; I shall read his story with interest. You shall find me in the Library of Time should the need arise. Keep me informed my dear Chancellor, with every faithful beat of your rotten heart.'

The Chancellor acquiesced with a flourishing hand, and bowed low before his master, delighting with the accolade. And down in the amphitheatre his army continued to listen in respectful silence.

'In due course,' concluded the Devil, 'all authoritarian records of Daniel Bonner shall be erased, so that he may be free to do your bidding. I alone shall see to that.'

The Chancellor gave another low bow, but before he could straighten, the Devil had disappeared back through the granite. The sudden loss of his presence to every one in attendance was appalling, and many standing on the bedrock, wept. Such was their love.

And I the Scribe recorded it so.

Anthony Windrow found Daniel Bonner, wandering aimlessly along an unbeaten track, dog tired and close to desperation. Escape was one thing but without adequate food and shelter, he was, in the prison vernacular, a dead man walking. He shivered against the wet and the cold, his guts cramped and churned with the sour fluid of desperate hunger, and above, the sun was obscured by the dense banks of cloud, that rolled in from the east, threatening yet more rain.

Unaware of his presence, Windrow studied Daniel from an obscured vantage point. The lad was tall, broad-shouldered, with a heavy neck, sporting a dense covering of cropped black hair, a testament to his youth. His jaw was set square, giving him an air of determination and decidedly good looks. But there was something else beyond his impressive, somewhat lacerated physique. Windrow detected an aura of formidable inner strength, perhaps even the infancy of latent power. Regardless of the escapee's fragile situation, Daniel Bonner showed the hallmarks of one day becoming an entity not to be ignored. Windrow concluded his appraisal, as he stepped out from behind an outcrop of rock, and onto the track.

Daniel froze, standing stone-faced and guarded at Windrow's sudden appearance. Quickly he sized the other up. Windrow appeared to be in his mid- forties, though difficult to accurately discern his age through his rugged face, that was neither handsome nor ugly, but strong with a proud forehead and large Roman nose. As he shifted his stance, Daniel noticed a lithe swagger in the other, like that of a boxer preparing a strike; a physique of a man half his age. Beneath his wide-rimmed bush-hat, he matched Daniel's six foot three inches in height, and with his black leather coat draped from shoulder to mid-calf, he possessed a dangerous mien; collectively a figure belonging more to the Australian outback, a world away from this very Dartmoor. For long moments, it was a stand-off as they judged each other, but with Windrow's eventual disarming smile, and the offering of a water canteen, Daniel felt moderately reassured. However, an understandable level of distrust remained.

'Tony Windrow,' he said introducing himself, accompanied with an open palm.

'And you are?'

Daniel was deeply suspicious. Who on earth was this stranger, offering his hand and enquiring after names? He didn't like the situation at all.

Tony saw the look of concern, and the corners of his mouth broadened into a smile. 'Actually, I already know who you are, Master Bonner.'

Daniel took a step backwards. In the correctional facility he had heard stories of modern-day bounty hunters, who would bring their man in, using guile, and if necessary brute force, to achieve their goal. Windrow had to be a hunter; after all he very much looked the part. He couldn't be anything else.

Daniel was close to running, and would have done so had Windrow's following words not been so disarming.

'There's no cause for alarm, boy. You're in no danger…well not from this quarter anyway. You see, I know the situation you're in.' Daniel turned to face the unexpected revelation, but remained primed to take flight at an instant's notice.

'I also escaped from that particular holiday camp many years ago.' continued Windrow. 'Locked up for reasons we shan't go into right now, but from that time to this, I have remained free.'

Daniel held his uncertain ground, plucking up enough courage to shake Windrow's continually extended hand, and the stranger's grip was firm, confident, and surprisingly reassuring.

'I've learned the ways of the moor,' continued Windrow, 'and more importantly the knowledge of how to survive.' He looked directly at Daniel. 'Do you want to survive Danny? Do you want to stay free, because if you do, I'm the only one who can show you how?' He released the grip.

Daniel remained in the middle field of suspicion, but nodded sharply. In reality he had little choice.

'Good! Then we'll lead the bastards a merry dance, and I'll be damned if we don't enjoy it. There hasn't been much excitement out here for a long while, and I'm in the mood. But be warned, they'll search for you every daylight hour and more, but eventually they will give you up as having moved on. Trust me. I know how it works.'

Despite remaining sceptical, Daniel recognised Windrow was throwing him a lifeline, and so he clung to his every word. The unexpected prospect of salvation was all he needed to hear. And he really didn't much care why.

In the days that followed, and as Windrow had predicted, the search was relentless. Tracker dogs and ground beaters required constant evasive action. Yet no matter how often the authorities came close, Windrow knew exactly what to do. He was a master in the art of vanishing, seemingly into thin air, laying false trails, and giving the dogs and handlers the infuriating run-around. Daniel witnessed first hand, his astonishing ability to manipulate the animals, and throughout such chases, the merit of his skills were proven time and time again. On one occasion, a lone dog caught up with them. Its handler had unleashed the animal over a trail too strong and fresh to ignore. The huge canine tore at them across the rugged ground, and would have dragged Daniel kicking to the ground, had it not been for Tony's sharp command, that brought the beast to a skidding halt. What happened next would have defied belief had Daniel not witnessed it first hand. The dog sat panting placidly at Tony's side, waiting for instruction, as if he were its only true master. It was then sent blindly along a moorland trail in the opposite direction, much to Daniel's astonishment, and boyish delight. However, within an hour of that particular encounter they heard the pulsating rotors of an approaching helicopter, the noise of its powerful engine soon overriding all other natural sounds of the moor. They instinctively knew this was their biggest threat. With a view from the air the searching authorities held the upper hand; an eye in the sky, superior to all other search capabilities. Armed with a thermal imagery camera they could detect and target heat signatures from long range, even under dense foliage or thick cloud cover. Daniel looked helplessly at Tony for guidance, and in answer, Tony rose to his feet and stood tall above the sanctuary of the scrub, deliberately exposing himself to the oncoming airborne threat. 'The man's gone bloody mad,' thought Daniel, as Tony held his head high, willing the chopper to alter course and find a direct path towards him, and as was his death-wish, the G-FTWO Eurocopter banked sharply in the low afternoon sun, and began its approach.

'Sky Eye to Ground Search,' said the pilot calmly into the Air Band Radio. 'We have visual one thousand metres due east of your current position. The suspect fugitive is one hundred metres away on our nose, with what appears to be another male alongside. We'll guide you in.'

Suddenly, Tony crouched low and crawled deep into the surrounding scrub. Daniel, greatly relieved that he had at last seen sense, followed suit.

'Sierra Echo to Ground-Search. Suspects have gone to ground. Transmitting GPS coordinates and switching to thermal eye.'

Two hundred feet above their heads, the G-FTWO hovered like a hunting falcon following Daniel and Tony's every move.

'Ground-Search to Sky Eye, received and understood transmitted location. Initiating Ground-Noose. It looks like we have them.'

High above the ground the surveillance systems' operator stared at the screen, then spoke to the pilot through his helmet intercom.

'Bloody strange, I can only see one of them. His image is clearer than Blackpool illuminations on a clear night. But the other seems to have disappeared.' And the pilot held his aircraft steady as a rock, beneath the constant clatter of rotors. The screen faithfully depicted Daniel's crawling figure, not to mention the ever-advancing ground-search several hundred metres to the right. But of Tony Windrow, there was no sign. The trackers on the ground pressed relentlessly forward.

Suddenly a blinding flash emanated from the thermal imaging screen, filling the helicopter cockpit with such intense light, it momentarily blinded the operator, and the G-FTWO spiralled a hundred metres to starboard, before the pilot regained control.

'What the Hell was that,' he snarled through the intercom. 'What the fuck just hit us?'

The operator, stunned by the intensity of light, held his hand against the punishing glare, his vision still starred with the flash. Then, just as suddenly, the screen changed from dazzling white to a lifeless pewter, like that of a blinded eye.

'We have complete surveillance systems' failure,' he reported, his voice distorted through the sudden static of the intercom, and the helicopter continued its uncontrollable lee to the west. The pilot managed to maintain altitude, but was unable to counteract the drift, and below the bewildered ground-search followed their lead.

'Sierra Echo to Ground-Search, maintain your previous heading. We are experiencing major problems up here. I repeat...maintain previous heading, do not follow our flight...do you copy?'

More static answered his transmission, and the G-FTWO led the ground force yet further away.

Under the blanket of scrub, Daniel punched the air in triumph, as he watched the receding aircraft, but as he stared at Windrow, he saw a look in the other's dark eyes. His expression was deadly with hateful concentration, so intense the air seemed to pulsate around them with its energy, until at last the helicopter flew erratically from view. Eventually, Windrow's eyes softened, and with relief Daniel accepted, no matter how strange, that they had somehow avoided the airborne arm of the law, and the alarm regarding his guardian slowly abated.

The episode was consigned the back of Daniel's mind, as Tony continued to prove himself an extraordinary individual. Not so much a father figure, but more of an avuncular guardian; protective and yet so much more daring in his approach to life to that of any uncle. He felt safe in his company, and in the following weeks continued to do exactly as instructed. Tony had treated the cuts to Daniel's face and hands with great care against infection, and they had healed without fear of permanent scaring. As the scabs fell away they left only thin lines of healthy tissue, that under Windrow's assurance would in time fade to nothing. With growing faith in his tutor, Daniel's feeling of respect and trust, evolved into something stronger than he had ever experienced in his previous fifteen years of living.

The task of teaching rudimentary survival proved easier for Windrow than he had expected. Daniel was a natural, and in a few short months, had not only accepted his new way of life, but had begun to truly master the crucial art of bush-craft. With increased stamina, he was able to cross the uncompromising topography of the moor, better suited to the mountain goat, than two legs of the human. However, Daniel could now speed run over broken ground, scaling the craggy Tors, dips and the relentless upheaval of nature's chaos, that was the moor. In a relatively short period he had surpassed Windrow's expectations, and the freedom to run in such an unhindered way, became the backbone of his survival.

In and amongst a dozen other essential items, Tony presented his protégée with a throwing stick; a skilfully carved three-foot length of oak that was quickly to become Daniel's favourite hunting tool. On face value, it was a relatively innocuous item, but in reality proved to be a deadly weapon, when used in the correct manner for which it was designed. At each end, were identical hardwood nodules, the size of a cricket ball, creating a perfect balance. It could be thrown with surprising accuracy, either as a spinning missile, capable of bringing down several birds in flight, or thrown as a club-ended javelin, to strike a target with bone-shattering impact. It negated the use of snares; a practice, Daniel had thought from the outset as inhumane. He would much prefer to use the Hummer, so named for the sound it made in flight, rather than the slow and often unpredictable garrotte.

He quickly became adept with the required throwing skills, and was soon out-mastering his tutor. Tony, of course, reminded Daniel that it was his tutorial skills, that had elevated his ward to such a high standard. But in truth, Tony recognised the other to be more than just gifted with use of the weapon, and was heartily pleased with the results.

In the months that followed, the mental mapping of Daniel's surroundings became indelible, especially the whereabouts of every natural food store at his disposal. The blackberry cloisters, the mushroom fields, the sheltered dips of wild garlic, the watercress streams, the preferred roosting places of pheasant, partridge and pigeon and numerous rabbit warrens. He exploited the disused quarries, filled by a million rainfalls, in which trout, perch, eel and other species moved through the deep waters, fearless of hook and line. Under such competent teaching, Daniel was awarded one of Windrow's rare accolades, as being an undisputed survivor, won with a master's degree.

'I bet you were part of one of the Special Force Groups,' said Daniel one day. It was an unprompted question, and not without the leading edge of admiration.

'Been around a bit,' Windrow replied softly, staring into the middle distance. 'One or two testing exercises.' But that was all Daniel was given; there were pressing issues at hand.

'What do you think of your chances of survival in the winter, Danny?'

It was a good question that required due consideration.

‘Pretty damn slim,’ he said after little thought. 'It’s hard enough out here in the summer, can't imagine how tough it gets in the winter months?'

‘Glad you recognise the problem,' said Windrow. 'No man can live out here in all seasons without adequate shelter. Come with me Danny.’

Their first port of call was an isolated quarry, in which stood a stone cottage, that had, in most parts, been restored by the National Trust, until insufficient funding had brought the project to a halt, several years previously. The windows were boarded and weatherproof, with a solid oak door in the jamb, above which was a newly-slated roof, expertly laid and reassuringly secure.

Daniel noticed the heavy padlock on the door, linked through an equally robust latch. Tony read his mind, and showed Daniel the fruits of some of his previous handy work. With the point of a knife, he prised out four coach screws holding the galvanised flap to the frame, and the door swung open.

‘Took these out and enlarged the screw holes a while ago.’

Daniel smiled at the deception and followed Tony inside. The interior was a single room affair, with a discarded folding camp-bed and a fisherman’s chair left, behind by the restoration team. On the far wall a simple fireplace had been built into the dressed stone, beside which was piled a stack of seasoned firewood.

‘All the creature comforts needed, eh Daniel?’

‘This is bloody great. But what if someone finds me here?’

‘The Park Ranger periodically makes his rounds during the summer, but it’s very unlikely that he, or anyone else for that matter, will venture out this far in the deep mid-winter. Use this place only during that time, and only when necessary. Burn only dry logs, as they give off less smoke. Start gathering as soon as possible, it will keep you occupied. In the meantime I’ll show you some other natural shelters, that you’ll find more than adequate in milder weather.’

‘It makes me want to stay here now.’

'Don't even think about it Daniel my boy. Now, come on, before the thought of this little palace, and its home comforts, turns you soft in the noggin, we have a lot to do.'

I the Scribe, forever to keep busy my loaded quill, am proud to write that Daniel never once softened.

After a year on the run, Daniel Bonner remained free. The authorities had long given up the search, and the need of Windrow's close supervision, had become a thing of the past. However, Daniel wasn't entirely alone. On several occasions, he had chanced upon Jesse, a master poacher, and his rat-catching dog, Zip. He was a man of the moor, much like himself, who certainly had as many survival skills as in Daniel's arsenal. Jesse was a heavily-muscled man, with short powerful legs, a deep-water tan, and a ruff of tight curly blonde hair, that ran as an unruly thicket, down his bull neck. His eyes were bright and alert, green as topaz, set in a balding cannonball head of weathered skin. Several scars on his face denoted his prowess as a brawling man, in yesteryear's ignorance of testosterone-fuelled youth. Now in his thirties, he had slowly accepted Daniel's presence on the moor, and the early if not uneasy truce recognised by both, had more than just a potential of becoming a true friendship. Notwithstanding that evolution, Jesse was probably one of the best men to have on one's side in a fight. Daniel had quickly come to the conclusion that he genuinely liked the man, and each time they met, the bond of mutual respect grew strong. He had an ally, other than Windrow, out there on the moor, and one he knew he could rely on if ever he was in need of help.

Unaware of the growing alliance, Tony Windrow dutifully visited the moor with replacement clothing and survival equipment, though as time went by, far less frequently. His ward was safe, a genuine survivor in his own right. He had learned the art of evasion so skilfully, that it had become difficult for even Windrow, to readily counter his moves, leaving him with little option but to haul Daniel in, with the call of the cock pheasant, annoying perhaps, yet deep down met with silent approval. He had taught Bonner well, who had not only listened and learned, but had made his own subtle and thoughtful variations.

Over time, his and Windrow's relationship strengthened, and besides, Jesse, it became the only true friendship, Daniel had really ever known. On each visit the two would sit by the open fire, Tony telling Daniel of the lessening interest by the authorities of the boy who had escaped from the Young Offenders' Prison. On one such occasion, Windrow turned the conversation to the subject of Daniel's future. Surviving on the moor was one thing, but hardly a satisfactory or fulfilling vocation. But, as with any sixteen year-old, Daniel had no idea what he should ultimately become. With no parental guidance, an element tragically snuffed from existence when his parent's car had ploughed into the pathway of an oncoming forty-tonne truck, he had no compunction whatsoever to leave the moor. With diminishing memories of his parents, the wild place had become the missing haven he had long craved for, in which he had carved out a new way of life. Windrow was now his true guardian. Tony dropped the subject realising, Daniel wasn't yet ready for any major vocational decisions. There would be plenty of time for such matters in the future.

The seasons passed seamlessly into years, and Bonner entered the confident age of early manhood. All lingering garlands of puppy fat had long been burned from his body, replaced with hard muscle, sculptured by the uncompromising chisel of moorland life. His formidable height, broad shoulders, long black tresses, and equally resplendent beard, gave him a wild if not frightening persona, enough to throw all rambling visitors who chanced upon him, into fast reverse. As they avoided him, he likewise avoided them, forever conscious, that one day he might be exposed as the missing fugitive. He had no way of knowing, that his true identity had long ago been eradicated from the judicial files, and through that extraordinary release, had unknowingly become prisoner to a far greater authority.

He sat stripped to the waist, sharpening a bone-handled hunting knife on a slab of granite, the blade a much cherished gift from Tony. With his leather long-coat and tee-shirt removed, the sun beat steadily on his tanned back. Preoccupied hadn't noticed Tony's approach. He looked up when sensing the other's presence, only to find Tony staring at him with unusual intensity.

'What a difference five years has made on you, Mister Bonner, from a frightened boy, to how you are today. I would suggest very few could physically match your strength. You've come of age,' he said with a respectful grin, 'and I'm glad we walk the same path, as I now consider myself very probably outclassed.'

Daniel rose from his task. He returned a hand of friendship that had stood the test of time. Tony's grip was as always, firm and heartfelt, and yet Daniel noticed an unusual challenge in the contact, a squeeze to test his strength. In response he smiled and returned the pressure. Within moments their torsos were locked in a mid-air arm wrestle, their smiles frozen. Sinews, tendons and muscles, flexed on either side, and suddenly, and for a frightening moment, they embraced the inconceivable notion of being mortal enemies. Their eyes locked like bull horns in a territorial fight, unimaginably deadly, a deep-seated throwback from the beginnings of primal man, and the level of the contest soared rapidly to breaking point.

Slowly Daniel began to take control. The veins in Tony's neck bulged as he tried arresting the tide of power, forcing his arm downwards and sideways. Something had to eventually give, and with Tony's sudden capitulation, it was over.

With a burst of laughter, Tony relinquished his grip, and with a strong cuff to Daniel's shoulder, ended the contest.

'It's like I said Danny my boy, I'm glad you're on my side.'

he fire in Daniel's eyes took a little longer to fade. He shook his shaggy head, freeing himself from the spell with a smile that replaced his granite expression.

'What was that all about, Tony?' he said, nursing his bicep.

'Just confirming my suspicions, that's all.'

'What suspicions?'

'Not only are you an ugly bastard, but you also have a physical strength superior to mine, you cocky git!'

Daniel's smile broadened into a laugh, difficult to extinguish, given Tony's open insulting accolade which, in itself, was something unusual. It was then Daniel noticed the others thoughtful expression had returned. He relaxed his smile and asked for the reason.

'Sit down Danny, there's something I have to tell you.'

As always, Daniel did as he was told; more so when detecting the importance in the tone of the request. Something was troubling his friend.

'Spit it out you old bugger,' chuckled Daniel nervously, 'I've a pheasant to knock down.' He hefted the Hummer.

Tony cleared his throat. 'It's your brother.'

'Stephen! What about him?'

'Don't know quite how to say this, so I'll come straight to the point.' Frustratingly, Tony took a few moments to nip his lower lip in consideration, before inhaling a lungful of air. Daniel raised an eyebrow, urging him to continue.

Tony uttered the bad news through an expulsion of breath.

'Stephen died of an overdose three weeks ago…I'm sorry.'

The revelation was brusque and to the point, striking Daniel like a thunderbolt. He blinked as if grit had been blown into his eyes.

'Stephen, dead...You'd better be bloody joking!'

'Sorry Danny, I'm afraid it's true.'

Daniel lowered his head, his heart felt suddenly heavy, sorrow and grief moved like a fat slug in the pit of his stomach.

'I'm truly sorry Danny.'

Without knowing what to do or say, he walked silently away in a daze, and Tony understood the need for him to gather his private thoughts to begin tackling the pain of loss. Suddenly, Daniel turned.

'The funeral…what about the funeral?'

'Done and dusted I'm afraid.'

'Oh God, I should have been there.' He made as if to turn again but stopped. 'Was there any mention of me?'

'Well, Danny, that's the weird part. In the printed obituary there was no mention of any living next of kin. It's as if you never existed. Bloody strange if you ask me, there's no way I can begin to explain it.'

'But they must know I exist. Nobody just disappears from the records, especially me. It's a trap…the cunning bastard's are trying to lure me out. It's a dirty trick.' Daniel could feel his temper rising in the bewildering fog of frustration and grief.

'Daniel,' Tony paused to think, 'for some inexplicable reason your entire history has vanished into the ether. However, given the circumstances, I reckon it's got to be for the best. I took the liberty of doing my own research. It looks very much to me like you've been given the luckiest break in your life, and all because of some extraordinary administrative cock-up.'

'What the hell's going on Tony?'

'Beats me…but one thing's for sure, you can now move on to other things. Sorry for being blunt but that seems to be the way of it.'

Daniel temporarily laboured beneath an avalanche of emotions, but in a matter of moments swept away his tears. His friend was right. Hard nosed and true to form, he, as always, made sense.

'Sorry, Tony, fuck off. I need to be alone.'

As I the Scribe, make entry in the Chancellor's journals, I fear more for Daniel at this point, than ever before. This was a new obstacle to overcome, so much more powerful than anything physical, and my hand, forever armed with quill, and deep with interest, hovered above the parchment of dried human skin, upon which I write.

In the weeks that followed the bad news, Daniel's thoughts belonged entirely to his family, with scant childhood memories, cut short by the untimely death of his parents. Daniel and Stephen had been spared the details, apart from the one small mercy that their parents' deaths had been instant, as documented in the last paragraph of the coroner's report. The process of recovery, however, had been a long drawn-out affair for the two boys, especially Stephen, the younger and chronically-wayward brother. They had adored both parents, but more so their father, who throughout their childhood, had nurtured and guided Stephen though many difficult and rebellious times. He had been their rock, someone to look up to, respect and admire, but within three years of his death, Stephen had lapsed into periods of violent moods, and countless run-ins with the law, and not without reason. Cocaine had become the matrix of his new and lonely world, it being the answer to all things, or so he was told by those who would benefit from his addiction. But under the influence of an ever-increasing habit, Stephen had quickly fallen into unfamiliar territory, devoid of friends, wealth or health. His once more-than-adequate weekly allowance, the disbursement of a modest inheritance, was spent faster than received and the downward spiral of theft, deceit and debt had swamped his world. But now, suddenly, it was all over. He was dead.

Daniel sat deep in thought on Badger Head Tor, a rugged and barren place, where the wind scoured the rocks, a place visited on such occasions to contemplate. He fought back the corrosive anger that had blossomed beneath his initial feelings of sorrow. He had been betrayed and left to rot in the institution, after assisting his brothers' victim, stabbed in a bungled side-street mugging. Stephen's knife blade had remained embedded, deep in the victim's chest, and as Daniel had pulled it out in an attempt to save the dying man, his brother had run from the slaying, leaving Daniel a condemned man. Stephen had barely left, when a side-door, leading into the alley from the high street restaurant, had unexpectedly opened, and the dumbstruck chef, and later chief prosecution witness, took justifiable stock of the situation, beneath the glare of the kitchen's neon lights. Daniel might just as well have been holding a smoking gun, despite his pleas for assistance and immediate ambulance attendance. He never left the victim's side, unfortunately a loser in the struggle for life. But no matter how damning the evidence, Daniel could never expose his brother as the perpetrator, either at the time of his arrest, or indeed at any other appropriate moment, that could well have saved him. As he languished through the seemingly endless judicial process, and subsequent incarceration, he always believed his brother would eventually step up to the mark, confess his guilt, and initiate Daniel's release. But Daniel was to discover, he had been abandoned.

Now high on the Tor, his anger slowly abated, and eventually gave way to a more considered view of Stephen's death and, if what Tony said was true, he was now a free man, with a wholly unexpected set of options before him. The more he pondered his brother's failures, the more he questioned his own rather surreal existence. Stephen had been the victim to the darker side of life, but what practical good was there hiding, like some hunted animal, doing nothing with just a tainted memory of his brother's failings? If in the eyes of the authorities, he no longer existed then he would put it to the test. And in that moment, Daniel Bonner arrived at a life-changing decision.

The Chancellor's army had travelled from their alcoves along the gabion causeways, to gather at the centre of the Exchequer. They were ebullient and noisy, spitting insults and crudities at one another in the foetid air. The noise was intolerable, until out of nowhere the Devil, wearing nothing more intimidating than a loose pullover, casual trousers and flip-flop's, crushed the head of the noisiest imp like that of a ripe grape. Another foul creature came to him, and licked the bloody matter from his palm, like a lapdog eager to please. The lair fell quieter than a crypt, and the Devil floated up to the Dais, with the blood-hungry leach still clinging to his hand, as he sat on the hot-rock throne, waiting for the Chancellor's report. There were important matters to discuss, and with a heavy hand, he slapped the subservient imp away, to fall from the Dais into the broiling masses below.

'My Lord,' began the Chancellor. 'He wishes to leave the moor as we planned, but he wants to create wealth, in order to assist others like his late brother. His cause is disgustingly philanthropic, running entirely against the doctrine of this house. He is full of charitable vomit, and I now question the wisdom of my somewhat hurried investment. That being the case we may lose the power of control over his soul. Perhaps you can advise me, my Lord? Do I drag him down to face the wrath of this sea of filth, or do I simply kill him?' The writhing army below pressed closer to the Dais, in foul anticipation.

The Devil leaned forward, the skin on the palms of his hands, crackling under the heat. He lifted the smouldering digits and covered his face, inhaling a cloud of greasy smoke before answering.

'Let us take the gamble. Put this human to the test, my dear Chancellor. Let him make his money, and plenty of it. His friend Anthony Windrow will make available two hundred thousand pounds to begin his venture into capitalism. And we all know how money corrupts. I shall reinstate his records, with a history as a law-abiding citizen, and with your expert guidance, who knows, we may yet darken his soul to a blackened crisp, worthy of this world?'

'Very well my Lord, it shall be initiated.' And the Chancellor bowed low.

The Devil acknowledged the subservient gesture, with a glib wave, and moved from the hot-rock seat. He floated down the granite steps. He stood before his army, and reached down to extract an unrecognisable life-form from the masses. It slopped on the bedrock at his feet, in a tangle of slippery limbs, and the Devil raised it gently to a standing position. The Chancellor barely recognising it as being human. Fascinated, he looked on.

As the Devil walked away, the creature held his hand; an ancient crone barely able to walk. But the further they moved away, she transformed. With every step, a young woman emerged, naked and reborn. She became an image of unparalleled beauty, the finest form the dwellers of the dark environs, had ever seen. Her very presence touched even the Chancellor's rotten loins, influencing his normally dismissive attitude, and he wondered at the power his master held over time and matter.

Draping her arm over the Devil's shoulder, the girl tore her eyes from the side of his handsome head, and glowered at the gathered army, with eyes of unquestionable power, like that of a Pharaoh Queen, being led willingly down into the carnal quarters by her king. Then they were gone, with her bright laughter ringing in their ears.

The Chancellor sank thoughtfully into his throne. What he had just witnessed, had not been merely coincidental. The Devil had set him a task and should he fail, the consequences would be dire. The demonstration was plain. Whatever the Devil destroyed, could be returned, and likewise all that he gave could be taken away. It was a blatant warning.

When the mighty Marlin comes to feed, he is but a minnow when hooked on the unbreakable line. Fabled words from my master, the Chancellor, and yet I the scribe wish nothing more, than to test that theory, for I see no minnow in Daniel Bonner. I write privately in my side journals, wishing for the line to break.

‘Two hundred thousand pounds, that’s a bloody fortune,’ said Daniel with a detectable ring of disbelief in his voice.

‘Not really,’ replied Tony in his casual manner as if it were a thousand times less.

‘Well it is to me, and no mistake,’ he blurted. ‘Two hundred thousand, Jesus Christ, you must be bloody kidding,’ and Daniel noticed, not for the first time, how Windrow’s right eyelid momentarily fluttered with a flurry of micro spasms, at the mention of that name.

‘I have genuine trust in you Daniel, and feel confident in the investment, I know you'll do well with it.’

‘Do what with it for crying out loud? Daniel retorted, searching Tony’s face for the slightest tell tale sign of a leg-pull. There was none. ‘Are you serious Tony?’

‘I am serious Danny. I want you to play the stock market on my behalf. I’ve found commercial premises, in the high street of Delamere town, with modest living accommodation above the offices. It’s forty miles north of here, and from there you’ll launch your career. Within a year, I want you computer literate and learned in the art of hedge-fund speculation. Trust me Danny; I’ve a gut feeling that before long you’ll be making money…good money.’

‘You must be bloody dreaming Tony. I wouldn’t have a clue where to start.’

‘On that matter I have to agree, however, I’ve appointed a colleague to assist; a man by the name of Norbert Morris, an officious little tic, with some rather unsavoury personal habits. However, he's blessed with an unparalleled expertise, to create fantastic returns, on almost any investment that most can only dream of. He is disliked by many, but begrudgingly admired by all who know him in the business. Don't let your dislike for him disrupt his teaching, should a dislike arise. You’ll be in excellent hands; you must use the opportunity well.’

‘But why choose me? Why not do this hedge-whatever-thing yourselves?’

Windrow's gaze went to that recognisable look of steel, that Daniel had grow to respect, if not slightly fear. 'We're in need of a new face on the block,' Tony said eventually. 'I have a criminal record which doesn't sit well in this particular world of business; insider dealing for a start. I am too well known. This is no favour I'm asking of you Daniel, just a straightforward business proposition. We need a new front man, and Daniel, please don't make me have to remind you just how much you owe me.'

Tony could see the seed had been sown, notwithstanding Daniel's unquestionable loyalty. He wouldn't have to remind Daniel of the debt again, but nonetheless gave him time to consider.

'Do you really think I can pull this off Tony?'

'Yes Danny, I do…and you will.'

'Tony.'

'Yes my friend.'

'It's one hell of a lot of money…please don't be offended, but is it legal?'

'My dear Danny, being caught for, let's say, slightly dubious activities in life, doesn't mean that everyone has to know about the little slush-funds one might have squirrelled away from time to time. Don't worry, it's cool.'

'Ok, Tony, I'm in,' said Daniel with the detectable warble of trepidation betraying his voice. 'But by God I'll need help.'

'Welcome aboard,' said Tony, with a wide grin and that funny little micro spasm in his eye. 'I'll make absolutely sure you come to no harm, in fact on the absolute contrary.' The proposition was sealed with a handshake, not only cementing the deal, but also furthering the almost family bond that now existed between them.

Daniel found Norbert Morris, stooped over a bank of papers in the small, somewhat claustrophobic offices in Delamere, trading under the new name of Bonner Tonrow, tooled into a small brass plaque, fitted to the freestone door frame, through which he had just entered. On first impressions, Morris was a Saville-Row suited, well groomed, demure-looking gentleman. However, within an hour of their meeting, Daniel was to discover, the man suffered from catastrophic dandruff, that had settled like a sprinkling of snow over the fine cloth on his shoulders. More alarmingly, the air in close proximity to the man, was foetid, and clinging with the unmistakable odour of stale sweat and chronic halitosis. Clearly he couldn't have cared less, quite the opposite, seemingly to enjoy entering Daniel's close proximity, as he studied his protégée with small enquiring eyes, and wearing a thin wet smile. Revolting as his personal hygiene may have been, within the week, Daniel was to discover that Norbert possessed another quality, far outweighing any first impression. A metaphorical row of canine teeth became apparent, with a vocabulary capable of demolishing anyone brave enough to stand in his way. Describing him as a Rottweiler, although fitting, was probably too harsh on the breed, mused Daniel, as Norbert rounded on him yet again, with the same tedious warning.

'You're here to learn boy, and learn you shall. So I'll make it plain… I doubt if I'll ever fuckin' like you, as I don't like anyone or anything but money, but Windrow has given me instructions to do this thing, so I'll go along with it. You're here to do, what the fuck I tell you, and do whatever I say, so don't ever…ever piss me off! Norbert's thin smile returned, more akin to a sneer, as a clear droplet of mucus hung precariously, from the tip of his beaked nose. Do I make myself clear, Bonner?'

What a disgusting little... Daniel told himself, but capitulated with little choice.

'Clear.'

Daniel also discovered that Norbert was never one to prevaricate, or waste time, a rare commodity squandered only by fools; a Morris tutorial preached at every given opportunity. His efficiency, however, was legendary, and Daniel would soon learn, that he had indeed been appointed the very best, in the field of speculative investments.

The following week, state-of-the-art computer systems, along with several user manuals, appeared on the central desk, and after a several days of Norbert's tutelage, Daniel found it all rather daunting. Norbert seemed to gloat at his discomfort, and what he described as gross ineptitude. And in the stuffy air of the small office, Daniel longed for the open terrain of his beloved moor. He would gladly have thrown the PC clean through the front window, followed closely by Norbert Morris, but the binding promise made to Tony constantly prevailed. Slowly he began to get to grips with the mechanics of the machine, and backed up his growing understanding of the discipline, by working late into the evening, after Morris had thankfully left the building. He began proving himself to be a competent student, steadily wading through, and most importantly, understanding the meanings of the manuals written reams.

During the following month, the central desk was fitted with an array of monitors, keyboards and laptops. A two-man team of dedicated engineers worked double time to meet Norbert's installation requirements. Under his dogged insistence, the remit was finished ahead of time, its success, due to in no small part, to regular and personal remunerations, handed over in discreet plain buff envelopes. The engineers were only too willing to install customised upgrades, above and beyond what was written in the official order.

'Cash is king,' Norbert mumbled to Daniel. 'No better incentive in the world.'

Daniel nodded with a rare smile, not returned. The contract was completed and signed off, a week ahead of the estimated schedule. Norbert's uncompromising insistence, along with a generous underhand payment scheme, had worked its unbeatable charm.

The office was illuminated by computer screens, accessing the world's hundred or so stock market exchanges twenty four hours a day; the all important Dow Jones, the FTSE, TIFFE, SIMEX, NASDAQ, and NYSE, with others spanning continents from Tokyo to Venezuela, in a truly global fashion. Norbert and Daniel now had real-time access to the world markets, and were poised to play the most volatile, risky, yet potentially rewarding game in the living world.

For Daniel it was a mind boggling array of information, that was to test the limitations of his previously curtailed academic career. However, he further proved himself to be grammatically and numerically adept, evident to Norbert from the outset. In just ten months he had fulfilled the promise made to Tony, until there was nothing much left for Norbert to teach, allowing Daniel some much welcome free time. Increasingly, he escaped the claustrophobic lodgings above the office, to venture out for a pint or two, in the Pink Pig public house mid-way on the high street.

With a moderate allowance, and less dramatic attire as once worn on the moor, he soon became accepted in both the bar, and the town itself. Indeed, there were several young ladies in the local vicinity, who would have dearly liked to know him a lot more intimately, one of whom, Daniel was very fond. On several occasions, he was joined by Tony Windrow, who when noticing the attraction, reminded him that work must come first, and not to get sidetracked with affairs of the heart. Daniel reluctantly agreed; after all it was the least he could do to repay Tony's life-changing generosity. This ruling, however, seemed not to apply to him, and more often than not, Daniel walked home alone, as his mentor remained at the bar, in the company of single women. Daniel forcefully put aside his feelings of envy, and strengthening frustration; his time would come soon enough, though the idea of making love to a woman ranked high and often, in his innermost thoughts.

The highlight of any evening, was when Jesse made an unexpected appearance. They propped up the bar, and talked about matters of moor, and the way of life Daniel so often missed. Although Jesse knew where Daniels heart truly lay, he understood the lad now had other commitments, strong enough to turn the young man away from the magical and compelling open spaces, within tantalising reach several miles to the south.

Achieving all that had been expected, Daniel was now ready to enter the big game, solo. Each day a pile of newspapers appeared miraculously on his desk, and he religiously studied the business pages for news and views, both political and commercial, that might help him identify any possible forthcoming potential trends. And at each step, Norbert explained in his icy way, the rudimentary mechanics of world trade, and his protégé realised it was far from the mundane pastime, he had originally presumed it to be.

He was attracted initially to zinc and copper, already reaching record levels. Norbert, however, was quick to point out, that investing in commodities already outperforming, was an expensive acquisition and that no major financial killing could necessarily be made. Safe perhaps, but not as profitable as other emerging markets. 'The true art of speculative investment, is the ability to sense what lies in the near and distant future; get the latter right by only half, and the future could pay spectacular dividends. It's like discovering diamonds on a deserted beach, knowing that one day the market will pay fortunes for them. The trick is in finding those deserted beaches. Another heartfelt Morris tutorial.

‘Remember, Bonner,’ he pontificated through spittle lips, ‘to build a comprehensive portfolio, you must look at both ends of the scale. Study the undiscovered or weaker commodities, seemingly worthless or in free-fall, recognise the crucial point when they are either discovered, or about to bottom out, and look for the potentially all-important upturn. Buy as much stock as you think is an acceptable risk before that happens. Sometimes it can be a longer-term strategy, but if you get your timing right and spread the risk, your portfolio and profit will grow accordingly.’

‘It’s a definitely a gamble,' said Daniel. 'Gambling can be risky! What happens if there is no upturn?’

‘Man-up Bonner! It’s always fuckin’ risky. There's no place for the timid in this little organisation, mark my words... but as I said, get your timing right, spread your investments to support your portfolio, and good money can be made… Have you listened to nothing I have told you over the past ten months... idiot!!’ Norbert licked his lips wetly, happy with the measured degree of insult dished out.

Daniel forcefully turned his attention to the pile of newspapers, ramming his tongue to the roof of his mouth, to prevent any rebuke from spilling out, justified or otherwise.

Norbert moved away to his own side of the desk, and Daniel surreptitiously blew several flakes dandruff from the uppermost pages in front of him.

It was then, that “soft commodities’’ caught his eye yet again, as a real opportunity. This was one particular sector he had been keeping close tabs on. The price of wheat and corn had the potential of rising dramatically, amid drought warnings and global shortages. He lowered the copy of the Financial Times and followed his hunch online. The more he researched, the more convinced he became, that “soft commodities” such as grain markets, were good for large investment. If the farmers and stock holders, could be enticed into taking a fixed futures payment, then, should what he was expecting happen, a good profit could very well be made. Daniel’s ear became hot and soft, with the hours spent making national and international calls, but everything he heard and gleaned only went to support his hunch. Already some of the more astute brokers and dealers were playing the potential down, and that for Daniel was all he needed to convince him the trend had been set. A while later he put his cards on the table in front of Norbert, to provoke an opinion.

Norbert smiled genuinely at Daniel for the very first time, or certainly for the first time that Daniel could recall. His rattish eye remained cold, but a recognisable grin creased his otherwise miserable expression.

'Windrow and I, have already seen it as a strong possibility, and it appears you've passed the little test we set. We've been watching to see if you'd notice the potential. You have, and this is one area where we'll invest heavily... but don't think for one fuckin' minute, you've wormed your way into my favour because of it. There is only one master at this game, and you're looking at him.'

Norbert continued to bait Daniel, like a chained bear, but he wasn't biting, realising that for what ever reason, he was being constantly and forever tested.

By close of play that day, Norbert had acted. He guided and prompted Daniel to talk monetary figures over the phone, as easily as if playing a board game. He recommended contacts dealing with home and international commodities, and Daniel, while nurturing a mutual and understandable dislike for the man, was nevertheless impressed.

That evening, Daniel saw Norbert for the very first time leave the office a happy man. He was back, trading at full capacity behind a new and respectable front, and although he disliked admitting it, Daniel had done exceptionally well, even from the outset. Despite Windrow's forthright directive to nurture his protégée, Norbert had tried hard to break the young pretender, but even at such a tender age, Daniel had shown great aptitude, even greater than that of the revered, and feared, Norbert Morris. Norbert was left with little option, but to aid and abet. The necessary funding had been electronically transferred, with no fewer than twelve acquisitions, and Bonner Tonrow's credit was Blue Chip in its stock purchases, at a highly preferable rate of exchange. With such large acquisitions, the rest of the sleeping market woke up and smelled the coffee, but the early low price gained by Bonner Tonrow, had been cast in stone for the benefit of their organisation only. Big money was now about to be made as other traders bought Daniel's stock at Tonrow's new inflated prices, the profit of which was automatically primed, to finance the next equitable stock of their choosing. Virtually overnight, Bonner Tonrow had arrived in the world marketplace, a meteoric rise, almost without parallel, boosted by an incredible ten million pound sterling boost, from sources known only to Anthony Windrow and Norbert Morris.

Time rolled smoothly by with exciting alacrity, and Daniel rose to dress daily in expensive tailored suits, a myriad of tailored shirts and an array of superbly-cobbled shoes, that shone like polished jet. For the first time in his life, he felt proud of his achievements, underlined by his finely manicured image, clean shaven jaw, professional haircut and fine clothes, all of which complemented the handsome man he truly was. As he stood one day, looking at his reflection in the full length mirror, standing in the corner of his upstairs accommodation, he couldn't help but wonder at the transformation, from a young man hiding on the moor, to this well-groomed commodity dealer. He leaned forward, and studied the now almost invisible scars on his face. That fateful day of escape, seemed so very long ago, yet at times of contemplation, it felt like only yesterday. He stood upright. Under a critical eye, he approved of his new image, that at least was in place. Now he had to succeed beyond his mentors expectations, thus repaying the debt to Tony Windrow, with every best possible return on his and Bonner Tonrow's multiple investments. This was his unstinting goal, and to that end, he made a silent vow to the reflection, standing rock steady in the mirror.

As Daniel matured with age and confidence, so did the way he was treated improve. He was invited to accompany Tony on excursions to the London Stock Exchange with increasing regularity. As a fast learner he soon understood the chaotic ways of that extraordinary place, a seat of power in which organized chaos so often ruled. Such were the exchanges world wide, and all one day would be home for him.

In just under a year his wish was granted. Prices of wheat on the 'Chicago Board of Trade' suddenly escalated, with the main 'futures contract' rising from £127 to £210 per tonne in a matter of weeks. For the commodity dealers, wheat was the new gold. Daniel believed it was the start of a 'supercycle'; a combination of falling harvests from drought-stricken Australia, global low stocks, growing populations and the demand for bio-ethanol products. This, he was convinced, would see the price of grain spiral upwards year in and year out. He was proved right yet again; another success in an increasingly powerful portfolio.

As my quill etches the human parchment with this very entry, I the Chancellor's Scribe, secretly fear greatly for Daniel Bonner's soul. Shall he be the mighty Marlin, or the minnow taken on the tide?

Tony Windrow sat opposite Daniel Bonner in the Pink Pig, as they saluted one another with raised glasses of single malt whisky, to celebrate their monumental successes. Within fourteen months, Daniel and Norbert had accumulated a net profit of one hundred and eight million pounds sterling, before tax, notwithstanding a full return of the original investment of two hundred thousand pounds, within the first six months. It was truly a story of mother capitalism at her best. And of that they were truly proud.

'Danny my lad,' said Tony with a lofty glass, 'I bloody well knew you'd come up trumps… knew it from the very fucking beginning.' With tumbler to his lips, Tony tipped back his head, and threw the fiery contents to the back of his throat. Daniel followed suit, smothering the resulting cough. He grimaced against the astringent liquid, with what he hoped would be mistaken for a smile. He swallowed hard behind his puckered lips, proud of being recognised as being the integral part of their rise to power.

'It wasn't just me, Tony', he said through a soft expulsion of breath. 'As you know full well, Norbert was the main man. No way could I have done it on my own.'

'Well, that's accurate to a point, Daniel. However, remember, you saw what we saw, you learned about this business faster than any man I've known. You have an instinct, that so few ever get even close to. I have studied you, but I am not the only one to do so. Your competitors, who once dismissed you as a pretender, including our dearest Norbert, have since learned the bitter truth. Despite their negative protestations, about the undoubted failings of a new kid on the block, they held no sway over the majority in the roll-call of commodity experts. I'm glad to say that you are now a respected member. That's quite an achievement Daniel, I mean... really something! Many never get that recognition in a lifetime of work, so don't knock it.'

What Tony said was mostly true. Already, increasing numbers of speculators, had begun to gather slavishly around Daniel, for advice on his visits to the London Stock Exchange. Some even saw him as being an emerging market guru, a ridiculous accolade that never failed to embarrass him.

Tony pulled an envelope from his inner pocket of his jacket, and slid it across the dry side of the battered drinking table, indicating its importance by tapping his index finger several times, on the Manila sleeve. Daniel raised a questioning eyebrow and extracted a bankers draft, from 'Bonner Tonrow Market Fund', for the sum of four hundred thousand pounds, Tonrow being an adaptation of Tony's full name. Daniel was certainly expecting a pay off, but nothing quite so large. His jaw dropped, long enough for a swarm of bees to take up residence.

'Congratulations Danny!' suggested Tony, breaking the spell with a grin, 'it's yours to do with what you want. The beginning of a personal fortune. You've certainly earned it.'

'Bloody hell, Tony! Have we really done this well? I knew we were certainly on the up, but I had no idea it was this good. Norbert keeps things very close to his chest.'

'Not only have we done well, but the returns on your initial investments continue to grow daily. Daniel, my boy, don't think for one moment this is the last pay day,' he said with a fruity chuckle. 'Keep up the good work, and you and I are going places far deeper than you might imagine.'

Again they raised their glasses, and Daniel downed the fiery contents. Life was suddenly good. He smacked his lips, coping with the burn, and Tony responded by ordering a generous refill. Daniel looked at Tony standing at the bar, with deep admiration and gratitude, as the whisky warmed his belly creating a strong sense of bonhomie. He touched again the envelope tucked in his pocket, to reassure himself this was no dream. He pinched his hand, he was fully awake, This was no dream.

In the polished reflection of the back bar mirror, Windrow watched as Daniel surreptitiously lowered the envelope to his lap and part extracted the bankers draft beneath the table. He watched the look of wonder on Daniel's face change to that of undiluted triumph, and Windrow grinned beneath those calculating eyes of steel.

As Daniel replaced the draft securely in his pocket, he was distracted by the sudden appearance of a small scruffy looking dog sitting at his feet.

In the past he had little reason to find time for the species, given his experience in prison and the year following his escape. More than that, he had actually gone out of his way to avoid them, and yet this little urchin was utterly appealing, as it looked up with its large searching eyes. In the light of his current mood, he reached down to stroke its head, and Daniel, whether he liked it or not, had found a friend. He hauled it onto his lap and it sat surveying the surroundings, as if it belonged to no one else on earth. The breed was indeterminable, a mongrel bitch puppy of the lowest cast, with a tan coat of coarse hair, shot through with streaks of white and sable along its back and ears. Utterly endearing nonetheless.

'What's that on your lap?' said Tony, laughingly with charged tumblers in hand. 'Looks like a lump of shredded tobacco.'

'Belongs to the pub I guess,' said Daniel, 'but I see what you mean, scruffy little bugger.' They chuckled before resuming their plans for Bonner Tonrow's future, and yet, even with being ignored, the little dog stayed stuck to Daniel's lap.

Another hour elapsed, but eventually it was time to leave and Daniel turfed the dog to the floor, but as they made their way to the door, the animal trotted happily behind Daniel, as if following his long-standing master. He scooped it up and made towards the bar, with the intention of handing it back to the landlord.

'It's not mine,' the barman said with a shake of his head. 'I thought it was yours, Danny.'

'Then who's is it?' Daniel directed the question as a general enquiry to the few patrons scattered about the bar, but it was soon clear the dog belonged to no one there present. He felt guilty with the idea of deserting the mutt, especially when the landlord made it clear that his Doberman bitch would prefer eating the hairy little morsel, before sharing its territory.

'Looks like you've gained a companion,' said Tony, and with his words, the pup threw out a yap and attempted to lick the point of Daniel's jaw.

'OK Tobacco, looks like you're coming with me, for the time being at least, but no way am I keeping you.' The dog tried again to wash Daniel's face. It was then he noticed a silver talisman, of three leaping flames, on its leather collar. Thinking it to be an ID tag, he turned it in his fingers and was surprisingly happy to discover it held no inscription. However, the longer he held the bright silver, the more he became aware of an odd tingling sensation running through his fingers. It had to be his imagination, or perhaps the effects of the whisky. He let it drop onto the dog's chest, and he, Tony and Tobacco, left the building, with the door closing with a well-oiled click behind them.

The Library of Time was dedicated entirely to the written word, a subterranean cathedral of colossal proportions, with vaulted ceilings of natural rock, higher and longer than the eye could calculate the true distance. Countless rows of books, written in every conceivable language, crammed every shelf, the higher volumes lost in the gloom, their end out of sight to the human eye.

The Chancellor found the Devil a mile along the central isle, sitting comfortably in a large wing-back chair, concentrating on a loam of current reading.

'The eye is in place my Lord,' said the Chancellor. 'I have placed the talisman on the mongrel bitch, which, Bonner, as we planned had little chance of resisting. His every move can now be monitored. It has to be said, my Lord, Bonner never wanders far. My task is made easy by this.

The Devil squinted his beautiful eyes. His subjects, including his Chancellor were minions of the underworld. Nothing should be easy, especially for him. Idle tasks breed idle minds. This was the hallowed place of purgatory, and by the doctrine of the underworld, so shall they all must suffer, forever in the broil of physical and emotional torment. He would see to it.

'More importantly' continued the Chancellor, unaware of the Devil's innermost thoughts, Bonner has an unnerving gift to make money. Before long it will without doubt corrupt him. He no longer mentions idiotic good causes. I believe we have turned his charitable mind into a tool of our making.'

'Interesting,' replied the Devil, raising an enquiring eyebrow as he looked up.

'He has become a money magnet as you rightly predicted, my Lord. Speculators cue for his advice, making it easy to snatch a few of the more greedy souls along the way. That alone has proved most fruitful. They clamour together and lust for the power of money, not knowing of what they are truly wishing, and indeed with whom they wish it. The investment in future body-counts increases daily.' The Chancellor looked for a reaction in his masters sublime features, with such love he thought his heart might burst. It was an intense moment, for the Chancellor only.

'That's good to hear,' the Devil replied... 'but don't for a single moment be complacent. Do not let Daniel Bonner get away. You know how much I detest failure. Now leave me, I have several wars and some global financial mischief to manipulate.'

The Chancellor bowed low, as he shuffled back a dozen paces, before turning briskly, to walk back along the mile long causeway of flagstones, to the colossal doors that were entry to the Library of Time.

The oakwood table ran over twenty metres in length, plain in design, robust and practical. At each end the timber had been worn, and battered, by the slamming of palms and fists in countless debate and argument, by rested elbows in concentration, and the sleeves of heavy robes, that had countlessly swept the surface, with arms in expansive gesture. Solid oak chairs stood sentinel behind the antique ends, upon which sat respectively, Lucifer and Abdiel, the dark and light angels, ready as ever to do battle. This was their middle world, a place of great council, where neither one could manipulate or control the other, but where through the power of argument or reason the all important status quo between good and evil was upheld.

I the Scribe sit as usual, at a separate desk, halfway along the length of the table between them, set back in the shadows, with quill rock steady over the page of natural paper. Abdiel utterly refuses the abhorant use of human parchment in this hallowed hall, and not without my inner and most humble blessing. A silence filling the hall, and keeping my head bowed over the clean sheet, I hardly ever dare to look up, unless addressed directly. The air is electric with latent, brooding power.

As had been the same for thousands of years, Abdiel opened the proceedings, amid almost instant protestations from the Devil. They debated hundreds of topics, arguing back and forth, on who had pushed the boundaries, on pacts and agreements formed in previous council. I write fervently to keep up, fascinated. They argued deeply, on the rise to power of despotic leaders, assisted as ever by Lucifer, Abdiel using thousands of past cases to press home the importance of the status-quo in his argument. The Devil maintaining it was the will of man who elected such people, not he, and whatever they did in human life, determined their future in the after-world. The consequences of their actions therefore, made them fair game to his manipulations, later to swell the numbers in the darkness of his very Hell. The same indeed, he argued contemptuously, as being no different to what his opposing brother might do, to swell the numbers in his spiritual world of light. It was the supreme court for the future of souls. The difference to that of earthly courts, being that Abdiel and Lucifer were both defence and prosecuting councils, adroitly entertaining opposite rolls at an instant, in the battle for ultimate supremacy, both knowing it was a war, they could never win. For me it was difficult to be swayed by one or the other, perhaps that is why I have been chosen by them, to act as scribe for the supreme council. They were twins, both beautiful to the point of perfection, Satan with an underlying aura of mischief and malevolence, Abdiel with a forceful yet calm countenance, and what I can only describe as fascinating grace. Both commanders in the spiritual field, both ultimately powerful, answerable only to their father, their creator.

'So what of Daniel Bonner, have you sent him to torment me, brother Abdiel?'

'You know full well, brother Lucifer, the will of humankind is sometimes strong as it is weak, and it is from their own gene-pool that they send their own to walk on the light or dark side. All we can do is gather them respectively.'

'Do you aid and abet him?'

'No more than you do already, my dark sibling. I shall however, endeavor to maintain the crucial balance. I have heard of this young man, soon to know him better than he does himself. It is written in our Libraries of Time, his life of which I am sure you have already read?'

The Devil despised the fact that Abdiel had the equivalent power over the future. If one day he could destroy his brothers library, then he could truly dictate his own design of equilibrium across the globe. For the moment he pushed aside his inner feelings.

'The scriptures tell of a forerunner to the man who shall one day unite mankind. Is this, Daniel Bonner, the forerunner, or perhaps the man himself, brother of mine? For the scriptures hold no name to either.'

'As you know,' replied Abdiel, all that is written in the Libraries of Time, are in most parts cast in stone. But we also know that the scriptures do not disclose his name, I assume to protect him from one such as you.

'You also,' snorted Satan. 'the equilibrium, remember brother?'

'We also know, the vagueness of the writings, deliberately cloaks the chosen one,' Abdiel continued, with an acquiescent slight of his head. 'And it is only when events unfold, that the scriptures shall change within our libraries. If Bonner is the one, so shall his story change, in no less than the passing of his lifetime. We shall not know until he has completed his path in life.'

'Then, we must watch Bonner, with great interest. Test him also, for we know not if it is he who walks this world, to unite mankind, and indeed, in which way. Yours or mine, Abdiel?'

Abdiel remained expressionless, although begrudging the truth in Satan's words, hoping the quick flash of annoyance that danced across in his brown eyes, had not been noticed by his sibling angel.

'We shall reconvene in this hall, at the twenty fifth alignment of the planets, to discuss the matter further. In the meantime, let us indeed test Bonner in our very different ways, and discover the true direction of his soul. '

The Devil squinted thoughtfully, calculating in his minds eye the time-frame of the twenty fifth alignment. 'So soon? He has you vexed?'

'You also, my dark-hearted brother. You too.'

There were never any greetings nor goodbyes. The hall for the future of souls faded into darkness, and I the scribe was transported back to the Chancellor's chambers' to sit at my desk awaiting his arrival. Heady am I, with having been once more in the company of the Dark and Light Angels. But how soon it is, that I miss them so, and sit with empty heart.

In the following months, Daniels success snowballed. Tony Windrow looked on with deep admiration, and even Norbert Morris, despite his inner loathing, had to admit he was genuinely impressed. Daniel was indeed, the magnet the Chancellor had hoped he'd become, and unbeknown to him, increasing numbers of men and women, were willing to sell their souls, in return for instant wealth, naturally, though undisclosed, for the Devil's ultimate price.

Later, the London Stock Exchange launched a series of 'exchange traded funds', which for the first time, allowed private investors to invest in commodity indices. Soft commodities, energy and metal equities, continued to rise and many investors made a killing, while the consumer continued to pay the price. But things were about to change. In the following years, the Devil would reap his reward, with the collapse of sub-prime mortgage lending, and would revel in the human misery that was to follow; to snatch the desperate souls, laid bare and vulnerable, in the icy shadow of financial ruin.

For the time being at least, it seemed that everything was in place for Bonner Tonrow, and yet a growing feeling of disquiet, had entered Daniel's inner well-being. Increasingly, he remembered his late brother, and more importantly the circumstances in which he had died, and in tandem, memories of life on the moor, entered his thoughts like long-lost friends. The sudden yearning for a simpler way of life re-emerged without justifiable reason. But it soon became more than just a wishful notion, in those unpredictable hours when a man is left alone to think. Be that as it may, he was devoted to Tony, with a loyalty that would quash any idea of returning to that wild place. He had no choice, and for the sake of his friendship would continue servicing his debt until Tony decided otherwise. And yet despite such dedication, Daniel Bonner's life was about to change yet again.

London's inner city streets were hot, and seemingly more polluted than normal, on that particular mid-summer's afternoon. Norbert was a passenger in Daniel's newly-acquired Aston Martin Vanquish, gloating over the success of that morning's session of trade, while harvesting dead flakes from his scalp with effeminately long, yet grubby fingernails; another singularly disgusting habit noted.

Daniel looked at the side of Norbert's head, and a sudden feeling of revulsion swept over the new millionaire, like an Atlantic wave. But it wasn't just Norbert that bothered him. Other issues had set alarm bells ringing. His loyalty to Tony Windrow went without saying; after all it was he who had saved him in so many ways, and who had laid such wealth at his feet. Yet he found himself questioning the next proposed field of investment - the International Arms Trade. Globally a dozen wars were raging. Windrow had argued, with some justification, that the supply of arms was a crucial factor, in maintaining the often fragile political balance. Be that as it may, the idea of making personal fortunes, from such bloody suffering, went wholly against Daniel's inner moral standards. It had been the catalyst of his, and Tony's, first major disagreement.

Daniel looked out through the smoked window of the Vanquish. Even with the air-conditioning on full, Morris's halitosis remained thick and claustrophobic. As he tried mentally to remove himself from his passenger's presence, Daniel threw a cursory glance along the teeming pavement, catching sight of a huddled form, in the shuttered doorway of an abandoned boarded shop.

'That could be my brother,' he said in a whisper, not wishing to engage Norbert in any way whatsoever. But Norbert's acute hearing was legendary. Countless times he had overheard conversations that others found hard to discern as anything more than a mumble. It had proved an invaluable asset in the halls of trade, but on this occasion, not so for Daniel.

Norbert gave the down-and-out a fleeting glance, and snorted through clumps of coarse hair, protruding from his beaky nose.

'People like that are nothing but fuckin' parasites, incapable of helping themselves. It's despicable. They're nothing but a bunch of bloody spongers. They should be drowned at birth if you ask me. Just look at the filthy fuck.'

In the following silence, Norbert believed Daniel had simply agreed, until he turned and saw the other's shocking rage. Daniel's normally calm face was creased and deadly, his fists clenched, knuckles translucent white beneath his grip on the steering wheel.

'Norbert, I want you to get out of this car,' he said with a voice thick with fury. 'Right now you grubby bastard, before I break your disgusting neck!'

'But the hotel is a couple of miles away,' Norbert countered with a shrill protest. 'What the fuck's got into you, Bonner?'

'I only wish the hotel was further,' Daniel said bitterly. 'Now get the fuck out!'

The look on his face said it all. He was on the brink of losing all restraint, and Norbert knew he would be a wise man to follow the instruction.

'Before you go I want you to take this tenner,' he said, stuffing the bank note into Norbert's top pocket.

'What the fuck's that for…I don't want your bloody money. What's going on, Bonner? Remember, I told you, never piss me off, or there will be consequences.'

Norbert's threat seemed suddenly to lack any substance whatsoever.

'I want you to give it to the man in the doorway,' he said through a set jaw. 'Prove to me, just this once, that you have a bone of humanity in your money-grabbing body.' And wisely, Norbert piled form the car as athletically as was possible in a singularly unimpressive manoeuvre. He slammed the door and Daniel winced at the treatment of his beloved car.

Norbert made his way along the pavement as Daniel crawled alongside in the slow moving traffic. However, instead of doing as asked, Norbert suddenly turned and began walking in the opposite direction.

The last thing Daniel saw of the revolting little man, was his two-fingered salute, as he ducked into a conveniently passing taxi, fluttering the ten pound note like a banner of triumph.

That night, Daniel drove the five-hour journey back to Delamere. He couldn't trust himself to go back to the hotel, as Norbert Morris would probably have suffered gross injury, or perhaps worse. Placid by nature he began doubting his normally passive attitude, but more importantly his vocation, and the feeling of disquiet persisted, as he made the journey west. He yearned for the warm, uncomplicated summers on the moor, the harsh winters survived only by bush-craft and guile, the everyday challenges, the often dangerous conditions. He had made huge tracts of money, but ultimately his success meant very little. It was time to initiate what he had originally set out to do, and would accept the consequences. In his view the debt had been paid. After all, Tony was his dearest friend and was sure to understand.

Daniel rose later than usual the following morning, to find Tony Windrow and Norbert Morris waiting for him, in the lower office at Delamere. The atmosphere could be cut with a knife, the silence brooding and ominous. Tony broke the deadlock with a thin smile, and came immediately to the point.

'We don't have petty squabbles at Bonner Tonrow,' he said behind an ice cool stare. 'I want you and Norbert to shake hands and forget your differences. I'm travelling to London within the hour, leaving you two to sort out this ridiculous misunderstanding. Trading will, of course, resume immediately. And that my young friend is an order, for our friendship's sake, if nothing else.'

Daniel had always recognised Tony's underlying toughness, but regrettably, for the first time, saw a very different person. His words were colder than steel, with an expression to match, and all the while Norbert concentrated on harvesting organic matter from under his fingernails, without once looking up. Daniel suddenly realised that, despite his uncompromising officious exterior, Norbert Morris was actually wary of Tony Windrow, perhaps even scared. But for what reason? And for the first time in their somewhat tumultuous relationship, he even felt a pang of pity for the man, as shadows of fear flitted through his expression.

'Get things back on track without fail! I'm sure you both understand me,' said Windrow.

For Daniel, it was nothing more than a sharp request. For Norbert, it appeared to be a lethal warning.

'My Lord,' said the Chancellor, to the Devil sitting in his wingback chair in the Library of Time. 'My Lord, it would appear Norbert Morris has failed to keep Bonner on the programme.' His words were mimicked in the distant echo of the vaulted ceiling, and he heard a bitter tone in his own voice.

The Devil sat motionless, his eyes unblinking in his handsome head as he continued to read without looking up.

'He would have gone anyway,' he said evenly. 'Remember, my squalid Chancellor, I know everything.' It wasn't the entire truth, for if Bonner was the one, the ending had yet to be written.

The Chancellor momentarily preened at the accolade, before remembering the severity of the topic.

'Indeed so my Lord, then it will be of no surprise for you, to learn that Bonner has given away his fortune.'

The Devil looked up wearily from his book, surprised that his Chancellor had even thought it necessary to mention the fact, given his first reply. This he had read, as chronicled in the ledger of Daniels life.

'He's given away most of his money to drug rehabilitation and AIDS Research; those charities in particular, my Lord.'

The Devil grew thoughtful, recounting how in the late fifties, he had actively inspired several leading military scientists of the time, to embark on a so-called biological defence weapon, that would destroy the human body's immune system, first tested on bush meat. It had only been a matter of time before it broke out into the human population. One day the stark truth would be realised, and on that day, half the living world would sue the other half with catastrophic consequences. It would be a modern-day Armageddon and he would reap the whirlwind.

'My Lord, I repeat, he's given away his fortune, don't you hear me?'

Again, the Chancellor stated what was already known, questioning his master at the same time, a foolish thing to do at the best of times, and the Devil's anger blossomed into a terrible thing.

Suddenly the Library of Time stank of sulphur, as the Lord of the Underworld rose from his chair, amidst a blinding cloud of acrid yellow smoke. His form grew rapidly upwards, until, reaching almost to the vaulted ceiling height, his body passed row upon row of priceless books that burst spontaneously into flames but never chard. And in the ensuing inferno, the Devil's true form was revealed.

In the two thousand years he had served his master, never had the Chancellor seen such a magnificent sight. The Devil was magnificent in ultimate beauty, incredibly outstripping his normal form. His skin was like flawless alabaster, his body superbly sculptured wrapped only in a loincloth. His face was the most handsome in all time, sculptured to a level beyond perfection, and with his eyes shut he was angelic. White feathered wings, born only to the angels, were folded high on his back, completing the mesmerising spectacle.

Slowly the Devil bent low until, coming face to face with his Chancellor, who in turn wanted to reach out and touch those perfect features. For long moments the Chancellor stared transfixed, eventually he found the courage to extend his hand.

Suddenly the Devil's eyelids opened like scythes, exposing orbs of polished anthracite, so dark and utterly soulless. A crash of thunder rumbled in the dry air, high above the Library of Time, and the Chancellor looked into those cacodemon orbs of death. They held the spite of a million Godless souls, of countless numbers from warlike generations, the pain and suffering of nations and the eternal terrors of an uncertain, inhumane world. And in the light of the burning library, those pools of jet exposed the truth. The Lord of the Underworld was truly the Dark Angel.

Not a word was spoken. None were needed, for the Chancellor saw everything, in those horrendous gateways. His master was the ultimate power. He possessed the books of time, and therefore had power over all things, the Chancellor's strengths rendered insignificant by comparison. He had been utterly cowed, and he lowered his head.

Slowly the Devil shrank to mortal size and resumed his seat, and the Chancellor looked up to stare at him, with unparalleled love and awe.

'My Lord, I am your servant of the ages. What should be done?'

'We have lost the hold on Daniel Bonner's soul. Through selfless philanthropy, he has proved himself perhaps worthy of another world. He has escaped your net and regained all he gave away on the night of his escape. He is free.'

'My Lord, I am to blame. I shall accept my punishment, your command is law.'

'My dear Chancellor, I would readily cast you down, to languish forever in the putrescent pit of anguish and suffering. However, before I change my mind, prove to me you can still be of use.'

'In any way I can, my Lord. What is it you want of me, your command is my existence?'

'You have failed to bring him down. He has inadvertently rejected our gracious invitation to dwell with us…therefore we must put him severely to the test. You shall now take the great game to his own world. Chancellor, from this day on you shall make Daniel Bonner's life... Hell on earth.

'Now get out of my sight.'

The rain had done its worse, flattening Daniel's hair into dripping rat-tails, as he trudged the moorland road a happy man. The rain was inconsequential; as for its effects, he couldn't have cared less.

On his feet he wore a new pair of stout walking boots, a small concession for a pauper's return, over his shoulders his much loved long-coat. Under his arm, Tobacco sheltered from the rain, over the other shoulder hung a duffel bag, containing a number of items for survival, including his hunting knife, fire-making equipment and an assortment of essentials. In his hand, he held the Hummer, which had hung as a memento on the wall at the office in Delamere, completing the menagerie. The real world was again at his fingertips, with all its good and bad points, balanced on the scales between adventure and survival.

'So, Danny my boy, you've returned.' Daniel spun to face the familiar voice of Jesse, who had appeared magically from behind a tree, with Zip close at heel. Daniel could never have imagined just how good it was to see the old rogue, more than could be said for Zip and Tobacco who stared at each other with fight in their eyes. With a crisp command, Jesse prevented a canine punch-up and Zip sat reluctantly at heel.

'Rumour has it that you made yourself into a bit of a millionaire.' said Jesse. 'So what the fuck are you doing back out here?'

'Money isn't everything, Jesse. I gave it all away.'

'You did what?

'Want to hear a story, Jesse?

Jesse answered by dumping his backside on a knoll, placed his hands on his knees, with the gap between his eyes pinched with enquiry.

Daniel moved as quickly as he could through the catalogue of events, after which, Jesse sat quietly for a while with a look on his face that was difficult to decipher. He rose from his makeshift seat, and stepped forward to stand directly in front of Daniel.

'Bloody fool,' he said, taking the others hand with a hard shake, 'but bloody respect…nothing but bloody respect. There is not a man living I know who would do the same. Welcome back Danny.'

Without giving more, Jesse walked away some twenty metres. He turned, scratching the nape of his bull neck. 'Danny, it will be a pleasure when we meet again.' And the friendship, that had been waiting quietly in the wings, was born.

Anthony Windrow came across Daniel the following day, sitting on a log in the gully of a dried out stream, and strode towards him with purpose. At his side trotted an overweight black Labrador labouring to keep up. Eventually they stood square and Tony stared long and hard at the young adventurer. After all these years, Daniel found words difficult to find for his friend. The ensuing silence was awkward and alien to both. Windrow eventually broke the silence.

'Why do you feel you have to give it all up Daniel…I never gave up on you. Didn't I give you everything?' His eyes were searching, cutting deeply into Daniels return gaze. For Daniel it was time for the truth. Choosing his words carefully, he began his regretful, nonetheless heartfelt, explanations.

'I'm sorry, Tony. The whole business with Bonner Tonrow suddenly felt wrong.' He was lying, the feeling of unease had been present for a while, but he chose not to labour the point. 'Besides, unknown to you and perhaps somewhat selfishly, I had set myself a private goal a long time ago.'

'Then what of our partnership…the ongoing success?' Daniel detected traces of a plea in the question.

‘Look Tony, I don’t want to sound ungrateful, but it’s over. I’m sorry but it’s the way I feel, especially with Bonner Tonrow now planning its entry into arms trade commodity's.’

‘Daniel…dear Daniel,’ said Tony, his voice at first sounding placatory. It then hardened to steel. ‘If it wasn’t us, it would only be someone else. It’s the bloody world we live in, no matter how unpleasant it may seem. Wake up, smell the fucking coffee. Get used to it. Danny, you could sell sand to the Arabs...think of all that money...the world is at your feet.'

‘At yours, perhaps Tony, but for me it’s a no can do. Please don’t ask again as my refusal will only offend.’

Tony noticed the set of Daniel’s jaw and the rock steady look of determination in his eyes.

‘So your answer is to return to the moor…to run away?’

Tony’s features hardened to match his voice, as Daniel gave his curt answer. ‘I have learned never to run, only to walk,’ he said, feeling prickles of annoyance run through his brain at the accusation that he might somehow be a coward.

‘Then it’s poverty for you once more, Mr Bonner! Flea-infested clothes, hunger that will tear at your empty stomach like blunt razors, winters that will chill your bones to the very core. And for what. Daniel. My dear friend, I have to ask, is this really what you want?’

‘You taught me how to avoid hunger and being unwashed. You of all people should know that. I’m back where I belong, and glad of it, believe me.’

Tony lowered his gaze, and then looked up with an expression to outstrip the one given in the office at Delamere.

‘Oh we do believe you my friend. The lower world believes every word you say.’

‘The lower world? What the fuck do you mean by that?’

‘Wake up my friend,’ said a voice at ground level.

Daniel looked down, and his senses reeled. The fat Labrador at Windrows side now bore the face of Norbert Morris, staring up at him with an expression of incalculable hate. It was Norbert Morris. 'My punishment for failing to keep you on the programme,' he whined.

'All that wealth gone to philanthropic causes,' cut in Windrow. 'What idiotic waste.'

'What kind of dream is this?' mouthed Daniel. It had to be a nightmare from which he would wake at any moment. Tobacco began to growl. Sudden droplets of sweat oozed from every pore in Daniels face, neck and powerful chest, cutting rivulets down the valley of his broad back, his face blanched like that of a skinned carcase of bled veal. He felt nauseous and vomited. And Norbert feasted on the mess at his feet. He vomited again. More dog food. Daniel eventually took control of his bodily functions and wiped his mouth clean with the back of his hand and found his voice.

'Tony…what is this? This can't be real. Who the fucking Hell are you really?'

'An aptly-phrased question,' answered Norbert, cleaning his own lips with the use of a long pink canine tongue. 'Meet the Gatherer of Souls, my lord and master, the Chancellor, or as you know him, Tony Windrow. Works in the pit of souls, second-in-command to the big boss, the Devil himself.'

'Sorry…I don't understand…What in Jesus name is going on?'

The Chancellor's left eyelid twitched spasmodically at the mention of that name, as if it were full of grit, but continued regardless.

'Prior to being pulled from the wire, as you attempted to escape all those years ago, can you recall what you said?' His question sounded like an accusation.

'No Tony, I can't! And what the fuck kind of dog is that…I want to kick Norbert's fucking face. I'm dreaming, I'm bloody dreaming.' Daniel was in shock.

'Bartered your soul for freedom is what you pleaded, and my friend…we were listening. We are always listening.'

'This is some sort of joke? This is bloody ridiculous! Tell me you're pulling my leg? Damn it, Tony, you're my friend! Jesus Christ, I'm not even religious.'

'Oh, dear boy.' There was that micro spasm again. 'You don't have to be believe in the Devil to sell your soul, but in time you'll learn.'

'Oi…idiot. Do I look like a fuckin' joke?' interjected Norbert. 'This is no bloody dream, a living nightmare perhaps, and one you shall never forget!'

'We are real, Daniel my boy. Very real indeed,' said the Chancellor, and suddenly the clouds that had veiled so many anomalies rolled aside and the ugly penny of truth dropped into its rightful place. Daniel had often wondered at Tony's extraordinary behaviour but had blindly accepted it as something of his youthful imagination. Reality had come home to roost. For years he had been running with the Devil's pack.

'So you've come for me. Is that it?' he said hesitantly, barely daring to ask the question. The initial shock subsiding.

'Hardly,' replied the Chancellor. 'You are of little use to us. You were neither greedy nor corrupted by the fortune we allowed you, proving yourself an unfit candidate for our world. You've managed to evade our gracious invitation this time, but perhaps there'll be another opportunity somewhere in the future. Who knows?'

'But why all this elaboration, to gather one soul…my soul?'

'Ah my dear friend! And I now use that expression lightly. We used you as an opportunity to move amongst humanity with impunity, exposing human greed, to gather up the unwitting. People are so wary these days it truly irks me. Takes time to win their confidence and lower their guard. However, we are part of a successful and wealthy organisation, therefore able to breach their defences with ease. I snagged a few avarice minded souls along the way. So in that respect it has been a relatively successful spree.' The structure of the Chancellor's words were strangely old-fashioned to Daniel's ears; but then the Chancellor had been around for countless years.

'So what happens now? I can't believe this is real.'

'Oh it is real. As to what will happen next? Why nothing. You're now free,' and the Chancellor tapped his thigh with an open palm, beckoning Tobacco to his side.

'What do you want with my dog?' demanded Daniel protectively, suddenly aware of how strangely placid Tobacco had been throughout the encounter.

'Your dog?' snorted the Chancellor. 'She was never anything of the sort. In my absence she's been my eyes from the day she sat on your lap in the Pink Pig, trained to keep a tag on my investment so to speak.'

Daniel looked at Tobacco, now hesitating between the two parties.

'If that's true, if she's one of yours,' Daniel shook his head sadly, 'I don't want anything to do with her.' A sudden sadness entered the pit of his stomach at the sound of his words.

The Chancellor stooped to retrieve the silver talisman of three leaping flames from around Tobacco's neck, snapping it from her collar. The tug was unkind, and in response she moved unexpectedly to stand beside Daniel, a little shaken yet staring defiantly into the Chancellor's dark eyes.

'Without this particular bauble she no longer has that all-seeing power, Mr Bonner. And besides, the less I see of you the fucking better. I have failed to take you down. An insignificant failure I'll warrant, but one of which I do not wish to be reminded. In the meantime allow me to leave you something, to remember me by.'

Suddenly the air around his body reverberated with a barrage of shock waves, his body vibrating violently, as that of a bull crocodile warning its closest rivals. Norbert moved his plump body aside as nimbly as possible on stiff canine legs, as the Chancellor became metamorphic. His body bulged and disfigured, undulating like a sack of angry serpents, fighting for freedom through his skin. His body towered over Daniel, as Tobacco stood loyally at his masters side with protective barks and growls, darting bravely forward then back again, highly unsure. Sputum fangs crowded the Chancellor's heavy open jaws, as strands of rotten flesh hung in gruesome packages between. His now scabby skin was livid red, interspersed with rivulets of pungent yellow discharge, and a stench from the grave of a thousand dead, corrupted the sweet moorland air.

Daniel reeled, trying to avoid the trenchant assault, but ultimately stood his ground with admirable courage. He felt woefully betrayed, sinfully used, and more importantly, one who had suddenly lost the only true friend he had ever known. Anger rose hot from his core and crowded his head, fury replacing fear. With a clenched fist, Daniel swung a superb right hook, catching the Chancellor by surprise, and knocking out one of his front teeth, with a crack to rival the lash of a bull whip. Puss and droplets of blood shot into the air under the impact, but the Chancellor never flinched. It was now a deadly time for Daniel. The chancellor moved a pace forward, and Daniel and the now frenzied Tobacco, were forced to give urgent ground. Again another step forward, and Norbert tittered through clenched teeth. He smelt death. Then without warning the Chancellor suddenly stopped, as if ordered by an unseen power to cease, and for long moments it was a stand-off. His vile head swayed in a slow figure of eight, heavy, bloodied and repugnant. Unexpectedly, he began a baritone chuckle. Norbert also began to laugh at the rictus of emotions etched on Daniel's face, then his right eye winked in a cocksure manner, before returning to a that of a Labrador head. The dog was complete once more, and the Chancellor slowly reverted into the man, who Daniel not twenty minutes previously, had loved and admired. In that instant, what had once been a remarkable bond of friendship blossomed into mutual hatred. It crossed the short divide, like a bolt of electricity.

'Not many escape me, Mr Bonner. Use your freedom well, and pity those unable to slip my net, for this particular episode has put me in the filthiest of moods, and somebody will pay.' Another short stand-off ensued, until he and the Labrador turned away, and eventually disappeared along the track, leaving Daniel to suffer the inevitable avalanche of emotions. He sat on the verge for many hours with Tobacco unmoving at his side, stupefied and in shock. He felt disgusted, horrified, scared and angry, but eventually rose stiffly to his feet, looked once more along the track and walked slowly away in the opposite direction. Surely he would wake soon?

The following months passed without further incident, and yet for Daniel the experience remained vivid, rendering it certainly no dream. At first he tried convincing himself it was nothing more than that, a strange and terrible nightmare, but ultimately came to realise, he had escaped the clutches of Satan's spawn, and their unknown twilight world. Not a single day passed, without a different aspect of the five year roller-coaster, entering his thoughts. He revisited the place where he and Windrow had first met, and sat there until long after sunset. He was slowly coming to terms with the string of incredible events. When eventually the night air had chilled his back he stood up, hawked a fruity plug of phlegm from the back of his throat and spat onto the track where Windrow had once stood. It was a small but gratifying act of contempt.

# Dance of the Tarquills

Tobacco's right front paw had swollen grotesquely, each step awkward and hobbled. A thorn had pierced the pad of her front right paw, and the wound was corrupt and hard with infection. Daniel would have to bring forward his annual visit to Delamere, and test the charitable nature of the resident vet. It was a journey he would have preferred not to make, but, given the circumstances, it was one he could no longer avoid. That night he kept vigil over the fitful Tobacco, until sleep eventually claimed him in the midnight hours, as he lay beside the dying embers of his cooking fire.

With heavy droplets of dew sliding from the hem of his coat collar, he woke to a glorious sunrise. There could be no better way to start the day and he felt good, but in worrying contrast, Tobacco appeared forlorn, her coat crushed and crumpled, a true give-away she was sick. She offered no resistance as Daniel tucked her into the poacher's pocket of his long-coat. Then taking a bearing from the early sun he de-camped. He moved with purpose across the broken ground, through gullies and over crags and tors, crossing the streams and open plains of the moor until, by early noon, Delamere came into view.

He entered the veterinary practice as it opened for afternoon surgery, and a young female assistant led him into the examination room with a puzzled expression on her attractive face. Several times she looked sideways at the brace of pheasant hanging by the neck on a piece of string attached to Daniel's belt.

Conrad Sweet, the resident vet and owner of the business, turned round from looking at the wall mounted X-ray light box, with a look of mild surprise, behind a pair of steel half-rimmed glasses. Daniel smiled, unsure of the reception and hoisted the birds in what he hoped would serve as an olive branch.

'At this practice we prefer to treat animals before they reach such an irreversible condition,' said Conrad, with a rock steady gaze and raised eyebrow. Daniel realised how it must appear. He placed the brace of freshly-downed birds on the stainless steel table before carefully extracting Tobacco from his coat.

‘I was hoping you’d accept this offering as a down-payment in exchange for treating my dog...she’s in a bit of a sorry state and really in need of your help.’

Conrad Sweet, despite Daniel’s swept-back crop of raven hair and well developed beard, recognised him from his trading days with Bonner Tonrow. He made no reference to that fact, but had always deeply admired Daniel’s act of selfless philanthropy, which for some time had been the talk of the town. Ordinarily, one such as Daniel may well have been shown the door, with directions to the nearest People’s Dispensary for Sick Animals. But this was different and he beckoned Daniel and the dishevelled Tobacco closer.

After a relatively quick inspection, he concluded that Tobacco needed a minor operation, and would certainly require an overnight stay at the surgery. This was of little surprise to Daniel. He kissed the top of Tobacco's head and laid her into the basket, offered by the sudden appearance of Conrad’s assistant.

‘Incidentally,’ said Conrad, ‘this brace of pheasant is more than enough payment. Your dog, I’m sure, shall soon be as right as rain. Come back tomorrow and we’ll take it from there, does that sound acceptable to you.’

'More than acceptable, and thank you for your kindness.'

On leaving the surgery, Daniel was suddenly at a loss of how to pass the time. The idea of being confined to the town for twenty four hours held no appeal whatsoever. In something of a quandary, he meandered along the main street, with the townsfolk he passed giving little more than cursory stares. Unlike Conrad, no one recognised him as being the once smartly-dressed businessman, that had previously dealt in millions from a rented office, on that very street, and Daniel was not unhappy with the anonymity. He felt ill at ease being back, and certainly didn't feel like engaging in conversation. The memories were still strong, with flashbacks of happier times at Bonner Tonrow, making him both smile and frown as he walked.

It took little time to reach the far end of the town. He was about to turn, when his eye was drawn to a centre display, in a grubby shop window of an establishment he hadn't much noticed in the past. The façade of the building was in neo-classical design of yesteryear grandeur. Granite pilasters and elaborate cornices framed the front elevation, and Daniel guessed it had once been the town's bank, but those days had clearly long gone, even before his arrival. The window panes were grimed with road-film and the bottle-green paintwork on the hardwood frames was cracked and peeled with neglect. On the fascia board, below the upstairs windows was written 'Artefacts of Age,' in old-style gold font, the flaky lettering in the same disorder as the frames. But the real object of Daniel's attention, was an isolated book sitting on a small plinth just inside the window, its patina of age much at home with its surroundings. The volume was of a peculiar size, taller and narrower than the more recognised formats of modern print. The dust cover was missing, the hardback binding sun bleached, from what Daniel guessed had been midnight black to dirty grey, its title cracked and faded on a fractured spine 'Myths and Legends of England'. For some reason the book had caught his attention enough for him to engage. As he entered the shop, a small brass bell tinkled above his head, and from the inner recesses someone moved silently from the shadows and into the dim light.

Without wasting time, Daniel expressed his interest in the book and asked if it was possible to take a closer look. The shopkeeper however, on assessing his customer's appearance made a ruling that the book was for sale and not for thumbing through, placing Daniel in another quandary. He had no money, so to avoid embarrassment he quickly apologised, and began a hurried yet dignified exit.

'You have no money, do you Mr Bonner?'

The address stopped Daniel in his tracks. 'You know me?'

'Daniel Bonner! Yes I know who you are? I saw you several times in the Pink Pig, and despite that rather fine beard of yours, I would recognise your face anywhere.

Ruefully, Daniel inclined his head. So much for the anonymity; twice recognised in one day.

'Mr Bonner, would you mind if I asked a question?'

Daniel shrugged. ‘That depends on the question. You have me at a disadvantage; I don’t even know who you are.’

‘Apologies. I’m Jerry Green, owner of this establishment and all that you see in it.’ He thrust his hand forward with an eager grin.

Daniel took the other’s hand with a reciprocating smile. ‘Nice to meet you Jerry Green. Now, what’s your question?’

‘Is it true you gave away your entire personal fortune?’

‘Blimey, that’s a bit fucking direct,’ snorted Daniel.

‘Sorry, it’s one of my more redeeming characteristics,’ said Jerry with a friendly chuckle. ‘Did you actually do it Daniel, if I may call you Daniel?’

‘Yes I did and you may. But it’s no big secret, though thankfully rarely mentioned. It was simply a personal decision, that’s all.’

‘I’d like to hear your story. The very idea fascinates me. In return you can have the book without charge. It’s presumptuous I know. However, your generosity was the subject on everyone’s lips for quite a while, and has intrigued me ever since. In this day and age of snatch and grab, it’s a rarity to meet someone with such an extraordinary view of money. Tell me your story if you dare and the book is yours.’

Daniel thought for a moment. There could be no real harm in indulging this quiet-mannered rather engaging little man. After all, Daniel held the trump card by divulging only what he thought was necessary. Besides, Jerry had a distinct aura of kindness, accentuated in his eyes, by the round-rimmed glasses perched half way down a very symmetrical button nose. He was short and comfortably pot-bellied, with a dense mop of curly brown hair, above a blushed complexion. Daniel had taken an instant liking to the man, and after all, fair exchange was no robbery. But what was it about the book that had made him agree to the exchange so readily? There was only one way to find out, and what would have been inconceivable just an hour before, and against all the odds, he agreed.

‘I shall tell you on one proviso, that what I tell you stays strictly within these walls, and not to be even divulged to third parties, within these walls. I need your promise.’

‘My silence is my bond, Mr Bonner, I promise,’ he said, using the surname as if to underline the sincerity of the pact. He then ushered Daniel into the shops inner recesses, with an outstretched palm, like that of a top restaurant maitre d'.

The two men sat in the small back room, crammed with curios and artefacts, that Daniel found hugely claustrophobic compared to the open moor. However, the offered wing-back armchair was large and comfortable, made better by the magical appearance of a twelve-year-old bottle of Scotch whisky, and two crystal tumblers, from which a light film of dust was first removed, with the use of Jerry’s crumpled but well-laundered shirt-tail. Alcohol was now a great rarity in Daniel’s life, but no less appreciated when offered. Jerry poured decidedly stout measures, and handed one over before slumping into the sister chair opposite. Finally he was ready to listen to Daniel's story.

As Daniel talked, the hour hand journeyed effortlessly through time, and Jerry listened intently, his only intervention being to periodically refill the glasses. Outside daylight retreated, and the shadows of nightfall advanced, like phantoms across the shops well-trodden floorboards, and in the stark glow of a naked light bulb, the clock hands slid past midnight. Another hour passed, before Daniel reached the conclusion of the story. In all it had been a rather matter of fact account, without a single supernatural embellishment. However, under the affects of alcohol his tongue had been somewhat loosened. With another generous top up, he found himself spilling out the dark and baffling part of the tale, something he would never have dreamt of doing, had it not been for the liberating malt. Without pausing, he launched into every detail of the disturbing events concerning Tony Windrow - the Chancellor, and Norbert Morris. And as the words flowed, a great weight seemed to lift from his shoulders. For the first time he had an attentive ear, with Jerry sitting passively opposite, with only a small crease between his eyes as he tried to comprehend.

‘So there we are,’ said Daniel swallowing the remnants of his glass. ‘I’ve told you everything, a lot to take in I agree, but nonetheless, all frighteningly true.’

A few moments passed before Jerry answered it, with an offer of a roof over Daniel's head for the night. For a man used to sleeping under the open sky, Daniel surprised himself by accepting. Besides, he could suffer at least one night without dew drops dripping from the rim of his hat as he woke.

Reclining in the chair under a warm blanket his eyelids felt like lead, and Jerry crept from the room to leave him in peace. Daniel slept comfortably enough, however, in the early hours of dawn his dreams were vivid and disturbing. He woke suddenly, leaving behind some grotesque threat in his nightmare. Something in there had chased him into waking with a jolt, and beads of sweat tickled his temples. He felt hot and closed in. He threw back the blanket and wiped his face with the palm of his big hand. His mouth felt dry with the taste of stale whisky. Recalling what he had said the night before, didn't help either, and he instantly regretted his loose tongue. What on earth would Jerry Green be thinking of him? As he became fully awake, he was aware of somebody moving quietly about in the galley kitchen next door to the office.

The heady aroma of grilled bacon and freshly ground coffee suddenly filled his nostrils, the smell was superb and saliva flooded his dry mouth. 'Good morning Daniel,' said Jerry Green, as he entered and placed on the desk at his side, two thick wads of white bread sandwiches, and a large mug of coffee. With a return greeting and a nod of gratitude, Daniel began tucking in, aware of just how hungry he was. Jerry sat opposite him with his own crudely cut doorstep, and apart from a periodic grunt of approval from both men, they ate in silence.

When they had finished, Jerry took the plates and returned with re-filled mugs, and Daniel looked at the man's kindly face. How on earth could he expect him to understand, let alone believe, a word he had been told, about the Chancellor? It must have sounded ridiculous if not rather insulting to his intellect. Jerry appeared to guess what Daniel was thinking, looking at his face with searching eyes.

'Sorry about last night, Jerry. Do me a favour and forget what I told you; far too much whisky I'm afraid, enjoyable but embarrassing.' Open scoffing was all that could be expected and he wouldn't blame Jerry in the least. But, unexpectedly Daniel's apologetic request was received with nothing more than a raised eyebrow. Had Jerry already dismissed it as nonsense, or was there something else in that quizzical stare?

Whatever it was, Daniel became guarded; scared he might be thought mad.

Jerry Green sat in silence for long moments, which was worse than any due critical comment. He then took the silver hunter watch from his pocket, snapped open the engraved lid, studied the dial, closed the lid, drained his coffee and stood up.

'Mr Bonner, I face a busy day,' he said quietly. He walked through the shop, extracted the book from its plinth and returned with it in his hand.

'What's drawn you to this volume?' he asked, with genuine interest. It was more than Daniel deserved.

'No specific reason,' said Daniel, albeit relieved by the change of subject. 'The title I guess, nothing more.'

'Well, whatever the reason, as was our agreement, it's yours.'

'Look, Jerry. What I said…'

Jerry inclined his head, with an expression sincere enough to convince Daniel that his host was at least not thinking him entirely insane.

The book was presented, and Daniel reached out with both hands, and as if wanting to show gratitude he took it almost reverently. As his fingers curled around the loam he immediately sensed it as being an important milestone in his life. A curious tingle coursed up his arm as he held it tighter. He instinctively knew the book had something to do with his future, impossible to put into words. Jerry had already shown great generosity, not to mention having a very large pill of a story to swallow, and for those reasons it was time for Daniel to leave.

On exiting, it was made clear that he was welcome to visit at any time. It was an unreserved offer, one that Daniel believed he would never need call on, but it was a heart-warming invitation nonetheless.

With 'Myths and Legends' tucked deeply into his coat pocket, he returned Jerry's final handshake, stepped into the empty street and headed to the surgery for news of Tobacco.

'Tobacco has made outstanding progress,' said Conrad Sweet.

'You're dog has a remarkable power of recovery, Mr Bonner,' he said reassuringly whilst looking over his half-moon glasses, with a smile whiter than his lab coat. 'The surgery, antibiotics and a good night's rest seems to have done the trick.'

'Then I owe you more than just a brace of pheasant.'

'The birds are enough for me, Daniel. My time and surgery I give with my blessing.'

Daniel moved through the door with the same gratitude he had felt for Jerry Green. He thanked Conrad again and left with Tobacco limping gamely at his side.

With a renewed sense of faith in human nature, he tracked south beneath the arc of the sun, until the need to rest dictated a timely halt. He made camp as Tobacco padded around their temporary home, her injury almost a forgotten thing.

A cooking fire was lit, over which a hen pheasant carcase was soon roasting, victim to Daniel's acute accuracy with the Hummer. Tobacco sat salivating at the fireside, but she would have to wait. For the moment, Daniel had other things on his mind.

Digging into his long-coat he extracted the book. He would thumb through the volume until the pheasant was ready to eat. He opened the covers and in contrast to fresh moorland air the smell of musty parchment filled his nostrils.

The beginning of each chapter was headed by the same printed outline of the British Isles, with the position and shape of each county printed in solid black ink. The following pages recited the stories and fables of that area, and Daniel turned the pages until had found the rugged wilderness of Dartmoor. He found much had been written of legends, witchcraft, black magic, infamous highwaymen, lost treasure, religious persecution and other such stories, that had conjured the imagination of countless generations.

He lowered the book and tended the roasting bird. Tobacco was having none of the terrible neglect, nudging the palm of Daniel's free hand with a wet nose for a bit of fussing. After seeing to both and satisfied they were both doing well, Daniel returned his attention to the volume and flipped the next page. He would have read on, but on impulse he returned to the previous page, the heading of which had caught his eye.

'Dance of the Tarquills.' At first glance, the following paragraph seemed little more than a rhyming piece of folklore nonsense. And yet when read again the strange and threatening words seem to harden in his mind. Daniel read the lines three times, each time more chilling than the first.

Deep from underground they come, to feast to gorge, 'tis best you run.
They snatch and tear, even the wolf-pack lair, the yews all dead by dawn.
They dance and leap, with burst of flight, vitals torn from thee.
Two thousand strong, it takes not long, to clear the moor, a vicious spree.
Human screams in tortured ear, the carnage each five hundred year.
Bodies cleaved, dragged to the feast, butchered in this night of fear.
Beware the Tarquill's coming, a hoard, vile in fang and claw.
I warned them so, they repaid me thus, a madman behind asylum door.

An artist's drawing of the creature was etched in great detail below the verse. Ice-pick fangs crowded the Tarquill's mouth, with warthog tusks jutting laterally and vertically from both top and bottom jaw respectively. A mane of course hair ran down the animal's rat-like body, terminating at a spinal knot of muscle, from which stunted bat-wings spread in an unlikely bid for flight. Its lower body was crowded with arrowhead scales, its tail tipped with a scorpion's barb, raised and ready to strike. The creature crouched on hind legs, bulging with sinew and muscle with three large snatching claws like those of a hunting raptor. It was a clever and vivid depiction of a creature from hell. After long moments, Daniel eventually read the summary.

Author's note;

It is believed the originator of this strange verse, Phillip De Theiry, a Frenchman, reputedly from a line of Parisian nobility, spent the remaining five years of his life incarcerated in a place for the incurably insane. A stone cell, from where there was heard the ranting and ramblings of the reputed madman. Only upon his death, was this verse and drawing found etched on a stone slab, beneath the cot in his cell. Believed to be drafted in the final year of his life, the writing, although strange, is worryingly coherent, as is the skilfully drawn, strangely named, Tarquill.

It was later rumoured that De Theiry was, however, master of all his faculties, and as a result of his wrongful incarceration, is reputed to still haunt the open ground upon which the asylum once stood. It is a strange tale indeed; more so if he were actually sane.

Daniel laid the book down with a feeling of unease. Why something so fanciful should rattle his nerve was nonsense! After an inner dressing down he felt foolish, and not for the first time in the last twenty four hours. He thought again of Jerry Green. He was tired and in need of food. Clearly fatigue and hunger had prompted the verse to spook him. He shut the book and replaced it in his coat.

Daniel and his dog consumed most of the succulent pheasant meat, in double quick time, with Tobacco turning her nose up at the boiled potatoes, cress and wild garlic salad. With the freshly stoked fire warming their bodies, food in their bellies and a clear dry sky above their heads, Daniel lay back against his duffel bag, with Tobacco stretched along his lap like a draft stopper. What more could they possibly need and what worries could there be? But, try as he might, he could not shake the dogged feeling that trouble was soon to gatecrash their simple world.

Daniel sat up, stoked the fire with fresh logs, sending a serpent of sparks into the white smoke rising vertically into the still night air, and he gazed subconsciously into the caves and canyons of the glowing embers. There was something in the writing that still bothered him. De Theiry's incarceration, his drawing and the fearful verse were extraordinary enough, but Daniel felt there was something he had overlooked. He glanced once more at the etching. It was then he noticed the initials and date. P.D.T. 1518. And the dread penny dropped. Phillip De Theiry had completed the etching in the last year of his life; incarcerated for five, which meant the actual date of his living nightmare would have been 1513, five hundred years ago. For the Frenchman to initial and date the artwork, would surely not have been in the mindset of a madman. Daniel's eyes dropped to one significant line of the verse.

'Human screams, my tortured ear, the carnage each five hundred year'

He stood abruptly, and Tobacco fell from his lap without ceremony, and slunk into the darkness in a true huff, away from the big man's sudden pacing. Every instinct in Daniel's being screamed alarm, every nerve end had become active to what he now knew, was a menace stalking his tiny world, an imminent danger to be ignored at his peril. The book was not only a horror story from the ancient past, but more of what he now believed to be a dire warning on a personal level. He stared over the flames of his fire and into the wall of darkness beyond. He stood silent as a statue, scanning left and right with his eyes being the only visible movement. At the perimeter of heather surrounding his camp, a minute alteration in shade, caught his attention. He raised his arm, shielding the firelight from his eyes and looked over the immediate horizon of his hand, and in the flickering shadows, he saw further movement. With rapid eye movement, he was able to increase his night vision, a little trick from Windrow's school of learning, and he wondered when they had last enjoyed rabbit. He studied the doe grazing in the uncertain light, her long ears constantly scanning for danger. Periodically she looked up, checking her immediate proximity, with large auburn eyes, before dropping back to resume her nocturnal feeding.

Daniel reached for the Hummer, momentarily putting his fears to the back of his mind. Spit roast rabbit would be on tomorrow's menu. He moved smoothly, studying the range and size of the target. It would be an easy kill. The weight of the Hummer felt good in his grip and he cocked his arm. He was about to let fly, when something in the backdrop of undergrowth placed the doe in instant readiness for flight. She thumped her hind legs against the hard ground, a warning to others of danger, but within the blink of an eye, an unseen hunter snatched the luckless animal, in a blur of savagery, dragging it convulsing and kicking into the undergrowth. The speed of the dispatch deceived Daniel's night eye, and the doe's death scream was eerie and startlingly pierce. Seconds later the rabbit's pelt, hot and steaming in the night air was jettisoned from the now hushed thicket, to land at Daniel's feet. He squinted into the impenetrable undergrowth, the Hummer poised at the ready.

It was then that Tobacco squeezed through the barrier of undergrowth on the opposite side of the arena, in what, even for her low pedigree, was the classic stance of the trained pointer.

'Stay away,' hissed Daniel, but Tobacco, with excitement for the hunt in her adolescent mind, dispensed with the stalk, and bounded forward on her short powerful legs to flush out the rabbit killer. Whatever was in there had her full attention, and even Daniel's sharp command could not halt her dash.

A disconcerting hush descended as she disappeared into the scrub, before a scene from hell broke loose.

Two fighting bodies, the larger being that of Tobacco burst from the undergrowth, snapping, clawing and biting amidst unholy noises from the world of the beast. In the firelight, Daniel identified claw and fang, glistening scales, stumpy bat-like wings and a scorpion tail. The dreadful legend had come back to life.

To call Tobacco again, would be a distraction that could prove fatal for his dog. Without a second thought, he drew back his arm and pumped the Hummer forward. It cart-wheeled towards the fighting pair with its characteristic low tone, and struck the Tarquill with bone shattering impact. It had been a desperately lucky shot, breaking every bone in the creature's spine, and Tobacco sprang away from the fight, ruffled and bloodied.

The Tarquill twitched in its final death throes, as Tobacco darted in and out, testing the body from all directions, with an impressive array of barred teeth. Blood dripped freely from her right ear, soaking the hair on her neck, and Daniel pulled her away by the scruff, mindful of the wound.

Although frightening, the etching in the book went only part way to depict the sheer menace of the creature, and the stench from its body wrinkled Daniel's nose. He raised the crock of his forearm to stifle the smell, and looked down at the corpse. With use of the Hummer he rolled the carcass onto its back to make a full inspection, but as he did so the body began disintegrating until all that remained was a greasy patch in the flattened grass. Then that too was gone. All evidence of the creature had dissolved without a trace, reason enough, thought Daniel, that these vile creatures had never been preserved for science, documented only once by the unfortunate De Theiry. It was little wonder they had all believed him insane.

Daniel hefted the Hummer and squinted at the front-line of dense thicket, wondering at the havoc two-thousand of these creatures could wreak. What he had witnessed, dispelled any lingering doubts about the legend, or indeed of the power in the book's warning. That they truly existed and that all things in their path were in mortal danger. Ordinarily the manifestation would be impossible to comprehend, but given his acquired understanding of the Underworld, Daniel believed everything the book was telling him with one vital question. One had found him, but where was the legendary hoard? It was only a guess, but Daniel reckoned the lone Tarquill was probably an advance scout, like a soldier-ant, blazing a trail along the most profitable route for food, with an army sure to follow. For five minutes he stood motionless, with the Hummer hard in his grip, until at last he was satisfied that there was nothing else dangerous, close at hand in the scrub.

Just in case, he dampened the fire, so as not to attract further attention and turned his attention to Tobacco's injuries. The rip in her ear was as if it had been severed by a blunt cleaver and the idea of confronting another Tarquill, let alone two-thousand was a sobering thought. He pressed the wound closed as hard as he dared, until it naturally sutured, then cleaned the coagulated blood from her coat, with water from his canteen. Tobacco allowed Daniel's ministrations with complete trust, but like her master she remained highly agitated.

That night, sleep was a fitful affair. Tobacco had tucked herself deep within the folds of his long-coat and Daniel felt only slightly comforted, by the warmth and periodic movement of her body. The temperature dropped around them, and in the lost hour before dawn, he succumbed to a world of strange and vivid dreams. The apparition of Phillip De Theiry sat opposite on the other side of the embers, a startling-looking individual with greying hair, tied back in an unkempt ponytail and held back by a decrepit bow of faded black velvet. His chiselled face was set in dire expression, as if carved in grey volcanic pumice. His grimy white shirt with its tattered breastplate ruff, was ripped at the shoulder, exposing translucent skin upon which a rose tattoo of superior artistry, showed through the tear. He possessed an aura of the dead, but his inquisitive eyes were certainly not that of the insane.

'They're coming,' De Theiry eventually said, in a thick Parisian accent. 'They're coming as they did five hundred years ago, and five hundred before that. They come for the blood of man, for the hearts and flesh of beast and bird. And they come with ravenous hunger.' His eyes grew wide and vacant, driven by his own startling experiences, and for a short while, De Theiry was lost in a sea of dark and frightening memories.

'What have I got to do?' said Daniel, breaking the silence, hearing his own voice echo in the corridor of his dream.

Although De Theiry starred directly at Daniel, his eyes had grown suddenly lifeless.

'What must I do?' repeated Daniel, his words grew louder.

Slowly, De Theiry came back from the far regions of his mind, and his eyes re focused.

'Lead them away, Daniel Bonner. Lead them as far as you can from humans and livestock. You have been chosen to defend those unable to defend themselves and champion the living. You have slain one of their numbers and they grow vengeful. You have now become the hunted. You must lay a trail they will be sure to follow.'

'What sort of trail?'

'Blood,'

'Whose blood?'

'Your blood.'

'Jesus…how much of it?'

'It needs but a drop.'

'And what then?'

'Find the house with windows small. It is your only chance of salvation. And remember, fire be your only friend.'

'You talk in bewildering riddles,' said Daniel accusingly. 'Where is this sanctuary? Are you sure it will be me they chase?'

'For you the Tarquills already nurture hatred. Spill your blood on the ground where their number perished and they will hunt you down. But listen, and take note. A house with foundations true, stands alone on a hill in the east.'

‘More bloody riddles!’ hissed Daniel, with trepidation thick in his words.

Ignoring the second accusation, De Theiry stared long and hard at Daniel, as if making sure his words had been heard. Satisfied that they had, his apparition began to fade and in desperation, Daniel reached out to preserve the contact but without success, as the Frenchman drifted away into obscurity.

Daniel called to him along the disintegrating conduit of dreams one final time, before waking with a jolt. He sat unmoved for a while, his torso bathed in sweat. Unlike most dreams this one remained vivid. As he sat with his collar raised against the chill, he found himself quietly asking a worrying question. Had he crossed the line of sanity into the unfathomable abyss of madness? And what of the book. Was it actually a curse to torment his mind? He thought about that aspect long and hard. Indeed it had warned him of the Tarquills, and more importantly of whatever influence that had actually guided him to it? His head broiled with so many unanswered questions, but eventually his conclusions were both reassuring and deeply worrying. If he were mad, surely what remained of his sanity, would drift in and out like an unpredictable tide and Tobacco’s ear would not be torn and bloody. He looked down at his sleeping dog, and suddenly he knew himself to be sane, and with a sense of purpose he stood to gaze in the direction of the inevitable sunrise; a new day, and with it the truth. In the first uncertain light of dawn, all doubts about his mental well-being evaporated. He drew his hunting knife and made a cut to the pad of his thumb as instructed in the dream. Any uncertainty was replaced by a sense of duty, like some unavoidable ordination. He had no idea as to the consequence of his actions, but because of the appearance of Phillipe De Theiry in his dream, he inexplicably felt less frightened and alone.

His thumb exuded a fat pearl of blood, that dripped weightily onto the patch of grass where the Tarquill had been destroyed, and once he had carried out De Theiry’s instruction, he gathered his belongings, calculated a course due east, and walked from the camp with Tobacco trotting close at heel despite her wound.

De Theiry’s advice to head east proved to be the best direction in which to lead the Tarquills, in the main devoid of livestock and game, but not entirely of humanity. Several miles into the journey, they came across Jesse and Zip at the foot of a rugged tor. Their greeting was easy, which was more than could be said for the two dogs. Zip, with his bull terrier mentality, strained tirelessly at the makeshift leash of baler twine to get at Tobacco, who gamely stood her ground. And for the sake of Tobacco's size and tender years they were duly kept apart.

'There's big fucking trouble heading our way,' said Daniel, cutting to the chase, and with Zip partially subdued, Jesse listened to Daniel's obvious bullshit wind-up. He shot periodic glances of disbelief through his bright topaz eyes, searching Daniel's face for any sign of a leg-pull, but worryingly he could see none. Jesse was not given to fantasy, but then neither was his friend, or so he believed. Daniel wasted no time in showing Jesse the relevant pages in the book, but ultimately, he could see the king of all poachers was struggling with what was being described, in his own colourful vernacular, as a complete load of bollocks. It was sorely testing their friendship. Why the fuck should Daniel, a newly trusted friend, be spouting such crap? Suddenly Jesse felt angry at the lack of respect. Was Daniel truly asking him to believe the legend's credibility and the equally ridiculous dream? He tilted back his heavy head, and looked at Daniel down the short length of his broken nose, searching for the truth, but despite everything, Daniel remained resolute.

'Christ, Danny! Don't bullshit me. Do you honestly think I came down with the last shower of fucking rain?' The question hissed through his tight lips with meaning.

'I want you to get out of here Jesse,' Daniel answered with equal sincerity, whilst pointing north with the point of his chin, indicating the direction which he believed was the safest passage for his friend. 'As far away as humanly possible.' He leaned forward until their faces were just a hand span apart. 'Right now Jesse, and I don't give a fucking toss, if you believe me or not!' If nothing else, Jesse could see the utter conviction in Daniel's eyes, and hear the power in his voice. It was impressive.

'Very soon they'll come to hunt me down.' His eyes were as fierce as a pride lion. This was the first time Jesse had seen Daniel like this, and for the first time he realised that Daniel believed in every word of warning he was giving. Daniel softened his voice, but his words remained loaded.

'Go now, Jesse, and take the dogs with you...please.'

Despite his difficulty in believing what had been said, Jesse realised Daniel was reacting to something that had scared him enough to say things that remained beyond the poacher's comprehension. The tenuous shift in Jesse's eyes, was enough to convince Daniel that at least some of his words had sunk home. However, precious time had been squandered by his friend's stubborn prevarication, born primarily from Jesse's bull-headed refusal to run from anything on God's green earth, human or otherwise. He stood full-square in the direction of the supposed threat, as a statement of defiance, his trunk-like arms swung like war clubs, and the buttons of his shirt shot taut over the barrel of his puffed-out chest. But despite the formidable show of force the shadows in the heather had grown long, and Daniel sensed it was suddenly too late. Zip lost all interest in Tobacco, and a growl rolled from his throat. Tobacco, not to be outdone did likewise. The two dogs now stood side by side, and with differences momentarily forgotten, curled back their lips, snarling at the encroaching darkness, with an impressive combination of barred teeth. Jesse knew Zip's every mood, and prickles of unease rolled up his neck like a chill breeze. The dogs, with all their animal genius, felt a great danger approaching, and were reacting accordingly, and with very good reason. The Tarquills had begun to hunt.

The distant sound of four thousand beating wings, was at first like that of a gentle breeze, heard in some far off woodland treetops, mounting swiftly into a loud murmur, then into a roar, that rolled across the open ground, like an approaching express.

'We're too late Jesse,' Daniel bellowed. 'It's begun…run for your bloody life!'

Jesse deflated his idiotic upper torso, and as the sound grew, it became a terrifying noise, a tangible thing reverberating through the air, and with one last shout of warning, Daniel crashed away into the dense brush, with Tobacco close at heel. Zip bravely stood his ground, baring teeth, with hackles standing like wheat stubble along the length of his spine. In that moment, time seemed to slow, as though Jesse had been caught thigh-deep in a trough of molasses. His legs were not responding, and for the first time in his life he felt real fear. The will to survive flooded his soul, and with a sudden presence of mind he spun, like a weather cock in a fluke wind, jerked Zip off his feet by the lead, and took off after the fleeing Daniel and Tobacco. It was so alien for him to run, but the voice of self-preservation screamed into his ears. Something bad was coming at him fast from the land of shadows.

With his own breathing, ragged in his ears, Jesse eventually caught up with Daniel. He tried to speak. Answers were needed.

'Save your breath, Jesse, and run. This ain't the time for questions.'
For several miles, the going was good and they gained ground. Ahead, in the distance, the ground rose steeply to an isolated hill, crowned by a three acre spinney. Maybe there they could climb a tree, and from that vantage point hold back the Tarquills; no easy task given that daylight was fading rapidly.

'Let's turn and fight the bastards,' grunted Jesse, through tortured lungs, 'Or at least find out what the hell is really coming up behind us.' And for the first time in his fighting life, he appeared unsure what to do for the best.

'No, Jesse. If we stay we die. Trust me…just run.'

They reached the summit, and with lungs almost blown they looked west. In the last light they saw movement, so wide and deep it appeared as if the ground undulated with life. Through the passageways of heather and brambles, the Tarquills were running amok. A red deer was thrown into panic and broke cover on legs of spring steel, but the large buck was no match against the countless claws and fangs of the terrible legend. Within seconds the animal was downed under the ferocity of a hundred writhing bodies. Dismembering and devouring, the Tarquills tore the fine specimen to bloody tatters, until all that remained was a few scattered bones, and a large bloody smear.

That little distraction converted all that was left of Jesse's scepticism into lurid fascination. A hefty slap on his back from Daniel broke the spell, and as one they turned and fled.

The four fugitives ran into the sanctuary of trees, Jesse now leading the way, bulldozing his way unchecked through the undergrowth, like a wild buffalo at full charge, carving a passage for the others to follow.

Just ahead of his position, Daniel heard a deep boom, as if something had struck a tuneless gong. Jesse was propelled backwards, landing on his rump at Daniel's feet. He hurriedly lifted his friend from the woodland floor. Jesse had careered into the wreck of an abandoned pick up truck. He regained control and tried the doors, but they were fussed in their jambs with years of corrosion, denying any hope of entry. However, in the flat bed sat a large plastic drum, and instinctively, Daniel dragged it to the ground, unscrewed the cap and hurriedly pressed his nose to the spout. He jerked his head away from the escaping fumes of sump oil and fuel tank flushings, and it was then he remembered De Theiry's words, 'fire be your only friend.' He replaced the stopper, hauled the container to his shoulder and the four continued their frantic dash deeper into the wood.

'Remember the house of foundations true, with windows small.' The riddle crowded Daniel's head, his mind racing on its meaning. No one in their right mind would bother to build a strong house, with little windows, in the tangle of this wood, but then again, was the condition of De Theiry's mind qualified to suggest it in the first place? But incredibly, as if on cue the answer stood square in front of him, under a blanket of wild brambles and hawthorn. It was a concrete pillbox, built as part of the ring of defences in the early forties, to defend against the threat of Hitler's invasion. In the past, Daniel had stumbled across similar buildings and was familiar with their layout and construction. There was no doubt, this was the house in the riddle.

They could hear the Tarquills advancing through the trees, already dangerously close and Daniel tossed Tobacco unceremoniously through the low entrance, her startled yap echoing from the interior.

'Get inside,' ordered Daniel, and for the first time in his life, Jesse did as he was asked without even a backward glance, leaving Daniel alone in the dark. He franticly unscrewed the drum lid, tucked the container under his arm and began pouring the viscous liquid onto the woodland floor. His plan was to hold back the Tarquills with a ring of fire, giving them a chance to build their defences in the narrow gun slits and the crawl-through entrance. It would be a tight run thing. He managed to circumnavigate the perimeter, and succeeded in linking the glutinous liquid in a defensive moat. He replaced the stopper and dumped the still quarter full canister into the oily flushings. All around him came the sound of twelve thousand snatching claws scampering across the woodland floor, the clicking chatter of two thousand tongues behind tusk and fang; the beat of four thousand wings and the rasping of a million reptilian arrowhead scales. It was a frightening noise, but most dreadful was the overpowering stench of decay.

Daniel searched frantically in the pockets of his coat for his flint to ignite the moat, but in his haste it remained illusive to his trembling fingers, and in that terrible moment he realised his jeopardy. He gripped the handle of his hunting knife, the final weapon of defence.

Suddenly an unexpected light flared as Jesse came to his side, and the world held its breath, as he dropped the flaming match into the liquid. The sudden expansion of flames leapt high between the trees, sending the two men reeling backwards, the air sucked from their lungs. Daniel's brows and beard singed alarmingly under the combustion, and the dry woodland litter fuelled the inferno beyond expectation. Within seconds the pillbox was engulfed in bright orange flames and belching black smoke, with Daniel and Jesse crawling hurriedly inside, heavily singed but unhurt.

'Fuck me!' snorted Jesse, 'that will give those stinky little shits something to think about,' and through the rush of fear and adrenalin, Daniel's laugh was robust in volume.

As the fire raged outside, he took stock of the interior. The cramped room was half filled with wire mesh, numerous building bricks and wooden fencing staves. Daniel guessed it was the local farmer's fencing store to keep sheep from entering the spinney. There was more than enough material to block the low entrance and gun ports. They set to work jamming fencing stakes into the apertures, made secure with pieces of broken brick, hammered into place with the ends of other staves. The main entrance was then blocked with an entire roll of wire, secured by a stake driven at right angles through the mesh across the inside jamb. With the other end tight against the inner blast-wall, the obstruction could neither be pushed nor pulled without the removal of the timber.

The fire continued holding back the Tarquills, and it bought the besieged men valuable time. But even with extreme optimism they both knew it couldn't last. Their fears were quickly realised. The canister of sludge Daniel had dumped near the entrance finally reached flash point. In the resulting explosion a dozen Tarquills were lifted high in the blast, their body parts crashing into the waiting ranks at the back. The explosion had created a gap but had claimed only a few of the hoard. But more importantly the blast had extinguished the last of the flames. All that remained of the inferno were scattered embers, silence and sudden darkness.

‘Damn it, should have known that would happen,’ said Daniel grimly as he looked through the mesh and into the shadows. ‘Get ready my friend. They’ll be at us any moment now, I reckon.’

‘They’d come sooner or later,’ gruffed Jesse, his voice hoarse with smoke and emotion.

In the middle of the concrete floor he had lit another fire, with twigs and leaf litter that had blown in over the years, fuelling it further with the pointed ends of the spare staves. ‘Flaming spears,’ he told Daniel with a wry grin. There remained just enough ventilation in which to breathe, and through smoke-watered eyes, he looked round for his dog.

‘Zip where are you? Come here boy.’ But Zip had gone.

'Danny, have you seen Zip?' He crawled to the entrance, filled his lungs and called again through the convolution of wire. It was then he heard a single yelp somewhere out in the darkness, shrill and panicked.

‘I have to find him,’ he grunted, and began tearing at the pole holding the mesh. Daniel rushed him, expending a considerable amount of his strength to physically restrain his friend, and although only half his size, Jesse was a power ball of muscle and strong as an ox.

‘For Christ sake Jesse, pack it in...I can’t let you go out there. You know that.’

‘Want to make a bet, Matey,’ wheezed Jesse through Daniel’s crushing bear hug, expanding his torso in order to break the grip. But ultimately, and very deliberately, Daniel slowly won the test of strength. Minutes later, the poacher slumped in resignation, fully tested.

‘Sorry Jesse, your dog may be gone, but there's no way I'm going to let you go.’

‘If I know Zip, he’s out there hiding somewhere…I bet…’

‘Hold it Jesse…Listen.’

With a frown, Jesse cocked his ear.

‘Listen to what? If you think you can hear something I can’t…well…’

'For fuck's sake Jesse…Just shut it for a moment.'

Since the explosion, the wood had in the main remained silent, and with it, Jesse's hopes rose.

'They've gone, Danny. The dirty little bastards have bloody well gone.'

'I really wouldn't count on that, Jesse.' Daniel was right. The stench remained thick in the air. Only a day ago he knew nothing of these Tarquills, but he had seen them hunt with unprecedented savagery, and such creatures would never give up that easily. They were out there waiting to attack, and begrudgingly, Jesse had to agree.

'I'm sorry about Zip, Jesse. Really sorry, but there's no way you can leave. Believe me, it's for your own good as well as mine.'

'Ok, you've made your point.'

Daniel was about to reassure Jesse that Zip had probably got away, when a strange sound came at them through the entrance, a soft whisper from countless stealthily moving bodies. The Tarquills were advancing in grim silence through the ferns without a wing beat in a surprise attack.

The two men peered through the roll of mesh as hundreds of the creatures gathered at the entrance and without warning began their assault, tearing at the barrier with claw and fang. Scorpion tails darted forward over their tugging bodies dispensing murderous drops of venom. Rivulets of the clear liquid ran down the galvanised strands, saturating the outer threshold in sticky puddles and when one fell back with fatigue hundreds of its fellow numbers were there to take over. Slowly they succeeded in chewing through the outer coils, but thankfully it would take days to breach the entire compacted roll. Satisfied they were protected, from that quarter at least, Daniel crawled into the inner recesses. Suddenly every nerve in his body snapped taut, as a piece of brick dropped onto his back from one of the gun ports. The frontal attack was a smokescreen.

'Jesse! Get the fuck in here now,' shouted Daniel, from the other side of the blast wall. 'The bastards are coming in through the windows.'

Grabbing a burning stave, he thrust it through the gap and saw the burning tip disappear down an impaled Tarquill's throat. Seconds later the stave convulsed so violently it was close to being torn from his grip, and Daniel realised the alarming strength of these ugly, foul-smelling creatures. The contents of its belly exploded in a convolution of half digested meat, entrails and sparks. It fell from view.

Again he bellowed to Jesse for support, and Jesse responded, rushing in to stand alongside, thrusting and stabbing the burning javelins, through an ever-increasing number of holes. Daniel primed the fire with more ammunition, then returned to the ramparts, in time to dash a brick against a scaly limb reaching through the crumbling defences. The Tarquill retracted its broken claw, then burst through the gap in a shower of brick dust and relentless will. It dropped to the floor and Jesse sent it flying into the interior with a toe-punt from his boot. It slid down the opposite wall then scurried away; he would deal with it later, right now they had to prevent others gaining entry in the same way.

Soon the pillbox was a smoke-filled hell-hole, and a raging thirst tore at both men's throats.

'Better a thirst than a Tarquill at our windpipes,' Daniel croaked, as he stabbed the point of his hunting knife deep into a Tarquill's eye.

Again and again they repelled the creatures with dogged brutality, but in the back of both men's minds the question hung like the gallows nose. How long could they stand against this never-ending assault?

For several hours the battle raged on, marked only by the number of attacks and necessary counter measures, but in reality, time was inconsequential. Their throats were drier than sandpaper, their limbs shook with fatigue, and the beleaguered friends knew it would be a fight to the finish.

Then as quickly as it had begun the attack ended. With no apparent reason the Tarquills disappeared from the gun ports and were suddenly gone.

For half an hour the two men stood in silent vigil, peering through the battered defences until, Daniel broke the silence, his words scratchy with smoke and lack of saliva.

‘We’d best plug these holes Jesse. They may well be back.’

‘I don’t reckon we can hold them again,’ replied Jesse. The sound of trepidation in his voice was telling.

In the hazy gloom their eyes met. Daniel held the gaze with piercing intensity, and in that expression, Jesse saw their fate.

Lesser men would have dropped to their knees and begged for divine intervention, some even choosing suicide, rather than face the prospect of dying in such a terrible manner. But with wry grins, Daniel and Jesse understood each other implicitly. There could be only one way to go. They would die fighting.

With renewed energy, the two men, galvanised by grim reality, went about the repair. Jesse even managed one of his appalling jokes, the gist of which fell on deaf ears but won a respectful chuckle nonetheless. With the defences finally reinstated, they sat slumped with their backs to the wall. It was then that Daniel remembered his dog. A Tarquill had gained entry, yet neither it or Tobacco were visible. Calling to her in the smokey gloom, he rounded the blast wall, and as his retinas adjusted to the darkness he saw the Tarquill and Tobacco, lying motionless on the floor at his feet. With the club end of the Hummer, Daniel crushed the Tarquills skull. He was taking no chances. He then scooped up his dog, and although her body was inert, he felt the merciful pulse of life in his hands. He took her into the main chamber and rolling her in his lap discovered a small puncture wound where the scorpion barb had pierced her shoulder. Unknown to Daniel, and luckily for Tobacco, the Tarquill was one of the numbers that had first attacked the entrance, and whose venom sack had been depleted, rendering his dog only unconscious.

‘Damn it Danny, you weren’t kidding when you described these stinking hell raisers. They’re fuckin' deadly! Sorry for not believing you, especially after that French bloke saved us with his riddle? All the same, I'm still finding all this difficult to get my fucking head round, but one thing I do know, I’ll never doubt you again.’

‘I would have reacted in exactly the same way, Jesse, and I hate to say it but we’re not out of it yet.’

‘But why is it happening, Danny. Why you? Jesus, I hope I wake up in a minute with nothing more deadly about my body than sweat.’ He looked at his friend and had to accept the awful truth. He left Daniel, and peered around the blast wall at the body from Hell's creation.

'Hey, Danny, come here! The bloody thing's escaped!' Jesse looked around for any possible hidden attack, before realising the blast chamber was empty with no possible exit. 'What the fucks happening Danny? It's gone.'

'They disintegrate on death, which means the bugger was still alive before I crushed its skull. Take no chances Jesse; make sure you kill them.'

Jesse rejoined Daniel, and Tobacco looked up from his lap with a feeble greeting.

'Zip,' Jesse remembered his own dog. 'I've got to find him, and this time I'm going out. Help me or not, I'm removing the barrier.'

'Can't let you do that Jesse. We have no idea where they are. It could be a trap and as a hunter, well you know it.'

'If they were out there we'd smell the bastards. Isn't that right Danny? We'd smell 'em, wouldn't we?' Jesse's eyes were wide and searching. This was certainly no time for another energy sapping trial of strength.

True enough. The woodland floor was devoid of movement and the stench had gone, enough to convince Jesse that the coast was clear.

'I'm going out Danny…with or without you.'

He began dislodging the stave and Daniel had little choice but to assist his brave, bull-headed friend. He felt a lift of pride at his courage.

'Stubborn bastard,' he muttered, and slapped the other's back. He then thrust the Hummer firmly into Jesse's calloused hand, as the poacher ducked into the exit tunnel.

'Take it my friend, and let's hope you won't bloody need it.'

'Doubt if I'll need this little piece of matchwood,' he replied, taking it anyway, with a grin that exposed the gap between his upper front teeth. 'Don't forget, Zip's the best ratter in the business.'

'These ain't fuckin' rats Jesse!'

Jesse grunted at Daniel's derogatory underestimation of his terrier, but nonetheless his grin became a farewell smile.

They shook hands, and seconds later, in the moonless hour before dawn, Jesse left the sanctuary. Outside, the sweet night air was clean and fresh, and he breathed deeply, clearing the remnants of wood smoke from his still stinging lungs.

Standing with his back to the pillbox, he peered into the darkness of the trackless woodland. Through dry lips he whistled a warbled note, and from beyond the tree line he heard barking. A smile of relief cracked his weathered face as he made towards the sound, but within thirty paces he suddenly sensed there was something behind him. Downwind of the pillbox the hoard had been waiting. The night breeze had carried their stench away through the whispering trees, but now they surged forward, craving human flesh as they came.

'Clever little bastards,' he muttered, realising the impossibility of making it back to the pillbox. 'It's a trap Danny,' he shouted, running blindly away. 'You were right, damn you. Close the fuckin' door.'

Inside, Daniel heard the warning, and the sudden beat of Tarquill wings, as they poured over the pillbox like a single organism, and without a second to loose he re-plugged the entrance. Some of the numbers played the original game of tug-of-war with the mesh, but the rest rolled over the bastion in uncountable waves with the irresistible scent of human flesh in their nostrils. They were hunting Jesse with ravenous hunger.

Coming from somewhere in the dark, Daniel heard Jess's distressing cries of fear and panic before they ceased abruptly. He fell back against the blast wall, dumbstruck. Jesse had to be dead. No man could survive the hoard. The beat of wings settled to a hum, and Daniel imagined the Tarquills feasting on his friend, like a gathering of giant sewer rats.

For minutes he held back, and then something dark and terrible erupted, from a place that no man should ever be made to go, and with all the anger and hate that one man can gather, he shouted through the mesh, deafened by the volume of his own voice.

'I'm in here you filthy bastards. It's me you're after. Come on! Come and get me!' He heard his rage in the challenge, an alien sound as if coming from another being. He goaded the Tarquills again and again with guttural profanities. And not surprisingly the Tarquills obliged.

An overwhelming wish for bloody vendetta, had blossomed from a dark place within Daniel's soul. He tore away bricks from a gun port, and draped his heavy leather coat over the opening. Within seconds, four of the filthy numbers spilled into the garment, crashing to the floor with the leather restraining them like rats in a sack. Daniel hastily re-plugged the hole, dashing away scaly limbs as he did so.

The coat heaved and pulsated on the floor like a disembowelled stomach, and he set about it with boot, stave and stone, pounding and pulverising, jumping and kicking, stabbing and beating with the passion and brutality of a man driven by vengeance for a lost brother. Claw and barb shot through the fabric in futile defence, useless beneath such a frenzied attack.

Then all movement ceased, and the coat deflated like a giant balloon, and Daniel heard the roar of his own breathing in his ears. He stood like a monstrous slayer, his chest heaving for air, his eyes wild, hunting the gloom like an apocalyptic madman, and a strange feeling of detachment replaced his fear, as though standing outside himself, and nobody could be more dangerous. He crouched, craving to kill again, praying more would breach the gun ports. Again and again they poured into his coat, their dispatch no less brutal, until eventually, with his coat covering the gap he waited for the next attack, but this time the Tarquills did not come.

For the next half-hour he stared into the empty woodland, slowly climbing back from the dark regions of his mind. He stood alone in the gloom, until eventually, the return of reason brought him back to the human race.

He picked up Tobacco from the concrete floor, and with her in his arms, he stood in silence for a period he couldn't calculate.

It was daylight seeping through the entrance, that gave Daniel a sense of time, and with Tobacco tucked into his shirt, he emerged blinking from the pillbox. As in the legend, the Tarquills had come to hunt in a night of fear, and then returned to skulk in the bowels of the earth, for another five hundred years.

Daniel found the Hummer, shattered and bloodied on the woodland floor and he wondered at Jesse's and Zip's final agony. He left the woods feeling numb as he walked west.

The further he travelled, the more time he had to think, and the more he knew it to be the Chancellor's work. The book was all part of it, a warning of what was to come in a strange and frightening destiny. He wasn't free at all, free from an existence in the lower world perhaps, but he had crossed swords with the Chancellor. Tony Windrow no longer existed. His battle was with the Chancellor, and should he fail he would nonetheless die fighting, as Jesse had done, making sure hell itself would remember the name Daniel Bonner for a long time to come.

# The Power of Money

The early sun had yet to warm the damp air, surrounding Daniel's camp-site high on Badger Head Tor, and with his front to the fire, he turned his collar against the chill. It had become his early morning ritual, as Phillipe De Theiry had ritually entered his dreams, just prior to waking. He had come to Daniel many times, since the Tarquills, to talk of mundane things in his search of company. No longer disturbed by the apparition, Daniel was also glad of the increasing visitations. Now awake he mused over their last meeting, happy with the thought they would meet again soon.

The temperature that morning was the first real indication of an ageing summer. The ground below his position, lay buried beneath a bank of autumnal mist, a beautiful sight, but nonetheless the harbinger to the onset of colder weather. He sat quietly watching the moor come to life, as he ate a breakfast of fat blackberries, from the makeshift bowl of his wide-brimmed bush-hat. Tobacco sat alongside, eating the remains of a brace of pigeon, brought down by the MK 11 Hummer. Her injuries received in the battle with the Tarquills had healed, the venom finally expunged from her body, but it had been a long recovery and all in all, a very close call.

Daniel popped the lid from a battered smoker's tin, and extracted a lollipop stick, around which was coiled a ten-metre length of six-pound fishing line. He inspected the weights and hooks, and cleaned away the light film of rust with his thumb and forefinger. Satisfied the tackle was in good general condition, he promised himself fresh trout for their evening meal. Replacing the lid, he looked casually down the slope that stretched before him, and at a thousand paces saw what appeared to be an inverted talon, poking through the white veil of mist, far too big for the creature of legend. Nonetheless, a cold wind blew through his Tarquill-minded soul. For a while he sat watching the valley, and as the sun warmed the air, it became apparent the object was nothing more threatening than the pole-tips of a makeshift wigwam.

'Well well, Tobacco, we have company,' he said, severely disliking the intrusion. Apart from the periodic necessity to enter Delamere for essential items, he was in most parts a law unto himself, abiding by his own rules, driven by the forces of the moor, not humankind. Mindful to avoid that particular section of the valley, he turned his attention to the duffel bag and exhumed a worn block of soap. The drop in early autumn temperatures, reminded him of the lessening opportunities to bathe in the quarry pools, and that he would soon be resorting to water heated in front of the fireplace, in the foreman's stone cottage that Windrow had shown him. Despite his unkempt appearance, Daniel's basic discipline of hygiene had never faltered, an essential element to overall health and well-being.

He left Tobacco on the high ground, and headed for his favourite pool. It was a deep lagoon, surrounded by high granite walls rising vertically from the clear depths, a flooded quarry, once used for the extraction of railway track ballast, now quiet and private, and more importantly close enough to his winter quarters. Daniel had learned its hidden secret. Beneath the deceptive tranquillity, the place was a potential death trap, the walls so sheer, it would vex even an expert climber just to contemplate an assent from the water line. Daniel, however, was one of the very few, who knew the location of a secret gully, through which he could enter and exit the water in safety.

Entering the overgrown entrance he began his descent, but after little more than ten feet into the narrow cut, he froze to sounds of crisis ricocheting along the gully walls, the unmistakeable sounds of someone drowning. He raced back to the ridge and arrived just in time to see the body of a girl sinking into the depths, her pale upturned face in the rictus of the dying.

The resulting removal of his clothes was a sudden feverish discard, and standing naked at the lip he took the plunge. Entering the water was like being hit in the body by a block of ice, and he grunted against the prickling assault on nerve ends in his skin. The dive took him in deep and as the effects of natural buoyancy took control he struck down. At a depth of forty feet, the pressure toyed with his vision, but through the darkening waters, he caught an ethereal glimpse of the girl. With a final lunge, he took hold of her wrist, and after what seemed like eternity, they broke the surface, in a chaos of white water and bubbles. Dragging air into his tortured lungs, Daniel swam for the secret path leading to the ridge, the girl held fast in the lock of his free arm. Water poured off their backs as he exited the water, with the lifeless body draped over his shoulder, like an abattoir carcass. On reaching the crest, he laid her inert body on a patch of short grass, and brushing aside the sodden hair from her face, he began mouth-to-mouth resuscitation. Her lips were a lifeless blue, fringed with purple, her skin pale, cold and translucent.

He rolled her onto her stomach, and with downward pressure, centre to the lower part of her shoulders, he forced water from her diaphragm, then turned her over to continue the resuscitation.

'Don't give up,' he hissed, pumping her heart, then covering her mouth with his, forcing air into her lungs, and suddenly water spewed from her mouth between instinctive gulps for air.

Placing her in the recovery position, Daniel watched the girl fight for her rightful passage to life. Slowly, she opened her eyes, blinking dumbly, seeing without seeing, until eventually the dark shadows rolled aside.

Daniel raised her body with a supporting arm, and she sat up. She looked up at him, her eyes still distant and bewildered.

'You're safe now,' and she managed a weak smile, struggling to comprehend her circumstances. Suddenly her shoulders shot rigid in his arms, embarrassingly aware of her nudity. She shuffled away on her backside, confused and frightened, and Daniel, realising his own lack of clothing, stood up and showed a respectful back.

'Please,' she said through a watery cough, 'I want my clothes.' She took in her surroundings, and pointed with a trembling finger. 'I think they're over there.' She sat with knees tight under her chin, teeth chattering audibly against the drilling cold, and Daniel couldn't abandon her in that state. He picked up his coat and began covering her shoulders, but something stopped him in his tracks. On an otherwise flawless skin was the De Theiry rose birthmark. But for the girl, Daniel's hesitation was clearly worrying. She snatched the coat folds and wrapped the heavy garment protectively around her body, looking up in confusion, as Daniel clumsily pulled on his clothes.

'Did I drown?' she asked eventually, breaking the awkward silence.

'Yes you did.'

'Then I owe you my life and I'm grateful, but please don't stare.'

Daniel shook his gaze with an apology. The birthmark had not been the only reason for his lingering gaze. Even in her half-drowned state, she was without doubt, the most captivating woman he had ever seen.

'You dived in from the ridge without knowing how to climb back out. Is that a fair assumption?' Daniel asked, and with the power of hindsight she acknowledged her stupidity. He was touched by her simple honesty.

Strands of blonde shoulder-length hair clung to her neck and neat pink ears. Her eyes were of an intense blue, wide spaced with long lashes. The line of her jaw was sculptured, with full, slightly parted lips showing small, very white teeth. Again she quietly asked for her clothes, and Daniel, doing the honourable thing, backed away.

He gathered her belongings from where she had made her fateful dive, and he looked down into the dark waters thirty feet below.

'The girl's certainly got guts and no mistake,' he said with admiration, 'daft, but bloody gutsy.' On his return, he again turned his back, while she climbed awkwardly into her jeans and loose pullover.

'Are you the owner of the wigwam?' he asked, throwing the question over his shoulder.

'Yes, my brother and I are here to sketch the moors. It's the first time we've been here. It's a wonderful place; well most of it anyway.' Her teeth still chattered as she enthused, but her passion for the moor was evident. Apart from his initial attraction, Daniel felt warmth for this girl, who clearly had empathy for the very thing he held so dear.

'It's OK,' she said. 'I'm decent…you can turn around now.'

He turned, and her unexpected smile, struck Daniel like a thunderbolt. Her eyes sparkled through the ramshackle tresses of her hair, and Daniel inadvertently followed the proportions of her body. When he realigned his eyes to hers, he saw sudden defiance in her gaze. Slightly embarrassed, he cleared his throat and picked up his coat.

'I think we should get back and warn your brother not to make the same mistake, in this or any other pool for that matter.'

The girl lowered her head in contrition; she owed Daniel her life and moved stiffly onto the track leading to the camp. They walked side-by-side, most of the way in silence. Several times her arm brushed harmlessly against his, and on each occasion, his heart moved in his chest, and for that he was not sorry.

Walking single-file through a short gully, they rounded on the camp to find her brother stoking a breakfast fire, oblivious of the dramatic events. Catching sight of Daniel for the first time, he rose defensively to his feet.

'Who the fuck's this…you all right sis?'

'I'm fine, Peter. 'This man just saved my life.'

'What?'

Suddenly tearful, the girl convulsed beneath an outpouring of emotion, with a somewhat spluttered explanation, and Peter moved forward to put a protective arm around her shoulders. For long moments he held her, before looking frankly at Daniel.

'Peter Carter,' he said, releasing her to extend an open palm, 'forever in your debt. Really can't thank you enough. Was she really drowning?'

'Drowned,' she reiterated through an intake of breath.

'It was serious,' Daniel said modestly returning the handshake. He turned to the girl. 'And I don't even know your name?'

'Bryony, Bryony Carter,' she said softly, with the ring of an apology.

'Bryony Carter,' said Daniel trying the name for size. It sounded good. But then had her name had been Fiffi le Dung, it would have measured equally well.

'And your name?' asked Bryony.

Daniel considered the question. He was still highly protective about his past, however unfounded.

'Daniel Bonner,' he said guardedly, and Bryony echoed his name as he had done hers.

Will you have breakfast with us, Daniel?' said Peter. It was a tempting invitation, given the warmth and sincerity in which it was offered.

'Thank you, but I have fish to catch and firewood to collect. But I'd like you to come and have supper with me tonight if you like fresh trout.' The sudden invite surprised him, given his earlier plans to avoid all contact, but if he were to openly admit it, the reason was standing only a few feet away. 'Your camp site is in the lowest part of the valley,' said Daniel, 'and if you hadn't already noticed its rather prone to morning mist. If you want a more comfortable night then strike your tent and join me later on the high ground. I'm up there on the ridge just below the overhang of Badger Head Tor.' Both followed the direction of Daniel's index finger.

'Sounds bloody good to me,' agreed Peter. 'What do you reckon sis?'

'Yes please.'

'Great, then we'll see you later, and Daniel...thank you again.'

That afternoon, Daniel succeeded in catching four brown trout, all over a pound in weight, but after that particular highlight, the afternoon dragged like a drunkard's foot. He tried to busy himself with preparations for the Carters' arrival, but there was little to do. Bryony remained in his thoughts and he felt from within, something strange and warm about the idea of meeting her again. He did the best he could, to spruce up his rugged image, by smoothing back the wild shanks of his hair, then pulling the makeshift comb of his fingers through his unruly beard, before trimming it with the honed edge of his hunting knife.

Eventually, Tobacco barked at the drone of an approaching diesel engine, and Daniel walked to the edge of the plateau and looked down the escarpment into the valley below. An early model Land Rover climbed the hill, with tent poles on the roof rack, the tips wagging like fishwives' fingers, as the vehicle jolted its way up the incline. He ambled down to where the vehicle had eventually been forced to make a halt, and with a flash of disappointment, he realised it was just Peter sitting in the cab.

'She'll be up in a while, Daniel. She fancied a little walk. I think what happened this morning has understandably taken effect, knowing how fortunate she is to be alive and all that. It's lucky you were there to save her. Fancy giving me a hand with this bloody wigwam?'

Daniel was glad Peter had breezed through the subject, without embarrassing accolades, and they were soon busy erecting the shelter.

Bryony ambled through the boulders and tussocks that peppered the lower slopes of the tor, periodically stopping to pick wild heather, adding it to the cluster of various floras, she already had in her hand. Eventually she reached the higher ground and entered the camp.

'Not exactly the best of Kew Gardens, but these are for you,' she said, noticing Daniels trimmed beard, but politely saying nothing, and Daniel took the gift. In an overhang of granite, he found a crack, wide enough to hold the bunch in the way of a makeshift hanging basket. Bryony openly admired the improvisation. She studied Daniel and noted again the strong but gentle manner he went about things, something she had always found attractive in a man. She had also seen him naked and this, though she dare not admit it, had secretly affected her. She consigned the image to the back of her mind, helped suddenly by Tobacco's demands for attention. Daniel's dog had taken an instant liking to her. She trotted at Bryony's side, and they moved to the fire as if they'd been together for a lifetime.

'Hey, nearly forgot!' said Peter getting to his feet, and he disappeared over the ridge, to return several minutes later with a crate of beer, that had been sitting pride of place on the Land Rovers front seat. He placed the crate near to hand, and snapped open the appropriate number of bottles and handed them out.

The baked trout wrapped in green dock leaves, were cooked to perfection, and beer and fish were savoured, without exception. Time passed easily with a flow of natural conversation and Bryony made frequent fuss of Tobacco. Because of this, Daniel was able to look at the girl, without it being at all awkward.

In a reflective moment, they sat quietly staring into the fire, each with their own thoughts, but as Daniel looked up he found Peter studying him.

'Can I ask you something?'

'If you like, Peter, but the answer depends on the question.'

'Where do you come from, where do you live?'

'Well, that was two questions and the second is an easy one to answer. I live out here on the moor.'

'What, really, all year round?'

'Yes.'

'Not all your life, surely…escaped the rat race eh?'

'Don't be nosey, Peter,' said Bryony.

'Your sudden appearance this morning scared the shit out of me,' he said, ignoring his sister. 'But when you spoke…well, you are obviously educated. I bet you once lived a very different life. Am I right?'

Peter was being uncomfortably astute, and Daniel wondered whether the line of inquisition was from him alone, or perhaps prompted by another. He looked across at Bryony, who lowered her head, as if to answer that very question.

Daniel remembered his former years and the fortune it had brought him. They had guessed something of his past and it made him feel a little put out. He gave no answer.

'Would you ever return?' Peter persisted.

'Leave him alone,' interrupted Bryony. 'What he's done is no concern of ours.'

'Oi, hold on Sis! It was you who…

'Peter! That's enough,' she retorted, with a blush and a flare in her eyes, that threatened a physical gagging of her brother.

Daniel smiled inwardly. Clearly he had been the subject of Bryony's inquisitive streak, and surprisingly, he felt more happy, than annoyed.

'My former life is long gone and money means nothing to me, a personal decision, but one I shall never regret.'

'I wish it were the same for us,' said Peter, 'but unfortunately struggling artists have to eat.'

'Ah! Bryony told me you were here to sketch the moor. Are you both professional?' Daniel was grateful for the change of subject.

'Yup, well more so Bryony. You should see her stuff. It's really good. If ever the right break should come along, she could go to the top.'

'Aw Peter don't exaggerate.' Her blush deepened, with a mixture of embarrassment and modesty.

'Now, you just listen to me sis, if you had a proper studio instead of that old tin shed you could do what you do best.' He turned to Daniel. 'Sculpting is what she does. You really should see them.'

‘I’d like to,’ replied Daniel

‘She’s only twenty, a mere strip of a lass, but she’s bloody good,’ whispered Peter, across the back of his hand.

‘Oi!! I’m still here. And don’t whisper, it’s rude.’

Hmm, she’s spirited, thought Daniel.

‘She sells almost everything she does, but after Dad lost his job in the City, we had to move to a smaller house. And with that, Sis lost her old studio. When he gets back on his feet, dad promises to find a replacement. But nothing is cheap, and while I’m at Design College, I can’t do much to help.’ Daniel sat listening, glad of the unexpected insight into their lives, especially Bryony’s, and a flow of varied conversations continued into the night.

Eventually, as Peter dropped the last empty bottle back into the crate, he engaged a yawn that seemed to engulf the entire site.

‘Sorry people, I’ve got to get to bed.’ He stood up, rounded the fire and took Daniel by the hand. ‘Sorry for poking my nose in earlier, it’s one of my better failings…but thanks again for all you did today.’ He moved over and kissed Bryony on the cheek, and with another yawn made for the tent, leaving the two alone by the fire.

They began talking at the same time and laughed, but Daniel got his question in first.

‘So what will you do without a studio?’

‘Well, actually, there’s one I’ve set my heart on. It’s a small converted chapel for industrial rent, only five minutes walk from my parent’s house. The stained glass has been replaced with clear, giving perfect natural light for my arty needs. In the early morning, sunlight streams in through the east elevation and again through the west in the evening, and there’s no light more critical than that. Six times I’ve been to look around, but the landlord wants an agreement on a five year lease, too much for dad to commit to. Oh, how I wish.’

‘Where is that, exactly?’ he asked, seeing the light of the dream in her eyes.

'The outskirts of Reading,' she said with infectious enthusiasm, and for the first time since leaving the world of hedge-fund speculation, Daniel found himself wishing for the power of money. He would happily give it to this girl who, in just fourteen hours, had so unexpectedly altered his view on life. It was certainly a growing attraction, and maybe in part something to do with the birthmark on her shoulder? On that subject, he would talk to De Theiry later.

They talked about all manner of subjects, oblivious to time, until she unexpectedly rose from her seat, and disappeared into the tent, to return a few moments later, armed with a sketch pad and pencil. In the bottom corner of the first sheet, she wrote something down.

'My telephone number and address,' she said tearing it off then offering it to Daniel. 'If ever you get a chance, come and see us. I know mum and Dad would be proud to meet you, after all you've done for us, especially me. So please don't be a stranger.'

Suddenly her white teeth flashed uncontrollably in the firelight, as she stifled a yawn to match her brothers. She covered her mouth with an apologetic hand. The hour was late and the evening had magically disappeared for them both. She crossed the ground, bent down and stared into the face behind the beard to give him a kiss on the cheek, but the close proximity of his smiling eyes foiled any platonic intentions she may have had. She lowered her face and kissed him fully on the lips. As they touched, they held perfectly still, unblinking and certain with a kiss that crossed the strangers divide. She lingered and saw in his eyes an unfathomable quality, so strong it took her breath away; if they never met again they had created a moment they would not forget. Slowly Bryony withdrew. 'Thank you for saving my life,' she whispered, not daring to say anything else, and walked quietly away.

Daniel remained by the fire, his head resting on his duffel bag pillow. He lay staring up at the night sky, memorising every detail of the day, the beauty of her naked body, the V of light blond curls, covering the pubis at the base of her flat stomach, pert pink nipples on her smooth breasts, the lines of her naked bottom, pure and symmetrical, and that final kiss? And the thought of her near death struck him deeply.

Bryony was also unable to sleep, and lay looking through the open smoke flap of the tent. Above her the night sky was so beautiful, the blaze of stars so dazzling it was as if she was seeing them for the first time, and she was transported to a place of great peace by its magic. Her hand reached involuntarily for her lower body, and with Daniel's naked image in mind, she uttered a soft sigh and closed her eyes, in that secret and personally intimate moment.

The following morning, she woke to the sun's warmth penetrating the fabric of the tent. She dressed quietly so as not to disturb Peter and stooped through the flap. Unsure of what might happen next, her immediate wish, was to be alone again with this quiet man, with unforgettable eyes, who had affected her so deeply.

She blinked against the morning light, and all her instincts told her he was gone.

A quick search supported her fears, and with a growing sense of bewilderment she moved to the ridge. From the plateau, Bryony searched the moor in every direction. But Daniel and his dog were gone.

Five miles to the west of Daniel's position, a storm front rolled its gargantuan shoulders, against what was left of a retreating blue sky. With a weathered eye, he took stock of the deterioration, and headed immediately for the Devil's Umbrella, a natural overhang of living rock, under which a cooking fire could be kept dry, no matter how inclement the weather, another Windrow tutelage. It had been sanctuary for Daniel and Tobacco on many an occasion, and for that alone he was begrudgingly grateful, to the man who was once his friend. They arrived just in time and outside the promised storm showed no mercy on the flora, fauna and earth below. Daniel watched the newly made firelight play hide and seek with the shadows of the overhang, and as on too many occasions, his thoughts of Bryony returned. Almost a month had passed since saving her life, and with that in mind he pulled from his back pocket, the piece of paper she had given him. With use of his thigh, he pressed the crumpled sheet flat with the palm of his hand, and re read the only link to the girl, whose image appeared in his waking moments, and so often in his dreams. He read it again, as he had done so many times before, and the only way to expunge her memory was to screw it into a ball, and with a heavy heart throw it into the fire. How could she know him, as anything but a vagrant, a recluse, a man reluctant to even give his name, a man without financial means, or indeed the wish for any? Above all, a man in combat with the twilight world, a world he could never begin to explain. And the thought of being mocked by her, was more than he wished to contemplate.

The paper ball flew through the flames untouched. It landed on the bedrock on the far side and, Tobacco, thinking it to be a game, tore after it, snapped it up and returned to dump it at his feet. A clap of thunder rumbled away across the moor, as if in closure for the girl who had taken his heart.

Daniel woke to a dull waterlogged morning, with the tail end of the storm moving reluctantly into the east. He stood and stretched, then walked to the edge of the overhang, and filled his canteen from the thin stream of rainwater falling from the ledge, high above his head. As he stoppered the bottle, he heard Tobacco's warning growl, and followed the direction of his dog's gaze into the gorse fields. A faint movement caught his eye. Thinking it a trick of the light, he was about to turn, when a human head appeared above the bracken, before ducking once more out of sight. It popped up again, this time to the left, traversing through the dips, searching for a way through. But one thing was clear, whoever it was, continued inexorably towards the Devil's Umbrella. Daniel was not in the mood for company and made a quick-fire decision. He plucked clumps of damp ferns and mosses, growing from the rocks, and piled them onto the fire. Belching smoke swirled around the belly of the overhang, and out onto the gorse field, and he and Tobacco disappeared behind the smokescreen, to make their escape. They made good time across country, and as the sun passed noon, Daniel was satisfied they had left the stranger far behind.

That evening found them ensconced beneath an old oak tree, and a golden sunset gilded the upper branches, a backdrop of slate grey sky lying behind. The sky later cleared and the appearance of a new moon was assured. The tree would provide shelter from the night air, beneath its turning canopy. Once more the Hummer had provided a rabbit supper, and Daniel sat fed and watered by the cooking fire, when Tobacco alerted him to sounds somewhere out in the failing light, too faint for the human ear, but not so for Tobacco. Trusting his dog's superior hearing, he realised he may well have company. He acted fast, draping his long coat over the propped up duffel bag where he had just been sitting. He then perched his bush-hat on top of the pile, creating a convincing human form in the half light, before melting into the gloom to spy on his own camp.

Fifteen minutes passed, beneath the light of the predicted moon, before Daniel detected someone heading stealthily towards the fire. The hat and coat decoy held guard, and from his position, Daniel watched the figure enter the outer perimeter, under the silver wash of the moon.

'Who the hell is tracking us?' he said quietly to Tobacco, holding her by the scruff. 'We left no trail.' Daniel had made sure of that, by periodically backtracking, to sweep any evidence of their passing. It perhaps wasn't his best work, but it was certainly good enough to baffle any novice, should they be looking.

As the intruder advanced, his approach was open and from the front. Whoever it was clearly meant no harm, unless there were others with him.

'Daniel, is that you? Speak to me...Daniel.'

The voice sounded familiar but Daniel couldn't place it. Apart from the Chancellor, there was no one else that had reason to track him down.

The weight of the Hummer felt handy in his grip, and instinctively he looked behind his position, for any danger possibly coming in from the rear. He sensed none and reassuringly, Tobacco remained alert only to the front.

The intruder called again. 'Daniel, it's me Jerry, Jerry Green from the shop.' He stood twenty feet from the fire, squinting in the low light, unnerved by the lack of response, from what he believed to be the man to whom he had given the book.

Still believing the duffel bag human, Jerry jumped a mile at the sudden appearance of Daniel, looming out of the shadows, in a wholly unexpected direction, and a nervous chuckle rose in his throat, as he at last understood the guile.

'That's not funny, Daniel.'

'Jerry? What on earth are you doing out here? And how the hell did you manage to track me down?'

‘Pure luck old chap, you lost me back at the Devil’s Umbrella from the get-go. Would have gone right past you in the darkness, had I not taken a rest bellow that hill over there.’ He pointed with the end of his chubby chin. The breeze shifted and I caught a whiff of wood-smoke. Had no idea it was you, but I had to find out. Actually I was completely lost.’ They shook hands.

‘How did you know to find me at the Umbrella?’

‘You told me in the shop it was your favourite shelter this time of year, so it was the obvious place to look first, took me ages to find, and then you buggered off leaving only warm ashes, and me looking like a right twit.’

‘Well at least you’ve found me now, Jerry. Come on in. Have you eaten?’

‘Not for twenty four hours, my stomach thinks my throat’s been cut. I’m bloody hollow and feel physically done in. I thought crossing the moor would be easier than this. How do you do it, Daniel?’

‘Sit by the fire. At least you had the good sense to wear waterproofs.’

Jerry was ravenous and after the magical disappearance of every titbit from Daniel’s travelling store, he then munched through a raw potato, as if it were a succulent apple. Daniel smiled inwardly with some compassion.

‘Daniel,’ Jerry said eventually, through the last bulging mouthful. ‘I’ve done something without your permission, it’s good news and of real consequence…but you may hate me because of it.’

Daniel shook his head. Make sense, Jerry. ‘Its good news, but I might hate you? Shit, does everyone have to talk in riddles around here?

'What does that mean?'

'Sorry, Jerry. It doesn't mean anything. Now start at the beginning, in sentences I might be able to understand.’ Jerry searched for the most appropriate place to start.

‘Six months ago I was propping up the bar in the Pink Pig when I overheard your name mentioned. A man I’d never seen before was making enquiries as to where he might find you…turned out to be John Oakley, from Ferry Coin Publishing.’

‘Never heard of them, but go on.’

‘He wants your story, all of it, from your upbringing, your school days, your life as a speculator, right up to the present day living out here on the moor.’

‘Not a bloody chance, Jerry. I hope you told him to fuck off?’

‘Hold on a minute, Danny. Hear me out. I’ve already written the first draft of your story, without of course divulging that little interface with that Chancellor character; I thought that might be a little rich, even for the more broad minded reader. However, although the manuscript is incomplete, the prognosis is that it shall get published. Daniel, it’s already one hell of a story, but I do need the rest of it.’

‘Hold it right there, Jerry, not another word. I want you to burn that first draft and stick the ashes up this bloke’s arse.’

‘I’m afraid it’s all a little too late for that, he already has a copy and wants more.’

Daniel’s anger began to rise. How dare Jerry make his story public? He had allowed this shopkeeper into his confidence, for the small price of an ancient book in what was seemingly an innocent exchange. Clearly there was nothing innocent about it.

‘But Daniel, it could make you a fair bit of money.’

‘My word is my bond. That’s what you told me, and now you’ve sold me down the fucking river.’ His anger reached instant boiling point and he rose abruptly to his feet.

‘Get out of my camp, right now, you bloody little parasite, before I do something I probably wouldn’t even regret!’

‘But, Daniel, I haven’t finished.’

'Get out now, Jerry…while you still can,' and the little shopkeeper lowered his head, realising the sudden danger he was in. He walked sadly into the moonlight and disappeared from view, leaving Daniel feeling outraged and betrayed.

The following morning, Daniel woke under a cloud of regret that persisted as he relit the fire. In his dream, De Theiry had convinced him that he had overreacted, and although still thoroughly dismayed, he made the conscious decision to find Jerry. He followed the shopkeeper's blundering trail and found him curled up, under a dense thicket of gorse. He looked down at the sleeping bundle ,and again deeply regretted his angry words. He bent down and shook Jerry by the shoulder. Groggily he sat up. His mop of hair was a comical tangle festooned with bracken litter, and with a sudden sense of affection, Daniel felt even worse.

'Come and warm up,' he said, and Jerry hesitated before clambering unsteadily to his feet to follow. He sat somewhat sheepishly in front of Daniel's fire, when he remembered he had a present, and digging into his jacket pocket he extracted a small package.

'Brought some of that coffee you liked so much.' And Daniel could have shed a tear of affection and gratitude. He would thank De Theiry that night for the advice.

They shared the only mug Daniel possessed, and with a fresh brew in his hand, Jerry looked up.

'I'm sorry Danny, you're a private man and what I did was wrong.'

'Look, Jerry, I'm sorry for what I said.'

'You have every right to feel angry. Until last night I thought I was doing the right thing; now I feel I've let you down.'

Yes, I was angry, and if I'm honest I probably still am, but you've come a long way to find me and I bet with all the best of intentions. The least I can do is let you finish what you have to say.'

That was all Jerry needed to hear. Suddenly the fire of optimism was back in his eyes. Clearly he had no intention of giving up that easily, and without further prompting, launched straight back into it.

'I listened to the words of your story a thousand times in my head. I read and countlessly re-read your narrative, that I subsequently compiled. Each time it became clearer to me that you are here for a reason. And I believe you know exactly what I mean, Danny.'

'Go on.'

'There are forces at work, with which you have already crossed swords. As you told me, they are capable of many things, including the misuse of the folding stuff. Money, Daniel, I'm talking about money.' He scuffed his fingers together in the age old symbol of holding cash. 'I believe it's the most powerful weapon the Underworld has, and why, because we mortals blindly allow it to be that way. They use it to entrap and manipulate, and without a similar weapon in your arsenal your future battle plans, if I may say so, will prove utterly wanting.'

'Blimey, Jerry, I never mentioned anything about my plans. Where the fuck is this all coming from?'

'Daniel, I just know it. You need money.'

'And your point being that in the unlikely event of my story ever being published, I should use the proceeds as some sort of counterbalance, like for like, and all that sort of good stuff?'

'Well yes, in part at least,' he said, hoisting his round rimmed glasses onto the bridge of his button nose with his index finger, with a deliberation as if to emphasise the point. His eyes were resolute. 'And I want to help.'

'Sounds like you've already started,' said Daniel. He looked down at Jerry, and remembered why he had genuinely liked this courageous little man from the outset. Jerry's argument was beginning to hold water, but Daniel remained unconvinced that the shopkeeper had any true understanding of the situation, although what he said was certainly making sense.

'We need the clout, Danny. As I've already pointed out, it would be a potent weapon in your arsenal.'

'Hmm….money can certainly affect those who have it against those that don't. I've seen what it can do first hand, and have never liked the stuff ever since.' He remembered Norbert and Tony's highly questionable proposals to further their empire, large tracts of money always being the manipulative key. 'Money is powerful stuff.'

'My very point exactly, Daniel, and with it we can do a little fighting back. Look what you did with your original fortune; you gave it away to make a change for the better, am I right? Tell me if I'm wrong.'

It was then, that an idea sprang into Daniel's mind. What if his story did make money, what if he found himself in a position to help Bryony? Guarding that somewhat selfish thought, he admitted the project had merit, if for that reason alone it showed in his face.

Jerry proffered his hand, and after a moment's thought, Daniel took it for the second time. There was a mutual strength to their accord, sealed by the grip. However, there remained one important question.

'What about the press, Jerry?' said Daniel, disliking the possibility of tabloid hacks swarming over his moor. 'They are bound to come the moment I poke my head above proverbial parapet.'

'Daniel, with your skills of deception you could have them whistling Dixie, and interviewing a duffel bag, before they got a rugged mile near you.' And for the first time they both openly laughed.

'Tell me Jerry,' he said, changing the subject. 'We've only met once, so what made you believe the story I told you that night. For all you know I might have been drunkenly pulling your leg.'

'I believed every word you said, then and more so now. Call it gut feeling, but the moment you entered my shop, I knew you and the book were somehow instrumental in what we are about to do. I already knew most of your business story to be true, so why on earth would you lie about the rest? It just wouldn't make sense. The way you became secretive convinced me further. If nothing else, Daniel, I'm a bloody good judge of character, and I recognise bullshit when I hear it. What you told me was incredible, but it was no bullshit. I've always had an open mind on such matters, all you said just convinced me.'

Daniel grunted. Apart from De Theiry, it appeared he was no longer alone.

'What happens next, Jerry?'

'I need the story of your life.'

'Strewth, how long have you got?'

'As long as it takes.'

'What about the shop?

'My sister, Florence has travelled down from Bristol, bit of a battle-axe with an ability to guard the shop like a cruising shark, but her heart's in the right place.' And with that comment, he pulled from an inner pocket, a half-bottle of single malt whisky.

'It's a bit early,' said Daniel, through an appreciative grin.

'There's no time like the present to celebrate,' said Jerry. 'Now take a slug and prepare yourself. We have work to do.'

'Oh! I forgot to ask, the book…how did you like 'Myths and Legends?'

'Like' is not the word I'd use. Had a bloody run in with a hoard of little bastards, described in one of the chapters. But before I say anything more, I think it's important that you know, I believe I was guided to that book, as a warning if for no other reason, but a warning, from whom I've yet to find out.'

'Were those little bastards, as you put it, were they Tarquills?'

'Yes Jerry, Tarquills. But how the hell did you know that?

'After you left the shop, I tracked down another copy on the internet, rare as rocking-horse shit to find they are. But I realised, this book is important to us both. In the end, I had to find out for myself, and from all the other tales the one that drew my attention, was 'Dance of the Tarquills', the most incredible story depicted in this part of the world. Tell me Danny…were they as bad in real life?'

'Worse,' Daniel said softly, 'far worse…lost a good friend and no money in the world could have helped him that night.'

'What do you mean lost?'

'Look, Jerry, if you want my advice stick only to my story and don't get involved in anything other than that.

'As you wish, but I honestly believe our meeting was a lot more than just coincidence. I really want to help.'

It was extremely doubtful, that Jerry had the slightest understanding, of the twilight world he seemed to be so willing to enter. He needed protecting.

'Right, Jerry, you've convinced me of your reasons, so let's get to work.' And Jerry firmed the crossbar of his smudgy glasses to the bridge of his nose, and aligned his teddy-bear ears to Daniel's story.

John Oakley sat in the chief editor's office of Ferry Coin Press, Wardour St, west London. Either side of the door, the walls were tiered with shelves and books of all genres, published testaments to the press's ongoing success. On an uncluttered desk, in the centre of the room, were several hard copies of a new addition to the family. The owner, Drew Theodor Llundorf, silent partner of the business, sat in a leather upholstered chair with a copy of Rags to Riches in his hand, congratulating his chief editor sitting opposite.

'It's a winner, John, and well done. But then I knew it would be from the outset.'

'Well, Drew, working with Jerry Green was a pleasure. His initial submission needed work, but given it's a true story the facts spoke for themselves, and therefore easier to edit. But let's not forget, without your direction, it would have never have come to my notice. Your insistence of fast tracking it onto the shelves, certainly added to the incentive. Your past record of picking a winner, goes without saying, Drew.'

Drew waived airily, with a circle of his manicured hand.

'The crazy thing is, I've never even met Daniel Bonner. All negotiations were made through Jerry Green, on Bonner's insistence that he personally remained well out of it, so where you got all those childhood photographs, business credentials and subsequent life on the moor beats me. Without them, the book would lack an important part of its appeal. Drew, you're a bloody genius.'

'I have my contacts, John. As you know, Jerry took shots of Bonner on the moor, the rest are from contacts that shall remain anonymous, and I would loathe to betray their trust.'

'Of course, Drew. We must keep them sweet whoever they are. After all, look what they've done for us in the past.'

'My sentiments exactly, John. Now tell me more about the book.'

'Well, as instructed, our New York office has been working on the State Side distribution, and it's already caught the imagination of the American reader; revenue from both sides of the pond has already started coming in.'

'And the royalties, has Bonner received what is due so far?'

'Yes, of course, as instructed.'

'Good, you're doing a great job.'

'You know what, Drew. I'll never fully understand you. I thought the whole ethos of this business, was to hold onto any outgoings for as long as possible. 'Let them fuckin' wait', quote, unquote. And yet here we are making damn sure Bonner gets his dues, if I may say so, almost ahead of time. I've never known you to do such a thing. '

'I have my reasons. Every thing I do always has a reason.' He rose from his chair, rounded the desk and shook hands.

'As I said, you're doing a great job. Keep me informed, eh!' And he stepped abruptly from the office. As always, his sudden visits, and likewise departures, left Oakley mildly puzzled, and although he knew his boss's eccentricities from old, he would never fully understand his strange ways. But what did he care, Drew was indeed a genius, owner of one of the most successful publishing houses in the business. And below him, stepping through the doorway leading onto the street, Drew Theodor Llundorf, an anagram of 'Lord of the Underworld,' the very Devil himself, left the building with a smile.

'Artefacts of Ages' was outwardly no different from the time when Jerry had closed the shutters and ventured out to find Daniel, and yet subtle changes seemed to emanate from every corner of the building. The shop held more meaning to him, less dull, less melancholy, altogether brighter, and the jumble of artefacts suddenly seemed to have a greater purpose.

The bell above the door chimed, and Jerry watched from the back, as a customer stepped in over the threshold. His immediate impression was that the man was above average height, wearing a well-tailored suit, that only partially softened the lines of a powerful physique beneath. His raven hair was swept back to his collar, in a cavalier but suitable style. His features were broad, with eyes that could smile; perhaps even in anger, a man of obvious substance, with a natural presence, that could silence a room of strangers. His teeth were white and even, behind a warm smile, and the drop of his powerful neck to his pristine shirt collar, was deeply tanned. A perfectly knotted gold silk tie, lent to the overall aura of a man with money, and when a customer of such obvious means, enters the establishment, there is normally a sale in the offing. Jerry pressed tight his glasses to the bridge of his nose, and crossed the floor in an unhurried professional drift, the consummate expert in sales.

It was the deep chuckle, that first alerted him to the startling reality, furthered by Tobacco, slipping silently in behind. Jerry gawped in disbelief. 'My God, is it you Danny, I don't bloody believe it. Bollocks, I thought I was about to flog a curio,' he snorted.

'It's me,' Daniel confirmed with a laugh, his familiar voice, the final endorsement.

'Bloody hell, never would have guessed in a million. Christ, you do scrub up well. Did you find what you were looking for...did you find her number?'

Daniel already had the piece of paper in his hand.

Jerry had listened to the story of the drowning girl and could understand the obvious attraction. Daniel had already saved her life and clearly an embryonic friendship had evolved, in the short time they had spent together. And yet here he was breaking every rule of his wanderer's code, dressed all spiffy to impersonate a solicitor's clerk, in order to give the highly fortunate girl, a gift from some invented, anonymous benefactor. He wondered at the powerful interest Daniel was evincing towards the girl, and his highly inquisitive trait was not about to let it go. Daniel was holding a little secret, yet to be winkled out, and although ignorant of what it might be, Jerry had sensed it from the outset.

'I have secured the lease papers for the chapel as you asked,' he told Daniel. 'Although it's been on the market for over a year we were bloody lucky to get it. For some reason, another party decided it was the building for them, so we got into a bit of a bidding war, but we won in the end. But it does seem we're going to great lengths to benefit this girl. What's the real reason my friend? It can't be the leverage of money to gain her respect, of that I'm bloody sure. So what is it Danny? And remember, I recognise bullshit when I hear it.'

Jerry was exercising finely-tuned perception, and Daniel, although disappointed at being so obviously transparent, actually liked him all the more for it. After the initial misgivings concerning the publishing of his story, Jerry had proved himself the man to trust, therefore it seemed only fair to reveal the true reason for his generosity.

'When I pulled Bryony from the lake, she lay naked in front of me.'

Jerry raised a salacious and inquiring eyebrow.

'Apart from the obvious, my lascivious friend, there was something I saw that stopped me dead in my tracks; something I'd seen in my dreams that I first thought was a tattoo. It turned out to be an extraordinary birthmark, on the shoulder of the apparition who saved me from the Tarquills, with that life-saving riddle. She bears the birthmark of the De Theiry rose. When I saw it, I knew that saving her life was beyond coincidence. Phillip De Theiry saved me for a reason. I, in turn, saved hers, for reasons more important than I know. I'm convinced this is all a part of a greater scheme, a small part perhaps, but it's an unknown that fascinates me.'

'There you are, you see,' said Jerry. 'I knew it wasn't just physical attraction.'

'Well, what she does to my soul, is one powerful piece of the equation and I'm not scared to admit it, but it's like I say, I'm convinced there is another and more important reason why we were thrown together, which I've yet to discover. Quite exciting really.'

'Yes Daniel, it is indeed. So why almost destroy the only link you had?' He lifted the scrap of paper.

'Jerry…until the sale of the book, I could offer her nothing. I can now at least fulfil her dream, a compulsive thing to do perhaps, but I feel driven. As for my personal feelings, well, lets just say I live in hope.'

'Hmm, don't leave it too long. In my experience if you don't tell her how you feel, she may move on, no matter how deep her feelings. Some can drop you like a stone in water and secretly cry their hearts out, as they watch you drown. But it changes nothing. They will still let you go, for what they believe to be a better and more secure life elsewhere. Remember Daniel, faint heart never won fair maid and all that bewildering stuff.'

'I shan't ask where all that came from, but it sounds like the voice of experience.'

'Let's get to work,' said Jerry, changing the subject. He took the crumpled sheet into the office, picked up the telephone and dialled the number.

'Ah! Mr Carter, glad to have got you,' he said into the mouthpiece. 'I represent the law firm of 'Harrison Talbot Solicitors', conveyors of wills, deeds and legacies. Pardon, no Mr Carter, I have no intention of selling you anything. On the contrary, I have something rather exciting to impart to Miss Bryony Carter, whom, if I'm correct in thinking, is your daughter'. Jerry looked across to Daniel, with a confidential wink. 'Yes, yes, I see, Mr Carter, no that's fine…yes good news, well actually it's really very good news. If I may come straight to the point, I have on my desk in front of me a hundred-year lease to a certain property, donated to your daughter by an anonymous benefactor. No, Mr Carter, I can assure you this is not some sort of scam, as you like to put it.' Jerry looked skyward and Daniel moved closer. 'Well, before you put the phone down, would you please consider an appointment with one of our representatives, to verify the legitimacy of this call? Yes, that's correct, 'Harrison Talbot.'' There followed a long pause, as a muffled conversation took place on the other end of the line. 'You will? Excellent, Mr Carter. Now, there are a few questions of formality, that we are obliged to ask, in order to ascertain whether we are conversing with the correct party. If I may take the details of your address, and confirmation that it is indeed the present abode for Miss Bryony Carter?'

Jerry chatted on with professional ease, to the point that even Daniel found himself believing in 'Harrison Talbot's' existence. Several minutes later, after scrawling details on a sheet of A4, Jerry concluded. ‘Yes that’s right Mr Carter, one of our most trusted employees, Paul Danton, shall be with you at twelve noon tomorrow with the paperwork. Oh, and Miss Carter’s presence shall be required as our instructions are to deliver the lease papers person to person…absolutely Mr Carter, and a very good day to you sir.’

With a smile, Jerry lowered the handset, and Daniel shook his head and grinned.

You’re going to need this,’ said Jerry, handing over a large water marked envelope with the ‘Harrison Talbot’ motif printed in the bottom left hand corner, and Daniel slid out its contents. The first sheet was a covering letter headed by the law firm’s name and logo. Connected by a security tag was a twelve sheet agreement.

‘Where did this little lot come from, Jerry,’ said Daniel looking at the headed stationary. ‘You can’t seriously tell me you designed and printed this off overnight.’ Jerry also handed him a business card with the name, Paul Stanton, printed in the centre. ‘The stationary was left in the vault below, when I bought this place ten years ago. I kept the blank side for spare paper, but never thought I’d need it for this purpose. Perhaps there always was a reason for keeping it, in this baffling puzzle we call life, eh! Daniel.’

'Yea, but does ‘Harrison Talbot’ actually exist? If Bryony's father looks it up on line, then we are pretty much shagged if it doesn't.'

'They exist, Daniel. Looked them up myself. This place is their old address, easy enough to bluff your way around, in the slim chance the Carter's should even notice, which they won't, old stationary needs to be used up in this time of economic unrest and all that guff. Besides, you're giving, not taking, so they won't be so much on guard. Trust me.'

Armed with everything Jerry had given him, Daniel took him by the shoulders. ‘You’re a bloody marvel Jerry, and no mistake.’ Jerry’s grin broadened with self satisfaction. ‘Listen, Danny, for the last three weeks, I’ve been traipsing backwards and forwards, signing this and signing that to secure this deal, don’t bugger it up.’

‘I have a feeling I should leave immediately,’ said Daniel, and with Tobacco at Jerry’s feet, the shopkeeper’s honoured guest, they watched the big man close the door behind him.

The Twenty Fifth Alignment of the planets hung in the heavens, for the Light and Dark angels to legalise their meeting, and I the scribe am seconded, as is my honour, to document the mysteries of their constant battle. They sat left and right of me, at the long table, to probe and test each others strengths. And as is the norm, Abdiel opened the proceedings, with the old quill of mine poised over parchment. There were many crucial items on their agenda, but what I found surprising, was the importance levied on Daniel Bonner, and how soon he was brought to the fore.

'So, brother of mine, your Chancellor has opened the Bonner account, with a barrage from the heavy guns that are the Tarquills. Your mind is as vile as they are repulsive, and yet he managed to not only destroy many of their numbers, but also escape their wrath.'

'It was my Chancellor who sent them to Bonner. I am merely the one who sculpts said repulsive creatures to the shape that lays fear in the human mind. It is the human mind that is to blame for my designs.'

'Then you are blameless?'

'Never am I blameless, brother Abdiel, merely the overseer of my world as you are in yours, so let us not waste time with things we already know. As my world sent the Tarquills, so did yours send Jerry Green and the book of ‘Myths and Legends’ to forewarn Bonner. It worked, and for that I thank you. My Chancellor has been made most busy. Excellent!'

They both looked at me and I lowered my head. As the scribe, there are certain things that cannot be documented, one being the game of ping-pong one-upmanship being played out right now between them. Abdiel trying to place his sibling on the back-foot, with the jibe at being blameless, Lucifer turning the whole thing round by thanking his brother for keeping the Chancellor busy. Although remaining outwardly calm, I felt their inner seething towards each other roll from each end of the table.

'So what plans do you have now for Bonner, to further test his abilities of survival,' said Abdiel, in the vain hope his brother might let down his guard.

'My darling brother, you know full well not to ask such ridiculous questions. However, I can tell you, he now journey's to the house of Miss Bryony Carter, for reasons that are most certainly aimed at her alone. We have toyed with his purchase of a certain property, as a second party interested in its sale, and I am happy to report that we have prised another ten thousand pounds from his bank balance, because of our interference. I do love doing that. Let him be on his guard, for my Chancellor is angry with his defeat.'

Abdiel looked down the table for a long moment, before speaking. 'Right brother Lucifer, we have many other things to discuss. Shall we get on.'

The Carter house was a modest, 1930s, red brick, semi-detached dwelling with a half-round double bay window, facing out onto a quiet suburban cul-de-sac. The small front lawn was well presented, with meandering banks of shrubs and flowers, breaking ranks with the more manicured formality, of its sister gardens in the horseshoe ring of houses.

Daniel stepped through the iron gate, strode up the path, ducked beneath the bunches of trailing wisteria festooning the porch, and pressed the doorbell. A woman of indeterminate years opened the door, and Daniel knew he had found the Carter household. Age had clearly been no enemy to Bryony's mother, her looks striking, the family resemblance immediate.

Daniel introduced himself as Paul Stanton, Harrison Talbot's employee, and that he had an envelope for Miss Carter, with the instruction to deliver it in person, and that hopefully he was expected.

Bryony's mother called down the hallway to her husband, who within moments, stood at her side.

'This is' she read the card. 'Paul Stanton. The man from the solicitors.'

Mr Carter studied the calling card and shook hands. 'Come on through. I'm sure Bryony won't be long.' And Daniel followed them in. 'I was rather hoping she would be here,' he said, as he was led along the hallway, and Mr Carter stopped and turned. 'We haven't told Bryony anything for fear of disappointment...I'm sure you can understand our need to protect her.' Carter searched Daniel's face, whose reaction was courteous, everything that could be expected and befitting of a legal emissary. He was suddenly rather enjoying the part, especially when considering Bryony's guaranteed delight. Carter continued to lead Daniel through the house and out into a small sunny garden at the rear.

The wait was pleasant enough, with Mrs Carter making a fresh pot of coffee in the kitchen, as the two men chatted, more so Mr Carter, attempting to pry more information out of Daniel, sitting easily on the cushioned swing seat. Mrs Carter had already noted his strength of looks, and through the open window, wondered with mild curiosity, at his deep tan and somewhat improbable stature for an office clerk. Nevertheless, he had arrived at the appointed time, with all the necessary credentials; therefore the possibility of disappointment was unlikely, and she felt excited for her daughter, unsure whether it was the man, or whatever he brought for her, that had suddenly made her smile. She decided it was both, and liked the positive feeling.

She served the coffee, and as Daniel took the cup, a movement in the hallway ended the wait.

'She's here,' said Carter, disappearing into the house, re-appearing moments later with Bryony at his side, wearing such an endearing frown, it made Daniels heart miss a beat. She was more beautiful than he remembered, a nimbus of sunlight outlining the blonde curls of her hair, in a fashion that was the nature of the human condition at its best. Daniel Bonner's heart punched against the inside of his ribs and he felt heady.

'Darling, this is Mr....?'

'Ah! Sorry...Mr Danton, Paul Danton, from Harrison Talbot Solicitors. I have some rather good news for you Miss Carter,' and without delay he dug into his lap-top case, and handed over the envelope with almost boyish haste. She didn't look up, but wearing a puzzled expression, opened the flap to extract the contents. A security tag held thirteen sheets of paper, the first being the letter of instructions. Quickly read, she then flipped it over to reveal the lease documents, and then back to the first to read it again. This she did three times before handing them to her mother, her frown replaced by a look of excited bewilderment. Was this dream real, or some sort of cruel joke? The covering letter was plain enough. The chapel had been acquired for the sole furtherment of Bryony Carter's artistic career; a simple instruction, but no less incredible.

'I don't understand,' she whispered. 'Who on earth would do such a wonderful thing?'

Daniel shrugged his broad shoulders. 'I'm only the messenger Miss Carter.'

Bryony crossed the small patio to shake his hand. Her grip was firm yet delicate and Daniel was momentarily arrested by the sensitivity of the touch. For the first time, Bryony looked up into his face, and the world rocked beneath her feet, as those eyes looked into her soul, as they had done on that fateful day on the moor. 'Daniel,' she mouthed, and could not let go the handshake. Daniel steadied her, as she fought for composure. Her father, too absorbed in the letter failed to notice, but as for her mother…nothing concerning matters of a daughter's heart goes unnoticed by a doting mother, and her eyes squinted into chips of concentration.

'Darling, release the poor man, before you stifle his circulation,' and as she said those words, she sensed the bond between them. This had to be Daniel Bonner, of whom Bryony had talked so affectionately, and who had clearly won her daughter's heart. It was a good feeling, a feeling that Bryony's place should be alongside him, a sense that they belonged together, as if destiny had already made its choice. It was a mirror of her own past, and she looked away before any silly comment got the better of her.

Bryony drew breath as if to say something. She had so many questions that desperately needed answering. Why had this beautiful man so suddenly disappeared? And a shot of anger popped momentarily across her eyes, with a host of emotions tumbling through her heart. Her gaze was transfixed to the clean- shaven, masculine lines of Daniel's face. She wanted to reach out and touch him with trembling fingertips, as if she had just found the most precious thing in the world, and she wanted to cry.

'All seems in order to me,' said her father, utterly wrapped up in the more technical side of the proceedings. 'Looks pretty damn kosher, Bryony. Looks like the place is yours.' He didn't look up from the documents, which in his wife's eyes was no bad thing whatsoever. If he had seen what was truly going on, he would have ruined it in an instant, with a typically blunt, insensitive question for which he was renowned.

As Bryony made to say something, a sudden commotion from the hallway heralded the blustering appearance of two young men, tumbling through the doorway in high spirits. Peter Carter strode in, gave his mother a kiss then rounded on Daniel with a genial hello, wishing to know who had come to visit, and Daniel realised Peter had absolutely no idea who he was. It was strange for Daniel to hide his identity to someone he truly liked, and almost let go his secret.

Peter's father made the introductions, unable to resist telling him the good news, and Peter stood momentarily gob-smacked.

'Bugger me, that's fantastic news,' he said, giving his sister one of the world's biggest rocking hugs, as if some kind of over-enthusiastic barn-dancer. 'Language Peter,' chided his mother primly. However, Bryony, despite the exuberant sibling buffeting, had grown suddenly silent.

'That is indeed fantastic news,' interrupted the young man who had entered with Peter. 'Charles Millington,' he said without shaking hands. He was marginally shorter than Daniel, with long well-groomed sandy hair. His pretty, if not slightly effeminate face, held unblinking steel grey eyes, over a long nose and thin but well sculptured mouth. His monogrammed, brass-buttoned blazer and finely pressed flannels gave him an air of sartorial elegance, like something from a thirties novel, striking to a fault, though certainly not to Daniel's taste. He brushed passed Daniel, seemingly not to have noticed the proffered hand, and moved across to stand at Bryony's side. With a protective arm around her slender waistline, he delivered a tender kiss to the corner of her mouth, and with it, Daniel's world faltered. He looked across at Bryony and saw the turmoil of sadness and regret tumble in the confusion of her eyes, and time stood still. Eventually, galvanised by the hand of reality, Daniel knew it was time to leave. Exercising great reserve he made his excuses, amidst genuine offers of further hospitality from both Peter and his father. But their well-meant words echoed hazily in his head, as if he had been drugged, and that sunny garden, which just a short while ago had been the brightest place on earth, had suddenly become a living hell.

'Allow me to see you to the door, Mr Danton,' said Millington, with a cheery offer. Daniel's discomfort had not gone unnoticed by Millington, or Bryony's mother and she agreed that is was a kind and thoughtful thing for Charles to do. As Bryony watched him go, her mother watched Bryony's body tremble, like a fledgeling bird.

'It's him, isn't it darling?' she said in a sympathetic and confidential tone. 'That was Daniel.' Huge tears appeared in Bryony's eyes, and rolled fat and fast down her cheeks.

'What on earth's the matter Sis?' Peter laughed. And his mother rushed to the rescue. 'Leave her alone, Peter…for goodness sakes. It's not every day one receives an unexpected gift like that,' and mother and daughter's tearful eyes connected in a secret bond.

Charles Millington led the way through the house, and down the garden path to the gate without a single exchange. Daniel passed numbly through the opening, and it was only then that Millington spoke.

'Well, well, Mr Bonner…you really do have the love bug, and bad I think.'

Daniel looked at Millington in astonishment, and the hair on his neck lifted as if touched by a chill breeze.

'You know me?' he mumbled.

'Personally, no, but my boss does, in fact he knows you very well indeed.'

Suddenly Daniel was forced to shake himself free of self pity. He sensed an aura of deep malevolence surrounding this man who stood on Bryony's side of the gate, his good looks had altered. They were now rattish and mean looking, as if spoiling for a fight, and in that moment of clarity, Daniel understood the terrible danger that had entered Bryony's innocent world. He was in the presence of a Chancellor's cohort.

'You touch one hair on her head and I'll…'

'You'll do what exactly, Mr. Bonner? I intend touching much more than just the hair on her pretty head, and rest assured I shall relish every moment, especially knowing the extent of your pain. These are my instructions and I shall, of course, carry them out to the letter, against which you are powerless.'

Daniel reeled. 'How did you get your filthy hooks into her…Milton, or what ever your bloody name is…and why?'

'How? Well, that was the easy bit. Drowning people often make irrational plea's to survive, the same way you did at the wire. And Mr Bonner, as you well know, we are always listening in the vast sea of souls. As for why, well let's just say it's the boss's whim to see you writhe in the agony of unrequited love. Personally I think it's all rather funny, to the point of laughing openly in your face. I shall, however, spare you that nicety on this occasion, but rest assured I shall enjoy the task of taking you from her heart immensely. Oh! And the name is Millington, Charles Millington, a name you shall hear a great deal more of. A name you shall not forget.'

Daniel's body slumped in tragic resignation, as Millington teased out another humourless grin, and a flash of hatred from his cold grey eyes. He was delighting in what he had said, convinced Daniel was crushed. But Daniel had only feigned defeat. He unleashed a fist with savage speed, bunched so tight it might have been granite. Millington's reaction was commendably quick, almost dodging the blow. However, Daniel's knuckles thumped into the other's left temple, with enough force to bowl him over on his white flannel backside. Millington was deposited on the path, with an alarming but satisfying thump, his features creased in surprise hurt and hate. Then, as if a switch had been thrown, he smiled. He rose to his feet, dusting the grit from the seat of his flannels with one hand, nursing his temple with the other, before smoothing back his sandy hair with an exaggerated flourish.

'Hmm, not a bad punch, however, it won't do you any good, Bonner.'

'On the contrary, you little weasel. I feel considerably better already.'

'We both know you are lying, Bonner. Goodbye for now, but rest assured that I'll update you every step of the way, on mine, and Bryony's forthcoming union. From here on in her sweet body will be mine. You shall learn to hate me, Mr Bonner…that I promise.' And with a courteous inclination of his objectionable head, Millington disappeared back inside the house, wearing the unveiled look of triumph.

He found Bryony sitting with her mother in the back garden, the tear spattered lease held tight in her lap. She became aware of his presence, and, given her mother's advice, knew what she must do. Charles Millington was about to become a very unhappy man, and with every heartbeat, Bryony's resolve strengthened. Mrs Carter rose quietly from Bryony's side and kissed the top of her head. 'Follow your heart,' she said in a whisper. 'Go to Daniel,' and she looked up and smiled briefly at Millington, before disappearing into the house. From the kitchen window, she watched as he took her place, to drape an arm over Bryony's determined shoulders. She turned to look at him and was about to speak, when Millington pressed his index finger against her lips, as if expecting the rebuff, and then with his free hand, hung a silver chain and pendant of three leaping flames around her neck. Agonising moments passed, and against all odds, Bryony then wiped away her tears, and astonishingly returned Millington's embrace, before tucking her forehead into the crock of his neck.

'Oh my darling girl,' whispered her mother from the shadows. 'Tell Charles how you feel and go to the man who really holds your heart. You may never have another chance.'

At the front of the house, Daniel waited, convinced that Bryony was sure to come to him. For two hours he paced the cul-de-sac pavement, but Bryony never appeared.

For Daniel, the train journey home flashed by unnoticed, as if travelled by another. For the first time he was beginning to understand the true power of the Underworld. His love had been undermined, and lost in a single moment, by one of their snivelling human cohorts. Losing Bryony to another man was one thing, but this was so very different. His enemies had been busy in his absence, and Daniel's anger began to blossom.

He travelled deep onto the moor, and for three days ensconced himself on Badger Head Tor, seemingly more isolated than ever before, as the wind howled around the high escarpment. It was a place to divert his mind from the avalanche of loss, fear and foreboding, that had destroyed his expectations. In all his twenty-eight years he had never felt such desolation. Not even the death of his parents came near to the mark. Still hanging in the crack of the overhang, was Bryony's decimated posy of heather, a fitting wreath to something that was now lost.

On the fourth morning, with the promise of dawn just a faint glimmer in the east, Daniel slept close to the hearth of his cooking fire, as De Theiry crossed the divide and entered his dreams. He administered an immense pinch of snuff to his Parisian nose, before speaking softly.

'A force has been created and grows strong,' he said, snapping shut the snuff box, with a sharp metallic click.' A force to counterbalance our very different worlds…and that force, Daniel, is you. Someone has chosen you, as I was once chosen and others like us around the world. However, I am convinced your strength shall prove far greater than mine ever was. I also know the Chancellor. Five hundred years ago he came for me. For five years, I languished in that despicable asylum, in a section for the chronically weak of mind, but in all that time, declined his magnanimous offer of care-taking my soul, until the day came, tired of my fortitude, he had me executed. I was suffocated with my own pillow, held by three warders, one of whom wore the Chancellor's talisman. My death was inconsequential, ending with a pauper's burial that passed unnoticed. The inscriptions chiselled into the flagstones of my cell seemed only to prove my madness to the judiciaries, and therefore, justification of my internment. They believed me dangerously insane and the world was well rid of me. But I was angry, Daniel. I wanted revenge and I lingered too long, until one day, I found myself trapped in the spiritual world of limbo. So be warned. Let neither hate nor anger blight your judgement, for that is a weakness they can exploit.' De Theiry took another pinch of snuff in a moment of reflection, before continuing. 'You shall be reunited with Bryony,' he said, with an unexpected prediction. 'The Pool without Water shall bring you both together, against force and flood, but not this day my friend. Not just yet.'

De Theiry was talking in riddles again. However, Daniel allowed the words to sink in. It was wise to listen, even if the Pool without Water had yet to be understood. De Theiry drifted between words of wisdom, and confusing injections of seemingly superfluous nonsense. But eventually, as the new day dawned, the apparition faded and Daniel woke with a start. With dry kindling, he rejuvenated the fire and as it burst into life, he pondered De Theiry's strange prophesies, with one part fresh in his mind.

'You shall be reunited with Bryony. The Pool without Water shall bring you both together.'

He repeated it several times word for word, and in the heat of the fire, the chill of apprehension that had clung so doggedly, lifted.

Strengthened by De Theiry's prophesy, Daniel decided it was time to leave the tor. His destination was Delamere, and after calculating due north from the position of the sun, he descended through the slopes of heather.

As he picked his way down, the wind changed direction, strangely chilling as it tumbled from the escarpments, and in the breeze he heard the sound of triumphant laughter. The Chancellor had begun his heartless goading. The Underworld sensed victory, believing him weakened if not crushed by Bryony's apparent rejection. But Daniel faced the wind and made his reply into the spoiling vortices.

'We shall see who's finished,' he breathed, and the hunting breeze suddenly stilled around him as if to listen, and with an act of calculated contempt, Daniel turned his back and walked away.

## Bruinscrofa

In the week of Daniel's absence, Jerry's life had returned to the trading of artefacts. However, his primary concern was now for his friend. Despite the outward bonhomie seen on his return, especially towards Tobacco's feverish joy, Jerry soon detected a sense of emptiness in the other's mien. The anticipated reunion with Bryony had clearly not gone according to plan, and he would have given his back teeth to find out more. Instead he allowed Daniel room to brood for as long as was necessary, as a mark of respect if nothing else. But Daniel quickly built the necessary fortifications around his emotions and there was no other mention of the trip, only his wish to return to the moor. And on the third day they exchanged farewells. Daniel and Tobacco were going back out.

The following three weeks passed laboriously for Jerry, and the new adventurer found himself concocting reasons to go and join his friend in the wilds. His boyish wish for daring deed and do had grown, and given just half an excuse, he would have ventured out that very day, but as evening shadows fell, he thought better of it, choosing an early night with a drop of Scotch instead. He made a final security check around the shop before retiring, in one hand a good measure of the golden liquid, and in the other his copy of 'Myths and Legends.'

After a little reading, the Scotch began soothing Jerry's senses, immersing him in a jumble of pleasant dreams. The volume lay open on his chest, rising and falling to the steady rhythm of his breathing, and below the endeavours of artisans, engravers, sculptors and craftsmen from times gone by lay hushed. Most pieces carried little more than intrinsic value, simply a mark of social history. And yet what was to emerge from the ordered clutter, was about to severely undermine his present thirst for adventure.

He woke unexpectedly to the sound of shuffling. Something was prowling around below. From his bedside cabinet he extracted a torch, looked into the lens and pushed the switch. The halogen filament flared, stinging the retinas of his eyes like needles. 'Bloody idiot,' he grunted, and with impaired vision, he crept clumsily from the room. The staircase creaked like an alarm bell, as his bare foot trod on the only loose tread in the flight, and he could have kicked himself. Any attempt at stealth had been compromised, leaving little option but to pelt down the last few treads, and throw on the main fluorescent lights. In what for Jerry was the nearest thing to being quick, he reached the electrical box, and after a fumbled moment, found and threw the switch. With frustrating slowness, the electrical starters kicked in, and the tubes blinked several times, before bursting into life. He took stock of his surroundings. On the face of it everything appeared to be in its place, and after a brief search, he had found nothing out of the ordinary. However, on his return passage upstairs, he noticed the taxidermy example of a brown bear was no longer in its normal position, perhaps no more than a pace out of line, but Jerry prided himself on knowing where everything was, to the millimetre. It was puzzling, but hardly serious. He slid the long-dead animal's steel footplate back to its rightful setting, then bid the inert bag of old stuffing a good and peaceful night, threw the light and returned to bed.

He lay reading for an hour, periodically listening for further sounds, but heard nothing more threatening than the sluggish ticking of his bedside clock, and eventually he closed his eyes.

In the morning he was a busy man. A recent order for artefacts, bound for the television studios ninety miles away in Bristol, needed assembling in preparation for a midday collection. Jerry was proprietor to one of the very few remaining treasure houses, capable of supplying authentic props for the film and photographic industry, and in recent years it had become a lucrative piece of repeat business. Part of the remit, was for several wall-mounted game specimens, but sadly he had none in stock, his only stuffed animal was the bear, too big, old and bedraggled.

However, the majority of the list was assembled, and after a labour intensive morning, the consignment was placed in a long row, in the centre of the shop floor. Making a fresh pot of coffee, he sat in his favourite wing-back chair, and was about to swallow his first mouthful, when the previous night's disturbance came to mind. He had overlooked the basement on his nocturnal rounds, and with twenty minutes to kill, this was as good a time as any to take a look. Expecting nothing of consequence, he made his way through the doorway in the back wall of the office, down a flight of stone steps and into the old bank vault. He had long ago converted the area into a repair workshop, as not all the antiquities were necessarily in the best condition on arrival. Along the left hand wall, ran a workbench sporting a lathe, large pillar drill, band saw, grinding wheels and a comprehensive variety of hand tools, hanging from a row of rusty screws, drilled into the whitewashed plaster above, all just as he had left it. At the other end of the vault was the strong room, a barrier of tempered bars, reminiscent to a Wild West jailhouse, protecting a walk in safe, set in the far wall of reinforced concrete. The door hung half open and he made an inspection of the interior. Apart from a convolution of cobwebs, a few dusty cases, containing antiquated light fittings, and several boxes of the law firm's abandoned letterheads, there was nothing more onerous than the musty smell of mildew. Reassured he left the vault to oversee the noon dispatch.

He spent the rest of that afternoon rearranging the shop, closing the gaps created by the outgoing pieces, and once done he shut the front door, and strode off to the Pink Pig, in search for some convivial company, not to mention a well-deserved pint.

An unusual quantity of Pig's Ear ale, carried Jerry Green happily into the late evening, and he eventually left the bar, with a distinct feeling of goodwill with the world, and everything in it. Trundling happily along the high street, he reached the shop, and on opening the door, he noticed a calling card lying on the mat. He pressed the crossbar of his glasses to the bridge of his nose, released a soft-fermented belch, and swaying gently on his feet, read the print. The name meant nothing to him, but when reading the handwritten flip-side, it was apparent the owner of the card had several curios for disposal, one of which was a wall mounted boar's head, in tip-top condition. Instantly, his interest was aroused. This had to be his lucky day; a money spinner to add to the Bristol studio order. He would phone the vendor, first thing in the morning, but right now it was unquestionably time for bed. He let out another belch, and with a request for whoever may be listening, to beg his pardon, he climbed the stairs, entered his room, kicked off his shoes and fell backwards onto the bed.

Outside, an unusually dark moonless night hung over Delamere, and as the world slept, something began to stir again in the shop below.

Woken by the weighty sound, of something being dragged across the wooden floor, Jerry sat up confused and annoyed, at being disturbed two nights in a row. Feeling horribly beer-muddled, he made a valiant effort, of hurling open the door and bounding down the stairs, and for the second night in a row turned on the lights to make an inspection, behind eyelids heavy with alcohol induced sleep. And this time he made a startling discovery. The stuffed bear had moved along the entire length of the shop floor. It now stood staring out of the front window, through its lifeless eyes. Feelings of deep alarm crowded the nape of Jerry's neck, as if a cut-throat razor had been placed at the base of his skull, threatening and dangerous.

The bear stood, as if expecting something to emerge from the darkness, beyond its reflection in the glass, and Jerry's new-found lust for adventure waned. Being regaled with extraordinary stories, in the security of Daniel Bonner's presence was one thing, but facing the unknown, alone and in the dead of night, was a different matter altogether. It was a reaction he had not expected of himself. Without moving closer, he studied the lock on the front door, and as best as he could make out, from that distance it appeared to be intact. He backed away, climbed the stairs, entered his room and turned the key, and just for good measure, placed a chair under the door handle, before climbing into bed. Throughout the remaining hours of darkness, he lay listening to the continued crashing and bumping below, petrified that whatever was down there might climb the stairs. But thankfully, the loose tread remained silent and undisturbed, until in the small hours of the morning, the noises eventually ceased.

Sunlight streamed in through the bedroom window, and the sleep Jerry had eventually found, was interrupted by a chorus of birdsong. A persistent headache reminded him of his Pink Pig indulgences, and the need for strong coffee was paramount. However, it wasn't until he saw the chair wedged under the door handle, that the night time shenanigans returned to mind. He pulled the seat away, gingerly unlocked the door, and descended the stairs, with palpable uncertainty. When standing in the centre of the shop floor, he was happy to find everything was in place, even the bear. Jerry tousled his unkempt top knot with trembling fingers, due in some part to the effects of alcohol, and the vengeful persisting headache. It had all been a ridiculous dream, and he vowed in future, to give that particular real ale the respect it so rightfully deserved.

Freshly ground coffee was soon navigating his throat, and feeling several degrees revitalised, he remembered the calling card found on his doormat the night before. Moving to the desk in his office, he exhumed the telephone from the general clutter that was his desk, and had just began dialling the number, when a knock at the door stopped him from tapping in the last two digits.

'Who the hell is that?' he muttered. His face was unshaven, his hair almost in orbit, and his clothes crumpled like paper. He moved irritably through the shop to the sound of the second knock.

In embarrassing contrast, a smartly-attired, suave-looking individual stood in the doorway, with the unmistakable aura of breeding and wealth. In his hand was a fine Victorian oil lamp, complete with its original etched glass shroud, and at his feet, sat a colossal boar's head mounted on a mahogany shield. Its brutish head and tusks took Jerry slightly aback. He steadied his already jangling nerves, and despite being thoroughly unprepared, ushered his visitor in over the threshold.

'Apologies for my appearance, had a bit of a binge last night. As you can see, I wasn't expecting anyone quite so early.'

'No need to apologise. It's important for a man to indulge from time to time, if only to celebrate life itself.' The customer's accompanying smile was pleasing and easy.

'Can I offer you a mug of coffee?'

'Love to, but I won't, things to do and all that. Give me a hand here would you?' and Jerry's interest quickened, as they lifted the boar's head through the door. It really was quite magnificent, more than adequate for the studio's discerning demands.

After some brief haggling, Jerry procured both artefacts with a small wad of cash from his wallet, and the deal was sealed with a handshake. He had paid a marginally inflated price, but would recoup the expenditure soon enough. He opened the door to let the gentleman out, but as the other stepped into the street, he turned and spoke in a manner that Jerry found out of pace, if not strange, but at the time he gave it little thought. The seller dropped his voice to a confidential tone.

'You'll find the boar's head an absolute bargain, in fact more than you bargained for,' he said with a silky smile.

Jerry read the calling card again, 'Charles Millington.' The visitor's eyes narrowed, focusing on the top of the shopkeeper's bowed head, with a cruel twist appearing at the corners of his smile. 'At your service,' he said, and as Jerry looked up, Millington's face was again flushed and sunny. They shook hands for the final time and then Millington had gone. Jerry hauled the boar's head further into the shop, and with all his strength, hoisted the shield onto a cast iron hook on the wall, used for the suspension of weightier artefacts. He stood back to admire the item, but it wasn't admiration he felt, more a strange feeling about the latent expression in the animal's face. He moved forward and touched the great head, and although the beast was long dead, the unaccountable feeling persisted.

Abdiel looked down the long table. 'So brother of mine, you seek vengeance on both our poor shopkeeper, and Bonner, simultaneously. For Jerry Green it is the 'Bruinscrofa', and for Bonner, the sucking dry of his spirit, languishing with a broken heart on the moor, with thoughts only of self-destruction as company. Both are powerful weapons you have unleashed, but somehow, with Bonner at least, I feel you may well fail again.'

'And you brother Abdiel, are you just going to sit there, in your pleasant world of the righteous and pretend to do nothing?' Now it was the Devil's turn to prize information from the other. But with little hope.

'Certain things are being done as we speak, Lucifer. And that is all I am prepared to say right now. So let us now turn to other things.'

And I the Scribe, documented the exchange with greater interest than usual.

Daniel crouched low in the cluster of wind-stunted trees, with the Hummer ready to hurl at the fast incoming flight of wood-pigeon. Tobacco sat motionless, watching expectantly, as their evening meal winged its way towards the cooking pot, and the Hummer span through the air, with a perfect interception. It struck two of the ten birds, and they tumbled to earth, in a cloud of secondary feathers. Tobacco sprang from her hiding place to retrieve them. As she dropped the second carcass at his feet, Daniel noticed a small tube attached to one of its legs. It was a message canister, normally used with carrier pigeons, but what was it doing on a wild bird? Carefully he extracted the tiny roll of wafer thin paper and read the neat print.

'Dear Mr. Bonner.'

'How much does it hurt knowing that Bryony is lost to you forever? Soon she will be lying next to me, as you languish on the moor. You have lost, Mr. Bonner. Did you really think you ever stood a chance? When she is fully mine, I shall inform you of how badly I treat her. She shall bitterly regret our wedding day, but never can she be free. And remember, all those that stand in our way shall be crushed from existence.'

Knowing I have kept you informed.
Kind regards
Charles Millington.

Daniel dared not read it again, for fear of further stoking a sudden rage inside, already on the brink of overtaking reason. It had been three weeks since leaving Delamere, and already, apart from Millington's first exchange, the Underworld had found a way of getting to him. This was far removed from the physical test with the Tarquill's, and he realised his enemy was capable of goading him, in every conceivable way. His heart thought it might break. He desperately needed De Theiry's help.

His cooking fire was hot and lively beneath the roasting pigeon, on a makeshift spit of green willow, and as he rotated the birds, his eyes dropped to the billy-can of water, heating against the lower bank of embers. It had begun to vibrate, with tiny ripples breaking the surface, as if the earth had trembled. Suddenly the container tipped unaided into the fire, and he and Tobacco leapt back with surprise. Steam and smoke billowed skyward, before coiling over the spit, to hover several inches above the ground, on the opposite side of the fire. It held station against the breeze, and Daniel watched the apparition of Phillip De Theiry emerge in the fog. Tobacco curled back her top lip and growled, and Daniel pinched his forearm to make sure it wasn't in his dream.

'This is no dream, Daniel,' confirmed De Theiry. 'I appear before you in your waking hours, as entering your dream saps valuable energy from my being. It was necessary at first, as I needed your attention without you overreacting, but now you know me, and that I mean you no harm, I shall come to you in this manner from now on.' He took his ornately engraved silver snuffbox from his waistcoat pocket, and with a large pinch of the stuff between forefinger and thumb, offered it to his nose with theatrical panache. 'Bryony is in no danger at present,' he continued, flicking the residues from his fingertips back into the box. 'However Charles Millington wishes you to think otherwise. He and the Underworld expect something foolhardy from you, at any moment, but I cannot allow such a thing. You are Bryony's protector, therefore I must protect you.'

Daniel visibly controlled his anger, at the mention of Millington's name. And De Theiry understood the inner battle raging.

'What have I got to do Phillipe? How do I fight them?'

'Outwardly you do nothing, but make them think their efforts are feeble. You must learn to mock them. Turn the table on their strategies, and throw whatever trickery back at their feet. They shall hate you all the more, and will come to realise you have grown stronger, since the first encounter. But be warned, it is a dangerous strategy. Control blind hate and raw emotion. Exercise it only when in mortal conflict, and you shall overcome the devious and dangerous games they play. They may even begin to fear you for it. Their doctrine stands strong because they understand mortal frailties. They manipulate the living world's emotions of greed, love, hate, envy, and most importantly, fear. There are many ways in which they will try to undermine your increasing strength. They may also attack those nearest to you, so try not to make unnecessary friendships. You have unwittingly embarked on a long and lonely war, that will follow you all your days. Be on your guard, and in the meantime I wish you bon chance.' Before Daniel could reply, De Theiry's form began evaporating, and the sullen fire burst back into life. When the smoke had all but gone, Daniel heard De Theiry's distant parting words.

'Call me whenever you need. Throw water on the fire and I shall come.'

The weeks that followed passed without incident, but De Theiry's instruction of indifference, began scoring heavily. Convinced Daniel was sure to react to Millington's goading, the Chancellor waited, taking odds with some of his more senior cohorts, as to how long it might be, before they could exploit the weakness. But he slowly began to understand his mistake, and moved amongst his army, brooding and vicious, loathing the notion that he had been, most probably, outwitted for a second time, and by the same, and possibly dangerous mortal. He decreed to be left alone, and his army did well to place themselves out of harm's way. They travelled the exchequer's causeway's, consigning themselves to the tunnels and distant vastness of the lower catacombs.

Alone on the dais the Chancellor, began planning the scenario to a much more deadly game, one he had conjured up on receiving information that Bonner was once more a man of substance. Jerry Green would now suffer the consequences for writing the book, a subject the Chancellor found particularly irritating, given it was his generosity that had made Bonner rich in the first place. Now he was a free soul, with a personal exchequer that grew daily, and to add insult to injury, Tony Windrow had not once been written of in a favourable light. Jerry Green would pay dearly for the insult, and Bonner would lose one of his closest allies.

It was Tobacco's animal instinct that alerted Daniel that something was wrong. She growled with a sound so unnerving with its cadence it gained his immediate attention. 'Myths and Legends' was suddenly the centre of her attention, as she sprang backwards and forwards to harry the inner pocket of his long coat. Daniel extracted the book and laid it to the ground. Tobacco ceased growling, stared at the volume, then back up at Daniel who instinctively began flicking the pages. Her head shot back and forth, as if expecting something to emerge from the folds, like a cornered rat in a grain store. Suddenly she shot forward, and pressed her nose into the chosen page, sniffing the musty print. She then sat, without once removing her gaze.

'Blimey! You daft dog! What the Hell's got into you?' Daniel lifted the book to take a closer look.

'The Dorset Ooser', headed the left page. The illustration showed the once high-priest who officiated at ancient fertility rituals, a figure wearing the horned mask of a ferocious bull, believed by some to be the 'Christmas Bull.' Legend tells of a terrifying creature, that roamed through the streets of Dorset villages at the end of each year, demanding refreshments from whomever it met. Those who refused, placed their lives in jeopardy, often making the ultimate sacrifice.

On the opposite page appeared the 'Bruinscrofa,' another alarming beast, with the combined body of the all-powerful brown bear, and the head of a monstrous wild boar. Long tusks protruded like scimitars from its mouth, capable of disembowelling a lancer's horse, with a single stroke, and Daniel was drawn to it, like a moth to the flame. 'Bruinscrofa' was a creature with a collected title of two animals. 'Bruin', a personal name for the Brown Bear and the Latin word, 'Suscrofa' meaning wild boar. Daniel read on. Legend tells that when the two are joined, there shall emerge from the twilight world, one of the most deadly creatures, ever to walk the earth. It is said that 'Bruinscrofa' is unleashed when the Underworld's order is challenged. It is also written, that when sent out to avenge, none survive.

Daniel lowered the book, as the first tingle of alarm ran through his mind, and he looked around the perimeter of his camp. His clever little mongrel was in tune to the vibrations of the Underworld, and had delivered a clear warning of an advancing and deadly force, against which the Hummer would be nothing. This would require strength and guile, and under the orange blush of sunset, he sat, considering how to tackle such a brute adversary. From where and when would it come, and on what ground? He would certainly need the advantage of terrain. Instinctively, he began calculating an offensive strategy.

He sat sifting through the imponderables, as Tobacco walked to the perimeter of their camp, before turning to bark at him. Finally he looked up, realising his dog was urging him to follow. Daniel at last responded. Suddenly he understood, and in that instant, remembered where had he had seen the replica of the bear in the book. As Tobacco disappeared along the gorse trail, he gathered his duffel bag, and the last line from Charles Millington's message came to him... 'And remember, all those who stand in our way shall be destroyed.' At the time, Daniel had thought it a warning for him alone, but now as he ran, the feeling of dread strengthened for his friend Jerry Green.

The huge boar's head, was most certainly the best taxidermy specimen Jerry had seen in his career. The tusks shone like polished alabaster, the snout and ears almost pliable beneath his touch. But it was the eyes that astounded him the most. He cleaned a film of dust from the lens of his magnifying glass, and took a closer look. They were soulless pools of polished jet, windows into an unholy place, devoid of feeling, warmth or light. He ran his forefinger along the lower lid, then drew back to study the digit. 'Dry as a bone,' and he snorted, at the laughable idea they might be real, however, they were no less disconcerting.

On the up-side, the studios had agreed its hire, and were to collect the following day, and Jerry wondered again at his good fortune, not to mention his relief in getting rid of the head.

That night, De Theiry came to the little shopkeeper, in the shadows of his bedroom, to warn him of 'Bruinscrofa's' rejuvenation. De Theiry realized this man was an important factor, in the unnatural game they were all playing, and therefore deserved all the help he could get. If De Theiry could keep him alive, Jerry could further help Daniel, who in turn would stand a better chance of saving Bryony. But unfortunately, it seemed that dear Jerry Green, was utterly impervious to his presence.

De Theiry had to do something; anything to raise the alarm. In desperation, he called upon his hitherto untried powers of the poltergeist. He entered a distant state of mind, drawing on the forces of the dead, connected the living and spiritual worlds through physical contact, and with surprising results.

For the third night in a row, Jerry's sleep was interrupted, and this time by Myths and Legends flying off the bedside table, to land with a bass thump on his head. Alarmed he sat up, switched on the bedside lamp and stared incongruously at the volume lying open on his lap. With a palm under each cover he slammed the book shut, but was surprised when the sleeves fell open at the same page. Again he slapped it shut, and again it fell open. It was then Jerry realised its significance, and in the background, Philip De Theiry uttered a sigh of exasperated relief, albeit mute to the shopkeeper's ear.

At that point, 'Bruinscrofa' meant nothing to Jerry, and yet the drawing leaped from the page. It matched the great bear, standing sentinel below, the boar's head a startling facsimile, of his recent acquisition, now hanging on the wall. The previous night's disturbances, suddenly began to gel horribly. Could 'Bruinscrofa' be in the process of resurrection? He was in desperate need of Daniel's reassurances, last seen three weeks ago.

Silently he slipped from the bed and padded barefoot to the door. De Theiry was beside himself, shouting at him to get out, run, hide, dive through the window, climb onto the roof, fly to the bloody moon…anything rather than go downstairs. But Jerry was oblivious. Besides, with a sudden rush of unexpected bravado, he had other plans. If the said beast was coming to life, he would be ready.

On the far wall of the office, an antique blunderbuss hung in its dusty rack. Despite its condition, it was however, a fully-working piece of considerable fire power when loaded correctly, all that was needed, for the annihilation of anything stuffed and hairy standing in its way? He had fired it just once in the open field behind the shop, and the resulting, yet inexplicable thunder-clap, had been the talk of the town for several days. He of course denied having anything to do with it, but recalled being dumped on his backside, with his prime apple tree, cut in half like a ship's mast, hit by a nine pound ball from a Long Tom cannon. Nothing could survive it. He would re-load the weapon, and wait in the shadows to blow anything, even remotely threatening, to kingdom come. A unique thrill spread through his stomach, and behind him De Theiry raised his arms in utter despair.

The bear and the boar's head were unmoved, as Jerry flashed past into the recesses of his cluttered office. He hoisted the neglected gun from its cradle, and from his desk, he took a large tin of black powder. With pure guesswork, he poured a quantity of coarse granules into the muzzle, and damped it down with the brass-headed ramrod, but as he reached for the wadding, he heard movement on the shop floor.

'Sod the fucking' guesswork,' he whispered, and tipped most of the remaining powder into the gaping barrel. He pressed home a lint wad, onto which was dropped an impressive array of 12mm hardened lead shot, a fistful of nuts-and-bolts, an equal amount of old Dutch guilders, a few brass wood screws and twenty or so rusty tacks, just for good measure. Again he heard movement, this time the unmistakable sound of something heavy, moving about on the creaking floorboards; it was becoming a race against time. With trembling hands, he packed down the top wadding, tighter than a cork in a champagne bottle, then pulled back the heavy hammer and primed the frizzen. The powder tin chattered against the gunmetal, as he filled the flash-pan, but at last, Jerry Green was now in proud possession of a gunpowder-powered bulldozer. He need hardly aim the weapon. All he had to do was point the trumpet muzzle in the general direction, pull the iron trigger, and destroy all and everything in its path. His preparations were complete.

Somewhere out in the shop the 'Bruinscrofa' had come to life. Not that he could see it in the darkness, more that he could sense its predatory presence.

He pulled back the hammer to full cock, biting his lower lip, as if to somehow silence the sears loud click, and the shop became hushed. The minutes ticked by with unsettling slowness, as Jerry peered unblinking, into the ominous shadows. He rested the blunderbuss on a pile of magazines sitting on the leather desktop, the muzzle pointing menacingly through the office doorway; the only possible way in for 'Bruinscrofa.' And when it charged, Jerry would send it back to Hades. Half his shop would very probably go with it, but that particular consideration held no precedence. What a fantastic boast he would make, when telling Daniel the story of how he had destroyed the beast! Empowered by the weapon in his hand, it was his moment for adventure and victory, and he willed it to come. However, as time dragged agonisingly by, Jerry found the prevailing silence increasingly unsettling. He wanted to get on with it, pull the trigger and end it. But the minutes continued to tick slowly by through the longest hour, and not surprisingly he began questioning the plausibility of the situation. He had always considered himself a rational man. The fact that Daniel Bonner had crossed blades with the Underworld, was the only reason he now lay in wait behind his desk, with a fully-primed hand cannon. But there was no proof the 'Bruinscrofa' even existed, only perhaps in his lucid imagination fuelled by the book. As for the book falling from his bedside table, he had probably dragged it off himself in his sleep, he reasoned. How ridiculous it all suddenly seemed, and indeed how ridiculous he must appear, skulking in the shadows, lying in wait for some fictitious creation, from a fanciful book of legends. He was sorely tempted to break cover, when at last part of De Theiry's influence, began to pierce his armour-plated senses. Something was telling him to err on the side of caution, and he began wrestling with the flip-side of the argument. He had been disturbed two nights in a row, not to mention hearing something moving around the shop, a little more than an hour ago. He would hold fast until daylight.

At his side, Phillip De Theiry took a nervous pinch of snuff, continuing his partially successful attempt, at sending dire warnings along the supernatural corridor.

Time tugged relentlessly at Jerry's fortitude, until suddenly, to end the torturous waiting, the moon appeared from behind a cloud, illuminating the shop in its silver wash. In the revealing light, Jerry saw the boar's head shield abandoned on the floor, and beyond was 'Bruinscrofa's great hulk, lying patiently in wait. Jerry's spine shot straight with a start, but the blunderbuss felt reassuringly heavy in his sweaty grip, and for the hundredth time he checked the hammer, and curled his finger around the trigger. He peered through his misted glasses, over the barrel, and into the backdrop of the moon's nacreous light, for any further sign of life. And as if in answer, the great mound moved. At first Jerry thought it a trick, in the uncertain shining, before the monstrous creature rose on all fours. It had been waiting motionless in the darkness, and Jerry realised it was not only a beast of great power, but also cunning. Now that the moon had exposed its position, it rose on its hind elephantine legs. Unsheathed claws clicked ominously on the creaking floorboards, in a deadly staccato as it advanced, almost enough reason for Jerry to prematurely yank the trigger, but it was the boar's head that put the real fear of damnation into his soul. Its huge bill-hook tusks, slashed at the ceiling joists, tearing away huge splinters, littering the floor like an open graveyard of bones. The dust of ages, fell from the beams in silver falls, around 'Bruinscrofa's head and the tip of its snout rocked to and fro, taking in the scent of its quarry, through bullet-hole nostrils. Drool overflowed the corrugation of its lips, dropping in strands of phlegm to puddle the floor, and the stench assailed Jerry's nose. 'Bruinscrofa' was an image of unbridled malevolence, its eyes like that of a hunting shark. Even in the half-light, the terrible watery orbs, exuded all the awful truths, about this harbinger of destruction from hells environs. Goose-flesh erupted along Jerry's arms, as he loosely aimed the broad barrel at its torso. 'Eat lead and death mother fucker!' said Jerry, and pulled the trigger.

The already disorderly world of his office, disintegrated in the over-loaded detonation. The door-frame suffered instant annihilation, with most of the surrounding lathe and plaster wall disappearing with it. An opening the size of a large family car magically appeared, and into the shop the destruction continued. Everything hanging from the ceiling was blown to smithereens. Ten thousand artisan hours, fragmented under the onslaught of spinning coins, tumbling wood screws, the corkscrew trajectory of nuts, bolts, nails, and 12mm hardened lead shot. It was a combination of ordinance, capable of re-writing the scientific capabilities of small-arms ballistics. The floor and ceiling beams splintered like a galleon, hit hard by a murderous broadside, and the unstoppable ordinance tore along the entire length of the shop without faltering. Nothing could survive such devastation, and 'Bruinscrofa' was blown away!

Behind the detonation, Jerry had been thrown six feet backwards, his body slamming into the far wall, with bone cracking impact. The Blunderbuss had split apart into unrecognisable sections, the departing hammer and frizzen blowing a large hole in the plasterboard ceiling, above his head. The shock-wave had crashed through the disintegrating walnut stock, expanding every knuckle joint in his hand and wrist, shattering his collarbone and stunning his brain, like a nuclear-powered explosion. His hair was blown back, the collar torn from the fabric of his shirt, and hot black powder smuts scorched his nose, eyelashes and tortured ears.

‘Fuckin’ hell,’ he grunted, barely conscious, holding his head in the jangling aftermath, with what little remained of the gun, scattered across the floor at his feet, ‘overcooked that little cake!’ Gun smoke and the loss of vital spectacles, distorted any visual detail of what was left of the shop. However, there was enough evidence to suggest, that he had blown the ‘Bruinscrofa’ back to its dark place of origin, and the realisation of such an achievement, marginally counterbalanced the terrible pain of his injuries. He was now one of the victorious dueller’s against the dark forces, and Jerry reckoned himself as a bit of a hero. ‘Ha ha!’ he shouted, unable to restrain himself, but regretted doing so through his splitting headache. ‘Not so bloody tough were you, you ugly brute,' he continued. 'Thought you could outwit the likes of me…but I’ve blown the mouldy old stuffing out of you eh! Well good riddance Mr. Pig Bear. Give me a pint of Pig’s Ear any time!’ And he groaned again, as he laughed through the clearing smoke. True enough, there was no sign of the beast. Nothing could possibly have survived such catastrophic ordinance, and as the smoke thinned sufficiently, Jerry began lamenting his decimated stock. He stood damaged but upright, in what was left of the doorway and closed his eyes in relief, against the residues of smoke, that also stung his watering nostrils. He stood for several long moments, until two primary senses, alerted him to the close proximity of ‘Bruinscrofa’. He could smell the fetid odour of the carnivore, as something sticky dropped onto his blackened, sweat-beaded forehead. A cold, glutinous unguent, slid down to his chin, before dropping like bearing-grease onto the floor. He opened his eyes, and looking through crusted lashes, his entire vision was filled, with a living wall of rank hair.

The roar of the ‘Bruinscrofa’ was a noise from another world; at first a screech of shocking decibels, followed by the deep undertone rumblings, of a bull elephant in musth. But its saliva was decidedly the most objectionable thing of all. A globule found its way into Jerry’s upturned mouth, and projectile vomit splattered the ‘Bruinscrofa’s expansive front, with an odour sweeter than roses, by comparison. Jerry tried ineffectually, to wipe what remained of his spaghetti supper, from the beast’s colossal chest. in the vain attempt to pacify it, and in response, a deadly tusk slashed down at the top of the shopkeeper’s fragile skull. It was only raw instinct, that enabled Jerry to dodge the killer blow. The tusk struck the top of his cheek, parting flesh like a blunt knife would cut a ripe tomato. It plunged down, narrowly missing the vitals in his neck, and embedded itself five inches, into his already shattered shoulder. Jerry screamed as he sank to his knees, and would have fallen, had the 'Bruinscrofa' not lifted him high into the air, with an up-sweep of its colossal front paw. In those vital moments, he knew it was all over, and Millington's onerous words rang in his head like a church-bell: 'You'll find the boar an absolute bargain. In fact more than you bargained for'. In that maelstrom of hell, in a sudden moment of clarity, Jerry understood he was about to die.

His body crashed into the office desk, taking all manner of clutter with him, the agony of his wounds, tearing through his battered body. Blood flowed thick and hot from the terrible wounds, as 'Bruinscrofa' came in for the kill. And all Jerry could do, was pray that the end would be merciful.

It was in the darkest moments before dawn, when Daniel entered the empty streets of Delamere. Everything seemed normal, as he moved like a ghost towards Artefacts of Ages, but the closer he got, the more agitated Tobacco grew, skirting any direct approach. Ten feet from the shop, Daniel stood like a statue, as dawn's sudden light spread along the street. Initially he was unsure of what he was looking at, until the light was sufficient enough to reveal the disturbing details. Bullet holes peppered the window, like black stars on a silver sheet. Fragments of glass crunched beneath his boots, and from that he knew that the shot had come from within. Tentatively he stepped forward, and pressed his face to the glass, using the holes to see into the dark interior. He saw the devastation in the immediate vicinity, but could see nothing further than ten feet beyond that. Hooding his brow, he moved along the ruined glass, as Tobacco gripped the hem of his coat in her teeth, and began to tug. Ordinarily Daniel would have given only partial consideration to her behaviour, but this was different. She was trying to warn him of something in the gloom. It was then he caught his first glimpse of 'Bruinscrofa'. Its charge was deceptively fast, with no intention of stopping short of the window. Daniel instinctively dived sideways, as the brute burst through in a maelstrom of more fragmented glass. He rolled away and sprang nimbly to his feet. 'Bruinscrofa' stood twenty feet away, low, menacing, ready to charge again, and Daniel was taken aback by the bulk of the beast. It had grown twice its original size and weight, its head bigger than a cow elephant, with ten times the temperament. The congealed blood around its mouth and chest, told a chilling story. Daniel moved slowly to the broken window, ready to dive headlong through the frame of jagged edges to escape, preferring to have his body lacerated, rather than face down an un-defendable charge.

As 'Bruinscrofa' bunched its mountainous shoulders to attack, good fortune played its hand, and suddenly, the duel was over. Half-way along the high street someone shouted, as others appeared from their respective houses, to investigate the sound of breaking glass. 'Bruinscrofa's war was only against those whom it was instructed to destroy. It sped quickly away, before disappearing into the rugged topography of the moor, too quick for the gaggle of approaching citizens to discern its bulk, on the dark side of the street.

As a dozen Delamerians marched along the road towards him, Daniel noticed a tusk lying in the debris, snapped from 'Bruinscrofa's jaw in the impact with the window frame. He gathered the curved dagger and slipped it unseen into his pocket, motivated by instinct alone.

At first the small crowd was highly suspicious, as they gathered around him, until Conrad Sweet vouched for their acquaintance.

'What the hell happened here, Daniel?'

'I'm not sure, Conrad,' he said to the gathered assembly, who were equally puzzled at the destruction.

As Daniel and Conrad stepped through the gaping hole, their prime objective was to find Jerry. Cautiously they moved along the splintered floor and tattered interior, and through what remained of the office wall.

'Has anybody got a torch?' shouted Daniel, looking at the electric switch spitting blue sparks, as it hung by its cable, and a few minutes later a torch was produced. In the stark beam, Daniel identified what was left of the wing-back chairs, both torn apart in a tangle of shattered wood and horse hair stuffing, but most disturbing were the sticky pools of blood, smeared and trodden on the floorboards. More of the stuff decorated the walls in heavy splatters leading to the vaults below, and most of the crowd were not prepared to go on, the macabre evidence robbing them of any remaining courage.

Daniel and Conrad followed the trail into the dark confines of the lower level.

'No man can lose this amount of the red stuff without threatening life itself,' said Conrad quietly in Daniel's ear, and Daniel moved grimly forward without replying. The trail led them through the workshop, and passed the twisted bars of the jail-house, and they wondered at the power that had reduced the tempered metalwork to scrap. The door lay crumpled and twisted on the floor where it had been hurled, and the men moved through until, on the far wall, they discovered something to give them hope. Bloody hand prints decorated the heavy steel door of the strong room. Jerry had at least made it this far.

On closer inspection, deep gouges on the door surround were visible. 'Bruinscrofa' had clearly attempted to excavate the fifty-ton steel box from its foundations of reinforced concrete. The claw marks were deep and wide, some parallel, some criss-crossed, others jagged, random and frenzied.

'Claw and tusk,' Daniel muttered, praying he would find his friend alive on the other side. 'Jerry, are you in there? Can you hear me?' There was little hope of his voice penetrating the twelve inch thick steel door, its wheel handle snapped from the centre, as if nothing more substantial than brittle plastic.

'We need a crowbar,' Daniel grunted to Conrad, who had already begun searching. He selected a three-foot bar from the twisted wreckage of the cage, and inserted the end into a tiny gap between the door, and the impenetrable jamb, and together they heaved. At first it wouldn't budge, but with all the necessary force, the makeshift jemmy gained purchase, and the door began to swing far enough open, for Daniel to peer inside. He probed the interior with the torch, and saw Jerry's huddled form in the far corner. He faced them with wide unblinking eyes, his head covered in a profusion of his own blood, like an oil rig red-neck after striking Oklahoma crude. Daniel placed his boot on the wall, curled his fingers in the jamb and heaved open the door.

Conrad took over. He recognised the look on Jerry's face, the look of an animal about to die, and this time it was he who gave the orders.

Within half an hour, Jerry had been extracted from the safe, his eyes crowded, with the haunted look of a man close to insanity, his hands clinging desperately to the folds of Daniel's coat. He was shaking like a victim from a bomb blast, and as the paramedics stretchered him to the waiting ambulance, Daniel walked hurriedly alongside.

'I tried to kill it...thought I'd blown it to pieces,' he hissed, through bloody spittle, fear and shock rattling in his voice. 'Gave it a full charge from the old blunderbuss...enough to knock over three bull elephants, but it was no good...it was fuckin' useless Danny,' and rivulets of tears cut through the blood on his cheeks.

Once loaded in the ambulance, the crew were ready for immediate departure. Daniel would have gone with him, but was ordered to leave the vehicle given the amount of emergency work needed by the paramedics, just to keep Jerry alive. He had all but prized Jerry's hand from his lapel, when his friend mustered the last reserve of strength, and pulled Daniel's ear within whispered range.

'This is one really bad beastie...It's out there, and it's waiting for you Danny...be careful my friend. For Christ sake's be careful!' And with the warning having barely left his lips, Jerry Green tumbled into the abyss of thankful unconsciousness.

Daniel watched the receding ambulance as it moved off along the high street. The wail of sirens and flashing emergency lights danced across the surrounding buildings. This was not where Daniel wanted to be, but the moor was now an even more dangerous place. He looked out across the vastness and wondered what possible defence could there be against 'Bruinscrofa'?

The authorities insisted on Daniel staying in Delamere for several days. He slept in Jerry's room, and guarded the shop until the windows had been shuttered, but after intensive questioning by the constabulary, he was at last, free to leave. It was commonly believed, that an escaped animal from a private zoo, had attacked the luckless Jerry Green, when inadvertently cornering the brute. In response a group of local residents set out, armed with a menagerie of small calibre rifles, shotguns and hunting knives; eventually calling a halt to the ensuing three-day hunt. They returned to the village weary, cold and without success. Daniel knew they would draw a blank. 'Bruinscrofa' was a beast of the Underworld, a heinous incarnation controlled by the Chancellor, a creature that could disappear under his guardianship, to be unleashed at will. No man ever found 'Bruinscrofa' by chance! 'Bruinscrofa' would always find man.

As Daniel stood at the edge of the moor, his frustration and anger blossomed. Somehow he would find the way of continuing the fight, especially for Jerry lying critically wounded on a hospital bed, connected to a flux of intravenous drips and bleeping monitors. Jesse and his dog, Zip, sprang once more to mind, and with one hand on 'Myths and Legends,' the other on the tusk, Daniel calculated a new course and headed south.

# Eight Eighty

The Chancellor's Underworld exchequer was hellishly hot for Norbert Morris, the financial director who had failed to keep Daniel Bonner aboard the original program. He had been summoned once more by his master, and only a fool wishing total damnation, would dare disobey. He tugged nervously at the gap between the translucent white skin of his neck, and tatty rim of a grubby white collar. The knot of his tie had been pulled so tight by the cohort that had dragged him into the arena, that a sharp knife would be required to remove it. Despite his obvious discomfort, his beady eye was drawn uncontrollably to the gold block gabions, filled with the most fantastic wealth in the universe. If he were destined to spend the rest of his existence in the catacombs of hell, at least he could boast he had once touched the yellow metal, and smelt its hot metallic odour, a comforting thought if nothing else. The exchequer was an extraordinary place of beauty and ugliness, the rock constantly close to meltdown, but nothing burned unless ordained, and through the shimmering heat, the Chancellor appeared, high upon the dais. But he was not alone. At a writing lectern of solid gold, the Chancellor's scribe stood with an open book, and quill poised in readiness. The Chancellor beckoned Norbert to climb the steps, and join them with a flick of his heavily ringed fingers.

'My Lord,' said Norbert, as he approached, 'I am ready for your orders, your loyal servant, to any mission you wish to send me on, until the best has been achieved. Then my Lord, if what I do is found wanting, I will do better still.'

'Found wanting' has no place in my vocabulary,' rumbled the Chancellor. He leaned forward. For long moments the scorching bedrock trembled, and the air was heavy with murderous thoughts from the hoard, until the Chancellor reclined into his hot rock seat, in considered thought.

'I have summoned 'Eight Eighty', one of our number from the Holding Cage of Souls, and shall return him to the mortal world, to hunt down Daniel Bonner. And you, Norbert Morris, shall assist. It is a calculated risk, for the Underworld cannot take a man's soul twice. He already nurtures a deep resentment for Bonner, and that is the key. Should he fail, then this world will lose another cohort. You, Mr Morris, shall make sure he succeeds. Is that clear?'

'What is it you wish me to do, my lord?'

'Lead 'Eight Eighty' to Bonner who, in turn, shall lead him down into the pit of the Tarquills. They constantly demand revenge for the loss of their slain, and I intend them to have it. Do not return until the task is complete, unless of course you wish the remainder of your soul, to be handed over to my little lovelies?'

Norbert dared not look down from the dais. He could feel the very essence of evil pour over him, from the Chancellor's terrifying army. Through thin spittled lips, he burbled promises of unrivalled success.

With a click of the Chancellor's fingers, a demonic specimen slithered from the front row of onlookers, and sloped up the steps to where Norbert stood. It closed in, and pressed its loathsome carbuncled face to his. For a fleeting moment, Norbert returned the eye contact, and wished he hadn't. He saw awful things in that bloodshot orb. The corrugations of corrupt skin around its single eye, creased into a pitiless smile, before it moved away to coil at the Chancellor's feet. With bowed head, the creature raised a small casket in its serpentine arms, from which the Chancellor took a silver talisman, bound on a thin necklace of plaited human hide. For longer than was needed, he studied the intricacy of the three leaping flames, and its inscription in the language of the Underworld.

'Gokin Rab Griv Ultim.' 'Those that wear, obey.'

The Chancellor returned his gaze to Morris, and grinned.

'You will place this talisman around 'Eight Eighty's neck to safeguard the mission.'

Norbert responded to the order with a subservient bow, but looked up sharply at his master's following words.

'You shall lead him to Bonner in the guise of a dog. The black Labrador suited you well enough I think.' His humourless smile remained.

An expression of deep reluctance swept over Norbert's face, and the Chancellor leaned forward enquiringly.

'You question my choice of vehicle?'

'My Lord, let me lead 'Eight Eighty' to Bonner in the form I hold now. It's all the other dogs; you see they all took a disgusting liking to me, unwanted attention around the nether regions, and all that sort of thing. One even tried to give me puppies. I implore you my Lord, not the dog.'

The Chancellor's arena erupted into a cacophony of mockery, until the noise became intolerable.

'Record it thus,' he told his scribe, standing attentively at the lectern. And the scribe did his bidding.

'Do well, Norbert Morris. It is my intention to document all and everything, concerning my new enemy and, ultimately, second guess his intentions. You also shall be entered in the writing, that shall document success or failure. Should the latter be the case, it would prove a seriously dangerous turning point in your future.'

Norbert scraped low.

'Take him away!' roared the Chancellor, above the cacophony of noise. 'Throw him out as a dog…and be warned servant of Mammon…fail me, and you fail yourself.'

The Devil's Umbrella loomed large in front of Daniel, as he made his way along the haphazard trails of expansive gorse bushes, a rabbit carcass swinging from his belt, in rhythm to his long stride. Freshly-dug potatoes, harvested from one of his secret locations, felt comfortably heavy in the pocket of his long coat, as did the bags of blackberries, mushrooms and edible cresses; the finishing touches to his evening meal. In the hearth, the ash of countless fires lay inches deep, dense as talcum powder, undisturbed since his last visit to the overhang. He settled in with a new fire, a good quantity of fresh food, and a gathering of quiet thoughts. Tobacco sat quietly by his side

It had been a while since Jerry Green had been released from hospital, to convalesce under the matronly eye of his sister in Bristol. Artefacts of Ages remained locked and boarded, with the interior still in tatters, as was poor Jerry's mental state, further aggravated by an unsettled insurance claim with the underwriters, insisting that a great percentage of the damage, had been caused by 'the unlawful discharge of a firearm in a public place'.

Apart from initial visits by the police, Jerry's sister, a formidable individual in both mind and stature, forbade access to anyone remotely associated with the circumstances surrounding her brother's terrible experience. Daniel, with his wild appearance, stood little chance of being granted access, and this particular rejection hurt him, more than any other. Although understanding the reasons, it was no less difficult to accept, given that it was he who had got Jerry involved, and his feelings of guilt had not receded. For the time being, he had lost a good friend and ally. He pulled 'Bruinscrofa's tusk from his pocket, as a reminder of what he had brought upon his friend. Stuffing it back in his coat, Daniel forced the guilt to the back of his mind.

The spit-roast rabbit was superb eating; garnished with garlic and cress. The meat was beautifully tender, and the baked potatoes absorbed the natural juices, the best Daniel had tasted in an age. A dessert of plump blackberries followed, and man and dog sat as happy as was possible, as a galaxy of stars slid soundlessly overhead, across the expansive moor and their secretive world.

Despite his overriding concern for Jerry, Daniel felt a sudden sense of unease, a disturbance coming at him through the ether. He had become attuned to the various forces, and could no longer ignore even the smallest of inferences. Without hesitation, he poured water on the fire to summon De Theiry, for reassurance if nothing else. Steam billowed above the dying flames, and De Theiry appeared in his ancient likeness, seated on the other side of the fire. Although eager for information, Daniel did the kindness of patiently observing the niceties. He watched De Theiry perform his highly elaborate snuff-taking ritual, and noted it had matured theatrically. He smiled inwardly and wondered at what kind of man the Parisian had been when he was alive.

'Nothing travels to me along the Underworld corridor,' said De Theiry eventually, pre-empting Daniel's question with an accompanying smile.

'And what of Bryony?' asked Daniel, glad the conversation had at last begun.

'Only that our most favourite Mr Millington, has placed a potent spell over her world, and all that are in it. However, you will be glad to know she carries emotions for you, whenever he is not there to enforce the power of the talisman around her neck. Millington senses the bond between you, and feels threatened by it. He rarely leaves her side. Bryony's mother knows of her daughter's true feelings, and yet Millington somehow holds sway over them all. Be careful Daniel, he is devious and powerful.'

De Theiry delivered another pinch of snuff, through the back-draft of a heavy sniff.

'He is also party to one piece of the jigsaw, of which you are unaware. Daniel, it was he who delivered 'Bruinscrofa's head to Artefacts of Ages.'

Daniel raised his eyes from the embers, with a look belonging to a distant and dangerous place, and De Theiry would have been deeply concerned, had his name been Charles Millington.

'I say to you again Daniel, do nothing rash and you will prevail. And remember you shall meet her again at the pool without water.'

'That's twice you've mentioned this place. Elaborate for me Frenchy! For pity's sake.'

'My premonition is incomplete; too many imponderables. But you will soon be with her at that place.'

'You and your bloody riddles, Philippe. Will I ever get a straight answer?'

The Frenchman replied with a shrug of his ancient shoulders. 'Rest assured, I shall inform you immediately should the circumstances change.'

'Well at least you've put my mind at rest. And thanks. I'd shake hands with you if I could,' said Daniel.

'I should like to shake my own hand if only I could, but it appears I have lost a little weight in the last half century.' And with a raucous guffaw, De Theiry disappeared.

The fire spat back into life, and Daniel felt reassured by the Frenchman's humour. The mere fact he had parted with a joke, confirmed there was nothing of consequence in the twilight pipeline. He looked up in time, to see the fleeting trace of an asteroid, cutting a path across the darkened sky, and for reasons he was unable to explain, he thought of Bryony. It was then he knew, with utmost certainty, that they would meet again. With his back to the wall, the fire at his feet and a comforting sense of inevitability, sleep came easily.

The camp fire burned down to a sullen glow, its warmth giving way to the night's lowering temperatures. However, it wasn't the chill that woke him, but Tobacco's warning bark to the faint sound of someone approaching the Umbrella. In a whisper, Daniel commanded his dog to be quiet. He leant back, feigned sleep and waited. In the faint glow of the fire he looked through the veil of his own lashes, to catch movements in the moonlit gorse.

'Here we go again,' he whispered, and a low growl resonated in Tobacco's throat, and from the gloom a figure stepped boldly into the camp. There was no attempt at concealment as he stared at Daniel, who pretended to wake in surprise.

'Sorry to walk in on you like this. I've wandered off the beaten track and found myself well and truly lost…been blundering about out here for bloody hours.'

Daniel rose to his feet, and stoked the embers with several fresh logs, that burst quickly into life. He took stock of his visitor in the new light. They matched each other in height, but the other had considerably less bulk to his body. He possessed the aura of a person suffering from prolonged ill health, and yet his eyes were alert.

'You'd better come and sit by the fire,' said Daniel, reluctantly. 'Getting lost on the moor at night, is not one of my recommendations.'

A hundred metres away, Norbert Morris, in the unwanted form of the dog, watched with interest, as Daniel allowed Eight Eighty into the camp. Even from a distance, Daniel's body language was clearly that of distrust as Eight Eighty moved in front of him, and began warming his hands against the fire, blocking it from Daniel, and Norbert sniggered at the effrontery of his ward. Satisfied the task had been fulfilled, he disappeared into the night, leaving the two men sitting at uncomfortable odds beneath the Devil's Umbrella.

Eight Eighty looked at Daniel, with a strange nondescript smile. 'I don't suppose you have anything for me to eat?' he asked, and Daniel, unable to say no, reluctantly pushed a cooked potato into the embers to re heat.

'What are you doing out here?' he asked. 'I can see by your clothes you weren't planning a lengthy stay on the moor.'

'I'm looking for the Devil's Umbrella.'

Daniel returned the other's gaze. 'Why would you want to go there?' he asked, handing over the baked potato, and it was taken without a single word of thanks.

‘I have my reasons,’ said Eight Eighty waspishly, tumbling the hot potato from palm to palm.

‘Look mate,’ Daniel levelled his voice. ‘I don’t mind you sitting by my fire, I don’t even mind you eating my food. But try to be a bit more fucking’ civil.’

With a dismissive shrug, the stranger broke open the potato, and looked at the white flesh, but there was something missing. Through his shirt he touched the talisman, and silently made a wish. Instantly the tuber was full of writhing maggots, an accoutrement he had come to relish, in the Holding Cage of Souls. He bit into it, with almost animal gusto.

With a look of utter disgust, Daniel crossed over the fire and slapped the rotten food from the other’s hand, and for a fleeting moment, he could have sworn he saw hatred in the other’s eye. Clearly the stranger was unaware of what he was eating in the low light, and they watched the grubs wriggle away in all directions on the bedrock, from the fallen potato.

‘Bloody hell…sorry about that’, said Daniel, kicking away the rotten vegetable. ‘The one I had earlier was fine. I’ll get you another.’

As he turned away, Eight Eighty’s tongue shot out on Daniel's blind side, and snatched a wriggling maggot stuck to the flat of his cheek, then gathered it in and swallowed it with relish.

‘Don’t worry mate, I’m sure it wasn’t done on purpose, but if you don’t mind I’ll pass on the offer. Sorry if I was rude…perhaps we can start again?’

Daniel nodded sharply, the man had at least said sorry, and with reserve, he shook his hand and the rest of the evening, not one of Daniel’s choosing, passed without further incident. Their conversation remained perfunctory, without the likelihood of any understanding being forged. Daniel was not unhappy with that, but despite the mutual stand off, the stranger seemed increasingly familiar. During the many lulls in their monosyllabic exchanges, Daniel’s mind was racing.

‘Your face reminds me of someone I can’t quite place. Have we ever met before?’

'No.'

'You seem very sure about that?'

'Yes, I'm sure.' And without labouring the point, Eight Eighty reclined against the rock, as if to close the subject.

It was just after midnight, that the two men uttered something of a goodnight, and within an hour the camp slept peacefully enough. But throughout the evening, Daniel had missed a vital point. Tobacco had never once taken her distrusting eyes off their guest.

Just after dawn, Daniel moved quietly around the camp, in readiness to leave. His visitor remained huddled near to the fire, and only then Daniel did notice that throughout the entire time, Tobacco hadn't once gone near him. He called to her softly, and she responded, happy to be leaving at last.

'Where are you going?' Eight Eighty asked, in a low even voice. He, as Daniel had done the night before, had been feigning sleep. Daniel stopped and turned.

'Sorry mate, thought you were still away with the fairies. I was trying to leave without disturbing you.'

'But you can't leave.'

'Excuse me! What the hell do you mean by that?' said Daniel, and not without the first flush of resentment.

'Look Danny, I need you to help me find the Devil's Umbrella. It's bloody important.'

'How the hell do you know my name? Only friends call me Danny.'

Eight Eighty's mind raced.

'Sorry Danny. Didn't want to appear nosy but I read it on the lid of your fishing tin.' Daniel softened, not through the friendly use of his name, but more the plausibility of the explanation.

'The Devil's Umbrella is right above your head,' he replied. You've been sleeping under it all night.'

Eight Eighty looked up at his surroundings, then back at Daniel. 'Don't go Danny; I've got something to find that I know you'll appreciate.'

'I'll be back in a couple of days, that's if you're still here, and if you've found what you're looking for, I'll take a look then.' And before Eight Eighty could make any valid protestation, Daniel and Tobacco had left.

Eight Eighty stood with fists clenched at his side, hate burning like coals in his eyes, as he watched them disappear into the gorse.

In the days that followed Daniel, checked all seven hidden crop fields, in particular the potato earths. At each stash, he glumly expected to find a ruined crop, but instead the tubers were strong and healthy. He suspended a cooking pot over an open fire, into which he dropped the largest potato, and a selection of wild herbs, and despite the lingering feeling of deep irritation, he nonetheless regretted the embarrassing maggot-ridden example, he had offered his visitor.

For his own piece of mind, Daniel unearthed all he needed for the next five days, relieved the crop was uncontaminated and with Tobacco trotting alongside, he decided to head south towards the lakes. The weather was dry and mild, and without further thoughts for the Devil's Umbrella, it was an ideal opportunity to bathe. The trek would take several days, but they were in no hurry. It was what they did best; man and dog, masters of that wild place, with a lifestyle that most would shun, and few could survive, and without a single murmur from the Underworld, or so Daniel believed, it was the finest place on earth.

The sun had settled low on the horizon, when at last they arrived at the deep pool, where Daniel had saved Bryony. He sat at the point where he had revived her drowned body, and the image and events of that day tugged heavily on his memory.

He settled into the camp on the ridge, and as always sat quietly. With Tobacco away exploring the perimeters, his thoughts wandered back to the Devil's Umbrella, the familiarity of the stranger foremost in his mind. He remembered the distinct flash of anger behind the rotten potato episode, then asking Daniel to help find something he wasn't prepared to divulge. But most baffling was the fishing tackle tin. Sure, it was possible he had seen the name 'Danny' on the lid, but it was never opened, so how on earth could the visitor have known its contents? He needed De Theiry. Wasting little time, he followed the Frenchman's instructions and poured water on the embers. Steam broiled into the image of the Parisian who sat opposite in the usual way, but there was something pleasingly different about the once-dishevelled apparition. Daniel could have sworn Phillipe De Theiry's deathly pallor, had been replaced by a subtle infusion of colour. There was even a sparkle in his eyes, and perhaps, thought Daniel, the Frenchman was beginning to relish his new found usefulness. Perhaps his five hundred years in limbo, now had meaning; perhaps he was thriving on a sense of long-awaited purpose. Whatever the reason, he looked better now than Daniel had ever known. And as for the snuff-taking, he could have won a BAFTA with the performance.

'Greetings Phillipe, I trust I'm not disturbing you on such a fine evening?'

De Theiry waved airily, as if it were the least he could do. 'What is it you want my boy?' his Parisian accent thick with importance. Daniel explained all that had happened, from the sudden appearance of his visitor, the maggot-ridden potato, the fishing tin lid and the strange request for Daniel's help.

De Theiry grew thoughtful. He administered more snuff and Daniel wondered if he felt any sensation from the powder. As if to answer, De Theiry sneezed then coughed softly with pleasure, at the powerful inhalation.

'I think it's time to give this new fellow a little visit,' said the Frenchman, with watery eyes. 'I shall return, should my findings be of significance.'

With a brief but courteous farewell, De Theiry faded from sight, and Daniel felt confident his spirit friend, would expose anything remotely out of place.

The night passed uneventfully, until the first blush of a new day, outlined the grand tors on the eastern profile. As daylight crept over the moor, the complete opposite could be said of De Theiry's sudden appearance. Through his ever improving mastery of the poltergeist, he spilled water on the fire and uncoiled on the other side. In the broiling cloud, he sat impatiently, as Daniel climbed drunkenly from sleep.

'Daniel, real trouble has come to find you,' he said, bulldozing through his waking. 'I discovered your man by the fireside under the Devil's Umbrella, and took the liberty of entering his sleep.'

Daniel shook himself fully awake and sat up with interest.

'At first I found nothing, but the more I searched, it became apparent that he carries the Chancellor's mark. A talisman hangs around his neck, but there's something else I couldn't readily identify. A dark secret hangs over this one, Daniel.'

'Tell me everything you know, and without riddles, Monsieur Froggy.'

De Theiry openly ignored the derogatory title, with a sudden nonchalant interest in the state of his manicure. However, this was no time to play games.

'I saw a dog in his dreams, Daniel. He and this dog ran swiftly to find you.'

'Was it a black Labrador?' The question was spontaneous.

'It was indeed.'

'Norbert Morris,' guessed Daniel… 'the poor old sod.'

'Why you should refer to him as a penniless, aged, clump of dirt, eludes me Mr Bonner. I fear I shall never understand the strange meanings of your modern language.' Daniel fought hard not to laugh.

'However, my findings are serious. You will meet this man again. If you don't find him, he is sure to find you. It's important to you both, though I'm not entirely sure why, but it has connections with your past. You have to remove the Talisman from around his neck, for without its power to cloak him, you may well discover this man's true identity. But there is one thing I do know. As if the other ones weren't bad enough, he is the key player, in a new and very dangerous game.'

'Then I'll track him down today, and find out more,' said Daniel with conviction.

'There are other things, Daniel…important things. I saw you deep underground, and great danger raced up to meet you from the bowels of the earth. I saw a beam of light, but of you, I saw nothing more. Daniel, I fear for your life.' He took another pinch of snuff, but this time without theatricals.

Daniel was about to reply, but De Theiry held up his hand. 'I also saw the numbers ten, two, one and five on the time log of an astral chart. Although none of it holds any clear meaning, I believe them critical to your well being. I also saw the number seven on the same chart, representing the seventh day of this month, just a day from now.

Daniel frowned. 'Riddles and more riddles, eh Frenchy? You've given me a date and possibly a time, but it's hardly bloody concise.'

'There is one last thing,' De Theiry lowered his voice, ignoring the accusation. 'I see tragedy and death, so be on your guard. Bon chance, my friend. I think you're going to need it.' And De Theiry evaporated, leaving Daniel alone with a frustrating number of unanswered questions, but at least he now knew the stranger to be his enemy.

'So tell me, has Eight Eighty has been delivered?' enquired the Chancellor, leaning forward on his throne. Apart from the pinking of hot rock, there remained a deathly hush, as Norbert Morris gathered his wits, to deliver his report high upon the dais. A creature slithered across the arena's bedrock, its grub-like, legless body dragged along, by its suckered tongue. It climbed the steps and wrapped its grotesque appendage around Norbert's trembling legs, in a dark embrace, prompting Norbert's report.

'My Lord, Eight Eighty waits beneath the Devil's Umbrella, for his quarry. The talisman hangs around his neck, and he is in a murderous mood.'

The Chancellor's army exchanged glances of reluctant approval, and one plucked the eye from its nearest neighbour, with a barbed talon, in disappointment. It was hungry and needed to feed. In the ensuing squabble for the gruesome prize, the monstrous grub on the dais, relaxed its grip on Norbert's leg. With its single puss-rimmed eye, it looked appealingly at the Chancellor for permission to drag the messenger down to its appalling chamber, regardless.

'And the whereabouts of Daniel Bonner?' quizzed the Chancellor, ignoring the wishes of the undulating grub.

'He has agreed to meet with our number, but knows nothing of the other's identity,' replied Norbert. 'Soon he shall be delivered to the Tarquills.'

He felt suddenly empowered by another universal murmur of commendation.

'And, my Lord,' he said confidently, rising to the moment, 'let us hope that tomorrow favours the deception.'

Another fizz of agreement coursed the chamber. But the Chancellor grew suddenly quiet and suspicious. The hoard noticed the change, and the colossal arena was suddenly hushed.

'Let us hope…you say, 'hope'? You insignificant little turd!! Why in this very hell, should we merely hope? The Talisman is all powerful, and yet you appear, by your very choice of words, unsure.'

'My Lord, it would seem that Bonner has received insight into our plans.' He would have to choose his words wisely, if he was to survive, and as all his confidence evaporated, the suckered tongue tightened its grip around his trembling legs. The smell of ammonia drifted to the Chancellor's nose, as Norbert urinated.

'It seems he is receiving guidance,' he quavered. 'The source is yet unknown and seemingly beyond our reach, my Lord.' Morris straightened his body in an attempt to regain a little dignity. He was careful not to place the blame in any one direction. If it were implied the problem had anything to do with the Chancellor, then a long and excruciating death, of one hundred years in the lower world, would be assured.

'My Lord, I believe he has some form of contact with the spirit world.'

'Then why do you grovel before me now, you snivelling weasel, rather than staying out in the field, to ensure Bonner's fate?'

Since failing to ensnare Daniel at the outset, Norbert's status amongst his Underworld peers had been heavily undermined; even more so when he had told of his encounter with an amorous bloodhound. But this time there was no laughter from the masses. Deadly intent was their order of the day, and the Chancellor looked down at Norbert and smiled, as would a kindly head-teacher to a failed pupil, and the grubs body slumped in further resignation. The Chancellor beckoned Norbert closer, and when within range kicked the doomed man off the dais, as he bellowed three terrifying words.

'Take him down!' And his words resonated throughout the domain for all to hear.

The chamber held its breath for a moment, before erupting into a seething mass of hellish, fighting bodies. In their hundreds they poured and slithered, flew and dropped, sprang and clawed their way across the hot rock, to reach the luckless Norbert. Within seconds, his body was lifted high in the air, by tongue and tentacle, talon and claw tearing his suit and flesh to tatters. Then as one, they dragged him, screaming, down through a hole in the bedrock, too small for the human body to pass. But down he went, with the cracking of breaking bones, and screams from the matrix of his soul, eventually fading to a lost echo.

For the Chancellor, Norbert Morris's journey to the ultimate world of the damned, was nothing more than an inconsequential interlude. Who knows, he might even visit him from time to time, to ensure the highest level of cruelty was maintained. But for the moment, there were more pressing matters to attend.

With a single click of his fingers, he summoned a solitary cohort from its perch of stacked uncut diamonds, quiet and aloof from the ruckus. Vile Bird flew to the dais, landing at the Chancellor's feet. Once human, it was now the most improbable flying creature ever created. Its torso was round and fat, like a shiny blueberry, its six arachnid legs hooked and hairy, its beaked head heavier than that of a Malibu stork, in which were set rows of crocodilian teeth, its featherless wings pinker and more wrinkled, than a plucked turkey.

'So my lovely, shall I send you to finish this game?' And the creature cocked its head to listen.

Vile Bird watched Eight Eighty from a distance, with the patience of a waiting vulture. Perched high on a tor, it had undergone a remarkable transformation beneath the Chancellor's magic. A magnificent raven now took flight, spiralling high into the air to take its bearings, and banked in towards the Umbrella. It alighted high on the top ledge, and studied the ground below, before dropping to the bedrock for a meeting with Eight Eighty.

Soon after, Daniel also found Eighty Eight standing beneath the Umbrella, almost as he had left him. On his approach, he saw the raven perched on the stranger's shoulder, his head cocked as if listening to the bird, but as Daniel closed in the raven took flight. It soared away in the opposite direction, and they watched it gain height, until it was just a dot in the blue sky and disappeared from sight. Moments later, the two men stood face to face and Daniel noticed a marked change in the stranger's manner. The surly scowl had gone, his mood appeared warm, his handshake friendly, and the strong sense of familiarity returned, as they exchanged greetings.

'So, I see you're something of an ornithologist,' said Daniel pointing with his chin to the now vacant sky.

'Oh that,' said Eight Eighty with an insignificant expression. 'It came to me quite literally out of the blue, no idea where from, but a fine looking bird all the same, and so tame. It must have escaped from a private aviary.'

Daniel decided not to say anything more. He knew the man was a cohort, and would keep that knowledge strictly to himself. He had to maintain, what he believed to be the edge.

'You told me there was something you wanted to show me,' he said, changing the subject.

Eight Eighty smiled, as he drew from his pocket, what appeared to be a folded sheet of ancient parchment. 'Glad you haven't wasted time with idle chit chat.' he said, looking surreptitiously about as if checking no one was in the proximity, before joining Daniel's side in a conspiratorial manner.

Unfolding the jagged edged sheet, Eight Eighty handed it over.

The texture was smooth and waxy to the touch, unrecognisable to Daniel as a piece of Norbert Morris's flayed skin. On it was a diagram that Daniel believed to be in black ink. Norbert's dried blood, depicted a stone slab containing ten symbols, four of which were randomly circled in numerical order, reminding Daniel of a modern-day keypad combination. Written beneath was the line, 'Beyond this gateway your future awaits.'

Daniel shook his head. 'I don't understand. What is this?' he asked.

Again, Eight Eighty grew furtive, seemingly worried at being overheard by some unseen eavesdropper. 'I think it's time for explanations, Daniel. I know all there is to know about you, but you know nothing of me.' Daniel raised his head from the parchment, with a look of mild surprise, skilfully masking the overriding feeling of distrust.

'I'm a cohort of the Underworld,' said the other with a whispered admission. 'And I know you understand exactly what that means.'

Daniel was taken aback by the wholly unexpected revelation, but readied himself for any signs of him having walked into a trap. 'Go on,' he said in a deliberate tone, not trusting his own voice.

'They summoned me from the Holding Cage of Souls to find you, and then to destroy you. I agreed to their terms, in exchange for a new existence in the living world.' Eight Eighty cocked his head, as he studied Daniel's face, allowing his revelation to sink in.

'Why are you telling me this?' said Daniel, now thrown thoroughly off balance.

'I don't believe I can ever be free of the Chancellor,' he returned. 'I don't trust a single word he says, and when I have done what he asks, and killed you, I honestly believe he'll renege on the agreement, and drag me back to the cage.'

Daniel eyed him with deep suspicion. For what possible reason should this cohort have the temerity, not to mention the courage, to defy the Chancellor? What could he possibly gain from the betrayal? Eight Eighty read the question written all over Daniel's face.

'Before my release, I acquired a vital piece of information, exposing what I believe is the Chancellor's Achilles heel. I heard through reliable sources, that behind that underground door, lies the key to expose the bastard's underbelly. I think I've found the gateway. Daniel, if we can destroy him, then you and I shall be free.'

Daniel had to admit that the unexpected idea of ending the conflict, was more than just appealing.

'Why should I trust you?'

'Why shouldn't you? I've laid all my cards on the table, most of which you already know to be true. Look Daniel, I'm taking a massive risk here. I need your help. You've got to believe me.'

Yet again the nagging familiarity returned, and suddenly, against all better judgement, not to mention going against everything De Theiry had warned him of in the riddle, Daniel was convinced by the other's explanations.

'Ok, what do you need from me?'

Eight Eighty's face cracked wide with a smile. 'I've been told that pressure on all four symbols has to be applied simultaneously, and I can't do it on my own.'

Daniel knew that they could be heading headlong into danger, and yet felt powerfully drawn to this man, and what the other professed to be their mutual goal. Besides, he could snatch the talisman from the other's neck, and end the game at any time. But right now, he was deeply intrigued, and carried along by a sense of reckless inevitability.

'Ok, I'll help, but before I do, I want your name.' Eight Eighty appeared not to have heard the question, but became animated with the prospect of Daniel's alliance. 'Above us hangs a ledge, and on that ledge lies a hidden entrance roughly half way along. Trust me, I know it's there.'

Daniel gave in, knowing it was pointless to ask again and followed Eight Eighty's gaze.

'How do you propose we find this entrance,' he asked.

'We climb.'

Regardless of inexperience, Daniel was determined to follow Eight Eighty in the assent. Climbing the tors and outcrops was one thing, but this, thought Daniel, was quite different. He stripped down to his tee shirt, emptied his army fatigue trouser pockets of any unnecessary encumbrances and made ready to follow. His boots, although heavy duty, proved a good grip on the craggy face, and at first the going was relatively easy. The cohort led the way like a mountain goat; his wiry stature seemingly built for the task. His long sandy hair swung in rhythm to his lithe movements, and conversely, Daniel cursed his own heavy frame. They climbed ever higher, and soon each foot and handhold Daniel took, was made with increasingly ragged breath. The wall was deceptively high, and when they eventually reached the overhang, Daniel was almost spent. The tendons in his limbs burned hot, the height made him dizzy and he didn't dare look down. As he curled his fingers over the ledge, it occurred to him that the cohort had to be genuine. If the ledge was fictitious and the cohort wanted him dead, Daniel could never make it back down the same way, and through sheer exhaustion would eventually fall to his death. Spurred on by that thought, and with super human effort, he hauled his torso over the rim. Sitting with his back to the wall and his legs dangling over the edge, he for the first time, looked down at the bedrock a hundred feet below. He saw Tobacco patrolling aggressively, back and forth. It was the first time he had seen her since her disappearance on their arrival at the camp, with her ongoing dislike for the cohort. Ignoring her warnings, Daniel took in his surroundings. To the left, the ledge pinched out, and fell away to a sheer drop to the bedrock, but to the right it continued along the face, that he guessed would eventually lead out onto the open hillside.

'Ready to go on?' said Eight Eighty, interrupting his thoughts. He also sat with his legs hanging over the side, seemingly unfazed by the gruelling climb, and dizzy height. 'Yeah, I'm ready. But how come we didn't come that way?' said Daniel pointing along the line of the ridge.

'That's the long way round. Besides I knew you could make a simple climb like that.' Daniel shrugged, not wishing to admit any weakness. The cohort was clearly testing his resolve.

They lifted their legs and began edging their way along the ledge, until the Devil's Umbrella revealed its second secret. A low cave entrance appeared to their left, large enough for a man to enter on all fours, and Eight Eighty led Daniel in. They crawled into the forbidding darkness and down what Daniel estimated to be a twenty-degree incline, of an arrow-straight tunnel. Steadily they made the descent and after a painful age, Daniel looked back over his shoulder, and judged the distance to be at least a quarter of a mile, back to the surface. He was going to need significant reserves of strength, to crawl back to the top. Still they went on, without any sign of the tunnel letting up. Half a mile down, there was still no end and on reaching the three-quarter mile mark, Daniel began to severely question his judgement. They were vulnerable, fumbling along like blind moles into the complete unknown, until at almost a mile below ground, they at last saw the faint, but reassuring luminescent glow of what had to be the tunnel's end. Crawling forward on bloodied hands and knees, Daniel could just make out the outline of Eight Eighty, kneeling with outstretched arms, embracing the end wall of solid rock, as an infant would its mother. As Daniel moved closer, Eight Eighty moved away and in the centre, Daniel recognised the identical indentations to the pen-work on the parchment.

In the strange light, the two men crouched to study the face, and the cohort's fingertips caressed the symbols, carved by stonemasons of old, with a strange reverence.

'Well Daniel, are you ready to strike at the Chancellor's underbelly?' and Daniel looked sideways at him. 'I haven't a clue what I'm doing, but whatever it is, let's get on with it.'

With a reassuring smile, Eight Eighty selected two of the four symbols. Daniel followed suit, and on the count of three, they applied simultaneous pressure. Suddenly the ground began to tremble, and with a deep rumbling the colossal slab of rock, rolled aside. Both men knelt wide eyed in wonder, as it drew aside, beneath a shower of stone dust and grit.

They stared silent and motionless into another luminescent section, of a seemingly never-ending tunnel. At first they could see nothing, until

Daniel detected movement in the far distance. The floor appeared to be alive, too far for any accurate identification, but his nostrils confirmed his worst fear. For crucial moments he was rooted to the spot.

'Tarquills,' he hissed, finding his voice. 'You've led us into the lair of the fucking Tarquills…let's get out of here or we're both dead men.' He turned, but Eight Eighty was no longer with him. Like a sewer rat he had already disappeared back up the tunnel, and a long way off his laughter of betrayal rang down the tunnel.

Daniel turned alone, to begin the impossible journey to the top. With every tortured metre he heard the advance of six-thousand snatching claws, and the clucking of two-thousand rasping tongues, against rows of needle-sharp fangs. Daniel knew it was going to be an agonising death, and all through his own crass stupidity. The Tarquills would begin feeding on his thrashing feet, slowly working up his legs, until the combination of his screams, and unimaginable pain would eventually dull his senses into a much-welcomed death. There was no other possible scenario. The stench of a million dead assailed his nostrils and he vomited. He wiped the mess from his mouth, and like a cornered animal, fear and anger welled from the pit of his stomach, and spread like wildfire through his being. Suddenly he no longer felt pain in his body, and wearing a wolfish grin, he put an end to his futile retreat. He lay on his back and summoned his terrible anger.

'It's time to do some kicking,' he breathed.

It wasn't long before the leading Tarquills came at him and ran directly into a booted barrage. Under the press of following bodies the creatures momentarily faltered. Fuelled by adrenalin, Daniel pumped his legs like hydraulic pistons, smashing the front row to pulp. He began laughing like a maniac. He became murderous in mind and body, once more the apocalyptic madman, and in those terrifying moments the faces of Bryony, Jesse, Zip, and Jerry Green entered the forefront of his mind. Drawing untapped strength from the images of the ones he held dear, he drove another barrage home. Several times the Tarquills managed to breach his crushing defences, only to be ripped apart by the frenzied power of his bare hands. He shouted his defiance, until the crack of his own voice, deafened his ears like gun shots in foxhole. Again and again they came at him, until the eventual failing of his strength, warned him of the inevitable outcome. Bitten, clawed and on his last reserves of strength, the end was near. He lashed out with a final double kick and felt his boots drive into the hoard for the last time, and in that terrible moment, believing it was all over, Daniel Bonner closed his eyes. For agonising moments, he waited for the final rush, but instead felt an unexpected warmth crown the top of his head, and his shuttered eyelids glowed bright crimson with a sudden light. He lifted his hand to the sensation and felt the same warmth covering the back of his hand. From high above salvation had spilled into the tunnel, and against all odds, Daniel's luck had not failed him. He opened his eyes as the light intensified. It flooded the tunnel with such brightness, that it scorched the retinas of his eyes. The front wave of marauding Tarquills shied away from the intense beam, and in an instant, the hoard was a mass of disoriented, frantically-retreating bodies.

At that precise moment in the yearly lunar cycle, the low arc of the autumn sun crossed over the tunnel entrance. On the seventh day of the tenth month, at precisely two-fifteen, sunlight shone directly into and down its entire length, and Daniel laughed uncontrollably, as the seething carpet of Tarquills poured back through the slab, to escape the torturous rays.

'Lie flat and cast no shadow,' he told himself, and as he did so sunlight flooded over him, to continue its deadly work. The front row of retreating Tarquills combusted spontaneously, their burning bodies adding to the fetid air, until the last survivors passed through the gap, and with a violent rumble, the gateway to hell closed behind them, amidst the stench of scorched flesh and ground granite.

Daniel lifted his hand. He was shaking uncontrollably, his breath was panicked, but despite being bitten and clawed, he was alive! By some miracle he had avoided being stung and had cheated death. He lay deathlike, long after the sun had passed over the entrance, and darkness engulfed the tunnel once more.

It took three hours before Daniel, near to exhaustion, tumbled from the entrance. He sat on the ledge, breathing pure moorland air, the sweetest, most welcome elixir in the world. Slowly he felt his strength return, and despite the agony in his bruised and lacerated limbs, he began making his way along the ledge. He eventually reached the end and discovered the hidden exit to the open hillside. Tobacco, having found the long way round was waiting for him in a state of high anxiety. She was uncharacteristically nervous and Daniel made a reassuring fuss of her. After time they both settled, and Daniel made an examination of his wounds. Most were mercifully superficial. Nonetheless, Tobacco continued her wary behaviour.

Surrounded by a clump of gorse bushes, they remained undetected by the incoming flight of the Chancellor's raven. The big bird swooped in low to land, fifty metres behind his position, and ordering Tobacco to stay put, Daniel moved stealthily forward. The bird had to be a part of the conflict and it wasn't long before he was proved right. Eight Eighty stood in a low gully with the raven perched on his shoulder. The cohort was speaking to the bird, and from his place of concealment, Daniel heard the other's traitorous words, clearer than a bell.

'Tell the Chancellor that Daniel Bonner is dead. Tell him the Tarquills have their revenge. Tell him of my success, and my gratitude that I am once more in the living world, a free man.' Eight Eighty lifted the raven from his shoulder, and launched it from his forearm, into the breeze. Vile Bird took to the air, carrying with it, the mistaken news of victory.

Eight Eighty's expression was one of complete surprise, as Daniel stepped from the undergrowth, but was quickly replaced with an unveiled hardening of posture.

'You weren't supposed to survive down there,' he growled.

'You were supposed to die, you nine-life bastard.'

Daniel's grin was tight and humourless. 'But I did survive. And now it's time for the reckoning.'

As he stepped closer, Eight Eighty sidestepped, and in the blink of an eye drew a stiletto blade from the inner folds of his sleeve, beckoning Daniel closer with sharp flicks of his free hand. Daniel's fatigue evaporated and a predatory spring appeared in his step. This was the moment of reckoning.

They circled one another, with utmost caution, wary in the extreme of each other's next move, more so Daniel, aware that any false move could prove fatal against the blade. Eight Eighty was pointing the killing steel unwaveringly at his heart, but Daniel countered the threat, by wrapping his forearm with his thick shirt. He wanted to kill the treacherous bastard with his bare hands.

'Those fucking muscles won't stop this bad boy,' spat Eight Eighty, and as he made his first lunge, a sardonic grin creased his face, telegraphing his intention, and Daniel was ready. They crashed into each other with spontaneous frenzy, locking arms and legs as they came together. For a slighter man, Eight Eighty possessed the power of the Underworld, and for a split second De Theiry's words, 'I see death,' echoed in Daniel's ears.

In the backdrop of sunset, Tobacco had come to her master's rescue, now pacing around the struggling silhouettes. She rushed into the affray, sank her teeth into the cohort's calf muscle, shook her head like a true ratter, let go and lunged again for a better grip. Eight Eighty lashed out with his foot, and halted the valiant little charge, with a knock-out blow to the side of Tobacco's head. She left the ground, spinning like a rotor-blade, before crashing out of sight into a tumble of brambles. Distracted, Daniel lost the grip on the other's wrist. The vicious blade slashed out, cutting his shoulder. Daniel struck back and Eight Eighty's jaw cracked audibly, as he landed a brain-numbing blow, to the side of the cohorts head. Daniel grunted behind the power of the punch, as he bowled the other to the ground, but under the influence of the talisman, his enemy was back on his fighting feet, like a cornered leopard. Again and again they came together, stabbing, punching and gouging. Several times Daniel laid in what should have been the blow to end it all, but his efforts were rendered ineffectual, under his adversary's supernatural power. In the desperate fight for supremacy, he again grabbed Eight Eighty's wrists in the vice-like grip of his powerful hands, and with their faces only inches apart, he shouted the question.

'Who are you?'

Eight Eighty roared defiantly, 'I shall tell you as you die, Daniel Bonner,'

As Daniel felt the others spittle of fury splatter his face, he remembered the talisman. If he could reach it and tear it from his enemies neck, he could swing the deadly tide. With one fist clenched around the knife wrist, he ripped open Eight Eighty's shirt and with his free hand tore the talisman away. It was exactly the opening his opponent had been waiting for. He thrust the knife towards Daniel's heart, and with a deft flick of the wrist pierced Daniel's torso with the tip. In shock and pain, Daniel's rage was complete. With all his strength, he slowly pulled the blade from his flesh, and turned it against his attacker. With sickening ease, it entered just below Eight Eighty's sternum, disappearing like some magician's sword deep into his heaving chest. The cohort slumped in Daniel's arms, and together they sank to their knees under the dead weight. Eight Eighty attempted to stand, but his kicks were weak and feeble, without the talisman it was a fatal wounding.

'Before you die,' hissed Daniel, his mouth touching the other's ear, 'just tell me who you are.'

Eight Eighty raised his suddenly weary head, and managed a weak smile.

'Look into my eyes Daniel, and tell me who you see.'

Daniel looked down, and would regret the moment for as long as he lived. He was staring into the dying eyes, of his own brother.

'Stephen…tell me it isn't you…for God's sake tell me it's not you,' and in that moment of truth, his death grip turned into a hug of love, as he stopped Stephen falling to the ground.

'It's me Danny,' he said in a whisper, his admission cut short, as crimson froth erupted from the sides of his open mouth

'But why, Stevie, for pity's sake why?Stephen fought for breath, closed his eyes for a moment, and then raised his heavy lids.

'I grew to hate you, or so I believed. Everything you did was right. Everything I did was wrong. I killed a man and you took the blame. I stood by and watched, but you didn't resent me.' He fought for air. 'As you went on and became successful, I sank deeper.' A cough gurgled up from Stephen's chest, the blood was arterial.

'Don't talk, Stevie. Save your strength.' But Stephen wasn't listening.

'Then you gave your money away. Even after my death, you made me feel worthless…you fucking sanctimonious git!' More blood poured from Stephen's mouth, as he fought for life. 'My resentment turned to hate. But Daniel, it was a false hate, they had nurtured in me. They offered me a second chance at life, in exchange for yours. And I took it.'

Tears flooded his eyes. 'Danny, I love you bro…I always did, I'm so sorry.'

Daniel saw his own tears splatter his brother's upturned face.

Stephen again fought for breath. There was so much to say and precious little time to say it. 'I wanted to see you suffer, to cry as I had done, to see your world crash around you like mine, a wish driven by that fucking' thing they put round my neck. For a while it felt right, so good…but it kills me to see you cry. Forgive me brother.'

'Stevie, you are not going to die on me. Not again.' Daniel's words were barely discernible through the tears, but they both knew the truth. With his dying breath, Stephen managed a smile. 'Sorry bro,' he whispered as he died, the last sound Daniel would ever hear from his brother, in this mortal world.

Daniel lifted his face to the skies, with a guttural sound belonging to the mortally grieved. He rocked Stephen's body in his arms for hours, remembering how they had been together in the once carefree days of childhood. But how the world had changed?

Eventually he placed Stephen on the ground, and as he did so his brother's body crumpled like burnt paper until all that remained was powdered ash.

De Theiry's prophesy of tragedy and death had come horribly true, and tears fell from Daniel's chin, like drops of rain on a dusty road.

Slowly he lowered his gaze to the ashes in his hands, and made a silent vow of revenge. He was already an enemy of the lower world. But now it was utterly personal.

'Your blessed Chancellor, has wreaked mayhem and death in Bonner's life, brother Lucifer, but not the death he would have wished for. Through the incompetence of your second-in-command, you have further empowered your enemy.'

'I have been reliably informed, that Bonner was warned by someone of your choosing, instrumental in the outcome, brother Abdiel?'

'De Theiry has indeed been most useful, in the battle against your dark heart and all you stand for, brother Lucifer.'

A sly grin appeared on the Devil's face. And I the Scribe looked at them both, for the first time since I can remember. The most important cardinal rule had been broken. Abdiel had divulged the identity of his source. Abdiel noticed his brother's grin of triumph, and he was not happy at his own blatant indiscretion.

'You cannot touch him, Lucifer. He exists in the untouchable world of limbo. His soul already belongs at this end of the table, and one day he shall find a way of passing across the divide to sit with me.'

'Nothing is certain in the human or spirit world, Abdiel. You know that.'

For only the second time since I the Scribe had succeeded my predecessor, I saw Abdiel lose control, and smash his mighty fist onto the table top. The vibrations crashed along the solid oak, and up through Lucifer's elbows like a jack-hammer, whilst Lucifer roared with laughter.

'Oh brother of mine, how you fuel my victory. If you were to spend a while in your library of time, you would note that none of this appears in any loam. It is an unknown even to us, and therefore, so is the outcome.' This De Theiry may well still be mine.'

'Then the whole structure of our houses, will have to be re-written, and that is hardly likely to happen. No, De Theiry will find sanctuary in this house, never yours, brother Lucifer!!'

'We shall see, Abdiel. We shall see.'

## The Pool Without Water

At the very point where he had taken the plunge to save Bryony from drowning, Daniel stood looking down into the limpid water some thirty feet beneath the rim. With toes curled over the granite lip, he raised his arms and with bent knees toppled forward and kicked out. For several seconds, he flew free-bird before plunging arrow straight into the emerald depths. From the ridge, Tobacco watched his body dive deep into the water, before rising slowly to the surface in a shroud of bubbles.

Although shockingly cold, Daniel emerged with an exulted grunt that echoed around the ageless walls. Every nerve-end and fibre in his naked body told him he was alive. Again and again he climbed the hidden path to dive, plunge or simply jump into the water with the exuberance of a forgotten youth. And each time was for Stephen.

Eventually he lay floating on his back and looked up at the cloudless sky, immersed in some sad, some funny, even tragic memories until the chill of the water began lowering the temperature of his core. For the final time, he swam lazily towards the secret path to light an early fire.

After climbing into his clothes, he strode down an incline to a cluster of silver birch trees, from which he harvested the thin strips of tinder bark. With enough of the fire lighter in his hand, he happened to look down and noticed a boot print near to the base of one of the larger trees. He knelt to examine the impression that had been partially covered by debris. He reckoned the print to be several days old, and after careful excavation discovered another indentation. An animal was following the human tracks and he guessed it to be a medium sized dog. But was it stalking, or walking with its master? It was impossible to decipher from a single print. Daniel straightened. Men and animals were moving in and around the lakes using the trees as cover; he naturally hoped they had simply passed through.

Returning to the hearth, he crumpled the strips of bark and with the top edge of his hunting knife, struck down on his flint rod, the resulting sparks igniting the natural creosote in the bark. Once lit, Daniel studied the heavily-worn flint. It was early September and he had to seriously think about replenishing his stock of essential survival items, before the onset of another winter. Reluctantly he looked north. It was time for a visit to Delamere and the Out of Town Store where he knew he could exchange hare, pheasant and other game for such goods. Over the years he had forged an alliance with the storekeeper, Mrs Tucker, a somewhat dour, overweight, matter-of-fact lady, with a mutual understanding of the old-fashioned bartering system. It was a supply line he simply could not live without, and he decided he would head out at first light to hunt game, for that very reason.

Vile Bird bowed before the Chancellor. The cavern was hushed as it learned that Bonner had survived what should have been a foolproof plan. It was now clear that he was either charmed or had powerful guardians, or Hell forbid, both. Either way, the events leading to his salvation could certainly not have been mere coincidence. Be that as it may, Vile Bird was guilty of failure, and an example had to be made.

Unlike the late Norbert Morris, fellow members held Vile Bird in something close to high regard, and the Chancellor understood the situation well. He could order it to be taken down to the pit, but feared the killing frenzy would be, at best, lacklustre. This was a task he would have to undertake personally. As he sat on the hot rock throne, his victim recognised the kindly smile of death, and in that lucid moment, understood its fate. As the Chancellor's smile grew wider, so did his right hand grow larger until ten times its normal size, and reaching out he took the cohort's blueberry body in his grasp. The surrounding numbers looked up to the dais with morbid fascination, fickle loyalties suddenly replaced by the desire for deadly entertainment. The Chancellor beckoned them to join him, and they clambered over each other for the best view. This was going to be a primary execution, one of the very reasons for which they existed. This was Hell.

One by one, and with terrifying purpose, the Chancellor plucked Vile Bird's spidery legs from its body. until all that remained were eight ragged portholes of bloodied flesh. Unable to stand it rolled over, its long crocodilian beak making it top-heavy. The creature's head crashed onto the bedrock, its body rolled like a ball in orbit and it screamed in anguish. Far from done, the Chancellor again placed the hand around the blueberry body, and applied slow but increasing pressure until it ruptured. The cohorts pressed closer. Unable to resist free food, Vile Bird began feasting on its own crushed body parts. until its vicious beak became too feeble to gulp down the grotesque lumps of flesh, and a strange silence followed as its life ebbed and died.

With a dismissive back flip of his soiled hand. the Chancellor waved away the cohort masses from sight. Although killing always fringed on ecstasy, the Chancellor perversely missed those he had sent to oblivion. It was a mark of respect to annihilate a treasured number. rather than send it to the eternal nightmares in the lower catacombs. It was the least he could do, and it was a rare thing to show such compassion.

He thought again of Daniel Bonner, and the information given to him by his Lord and master. Bonner's secret informer would need destroying; they couldn't afford to ignore such a growing force. Although he had survived, Jerry Green was now out of the picture, but in the meantime, he needed something to lure Bonner into an inescapable situation, and he pondered hard. Slowly his face broke with a callous smile.

'Come to me my Jackanapes,' he roared, and the chamber miraculously re-filled with the crude creatures. Selecting a pair of bloated sucker worms from some ancient prehistoric sea, he shooed all others away. Holding both arms outstretched, he transformed their grotesque bodies into a pair of resplendent buzzards.

'Bring me Charles Millington,' he said to one, and 'Pinpoint Bonner's whereabouts,' to the other. He looked down at the pitiful remains of Vile Bird, then back to the raptor's perched on his forearm. The buzzards couldn't fail to misunderstand his meaning.

Daniel held the Hummer over his right shoulder as he waited for a foraging cock pheasant to come within range. Tobacco was close enough to flush it out and the pheasant took to the air. The Hummer flew true and the bird died instantly in mid air. Placing it in his game sack, along with another of its number, two wood-pigeon, a similar headcount of rabbit and a large buck hare, he set off on a direct course for Delamere.

For the first time in his vagrant life, there were a surprising number of people on the high street who actually acknowledged his presence, as he strode purposely through. He had become something of a talking point after he and Conrad Sweet had saved Jerry Green's life, not to mention them finding out about his original philanthropic decision to give his money away, along with his highly-successful career. With the knowledge he had once walked amongst them as a professional, they now felt less threatened by his periodic visits and wild appearance.

He respectfully returned their greetings and moved on. On reaching The Out of Town Store, he and Tobacco entered the shop, but unseen by both, a Chancellor's buzzard soared high in the blue sky above them.

'Good morning, Mr Bonner,' said Mrs Tucker, in an unusually jocular manner. 'It's been a while since we last saw you…lovely weather were having.' She eyed the bag of game. 'How's Jerry? How's the book? I hear its doing well.'

'They're both doing well enough.' His answer was polite, sufficient enough to indulge the woman, without being drawn in by her prying nature. She got the hint.

'What is it you need, Mr Bonner?'

Daniel placed the bag on the counter. I need a flint rod, soap, six pairs of socks, a new pair of boots, and what's left on this list should you find this bag of game fair exchange?'

She glanced at the little note pad Daniel had placed in front of her, then again at the bag.

'Boots don't come cheap,' she said. Pheasants are out of season and hare are protected. I'm taking a risk as it is. Poaching is illegal you know.'

Daniel knew Mrs Tucker couldn't care less how illegal the bag was, and what he took from the moor hardly constituted a threat to the indigenous fauna. Besides, her appetite for game was legendary. However, he accepted the fact that boots were expensive, and without them he was lost. He needed more than what was in the game bag, and he knew it.

'Can I ask a great favour of you Mrs Tucker?'

'Go on,' she said guardedly.

'Would we have a deal if I promised the next time I come in, to bring you a signed copy of my book with a personal inscription?'

Mrs Tucker's eyelids flared slightly. A personal inscription was indeed a good bargaining chip.

'There's a rumour going round, Mr Bonner, that you have money, and lots of it?' She smiled in a rather pathetic attempt at being alluring. Rumour has it that you could live like a king, and that you could afford everything in this shop to make a better life for yourself out on the moor. You can tell me, Mr Bonner, I can keep a secret. No other living soul shall hear a single thing from me.'

Not only was she prying into his financial affairs, but she was also delving with her sharp piggy eyes beyond the thick tresses of Daniel's beard, in an attempt to see the reputedly handsome face beneath.

'By God she's actually flirting with me,' Daniel thought, soon confirmed as she reached out and placed a hot podgy hand on the back of his.

'The power of money,' he told her. 'However much, I shall probably give it away as before. I have no need of it. For me, true wealth lies out there on the moor.' Her face fell. 'If I bring you a copy of the book, do we have a deal?'

The clammy mitt was suddenly withdrawn with a tart, humourless smile. 'Yes I suppose we have a deal.'

The items on the list were soon gathered and Daniel tucked then into his duffel bag.

'Remember, Daniel. I'm always here should you need anything…anything at all.' Her comely smile had returned.

'Thank you Mrs Tucker, I shall remember that.'

'Call me Gladys. It would be much nicer if you did.'

'Thank you Gladys, and I shall return with the book.' And precious little else thought Daniel. He left the shop with a broad grin at her blatant transparency, and above him, the sky was now empty.

Until that time, Daniel had thought little of the book's progress, but because of dear Gladys, he had a sudden brainwave. Jerry Green was, to the best of his knowledge, still fighting the insurance company over the wrecked shop. He had been as good as his word about keeping the new money aside for reasons other than personal gain, and if anyone deserved a financial leg-up it was Jerry.

Tobacco trotted alongside as Daniel made his way to Artefacts of Ages. Outside he stood staring at the half-boarded window, and peered through cracks in the whitewash on the surviving pane, and the events of that night returned like a bad dream. Through the glass he identified the damage in the close proximity, but nothing much else, and in the darkened recesses the unseen buzzard that had gained access through an open upper window, stared at his silhouette floating over the pane. As Daniel made to move away, he noticed a small area of irregular scratches in the whitewash. Taking a closer look, the scratches took on a different shape. It was a message that took him by surprise and one he found reading aloud in astonishment.

'Wait by the pool, and she shall come.'

Twice he read the scratchy line in disbelief. His mind was racing. The message could only be for him and him alone. Confused and elated, he backed away. It had to be a reminder from De Theiry, though why he had to do it in such a manner, was something of a mystery. No matter. Now he was sure she would come, but what would prompt her do so after almost a year? Of course he trusted De Theiry implicitly, but hoped that slimy toad, Millington was not instrumental. The thought of leading her into danger appalled him, and yet he knew that De Theiry's prophesy was about to come true. What if there was danger, what if he were to be goaded too far and that she should witness his dark rage? Stephen's death had affected him deeply and perhaps he had changed from when they last met because of it? There were more questions than answers, and suddenly he was unsure. He turned and strode away so quickly that Tobacco was forced to break into a canter to stay at his side.

Inside the shop, the buzzard blinked its fantastic golden eyes, and from a cross-member in the shattered office wall, flew the length of the shop to land on the plinth where 'Myths and Legends,' had once stood, and with the tip of its hooked beak scratched the finishing line to the message. 'And death shall find you.'

To date Charles Millington had done well. He had maintained the gulf between Bryony and Daniel Bonner. Now he was being summoned, he hoped with an opportunity to hurt his adversary yet further. He was in for a monumental shock.

'I want you to remove the Talisman from around the girl's neck,' commanded the Chancellor. 'It has served its purpose and my plans have now changed. I want to engineer a meeting between Bonner and the girl.'

Millington was stunned. 'With all due respect, my Lord, I cannot see how their coming together would be beneficial to our plans. After all, we know they have deep feelings for each other, and their meeting would only serve to increase Bonner's power. That surely would be folly.'

The Chancellor leaned forward thoughtfully on the dais throne. Heat shimmered around his broad shoulders, distorting the image of his handsome head. Why should Millington be so vocal against the change? Although Millington was still a member of the mortal world he had, however, sold his soul, and what he did in this life marked his ultimate future in Hell's eternity. Suddenly the Chancellor understood.

'Please don't tell me you too have feelings?' he chuckled, and leaned further forward to meet the mortals eye. He looked deep into Millington's soul, and realised the other had grown to love this girl. It was the most fascinating irony and one he could exploit. He reclined with one of his classic wry smiles.

'Deliver her to the pool, and in return I shall grant her yours for one hundred years,' he said, 'and neither you nor Bryony Carter shall grow old. Long after Daniel Bonner has shuffled his mortal coil, you will continue your life together. Then after one century I shall return and you shall be judged accordingly. Do we have an accord Mr Millington?'
One hundred years was an eternity in which to cherish the woman he loved. He would gladly deliver her to the drowning pool for such a reward, especially with the promised death of Daniel Bonner thrown into the bargain.

'Yes my Lord, we have an accord.'

'Record it so,' the Chancellor told his scribe sitting at his right hand side. And the scribe was diligent in his task.

Tobacco led the way through the secret tracks in the bracken fields, rarely leaving Daniel's sight, as they journeyed back to the lakes. It was a successful hunting partnership, with a fair chance of Tobacco flushing quarry out in the firing line of the Hummer. Suddenly she crouched low with only the tips of her ears visible above the wild grass. Something had moved in the thicket ahead. Her right ear twitched as Daniel moved up, but she never once broke her forward gaze. Ordering her to stay, Daniel entered the shoulder high tangle of undergrowth, and after a brief search discovered the reason for Tobacco's stealthy warning. A large buck hare was held fast by its hind legs in the noose of a poacher's snare. Its struggles became frenzied at Daniel's approach, as it leaped into the air in a failed bid for freedom. Daniel snatched it by the scruff of the neck in mid flight, and with his knife cut the line. The animal was badly injured. The snare had mutilated one of its hind legs and the animal stood little chance of survival. The Hummer struck down and humanely despatched the stricken animal. The snare was made of intricately woven lengths of hide made subtle with goose grease. He knew of just one man who had made such snares his trademark, and that poacher was long dead.

Puzzled by the discovery, Daniel folded the garrotte several times before severing through the multiple loops, reducing the noose to nothing more than ineffectual strands. In the sterile soil he also found a boot print similar to the one he had found beneath the birch tree, placing him in something of a dilemma. Should he continue his journey to the lakes, or should he lie in wait for the man guilty of depleting his winter stores? After a moments consideration he left the bracken fields and marched on.

As evening fell rain clouds clung doggedly to the western horizon, creating a premature sunset that brought Daniel to an untimely halt. Not even he travelled the moor under the promise of a storm, unless it was absolutely necessary, and without valid reason to the contrary he settled down for the night.

As midnight advanced, Daniel's billy can of water tipped into the embers and once more, De Theiry appeared in the infusion, ministering large pinches of snuff to his nostrils as he squatted opposite.

'Christ alive, Frenchy, this bloody steam business makes me jump every time,' snorted Daniel. De Theiry ignored the title as he dug again into his snuff box, and Daniel couldn't help noticing again how resplendent in stature and dress the Parisian had now become. His hair was plied neatly in a lustrous ponytail. His shirt was less torn and had the signature of ironed cleanliness, his once pallid skin possessed a sheen belonging more to that of the living. Daniel couldn't begin to understand the reason, and yet the change was heartening.

De Theiry was a spiritual star, once a lost and angry soul, destined to wander the desolate fields where once the asylum stood in which he died. Now through his mortal friend he had found great purpose. Solitude and loneliness had given way to usefulness. Daniel would have been saddened to know that sometime in the future, De Theiry's spirit would become a nova, a stunning bright light that would transport his soul across the divide, away from the lonely land of limbo, to a deserved and untouchable place, beyond the clutches of this or any other world.

'One day soon you shall see me as you would a mortal,' De Theiry told Daniel. The use of the fire and water shall no longer be required. You are becoming increasingly attuned to my spiritual existence, and I look forward to that day. Inhaling smoke can be so unhealthy you know.' He chuckled. 'But I digress. There are pressing matters to be addressed. They're coming for you Daniel, and this time they mean business. On my oath, you have surely tapped this particular cobra on its ugly head. Warning signals are coming to me along a multitude of corridors. Amongst other things, there is collusion between a certain mortal and the Underworld. And Daniel, the signals are strong.'

'OK, my French friend, I get the drift, but just for once can you be a bit more specific? I would be grateful of some straight talking.'

'It's as I say, they are coming, including Bryony, the unknowing participant in the collusion. She enters the moor as we speak. Her destination is the pool without water.'

'But Phillipe, there is no such place. I've been on this moor almost a bloody lifetime and I can tell you the pool without water doesn't exist. And if it doesn't exist, how on earth can I meet her there?'

'She shall find you at the drowning pool where you saved her life. Perhaps from there on things will become clearer. I can say little more than that. There is, however, something else. A powerful force travels at speed towards you, against which you must use the Devil's Dagger. It's your only defence and the only thing in your possession that can hurt it.

'What the Hell is the Devil's Dagger?'

'A weapon already in your possession.'

'Fine, but what is it?

De Theiry ignored the question and moved on. 'Should you survive, then the Underworld shall respect, if not admire you. But be warned, if you do win the battle, along with their begrudging respect, this war of yours shall enter a more deadly dimension!'

'Then you advise me to lose?' It was a pointless question. After what happened to Stephen he wouldn't know how to lose.

'I could never advise capitulation,' continued De Theiry. 'However, it is my duty to point out that the outcome remains uncertain. Oh! And there is one last thing. Someone from your past has returned, but as yet knows not of your existence, nor you theirs.'

'More bloody riddles again, my Parisian friend,' accused Daniel, and with his words, Phillipe De Theiry drew uncommonly close and whispered revelations into Daniel's ear, stunning him into silence. He looked into the indigo night, and entered a personal chasm of thought so deep he was unaware of De Theiry's magical departure.

Daniel knew he had visitors, not that he could see or hear them, but every instinct in his person told him they were there. Shadows of the living heading his way, true to De Theiry's prediction. They were behind him now, not twenty paces away and it was then that he heard the soft sawing of a panting dog. Daniel's broad smile was uncontrollable as he stoked the fire in a blaze of sparks, before talking over his shoulder into the night.

'That dog of yours sounds as though it has bloody asthma,' he said through the corner of his smile. The breathing stopped and the night held its breath.

'Here boy,' Daniel encouraged, then whistled, and Zip, unable to resist, tore forward, leaping and yapping at his side. Jesse stumbled into the camp a few paces behind, and Daniel rose from his duffel bag seat to greet his lost brother of the moor.

To the incredulous Jesse, it was the ghost of Daniel Bonner standing before him, and the poacher's face was the picture of genuine astonishment.

'Well, blow a gnat off my arse with a fuckin' punt gun…Bonner you git…is it really you?'

Zip continued to jump like a coiled spring, as the two friends grasped each other in a hearty bear hug and a staccato of heavy back slaps.

'It certainly is old friend…but I still can't believe it's actually you Jesse?'

'Jesus, Danny boy, I thought you were dead!'

'Yeah! I did you. When I found the broken Hummer I thought the worst. Bloody hell Jesse it's good to see you alive. Come and park your big fat, hairy butt by the fire, and tell me how the hell you managed to get away.'

Jesse sank onto a log on the other side of the fire. 'Before I do, tell me old friend, how the flying bucket of crap did you know I was coming?' Jesse had always prided himself on his ability to creep up undetected on any man or animal, a skill supposedly learned under the fabled tuition of a Zulu warrior chief. A load of bollocks perhaps, but one he enjoyed telling. This time he had been readily detected and so, not surprisingly, his pride was dented.

Daniel chuckled, thinking it best to leave De Theiry's ghost out of it; for the time being at least.

'You left your great hoof marks all over the moor,' he accused, parrying the question.

'You're getting too good at this game, Daniel. But how you knew they were my prints beats me. Perhaps I'll work that one out later, but in the mean time I think this calls for a drop of the old glow juice,' and he pulled a bottle of Scotch from his coat pocket. Together they passed the bottle back and forth, but as Daniel enjoyed his third ecstatic burn, he noticed that Jesse had grown suddenly reflective, his eyes were wide, staring blankly into the flames.

'They came for me Daniel, thousands of the filthy bastards, swarming over the ground like a stinking carpet. Heard Zip bark and I ran in that direction, found him crammed under the wheel arch of that old pick up truck. Feisty little bugger had fended off several attacks, though I reckon it was only a half-hearted attempt to winkle him out. Their real target was you Danny boy, and that's what ultimately saved me. It's amazing what strength a man can find when death comes knocking. Threw your hummer thingamajig stick at the fuckers then managed to break open the truck door.' He nervously tousled the tight curls of hair on the back of his balding cannon-ball head. 'We dived inside for cover and just in the nick of time. It was bloody close. I remember shouting at them at the top of my lungs, and for the first time in my life, I was fucking terrified Danny, and I don't mind admitting it…but only to you OK?' He stared at his friend. A sharp nod from Daniel was enough to reassure Jesse the matter would go no further, not that there was anybody else to tell. But for Jesse it was an important matter of credibility.

'They swarmed over the cab,' he continued. 'I thought their weight would crush in the roof. They began tearing away the windscreen seal and would have succeeded getting in, if it hadn't been for you. At first I couldn't hear your shouting over their noise, but then the stinky little clusterfucks fell silent. They heard your challenge and swarmed back to the pillbox. Thought it was only 'yours truly' that knew such fuckin' profanity, you foul mouthed bastard?'

Daniel sat in silence listening to Jesse's account, wearing a soft grin. He smiled for his friend, but in his mind's eye he could still hear and smell the hunting Tarquills.

'Stayed in the truck for most of the following day,' Jesse continued. 'Hardly dared raise my head further than the dashboard, even Zip knew it was best to be quiet. Late afternoon was the first time I properly looked out. The wood was silent, not a single bird was singing, the whole spinney was empty of life. I sneaked over to the pillbox and found your coat. It was a real mess Danny, all torn and bloody on the concrete floor. I knew you were dead so I started running until I couldn't run any further. I was knackered, physically and mentally, but when I at last found my strength I didn't stop travelling, until six months on I reached my old poaching grounds in Norfolk.' He looked up with haunted eyes. 'I've been there ever since.'

A natural pause followed, as both men entered into deep reflection until Jesse broke the silence with a question.

'So…tell me Danny, what happened to you?'

Daniel recounted his own battle for survival which was no less harrowing, but there was so much more to tell.

'Have you ever wondered why this all happened, Jesse?'

'Of course. A day hasn't passed without thinking about it. I think you owe me an explanation. Why did it happen, Danny?'

'Do you remember Tony Windrow?'

‘Yeah, your boss in Delamere.’

‘Well he proved to be much more than that. I hope you’re ready for what I’m about to tell you.’ Jesse nodded cautiously, remembering the last time Daniel had something to tell. But despite that, he now needed answers.

Daniel told Jesse of how he had lost his soul, regained it and subsequently escaped the Underworld, and of the frightening events thereafter. The first being the knowledge that he had run with the devil’s pack, the Chancellor and Morris and all their powers. The second being the Tarquills, of which Jesse was only too familiar. He told of Bryony, of Phillipe De Theiry, Jerry Green, the book and the ‘Bruinscrofa’ that had all but killed his friend. Of hell’s ongoing vendetta, and how De Theiry believed Daniel himself had been somehow chosen to fight the good fight, and that there were forces other than the spirit world of limbo out there helping him. As Daniel revealed everything, Jesse recognised great determination in Daniel’s manner, the same during their time in the pill box. But when it came to the slaying of Stephen, that determination gave way to an emotion from deep within. Jesse sat staring into the fire, hearing the loss and grief in Daniel’s voice as if suddenly listening to a broken man. Eventually Daniel fell silent, and Jesse raised his head. Daniel was fast asleep where he sat, the only way he knew of blocking the memory from his mind.

The following morning, there was no further mention of Stephen. However, Jesse had noticed something rather intriguing in one item his friend had said. Daniel couldn’t help but notice his wry grin over the flames of a re-kindled breakfast fire.

‘What on earth are you grinning at, you ugly Ape?’ he said, handing over a skewer of sizzling pigeon breast.

‘Danny old son, I’ve known you for some years and I’ve never heard you talk of a girl in such a way, apart from that flirty piece in Delamere. Bryony, you called her. You’ve got real feelings for her and don’t insult me by trying to deny it, you randy old git.’

Daniel looked at his friend. ‘Was it really that obvious?’

‘As clear as you cutting up my bleedin’ snares,’ he laughed.

Daniel quickly got off the subject, yet was secretly glad he had been rumbled. He was in the best company he knew, and trusted Jesse not to blurt it to others, for the outcome was far from certain.

While the men enjoyed the continued reunion, the same could not be said for their dogs. Tobacco had successfully avoided Zip all night. It had never been an easy relationship; Tobacco felt defensive to the bull-terrier cross and his aggressive body language at the time of the Tarquills. But the stand-off couldn't last forever, and inevitably they stood face to face. However, there was a marked difference in Zip's attitude. He sat quite peacefully, periodically endorsing the surprising pact with a short wag of his docked tail. Tobacco, risking her life, moved forward until Zip's wet muzzle was just inches away. They had stood side-by-side as the hoard had advanced, and during that encounter a bond had been forged.

'Well, bugger me, will you just look at that!' blurted Jesse, as the animals walked into the camp, then to the fire, warming their bodies with the best seats in the house. Both men sat with mouths agape, until Jesse changed the subject, just in case the unlikely truce was somehow compromised by their attention.

'So when are you seeing Bryony again then, lover boy?' Daniel shook free from his astonishment and told the poacher of his next move.

The buzzards hopped across the hot rock dais, and stood before the Chancellor to deliver their report. As ever, the expectant chamber listened intently, and it appeared that everything so far had fallen into place as planed. Millington had removed the Talisman from around Bryony's neck as instructed. Daniel Bonner was nearing the drowning pool, and the girl would soon be with him. But as was the Chancellor's decree, Bryony, the unsuspecting bait in the trap, would not be harmed. Also there were unforeseen yet potential bonuses. It transpired that one of Daniel's long lost allies had joined him, with the very real prospect of him being another unsuspecting soul for the taking?

'One of my darling brutes is on its way to find them, one which has never failed,' he said to his scribe. 'Mark it so.' And the scribe did his bidding.

Jesse had volunteered to accompany Daniel to the drowning pool, as there was much to talk about, mingled with general reminiscing. There still remained the debate about the better hunting tool, ending with Jesse grudgingly agreeing to try out the Hummer without breaking the bloody thing. Upon reaching the pool they scouted the surroundings and finding it clear of human activity, and with time on their hands the tuition began in earnest. Daniel showed him how to hold the stick and selected a tree stump as a target. It struck dead centre, making the affair look easy. After, Tobacco had retrieved it for the fourth time with equal results, Daniel handed the weapon over.

Jesse felt the weighty balance. 'Piece of piss,' he said. Don't know what all the fuss is about.' He drew back his arm and let the Hummer go. If, however, his target had been the large tuft of grass a metre to the left, then it would indeed have been the perfect shot, but in reality it was an appalling first attempt. Tobacco raced away to retrieve it, with Zip deciding the little Terrier needed all the help it could get. With each end of the Hummer in respective mouths, they raced back to the men. Again and again he tried to impact the stump, until he had moved in so close he might just as well have reached out and clubbed the already dead tree to another brutal death. He stomped back and forth in frustration, and Daniel realised that not everyone was a born thrower.

It was during Jesse's utterly grumpy tuition, that Bryony found them. She climbed unseen on top of a prominent knoll behind the two men, pausing for a moment to look at them both, then at Daniel. Suddenly he was the only one there.

In the last few weeks, she had been in a state of emotional confusion. Although extremely fond of Charles Millington, an attitude of which her mother was most unsure, she had somehow managed to fend off his amorous affections, and countless offers of matrimony. He, in turn, had shown incredible patience as if he had all the time in the world. Then suddenly, and for reasons she couldn't explain, he had unexpectedly encouraged her to venture back onto the moor, to pursue her love of drawing. She needed space, he had pointed out, time on her own, and he had said that he was sensitive as always to her needs. He had even taken her beloved Talisman from around her neck, telling her it was an inappropriate and too valuable an item to be taken onto the moor. He of course would safeguard it for her return.

For Bryony it felt like being released from school for the summer, after a term of strict tuition. A sudden, blissful sense of freedom, with a near constant tingle of excitement running through her stomach, like a warm cocktail. But there was something much deeper. From the moment the Talisman had been removed, overpowering feelings for Daniel had flooded her very existence, so strong that it was impossible to keep it a secret from her mother. Her father on the other hand had shown some forthright concern about allowing his daughter to go alone, but again, Millington had argued her case, booked her accommodation at the High Tor Inn, north of the moor, and ensured her mobile phone and charger were both in full serviceable order. Bryony's mother had even given Millington a huge hug of gratitude for his uncommon understanding. Perhaps she had been wrong about him all along.

Daniel handed the Hummer once more to Jesse, who, whilst concentrating wholeheartedly on the highly elusive target, remained unaware of Bryony's presence, and as Daniel turned to face the knoll, her heart missed a full beat, then returned with a thump inside her breast. She hesitated. Daniel walked forward and without a word lifted her hands in his and she stood at long last before him. Jesse successfully botched another shot, before realising Daniel was guilty of gross tutorial dereliction. He turned, armed with blunt protest, but what he saw stopped him from saying another word. Daniel and Bryony stood facing each other, their foreheads barely touching with eyes meeting in silent reunification. They were the only two people existing in that particular place in the world, and although normally monumentally thick-skinned, Jesse understood and politely withdrew.

Unaware of the poacher's comical tiptoed departure with Zip at heel, Daniel and Bryony, had they been witness, would have nonetheless been grateful for his thoughtful retreat.

Bryony led Daniel by the hand to the ridge where he had saved her from drowning. It was the place of their beginning, so the possibility it could now be a place of great danger was an idea that couldn't be further from their minds. For a week, Millington had worked a physiological number on Bryony, conditioning her with suggestions that she must at some point visit the pool and plunge into its depths, convincing her it was the only way to put that particular ghost to rest. At first Bryony couldn't even contemplate the idea, but in the end she had slowly come round to his persuasions. Now with Daniel at her side, she felt safe and assured, but had Daniel known of Millington's sudden interest, he would have guessed the deception and done everything in his power to stop Bryony from taking the plunge!

‘I have to dive in,’ she said, and Daniel saw shadows of trepidation in her eyes. But behind the fear there was something stronger, and those wonderful eyes slanted with endearing determination. She was free, she was with the only man to make her feel the way she did. She was going to take the plunge whatever. She made towards the edge, ready to discard a modest amount of clothing to save the embarrassment of premature familiarity.

Daniel reached out and held her forearm. ‘Then we do it together.’ And as she faltered, he began discarding his own clothing, to the last stitch. Once done he stood naked and proud before her. Bryony's eyes widened and her interest quickened with every living beat of her heart. 'I have never seen a man in his full natural state, other than professional models in the studio. This is different Daniel Bonner, and as I believe in what we may become, I shall gladly show myself to you, and you alone.'

She kicked off her walking boots, her shirt, jeans and underwear, until she stood unabashed, naked as the day she was born, and Daniel clasped his hand over the crown of his head in a somewhat boyish manner, as if to stifle something stupid he might say, to ruin the moment. She smiled and stood before him wearing nothing but pride. They walked to the rim, heady, elated, facing one another with the warmth of their bodies just a hairsbreadth apart, enjoying the arousal and intimate senses flooding over them like an irrepressible tide. Eventually they parted with an understanding in their eyes, and Bryony uttered the most wonderfully wicked, lascivious laugh, removing any lingering restraint they both may have had.

‘I think sir is in need of some cold water, for I fear otherwise this maiden might be troubled by this knight’s impressive lance.’

Now it was Daniel who laughed. He followed her wide gaze to his penis, now heavy and blissfuly unrestrained. He had never felt so natural, so at ease, and with a mischievous giggle, Bryony wriggled away before he could react. ‘Follow me if you dare Casanova.’ And she jack-knifed over the edge, twisting her body into a swallow dive, but before hitting the surface Daniel was alongside, entering the water just milliseconds behind. The height of the plunge took them in deep amongst a confusion of bubbles, until natural buoyancy held them in suspension. They took each other’s hands and kicked lazily to the surface. How very different the circumstances from when he had last hauled her out, and how very different the water, almost blood temperature; surprising yet delightful. Daniel should have known it was the Chancellor's work, and listened to the voices in his head, but he was deaf. He should have been more curious, but he was dumb. He should have observed the thin layer of surface steam, but he was blind. The water felt luxurious, and the Chancellor had them just where he wanted!

They broke the mirrored surface pushing hair from their faces and laughing freely. Hand in hand they floated on their backs, looking up at the cloudless blue sky. It was a magical moment they had long wished for, with hope it would last a lifetime, but as Bryony filled her lungs and sighed, they felt the shockwave from an upheaval way down in the limped depths.

'Was that anything to do with you Mr Bonner?' she laughed, but Daniel was not smiling, and the rest of what was intended to be a saucy joke lodged in her throat.

Another tremor shot through the water, followed closely by another and more violent. It sent ripples from the granite walls into the centre where they trod water, until they became aware of movement. Slowly at first the water had begun to spiral, but within seconds the entire surface became an unstoppable whirlpool. They began swimming for the secret pathway, but the surface speed made reaching their goal impossible. In ever-decreasing circles the vortex dragged them round towards the epicentre. Inexorably they were drawn towards the funnel, their vulnerable and ashen faces just visible in the melee.

'What's happening?' screamed Bryony, over the roar of water, and Daniel gripped her arm. 'I want you to do exactly what I say,' he bellowed. Bryony nodded trustingly. 'When I give the signal take a deep breath and hold on to me.' And Bryony nodded again.

Above them the walls rose higher as the water level dropped around their swirling bodies. They struggled on, refusing to go under until the power of the whirlpool began exercising ultimate control.

'Now!' Daniel shouted, and Bryony filled her lungs as they went under, spinning like dancers on ice. Daniel knew he had to drag them away from the centre which would lead directly to the drain hole and certain death, but the power of the vortex held them in its violent, unbreakable cocoon. Then something smashed into his shoulder. Through the blinding silt, he saw a huge static object, the top of which rose ten feet above the bedrock. It came round again with alarming speed, but this time he was ready and caught hold of a protruding metal stanchion. The force of drag nearly tore his arm from its socket but he held on. Suddenly the sickening spinning ceased as the funnel fell down around their legs, releasing its death grip on their bodies. But still their lower limbs were dragged horizontally in the relentless rip, their lungs dragging in air, and all around them the cacophonous roar of raging water.

After leaving Daniel and Bryony to their own devices, Jesse had trudged down a meandering game track, periodically hurling the Hummer with a modicum of success at various targets. A quarter of a mile from the pool, he found an ideal place to stop. He sat in the middle of a cropped circle of grass with the throwing stick close at hand, just in case any juicy morsel offered itself for dispatch. With a chuckle at such an improbability, Jesse pulled a pouch of tobacco and papers from his pocket and rolled a fat cylinder of Golden Virginia. Smoking for Jesse was something of a rarity, normally done when faced with a problem or something to celebrate. Daniel and Bryony were more than a reason to have a quiet smoke, and with a heavy intake, he blew a cloud into the air followed by a soft, satisfying cough.

'Filthy habit' he mused, as the smoke drifted slowly away to a distant smudge, and he watched as it disappeared. As he knocked the ash off with the tip of his little finger, he studied the glowing end, lost but happy in a world of his own. He had been reunited with the only person he truly admired, and felt glad for his friend. Bryony was a good and healthy development for Daniel's wellbeing, having lived alone for so long on the moor. He reminded himself of his own romantic interludes, and reminisced fondly of certain dalliances, but concluded that, given his own first hand experience, all his women had made rubbish poachers, and therefore, and most regrettably, leaving him to chance his luck in life alone.

He flicked away the tip and sat chewing thoughtfully on a blade of grass. Zip had nestled down at his side, twitching with dreams of some far-off chase when suddenly Tobacco raced in from nowhere. She tore over Zip's resting body to stand barking in front of the poacher, with obvious agitation. Having had his body used as a springboard, Zip woke startled and angry. The truce was over. However, the moment Tobacco began her graveyard growl, Zip stopped to think.

'We've heard that terrible malarkey before, eh Zip?' But before Jesse could say another word, Tobacco had turned and was heading back to the lakes at full tilt. Zip caught up with her and together they raced towards pool.

Breathing heavily, Jesse eventually joined the animals standing on the rim at the place where Daniel and Bryony had dived in. The dogs were looking down into the quarry, growling at something below. And perched unseen in the upper reaches of the birch tree, the buzzards looked on with special interest.

'Where the flying fuck's all the water gone?' panted Jesse, as he peered gingerly over the rim, the depth of naked rock an unaccustomed sight. It was a gigantic bullring, fifty metres deep, one hundred metres across, the walls sheer and green with algae, a myriad drops of water falling from hanging weeds onto the bedrock far below. The pan was littered with debris; shovel-heads, pipes and spas, an old heavy-framed butcher's bicycle, a fridge without its door, a liberal assortment of animal bones and a discarded car door hanging like a drunkard on what looked like the remains of a huge industrial machine. It was from behind the machine that Daniel stepped out and looked up, white-faced, but smiling.

'I'd be grateful for my clothes,' he shouted, standing as natural as the day he was born with just a fingertip on both his nipples as something of a joke. Jesse laughed openly and punched the air with a heavily muscled forearm in relief. Whatever had happened had clearly been close to catastophic. Daniel and Bryony were lucky to be alive.

'What the fuck happened Danny?' he shouted, with almost a ring of accusation, as if Daniel couldn't be trusted to be left alone for one minute.

'Never mind that now,' said Daniel, his arms now spread wide as if to emphasise his state of undress.

'And what about the young lady,' Jesse asked with a broad grin. 'Does she want her clothes as well?' He noted that Bryony was keeping the machinery very firmly between him and his direct line of sight.

'Just chuck them down, you lecherous old poacher.'

'Oi! Less of the old! As for lecherous, it's not me standing there in the buff, Mr Bonner.'

Their clothing sailed through the air, landing unceremoniously in the abundant puddles. Daniel scooped them up and rejoined Bryony with the soggy offerings.

'For your eyes only,' she told him, standing full frontal, but the warble of shock was clear and present in her voice. 'What on earth happened, Danny? That's twice you've saved my life in this pool.'

'It's my guess the water drained down some subterranean fault. We're lucky to be still breathing.' He studied the surrounding walls, and saw with dismay the secret path ended abruptly a third of the way down. Below that there was no obvious way up. The twisted spas and booms at his feet were all that remained of a large working davit that had been once secured on the rim to service the workings below. The huge cast piece of engineering he had clung onto was a steam-driven rock breaker, left behind when the mine was abandoned. He walked over to the two-metre diameter sink hole in the bedrock where the water had drained and wondered how much lose debris had been dragged away. Bryony joined his side and looked into the dark forbidding gateway. She shivered at the thought of such a terrible fate.

'Well, its not over yet. We've got to figure a way to get out of here,' said Daniel, turning away to study the vertical walls.

High above, Jesse looked down at the helpless couple realising their predicament. Any attempt at rescue would be impossible without a valid length of rope. Suddenly a movement in the drainage hole caught his eye.

'Daniel!' bellowed Jesse, 'I think you've got company.'

Daniel and Bryony heard the urgency in his voice, but neither could see what was emerging from the hole behind the crusher, and high overhead the buzzards circled expectantly, over what would soon become a murderous killing field.

'Bryony, get behind the machine and stay there. Whatever Jesse can see has him worried, and if it has anything to do with the Chancellor, then believe me we can't afford to be caught out in the open with our pants down.'

'Looks like you already have,' said Bryony with a weak laugh, noting that Daniel had yet to pull on the rest of his clothing. 'But who on earth is the Chancellor?' She turned to him., 'I don't understand, Daniel. What's going on?'

'No time to explain right now, but when the time's right, I'll tell you everything,' he said, tugging on his trousers.

'For fuck sakes, Danny. You have really got to get out of there fast.' Jesse's voice was in high pitch.

From behind the iron wreck, they saw a colossal body emerging from the sluice, like some gigantic mole breaking free from the confines of its burrow.

'Oh my god... 'Bruinscrofa'.' Daniel hissed. 'Now we're in the bloody shit.'

Bryony held her hands to her mouth. 'Sweet mother, what on earth…?'

'

Bruinscrofa' emerged fully from the hole, standing on all fours, taking in its surroundings through mean slits of unblinking eyes. It shook water from its fur, like a giant dog would after a swim. It lowered its massive head, its bullet-hole nostrils catching the sweet scent of humans, and with explosive suddenness, it charged the central machine, with all the rage of a gut-shot rhinoceros. It ploughed headlong into the ironwork with such force, it sheered the anchor bolts like rotten matchwood, shoving the entire structure almost a metre across the pan. Daniel's substantial frame was bowled away like a swatted fly, landing twenty feet from the only thing between him and the snorting beast. He was out in the open and vulnerable. Rolling off his back, he found his feet as 'Bruinscrofa' lumbered forward, passing Bryony's frozen form by a mere hand span. It looked directly at her for a second, before resuming its murderous intention towards Daniel, now in frantic retreat. However, there was nowhere for Daniel to run, and 'Bruinscrofa' followed his spirited but slippery course, with a loping ground-eating canter through the scattered debris. It gained ground as Daniel slowed to find the most likely spot for any kind of assent, and against all odds, Daniel succeeded in scaling the first fifteen feet. Despite his weight and size he clung to the slippery rock like a human fly, just above the flesh-tearing tusks that scored the granite like stonemasons chisels. He climbed again, only inches away from 'Bruinscrofa's lunge as it slashed with tusk and claw, but his position was perilous. The rock face was covered with slime, and Daniel wondered how long he could maintain the grip, soon answered as his fingers began to slip.

'Bruinscrofa' lunged a dozen times before accepting its quarry was frustratingly out of reach. It lowered itself back down on all fours and looked round for easier prey. In a lumbering search, 'Bruinscrofa' moved back to the centre of the pit giving Daniel a slim chance of survival. With every muscle and sinew in his body burning , Daniel finally lost his hold. On the ridge high above, Tobacco and Zip threw down a coincidental barrage of echoing barks, smothering the meaty sound of his body hitting the bedrock, as 'Bruinscrofa' continued to head directly for Bryony.

Selecting a rock at his feet the size of a large cooking apple, Daniel cocked his throwing arm and let fly. The missile struck 'Bruinscrofa' with a satisfying thump below its left ear, but to no effect. Another rock the size of a watermelon crashed into its back, with a bone-shattering impact that would have splintered the vertebrae of an armoured rhinoceros, a monumental throw by Jesse from the rim. 'Bruinscrofa' hardly flinched, but the next rock that exploded at its feet at last gained its attention, and the beast turned with all the menace of a battleship gun turret.

'Keep the ugly bugger busy, Danny boy, I'll get some more ammo,' shouted down Jesse, as he disappeared from view. 'Yeah thanks,' muttered Daniel under his breath, but at least 'Bruinscrofa's attention had been diverted. As Daniel stood facing his fate, direct sunlight suddenly streamed over the rim. It flooded most of the pan, blinding the beast momentarily, throwing the wall against which Daniel stood into cloaked shadow. In the cover of relative darkness, he slid unseen around the face, and ran to where Bryony stood, seemingly welded to the spot. As he reached her he realised, although scared, Bryony was standing with utter defiance rather than fear, and complete admiration swept through Daniel. In that millisecond as their eyes met, it was clear they were going to survive or die together, there would be no in-between.

Hunting along the rock face, amidst Jesse's almost constant barrage of rocks from above, 'Bruinscrofa' realised the deception and returned its attention to the crushing machine. Squaring its gargantuan shoulders, it bunched its body and with lowered head charged again. The ground disappeared beneath the onrush with impressive speed, and again it slammed into the crushing machine. Daniel and Bryony, hands firmly clasped, danced the jig of death around the block, as the heavy casting of the machine began disintegrating. Large chunks of corroded iron ruptured and fell under each colossal impact, and Daniel knew it was only a matter of time, before there was nothing left between them and their relentless attacker. He looked skyward as he heard the buzzard's delighted cry of sorcery. Daniel had been lured into this chosen place of death, through the innocence of his and Bryony's feelings for each other, and the Chancellor's emissaries gloated over the inevitable outcome, as they circled lower. But there was one part of the equation that was impossible to calculate. As they reached for each other, the bond between Daniel and Bryony became beyond doubt. Apart from the swell of inner emotions, they now possessed an incalculable will to live. Inspired by the tremendous courage Bryony showed, Daniel became focussed, and in that moment something in De Theiry's prophesy sprang to mind.

'The Devil's Dagger,' he grunted, without fully knowing its meaning, and they dashed to the blind side of the machine to dodge yet another charge.

Bryony turned. 'The Devil's Dagger?' Hope lifted in her voice. 'Have no idea. I'm thinking aloud. Just repeating something someone once told me.' Suddenly he understood. He squeezed Bryony's forearm and looked up to the ridge high.

'Jesse, for God's sake, can you hear me?' he roared.

From the rim, Jesse ceased hurling what remained of his ineffectual arsenal and listened to the voice beyond the sound of his ragged breathing.

'I hear you Danny.'

'Throw down my coat.'

'Your coat?

'Yes, my bloody coat, and do it now!'

Jesse disappeared and returned moments later with the heavy garment and without hesitation, catapulted it over the edge. They all watched it float agonisingly through the air as if sinking through water. Then came the real agony as it snagged on a corroded support spa protruding from the rock face six metres above the pan. Across the divide, Daniel's and 'Bruinscrofa's eyes met. With a deep intake of breath, Daniel left the scant cover and began his run. 'Bruinscrofa' made a side swipe at him with its tusk, but was outclassed by the human's agility. He bypassed the beast by the skin of his teeth, reached the face and began climbing. But 'Bruinscrofa' turned and was already making its charge. As it ploughed into the rock, its tusks narrowly missed Daniels torso, but a tip tore through his calf muscle like a blunt knife through butter. Blood covered 'Bruinscrofa's snout and it grunted ecstatically at the sweet metallic taste.

Bryony watched on in horror. In her wildest dreams she had never seen such a thing, but this nightmare was real and she was part of it. If immediate action wasn't taken, Daniel was going to die. Trembling at what must be done, she slipped silently from what was left of the sanctuary to stand unprotected in the open.

'Hey bad boy,' she screamed. But 'Bruinscrofa' ignored her.

'Hey ugly bad boy,' she repeated with yet more aggression. 'I'm over here!'

It was the most courageous act Daniel had ever seen, and the beast obliged. It thundered back across the pan, its head down with its tusks pointing like javelins at Bryony's undefended belly. The gap closed with terrifying speed, and Bryony heard the surreal and distant sound of Daniel's anguished cry. He dropped from the ledge but his legs felt heavier than soft lead. He had felt it only once before at the wire, but he wasn't going to repeat the same mistake in asking for help, even though the world had fallen into slow motion, around his powerless.form.
A second later, he heard a wing beat as one of the buzzards swooped deep into the pit, with a shriek from the underworld. It flashed passed 'Bruinscrofa's drooling snout and Daniel stood dumbfounded. Hell's creation slid to a halt a metre from Bryony's slender body. It blew hot snot through its nostrils, splattering her face and front. Incredibly she stood unmoved, almost serene, and the colossal bulk of 'Bruinscrofa' loomed over her, with the point of its bloodied tusk just a lunge away from her face. She saw Daniel's blood on the tusk tips, and her resolve

hardened. 'Bruinscrofa's powerful head swayed back and forth, unsure of what to do next. Again the buzzard called, Bryony was not to be harmed. 'Bruinscrofa' inched forward and sniffed Bryony's face with the huge disk of its rocking nose. Remarkably she reached out to smooth the coarse hair along its corrugated snout, and the beast rumbled deeply with satisfaction.

She was buying time and Daniel made good use of it. From the coat he wrestled the shaft of broken tusk and, using the machine as a screen, and with blood pouring from his wound, he began his run. Moving onto the creature's blind side, he vaulted on top of what was left of the machine and with his good leg launched himself from it, in an utter leap of faith. It had come down to all or nothing. Sensing danger, 'Bruinscrofa's malevolent eyes scanned the pit, but Daniel had lept high with the sun behind him. He landed heavily astride 'Bruinscrofa's massive neck, and in a single downward stroke drove the tusk into its head. With a squeal, 'Bruinscrofa' reared its monstrous body, with trails of drool spinning from its snout like strands of gossamer. The tusk had pierced the skull but missed the brain. It fell back to earth on all fours with a thump, narrowly missing Bryony, who just managed to duck away.

Daniel clung on for dear life, as 'Bruinscrofa' charged the granite walls with the fury of its calling. In the collision, Daniel was thrown from its neck like a rag doll in a rodeo, crashing to the ground in a tangle of limbs. Ignoring the impact and the wound to his leg, he rolled to his feet and moved round to 'Bruinscrofa's side in an attempt to thrust the tusk through its ribs, and into what was once its beating heart. But 'Bruinscrofa' was ready and with a half turn of its body, swung its broad front paw in an upward swing, lifting Daniel high into the air. As if shot from a cannon, he flew backwards into the wall, with the wind being blown from his lungs. But fate was playing its unpredictable game. The same spa that had snagged his coat was about to save his life. Although badly dazed he had landed belly down over the broad spa like a piece of meat on a curing rod, but despite the pain, he clung on doggedly to consciousness and to the tusk. The pressure of blood in his head was threatening a blackout, and he opened his bloodshot eyes to see 'Bruinscrofa' searching the pan once more for Bryony. Suddenly he was aware of a dark shadow behind him. He felt pressure on his back as a buzzard perched on his spine, with the full intention of plucking his left eye from its puffy socket. Daniel felt the tusk in his hand. He threw his right arm backwards, and believing its meat dead the buzzard was taken by surprise. It tried to flap away but its reaction was not swift enough, as the Devil's Dagger penetrated the side of its head with the point exiting the other side of its skull with geometrical surgery. The bird's magnificent yellow eyes bulged as they both toppled off the spa, falling as one to the pan below in a dance of limbs and feathers.

Daniel got unsteadily to his feet. His head pounded like a pile driver, his ribcage felt as if he'd been rolled over by a steam locomotive, and the lacerations on his body were matched in number by heavy bruising. As he stood facing the centre, what had moments earlier been a fabulous bird, reverted to its original form. Like a nylon stocking filled with wet clay, the prehistoric worm hung from the tusk. Daniel tilted the dagger until the remains slipped off the tip, like reject offal at Billingsgate fish market. He remained square to 'Bruinscrofa', legs slightly apart and holding the Devil's Dagger, like a swordsman confronting a challenging duellist. He hung his head and looked forward under his brows. His eyes were colder than steel, irrepressible, calculating and deadly. Daniel had once more become the Chancellor's true nemesis. He felt no fear, and as he moved forward Bryony witnessed the frightening aura that surrounded him. It was if another person had entered the arena, a trained gladiator with death on his mind. Suddenly she was more scared by the transformation, than of 'Bruinscrofa' itself.

'Bruinscrofa' screamed its fury at the challenge and charged. Daniel stood his ground as the gap between them dissolved. He stood poised and utterly still, then at the last moment span on his heel. With his back to the charge he drove the tusk between 'Bruinscrofa's eyes with a powerful backward swing to deliver the 'coup de grace.' Like a slaughter man's bolt, the tusk disappeared into 'Bruinscrofa's skull, splitting the beast's life force in two. The momentum took the great beast a further dozen paces forward, until it came to a halt swaying gently on it feet. Suddenly its legs buckled and the mighty body crashed to the puddled floor.

The pan shook under the collapse and from the wound in its skull, a pall of graphite dust rose and twisted, snaking its way passed Daniel's face. And as he stared into the column of the million swirling particles, he saw the engine room of Hell itself. At first there were kindly faces smiling at him in the multiple shades of grey ash; men and women with all the attributes of human beauty, laughing and happy, embracing and forgiving, swirling around Daniel's head, carefree in their abandon. But as they were drawn along the twisting column, they turned from things of beauty, to the stuff of nightmares, a transition from joy to the grotesque, the corridor of lost souls, from the innocence of youth to the gateway of the damned. All the while dark shadows appeared from the dark core of the plume, to snatch the floating faces away, to a place beyond the realms of imagination. Some of the beautiful cried in anguish, with outstretched arms, pleading for Daniel's help. But Daniel was no longer fooled by the countless tricks of his enemy. He watched impassively as they floated past on their tormented way.

Bryony, wide eyed, ran to his side and reached out to hold hands with a terrified young girl, and before Daniel could react, their hands had met. Bryony smiled sympathetically at the waif, who in turn smiled sweetly, before transforming into a lizard from the swamp of time. To the sound of cackles from those left in the swirling dust, the lizard began dragging Bryony in. Her scream tore into Daniel's soul, and with a savage up-sweep of the Devil's Dagger, he severed the link with such abruptness that it sent Bryony sprawling.

The tail end of the column eventually disappeared into sink hole from where it had come, and the cries and the screams died away, until blessed silence replaced the agonised noise of terrible suffering.

Daniel helped Bryony to her feet, and strode across the pan and stood astride 'Bruinscrofa's head. He looked at Bryony, and she watched her man return from that distant, unpredictable and dangerous place. He stepped away from the carcass and with tentative steps she slipped into his arms.

'In God's name what's happening? Tell me it's just a bad dream.' She buried her face into the wall of his chest, in a heart-rending attempt to hide her out-pouring of emotions. Daniel lifted her chin against spirited resistance before she raised her face to meet his, and he kissed a runaway tear from her cheek. Daniel had returned to reason and momentarily they were lost to each other.

From the opposite side of the rim, the remaining buzzard looked down in disbelief at its fallen companions, until Zip and Tobacco tore in to exact their revenge. Feathers flew in all directions like a detonation in a barrel of eiderdown, until the worm shed its frail bird body and fought back. It reared like a striking cobra, but out of its ancient sea, it was cumbersome and vulnerable. It suffered neither a merciful nor quick dispatch, but in its dying moments, sent telepathic news of the defeat to the Chancellor's chambers.

Far away, the Chancellor grew rigid with fury. The unimaginable had happened and in an act of vindictive retribution, he summoned the water to return with tempestuous speed. Volumes spewed back up through the sink hole, like the open sluice gate of a hydroelectric dam under a full head of pressure, and within seconds the surface broiled three feet above the bedrock. Daniel and Bryony were buffeted like flotsam in a storm; however, the Chancellor's wish to see Daniel drown had backfired. Bryony's life was charmed. It had been his own decree. Therefore, as long as they held on to each other, he would survive. The waters rose ever closer to the secret path and freedom. Within ten minutes they had reached the lower section and using the already heavily-tested power in his arms, Daniel hauled himself and Bryony onto the first step, until their bodies were clear of the turbulence. Near to exhaustion they crawled to safety and made their way to the rim, dazed, weary but so very glad to be alive.

They looked down into the swirling waters, as Jesse rushed to join them, but none were able to find words. Even the animals stood silently at their feet, as the water found its original level. It slowly calmed and normality returned.

They stood in a silent row and placed arms of friendship around each others shoulders, and in that moment the league was born. It had been a decisive victory over the Underworld. Their will to survive had been grossly underestimated, and because of it they had won through. 'Bruinscrofa' had been slain, sweet revenge indeed for Jerry Green, but most importantly, they had lived and triumphed.

'Should you survive, Daniel, the Underworld shall respect, if not admire you. But be warned, should you be victorious, your world shall become a much more dangerous place!'

Phillipe De Theiry's words filtered into Daniel's thoughts, and Bryony, noticing his mood, drew closer. She remained shaken and held on to Daniel as if she would never let go.

'I don't understand any of it. I'm scared, Daniel, I mean really scared. Wake me up! Shake me from this dream!' She looked up into his face and saw the dreadful truth. 'Who are you Daniel?'

Bryony certainly deserved to be told, but the appropriate words eluded him. He caught Jesse's eye who answered with a shrug of resignation. This was a task for Daniel alone.

'Promise me one thing, Bryony. Don't put the silver talisman you've been wearing back around your neck. Please do as I ask and I promise we'll meet again very soon. I shall explain everything then.'

She drew breath to say more, but Daniel raised his finger and pressed it softly against her lips, and in response, in an act of total trust she kissed the palm of his hand. She was strong and in love, but it had taken great courage and self-sacrifice to find the belief she needed in Daniel. Daniel could see it in her eyes as she fought to dispel any lingering fear, but as her expression cleared, he knew he had found his prop in life. The message was clear. She would stay at his side in a lifetime union never to be broken, even in death.

Jesse cleared his throat, breaking the spell. It was time to leave, and the three followed Tobacco and Zip's lead. They had won an important victory. However, the matter was far from over, of that, Daniel was more than sure. His hand tightened on the Devil's Dagger, as they turned as one from 'The Pool Without Water'.

It was a busy time indeed for my loaded quill. My Lords, Lucifer and Abdiel met more frequently than I could remember, and always with Daniel Bonner high on the agenda. Lucifer's creations, sent to Bonner by his Chancellor had indeed brought hell to earth for the mortal, but had failed to destroy him. It intrigued me to listen and chart with ink, the arguments that flowed back and forth along the long table in the hall of souls, and that being so, I the humble Scribe learned the strengths and weaknesses of my masters. And dare I think it, their fears also.

'After a thousand years, 'Bruinscrofa' has eventually been destroyed, my evil brother. So I have but one question, what mortal could achieve such things?' Abdiel sat at his head of the table, with robed arms open wide in invitation for his question to be answered. Abdiel was not one to gloat, that would have gone wholly against his doctrine. However, I do believe he was enjoying Lucifer's discomfort.

'The same mortal whom you have chosen to champion, brother Abdiel. I know it was you who made the dogs bark to smother Bonner's fall onto the bedrock. It was you who positioned my fallen beast to be blinded by the sun as it appeared over the rim. But prior to that, it was you who enticed Bonner to pick up and inveigle into his coat 'Bruinscrofa's broken tusk, to use as the only weapon that could destroy him.'

'Like for like, brother Satan. Sorry, I get confused, is that what you like to be called nowadays?

Lucifer chose not to rise to that particular line of questioning and returned to the subject in hand.

'That is how, in part at least, this mortal has survived, with your help!'

Abdiel nodded sagely. 'It was down to more than just those rather pedestrian details, my brother.' And he lifted forward his arms and from his palms, a white mist ran half the length of the table, to transform into a strange image.

Six men stood as a huddle on a bedrock of a deep open-cast excavation. Five of them wore thick woollen trousers, with rolled up sleeves, waistcoats and heavy boots, typical of late Victorian workwear. The sixth man wore a badly fitting suit and a bowler hat, and was deliberating with the other men. It was clear he was the gang boss, and their task was to recover a large rock crushing machine, standing pride of place at the centre of the excavation. A long boom-arm had been rigged high on the ridge, and from it hung a thick steel hawser, with an equally robust crane hook at its end. This was lowered through squeaking pulley wheels, with enough slack to wrap securely around the machine, and above, the steam winch took up the strain. The hawser began to hum as it became taught, but the machine refused to move. The six heavy nuts had been removed from the anchor bolts, but still it held fast. The hawser sang a tune of danger and one man looked up in fear. The steel spa suddenly gave way and fell towards the pan in a conflagration of rubble and twisted cable. The man looking up and hurled himself at the others, milliseconds before the crane smashed into the deck with a ring louder than a cathedral bell. All six were stunned, but unhurt. The first to recover was the gang boss, with orders to re-rig the davit and begin again. It was then he cocked his head sideways, as if listening to a voice in his head. Without another word he ordered his men out for the last time, leaving the machine to stand monument to what had once been a viable excavation. This was the very machine that had saved Daniel and Bryony from 'Bruinscrofa's brutal attacks.

Lucifers fist clattered the table and the story mist dissolved into nothing. 'You cannot go back in time to alter history, brother of mine. Even I acknowledge such practice is illegal in both our houses. I claim victory by default. You are guilty, brother Abdiel, and I demand satisfaction.

Abdiel laughed through his nose. 'Agreed, my brother, I was indeed present, guardian to those men at the time of the accident. I have never re-visited to alter history. Nevertheless, I of course knew the importance of the machine to act as an all important shield.'

'But Bonner's future is not listed in the Libraries of Time, therefore you must have gone back. It's as I say, I demand satisfaction.'

'Oh dear brother of mine, indeed, it's as you say, Bonner's future does not appear. But Bryony Carter's does. That is how I knew to leave the machine. I really do suggest that you read a little more often.'
It is rare, as you know, that I look up from my writings, but on this occasion I found it irresistible. Lucifer was in a state of utter rage. He cocked back his arm and let fly a ball of molten plasma. Abdiel reacted throwing back a ball of ice. They collided half-way and the resulting explosion sent shards of matter screaming over my ducked head. It was a magnificent spectacle.

'Save your trifling tantrums for the human world, brother Lucifer, and for that act of violence, I forgive you.'

The Devil soured features relaxed as he looked through the eyebrows of his bowed head. His eyes told of everything he was. And I could gaze no longer, my quill ready and waiting, my eyes focussed on the clean parchment alone.

'Like for like, I believe is what you said, brother Abdiel. The 'Bruinscrofa' tusk has slain the 'Bruinscrofa'. Then let it be so, like for like!!'

'Let what be so, brother Lucifer?'

It was a pointless question with no forthcoming answer. Lucifer had something in mind, and Abdiel was more than aware of the power of his brother's trickery.
'Let us move on, brother. There is much to discuss', said Abdiel. But his face told another story.

# Bengie Slink

Daniel Bonner was soon to discover just how formidable Jerry Green's sister truly was. Despite a clean shaven chin and slightly more pedestrian choice of clothes, Florence Green, a spinster and five years Jerry's senior, eyed Daniel with suspicion as he stood at the threshold of the family house in the Redland district of Bristol. It wasn't until Jerry came to the door, that Daniel was eventually allowed in.

'He's been to Hell and back,' she whispered sharply, as Daniel stepped past her into the hall, 'so don't be troubling him mister or you'll have me to deal with…clear?'

'Crystal,' said Daniel, as he caught Jerry looking skyward, shaking his head at the improbability of his sister ever even reaching Danny's jaw, should she be so inclined to take a swing.

'Leave him alone Sis, he's a good friend,' said Jerry, leading Daniel into the sunny bay of sash windows in the sitting room. They settled into matching armchairs and in the revealing light, Daniel saw the terrible damage inflicted by 'Bruinscrofa' on his friend. From the top of his temple to the lower drop of his jaw was a ridge of heavy scaring, a disfiguring cicatrix that dragged at the corner of his mouth when he spoke, and from which he periodically mopped a flow of undignified dribble.

'Tell me Danny, how's life on the moor? But keep your voice down. My sister has hearing like bloody radar and wouldn't understand what you might be about to tell me…if you get my meaning.'

Daniel began with all the normal things; Delamere, the 'Pink Pig,' and the moor in general, even Artefacts of Ages. To the would-be eavesdropper it was nothing more than casual chit-chat until without warning, Florence trundled in through the sitting-room door announcing she was going shopping, and asking her brother what he would like for supper. Jerry quietly asked for crispy roast duck which would require a special trip to one of the supermarkets in Clifton Village. It was a crafty but kindly manoeuvre to remove Florence 'Battleaxe' Green from the house, and would enable the two men to talk of other more important matters.

'I'll be gone for a while,' she said somewhat suspiciously. She knew her brother well. 'Will you be all right?' she said, throwing a scowling glance at Daniel.

'I'll be fine' said Jerry, giving Daniel a surreptitious wink, and they listened in silence as she bustled industriously from the house. The moment Florence had closed the front door, Jerry stood to his feet and raised the window seat in the bay. From under a pile of old curtains, he extracted a full bottle of malt whisky and two crystal tumblers.

'You certainly were expecting me,' said Daniel, holding the glasses to be filled, and Jerry grinned crookedly. 'Just like old times eh?'

Once alone, they started talking of matters that would have had Florence breaking into a hissy fit had she been listening, with the upshot being Daniel thrown bodily from the house, if that was at all physically possible?

Despite Daniel's awareness of Jerry's trauma he knew they could talk freely at last. Jerry sat forward in his armchair with his elbows resting on his knees, staring into the bottom of his tumbler. 'Tell me everything,' he said, 'I need to know.'

'Are you sure, Jerry? There's a lot to tell, about this and other worlds. 'Bruinscrofa' being just part of it.'

At the very name, Jerry's hand went involuntarily to the canyons on his face. 'Yes, Daniel, I really need to hear it all, and don't worry, I'm actually OK with it.'

So Daniel began by telling him the horrendous story of the slaying of his brother, Stephen. Jerry swallowed several large drafts from his glass as he wondered at Daniel's inner strength, to be able to even raise the subject. He listened intently to how Daniel and Bryony had survived the pool without water, but on hearing of 'Bruinscrofa's final destruction he broke down. Daniel couldn't determine if his tears were of joy, self-pity, revenge or all three. Nonetheless, the tears were distressingly real. He leaned forward and placed a comforting hand on Jerry's shoulder, who slowly controlled his emotions and eventually found his voice.

'Sorry old friend, it's not been a good trip,' and Jerry again touched again the ridges of heavy scar tissue. He took a deep breath, held it for a moment before exhaling. It did the trick, but for Daniel it was hard to imagine the physical pain Jerry must have endured in the immediate aftermath of the nightmare, from then to the present day. He felt inadequate in the presence of such fortitude. Likewise, Jerry had similar thoughts about Daniel and Stephen's story. They had a strong accord.

'You've had it tough Jerry.'

Jerry saw the look on Daniel's face and smiled crookedly.

'What you see is only part of it.' With his good arm he pulled away the loose fitting neck of his pullover to reveal even heavier wounds on his shattered shoulder, descending into his pectoral muscle as if cleaved with a blunt broadsword, and Daniel reached across to cover his friend's torso. A sense of shame and anger spread through Daniel's thoughts, and he wished above all things he had done more to discourage Gerry from entering the dark side of the world which he had initially invited in. He owed so much to this courageous little man, and his following words sounded inadequate.

'It's a wonder you're still alive, Jerry, and no mistake.'

Jerry nodded curtly, uneasy with the reminder he sank back into his chair. 'It seems you've had it even tougher Danny.'

'Hmm, I'm not entirely convinced about that.'

They each sat for a while in silence, lost in their own thoughts until eventually Jerry spoke. 'Daniel, there's something I need to talk to you about. It's in 'Myths and Legends. For obvious reasons I've not looked at the book for a long time, and believe me I nearly burned the bloody thing, as a form of a much needed exorcism. However, and don't ask me why, some sort of morbid fascination stopped me from throwing it on the fire. From the first moment you stepped into Artefacts of Ages I've been locked into it. I just couldn't burn it. Then one night I found the courage to pick it up again. I naturally skipped over 'Bruinscrofa'; can't find the guts to go there again in too much of a hurry.'

'I reckon you've shown more than your fare share of guts, almost literally,' said Daniel hoping to provoke a smile.

'Hmm, perhaps,' said Jerry modestly, through something of a grin, 'but that aside, I came across this rather disturbing story that caught my attention; it's been lodged in my mind ever since.' He took the book from an occasional table at his side and offered it to Daniel. 'Take a look at page one five four.'

'Do you honestly believe I'd come here without my own volume, my relic-selling friend?'

Jerry's face succeeded a proper smile, as Daniel extracted his copy from the overnight bag at his feet.

Simultaneously the binds were tested, opened at the appropriate page and the two men began to read.

'The Haunted Moors'

'Separated by a broad band of Devonshire farming country, the uplands of Dartmoor and Exmoor are quite different in character. Dartmoor is a craggy inland plateau of rough moorland, treacherous bogs and rocky outcrops. Exmoor curves gently across heather and pasture, to drop steeply from over one thousand feet to the sea.

In the remote northern part of Dartmoor, lies Cranmere pool. Now mostly drained, it was once the most treacherous of bogs, and a place to which evil spirits and their victims were reputedly consigned. The most famous was that of 'Bengie Slink,' a footpad of the most vile order, a brigand who in 1670 is reputed to have cheated and betrayed his two picaroon brothers, who in true buccaneer spirit, were feared marauders of the Spanish and French ships of the line. Captains of the ships, War

Piper and Drummer, they had gained both reputation and fortune under the protective mark of King Charles II, enabling legal pursuit in what can only be described as piratical practices. It is said that not all the gains were declared, and that that Bengie Slink found safe store on the moor for his brothers' illicit share of the fortune. However, not content with what he deemed a paltry share, he reputedly informed Spanish sympathisers of the exact time and destination of his brothers' next sailing from the medieval Cornish harbour of Fowey, down to the Spanish Main. It ended in a perfect naval interception, and the ensuing battle in the heart of the Bay of Biscay, was both bloody and brutal. War Piper and Drummer were heavily outnumbered, outgunned and subsequently blown from the water. It is documented that the captains, on guessing Bengie Slink's treachery, bellowed a curse across the water to England as they went down with their ships. Should his bones ever be cast into the sea upon those fateful coordinates, they would rise from the crushing depths and claim his treacherous soul.

Legend has it the curse has yet to be fulfilled. Centuries have passed and reputedly they still wait for him out in the watery wastes. Maritime folklore still insists that their rantings can sometimes be heard above the wailing wind, bellowing damnation and terrible threats of retribution.

In 1672, Slink's luck eventually ran out, and the enduring story has it that both his bones and his gold lie somewhere in or around Cranmere Mire. Bengie Slink is reputed to still haunt the area, forever guarding the illicit fortune and apparently still every bit as vile.'

'Ok,' said Daniel. 'That's quite a story, but what's it got to do with us?'

'Before I explain,' replied Jerry. 'Take a look at the following page,' and Daniel did as he was asked. He turned the page and read on.

'The following account chronicles the last days of Bengie Slink, written by a member of the militia sent out to bring Slink to justice. Found in the vaults of the local parish church some two hundred years ago, the writing of the time has subsequently been adapted to more modern day phraseology for the benefit of this book. Nonetheless I believe the following to be an accurate account of Bengie Slink's last days, and despite the passing of time, I find the idea of his existence, in whichever form, in whichever world, no less chilling.'

'The hunt for Benjamin Slink: By Jonathan Percival Miller, Member of Cranmere Militia, in the year of our Lord God and defender of the faith, King Charles II, Anno Domini, January, 1672.'

'Twas, I believe, ordained, praise be to my Lord and Saviour Jesus Christ, that I, Jonathan Percival Miler, in attachment to the six in number of volunteers, trod light of foot through Hell's creation and natural treachery of Cranmere Mire, in the most exacting winter of 1672, and through his good grace did survive. If diligence and courage had failed along the bloodied trail that we coursed, verily the same infamous trail upon which the wanted rapscallion, Benjamin Slink had murderously dragged the body of his latest victim, this account would have been lost to mind and memory. The merchantman, under the magistrate's protection did not survive. God rest his soul. T'would be travesty if I were not to impart that once below the escarpment of Fox Tor, it's very satanic presence did well to further beggar an already tested fortitude, and that I and my fellow members of the militia, were sorely tempted to return to the comforting bosom of our homes. However, we chanced upon the pitiful frozen remains of a disembowelled horse into which, t'was readily assumed, the merchantman had performed drastic surgery and climbed into the cavity, seeking respite from the exacting temperatures, that now did claw most thoroughly through our own wretched limbs. As inquisitors we were soon to discover, that this dark place was the very place of Benjamin Slink's chancing upon the aforementioned luckless merchant, and Slink, through infamous reputation, had proved himself again to be indeed grotesque of mind. A brigand without compassion, a murderer incapable of mercy, destined for expulsion even from Hell's roll-call. We, the militia, were given to discover this t'was most parts true...God protect us. In the foul surround to the equine disembowelment, we were able to unravel the most brutal event, printed in the snow by both innocent and dastardly foot alike, and thereupon conclude the last living moments of the luckless merchant. He, believing Slink his rescuer, had most naturally clambered from the morgue cavity, to be thus smitten to the ground by Slink's clubs of thuggery. The dispensing of human blood, disconcerting in its profusion, did trace the poor soul's final movements as he shuffled fore on bended knees, in the most undignified manner. Most like as not, he begged for mercy, as blood flowed gross to the snow, and did proffer pitiful coinage, in return for salvation, several pieces of which we discovered bright in the fresh fall. Slink had thereupon clubbed his victim to death; the signs clear, ungodly and violent.

In the light of such evidence, we did follow the bloody trail along which Slink had hauled the merchant, to the edge of Cranmere mire, and without remorse had cast him down, another murdered soul gone without fare thee well to kin or countrymen. T'was chronicled that Slink had lost count of his victims sent down in such manner, reputedly seventeen plus of which, through later investigation, t'was agreed an accurate accusation.

The blizzard that had delivered the ill-fated merchant to Slink, t'was to prove the cutthroat's undoing. The snowstorm had ceased abruptly thus failing to obliterate his murderous trail.

T'was then that we, the militia, did find the unsuspecting Slink, as he stood watchman to the merchantman's body going asunder. Sergeant Jeremiah Pratt, a man not given easily to acts of clemency, stole the ground between him and the dread Slink, to drive the butt of his heavy musket most savagely between the brigand's shoulders. Slink did collapse and the second blow to his pate rendered him unconscious, praise God. Slink's soul, were it that he possessed one, was devoid of mercy and, therefore, deserved none from us in return.

We did cast his unconscious body onto the mire, suspended so by spread cloaks given willingly for the task, despite the cold. Assumed by us all t'was the savage cold and pounding in his skull that awoke him. We watched as he understood his grim circumstance. Beneath his body he felt movement of the mire, and with due care Sergeant Pratt did press close to the edge. My first impression of Slink was the corruption about the inside of his mouth; blackened teeth stood like rotted stumps, several of which had been knocked from his mouth and had stuck sickly to his chin in a poultice of bloodied puss. We stared with hatred, and as God is my witness, Slink's loathing was mutual. From his neck a drogue rope ran to the bank, onto which a rock was attached, held aloft by a member of the militia.

Phillip Curme, our Captain pressed closer than we dared and delivered Slink questions, the answers in exchange for his worthless life. T'was fact he knew the whereabouts of his brothers' fortunes and t'was our intention to discover where the said gold was hidden, for the weighted rope would drag him asunder should silence be his return.

Phillip Curme, an authoritarian of repute, God rest his soul, laid bare our intentions, and we, a most expectant number, were certain that Slink would sing sweet, in order to save his wretched hide. God forgive me, but my wish to see Slink go head fore into the mire marked little on my conscience. But alas the coward gave promise of the gold, and it was others that did haul him from the mire. Captain Curme stood front to Slink and demanded inform, lest Sergeant Pratt should lay violent about his skull with the blunt of a musket. The sergeant moved with weapon raised, and Slink did then announce he would lead us to the gates of Hades before exposing the gold. Sergeant Pratt moved to silence the impudence, and the Captain stepped back for him to execute his duty. But we, as one in mind, did underestimate our prisoner. In a movement to befool, Slink held fast the musket butt, inclined the barrel over Pratt's shoulder and pulled the trigger. Captain Curme's face exploded beneath the full discharge and the sergeant's nose did split, as Slink swung the weapon round in the same action. We, the four remaining, did witness the capability of this murderer, as the back of captain Curme's head fell upon our frozen faces, grotesque and bloody. His body fell face to the snow, as steam rose from the wound like a lit pipe, and in that moment we realised the fate of Sergeant Pratt. Slink did fasten upon Jeremiah Pratt's throat with Lucifer's grip. Sergeant Pratt made stout fight for life, crying desperate through crushed windpipe as Slink dragged him into the mire, whereupon the unified weight broke sudden the surface. We did witness Slink and the Sergeant go lower into the freezing mire, and Slink's laughter was from a place insane. Within moments they were gone with one final up-swell, testament to the ending of both lives.

I, Jonathan Percival Miller, one year after the deaths, sound in body and mind, felt the profound need to document this account, and expunge the aforementioned nightmare from my mind. Alas it has not worked and I awake each morning in awe at the power of my wretched nightmares.'

'J.P.M 1673'

'Blimey,' said Daniel as he lowered the book. 'This Slink character was an evil son of a bitch. But why this story, Jerry? What's got you thinking?'

'I've just got a feeling about it Danny, can't ignore it any longer.' He raised his book again and read aloud the editor's concluding paragraph.

'It is said, that from that day to this, Bengie Slink's spirit, caught between this world and the next, has ceaselessly patrolled the area. Throughout the following centuries, it is reputed that he has sat on an adjacent crag, guarding the mire and, supposedly the gold. It is also said that the Devil himself cannot touch him, as he is a rogue spirit in the state of limbo, belonging to neither world, reason enough that the legacy of Bengie Slink remains unchanged to this day.'

'Ok, but I still don't understand what it's got to do with us?'

'I reckon the Underworld wants to set this Bengie Slink character onto our Parisian friend. Daniel, since the run-in with 'Bruinscrofa' I've started having vivid dreams. I saw you kill the beast, but thought it only my wishful imagination until you just told me otherwise. I can't ignore these dreams any longer.'

'You saw me? Don't tell me you're becoming a living De Theiry?'

'My dreams are strong, Daniel, and I'm slowly, but surely, getting them in order.

'Blimey, at this rate we'll be able to second guess the Chancellor before he's even had a chance to think. We'll slaughter the bastard.'

'Most of my dreams mean nothing, but from time to time they are highly accurate. Daniel, after reading Slink's story, I saw him tearing De Theiry apart, and it was the Underworld's doing.'

'But it's written in the book, the Underworld can't touch Slink, and if that's the case, nor can they Phillipe De Theiry.'

'But what if they find a way to fight like for like. What if they find a way to manipulate the spirit of Bengie Slink to attack De Theiry?'

'Do you think one spirit can hurt another?'

'Like for like, Daniel? Nothing would surprise me.'

'Hmm, nor me, good point well made. I think it's time to discuss this with Phillipe.'

'Not before we've made a colossal dent in this bottle you won't,' countered Jerry. And the two friends raised their glasses beneath the rare sound of Jerry's laughter.

Daniel looked long and hard at Phillipe. The Frenchman looked utterly resplendent. His hair well groomed; his clothes no longer in tatters and his complexion close to that of the living. Even his buckled shoes possessed a shine that any Parisian cobbler of that era would have been proud. And yet there was an unusual frown between his eyes, that Daniel couldn't quite fathom.

'Why the look of concern, Phillipe?' he asked idly, disguising his own concerns, given his recent conversation with Jerry.

'It's like I told you a little while ago my English friend, I think they are on to me,' admitted De Theiry. 'I can feel the negative energy, and it's powerful.'

'Look, Phillipe, I have to tell you, that Jerry believes that you and a particularly nasty spirit called Bengie Slink, who existed three-hundred and fifty years ago, will be thrown together in conflict. The Devil's Dagger dispatched 'Bruinscrofa', and we think the Chancellor is recruiting, through some nefarious channel, a 'like for like' force from your world of limbo. He is to hunt you down. I hate to admit it Frenchy, but it's looking increasingly likely. Can another of your kind attack you?'

'Yes, we can even destroy each other if we have a mind to do so, but it is very rare.

'Then I'd better read to you the tale of Bengie Slink.'

De Theiry listened to the story word for word, after which, Daniel looked across at him. 'Have you anything with which to defend yourself?' he asked, noticing the frown between De Theiry's eyes had now creased his forehead. Clearly the idea of Bengie Slink hunting him down was an unexpected development that had him rattled. He was entering new territory, and had no idea what to expect, but whatever was coming along the Chancellor's corridor of hate would be unpleasant in the extreme.

Vincent Wothe was a powerful clairvoyant, a mortal able to communicate with those lost in the vastness of the spiritual wilderness. Wothe, unlike his name, was a plain-looking nondescript man, capable of passing unnoticed through a crowd, with a non-giving face that any discerning poker player would give his back teeth for. He had however bartered his soul to escape a jail sentence for fraud, a pact he would regret in the future. But how he conducted himself with this particular contract would make a difference when it came to the harvesting of souls, and so far he had done rather well.

The Chancellor listened to Wothe as he explained what he had achieved so far. He had found Slink sitting on top of Fox Tor and told the ghost of his French enemy. Slink was incensed with the idea that Phillipe De Theiry was planning to expose the whereabouts of the hidden fortune, unaware it was a manipulative and blatant lie. Not that it would have made the slightest difference, as Slink revelled in the prospect of appalling thuggery anyway. He needed little coaxing and certainly wanted no reward for doing what he did best.

The Chancellor turned to his scribe sitting attentively at his side and told him to record it so. And I the Scribe did his bidding. My true master's were the light and dark angels, and with hidden reluctance, I did as was instructed.

For the sixth time in as many days, Daniel threw water on the fire in yet another frustrated attempt to summon De Theiry. A great upheaval had taken place, of that he was sure. It was a strange and uneasy feeling not being able to draw the Parisian to the fireside. Disturbing as it may have been for Daniel when De Theiry had first entered his dreams, it was vastly more disturbing losing him. The Frenchman had become an anchor, a bright vision in the world of the dark unknown and into the flames, Daniel made a silent promise. He would do everything in his power to guard De Theiry, as he had guarded him.

More water was poured on the fire and this time Tobacco sat suddenly upright. De Theiry appeared before them, and Daniel barely recognised the apparition. His long hair was dishevelled, more so than when they had first met. His clothes were tattered and dirty, and the pain etched in his ghostly features had transformed his suave appearance into something resembling abject terror. It was then Daniel saw the stump that had once been the Frenchman's right arm, a shredded shirtsleeve was all that was left, testament to the loss.

'Help me Daniel…for pity sake, help me! He hunts me down with a dark relentless hate in his once-beating heart. On so many occasions he could have sent me to oblivion and yet prefers toying with me, tearing pieces off my body with depraved joy. I fear I shall soon be broken into irrevocable pieces. This one is utterly evil. Daniel, I implore you to find the answer. Find a way through for me, I beseech you.'

Shocked, Daniel rose from the fire. There had to be a way to stop this horrific game, but before he had even begun to placate the distraught Frenchman, chaos tumbled into their meeting. Without warning De Theiry looked fearfully to his right, then tore away in the opposite direction. In front of Danny, the image of his friend was replaced with the figure of Bengie Slink. A dreadful predator, head slunk low, shoulders hunched over a thick neck, with heavily muscled arms dragging two skull crushing clubs. As he drew parallel, he turned his long dead neck and stared directly into Danny's face, and for a moment their eyes were locked in time. Slink was to Daniel the most appalling apparition imaginable. His puce green skin hung from his face like peeled bark, in places holed to the bone, but it was the catastrophe of what had once been his teeth, that Daniel noticed most. Rotted stumps dotted his gums, like ribs of a shipwrecked hull in estuary mud, and the appalling smell of corruption.

'Leave De Theiry alone, you murdering bastard,' Daniel shouted, and Slink pranced about in un-feigned joy. Raising both clubs high above his head, he brought them crashing down to earth, and Daniel realised the power of this poltergeist as the ground shook below his feet. He was helpless to do anything but watch Slink race after De Theiry, he would have to act fast if there was to be any hope of saving the Frenchman. He scrabbled in his coat for 'Myths and Legends,' and his hands poured feverishly through the pages. The key had to lie somewhere in the writing, and it wasn't long before the answer became apparent in one telling sentence. 'Should Bengie Slinks bones ever be cast upon the sea on those fateful co-ordinates, his buccaneer brothers would rise from the deep and claim his treacherous soul?' It was clear what had to be done. But to do it Daniel would have to desert his Parisian ally.

Jesse sat waiting in the foyer of Plymouth's largest commercial bank, as Daniel returned from the office into which he had disappeared only a short while ago. Unlike the queuing customers, the manager escorting Daniel back to the foyer couldn't care less about the strange menagerie of men and animals, as Tobacco and Zip strained on their makeshift leads of baler twine. The banker's parting handshake was respectful, putting it once more to Daniel in a whispered voice, that carrying such a large amount of cash was perhaps not the most secure method of transporting money. Had he known Daniel Bonner better, he would not have felt so uneasy.

In a pay and display one hundred metres away, Bryony's Volkswagen Golf waited in readiness for Daniel and Jesse's return. The passenger door swung wide and Daniel tucked himself into the front seat as Jesse piled into the back with the animals.

'Feels like we're on a bank job,' giggled Bryony.

Daniel grinned. He looked at the side of her head and wondered if she had aged a single day, since saving her from drowning five years previously. Her face had remained a flawless rose-tinted alabaster, and he compared the radiant colour of her hair to the ever-increasing streaks of grey, that had stole in like a thief around his own temples. Millington had tried on numerous occasions to replace the Talisman, but she had flatly refused and the mere thought of him touching her, brought a flush of anger to Daniel. He leaned over and kissed the crock of her neck and she smiled.

'What was that for, my darling man?'

'I just needed to do it,' replied Daniel.

'Well you can do it anytime you like,' and she smiled again, this time with a wicked grin.

'Shall we get on now?' said Jesse in the back seat, the two dogs his only company. 'Some blokes have all the luck!'

The journey back to the moor was full of humorous and easy talk, everyone setting aside, for a while at least, the task that lay ahead. Bryony was bound for Fowey. She was to charter a boat large enough for a channel crossing with the use of the five thousand pounds drawn from Daniel's book account. In the meantime, Daniel and Jesse were due to exhume the remains of Bengie Slink. The maritime curse of War

Piper and Drummer's battling Captains had to be realised, not only for De Theiry's wellbeing, but for everyone concerned. Slink had the absolute power of the poltergeist, and it would not be long before that power was brought to bear on the living. They were all in danger.

On the high moorland road, the two parties said their farewells with Bryony still insisting that she had the stomach for the exhumation, and that it was she who should be assisting Daniel, not Jesse.

Daniel took her aside and stared into her beguiling face. He gently held the lobes of her neat pink ears and drew her close with a promise of what they would do when next they met, and a wonderful blush spread across her cheeks.

'Go and broker the boat deal,' he said, with a smile. 'What I and Jesse have to do is far better suited to us low brigands. We know nothing about boats, so please, do as I ask.'

'So what makes you think I know anything about boats?' said Bryony, clinging to her protestations.

'Hey Pinky,' said Daniel, an intimate reference to her complexion, 'I'm afraid we don't have any other option. Do it for me please?'

For a moment Bryony's bottom lip protruded, but reluctantly agreed it was at least a workable plan.

'When it comes to payback time, you'd better be in a generous mood Mr Bonner,' and after a final kiss, Bryony climbed into her car, and in the rear view mirror took several longing looks at Daniel, until she disappeared from view.

Long after sunset, Daniel and Jesse continued forging ahead into the enveloping darkness. To travel at night on the moor was normally attempted by those somewhat touched in the head or lost, but the brothers of the tiny league navigated the treacherous cataracts with unnerving skill.

Midway through the following morning, they rounded on Cranmere Mire and from the elevated position of Fox Tor, they stared down into the far-reaching indentation that was once the notorious marsh.

Daniel and Jesse stared into the bright flames of their fire, wishing for De Theiry to appear. It was imperative for him to pinpoint the last resting place of Bengie Slink, and no one else could do it.

On the second morning, Daniel's billy can toppled over with unexpected suddenness, waking the friends with a start. Before them sat what had recently been an elegant Parisian gentleman. Both De Theiry's arms were missing with the remainder of his clothing in tatters.

Although Jesse had not yet been able to see the apparition, he sensed the atmosphere of fear, helplessness and desperation. It was a tangible thing and he could only guess at the turmoil running amok in the unknown place of limbo.

'Show me where the bastard Slink is laid Phillipe. Let's dig him up and throw his rotten bones to his brothers.' Daniel's anger was fast in the rising.

De Theiry looked fearfully about him. He had given his vicious tormentor the slip. But the reprieve couldn't last.

'Come quickly, Daniel. I have such little time.'

He floated down from the tor and Daniel tumbled close behind him with spade at the ready, and Jesse and Zip close at his heels. Tobacco, for some reason, chose to stay by the fire, but there was no time to coax her down.

De Theiry's form slowed over a flat piece of ground on which not a single blade of grass grew, as if the soil had been dosed with an astringent weed killer. De Theiry hovered above the eight foot diameter circle, and looked directly down the length of his body and into the ground below. With his head bent forward, his jaw on his chest, his body like a limbless crucifixion, De Theiry spoke over the corrugation of his double chin.

He's here, directly under my feet, not ten feet down,' and he floated aside for his mortal friends to perform the exhumation, he then looked nervously about, and for good reason.

They all heard Tobacco's startled yelp on the tor as she pelted away, ears flat back on her head, with her body zigzagging frantically left and right, and Bengie Slink's killing clubs pounding the ground close behind her fleeing form. Daniel watched in horror, as the grotesque figure of the profane murderer attempted to kill his dog.

'He is blind to what we are doing here,' De Theiry told them in a hasty whisper. 'Your dog knew he was coming and has led him away. I must go now and help lead that gutter filth yet further.'

'We shall need you to sail with us,' said Daniel. 'You have to join us on the south coast in Fowey. Now, go and save my mutt, and for pity sake be careful, Phillipe. Our friendship apart, you are crucial to the plan.'

'I shall do the very best I can, Daniel. But with this one there are no guarantees.' Daniel looked at Slink's rugged butchery and smiled at his friend in a way he hoped would cover the deep lines of concern.

The returning smile was of true bravery, as De Theiry floated back to the tor before disappearing over the crest.

'Cant see De Theiry yet, but I sure as hell saw Slink,' said Jesse. 'That's one bad boy.' There was no time to lose, and in unison the two men began digging feverishly in the soft soil. Within the hour the first human remains were unearthed and from his pocket, Daniel took a plastic rubble sack and began bagging the macabre relics. It was then they discovered the remains of two bodies, but which one was Bengie Slink?

'Bugger it Danny!' breathed Jesse. 'We can't take both…the friggin' bag's not big enough.'

'Look at the skulls, Jesse. Slink had rotten teeth. I saw them myself when he ran passed my fire. They look like stunted pegs.'

The identification was easy, but they wondered at the force that had shattered the nose and cheek bones of Sergeant Jeremiah Pratt's long dead skull.

'Come on matey,' breathed Jesse, 'let's get the hell out of here. This place is really giving me the creeps!'

Scrambling out of the excavation, Jesse looked down and made the sign of the cross on his chest, and with a dismissive shrug, looked at Daniel. 'Seems the right thing to do, that's all.' And with the ancient skull and bone fragments wrapped securely in the bag, the two men and Zip headed south. They had many miles to travel, and made the heavy decision to leave without Tobacco.

From his dais the Chancellor watched Vincent Wothe with interest, intrigued to know what the league was up to.

From a distance, the clairvoyant had watched the exhumation. Slink, unfortunately had been elsewhere chasing a little dog, and Wothe made his report accordingly. The Chancellor reacted with a wholly-unexpected invitation.

'Let me take you to a place I know you shall find fascinating.' He reached out to place a placatory hand on Wothe's forehead and the medium's world went out like a light. When he woke they were standing in front of two colossal teak doors rising three storeys to a vaulted ceiling of living rock. With a sharp clap of the Chancellor's hands, the doors drew aside on soundless hinges, and the clairvoyant followed his master into The Library of Time. The Chancellor remained by the door and watched Wothe grow small in perspective, as he walked down the aisle, and from nowhere a silent figure stepped from the gloom to meet him.

'I see you are impressed, my friend.'

'I've never seen such a place. I feel utterly privileged,' said Wothe, little knowing who he was addressing.

'Ah indeed, you are privileged. Very few have ever been here.'

'Then I have to ask, why am I here?'

The librarian inclined his head and studied the other's face. 'Let us just say that the Chancellor wishes to put your powers to the test. Somewhere in this seemingly endless vault there is a book containing all the information you need for the success of your mission. Find it and you shall discover the leagues intentions. After all, information is power, and those fully informed are therefore truly empowered.' And with an expansive gesture from outstretched arms, the librarian handed over the floor in silent retreat.

Vincent Wothe closed his eyes and filled his lungs, shutting his mind to the other who moved away to sit in a large wingback chair; the only piece of furniture in the otherwise empty avenue. Dressed in denim jeans and a casual floppy pullover the Devil reclined, opened the book he'd been reading and left Wothe alone to do his work.

Slowly Wothe began homing in. Section-by-section he scanned for readings. Bombarded with auras from countless volumes he moved on, nothing yet strong enough to influence his instinct. Within ten minutes his inner eye saw the glow emanating from his true target and he reached out and extracted 'Myths and Legends.' Finding the book demonstrated his remarkable power. He looked back at the librarian, who made a gesture for him to continue.

He stood examining the book page by page, turning the leaves swiftly until he came to page one five four. Wothe had unearthed the leagues intentions, he had witnessed the exhumation and had watched them head south to the coast. They had Slink's bones and it was now obvious they were going to cast them to the sea. Suddenly he felt as if he was wasting time. Bonner was already way ahead and it was going to be a race to the finish. Wothe couldn't afford another moment's delay, so without courteous farewell began to run the half-mile he had travelled to re-join the waiting Chancellor. In his haste he had turned around and ran full tilt into some form of invisible barrier that propelled him backwards onto his startled backside. The Devil moved up from behind and hauled him to his feet.

'From here to the door are all the books ever written to date, beyond the barrier are books of the future, to which only I am privy.'

Wothe was puzzled. The librarian was talking nonsense. How could it possibly be so? Suddenly remembering his mission he ran towards the doors and the waiting Chancellor, leaving the idiot librarian to his own devices.

'So, his paranormal skills are relatively well tuned,' whispered the devil. 'One day he could prove most useful to me down here.'

When the doors were finally closed, the Devil replaced 'Myths and Legends' then stepped easily through the barrier of time as if it didn't exist. He stood facing the immediate stack of shelves before floating upwards until elevated one hundred feet from the ground. From a lofty shelf he extracted his next choice. Drifting back to the floor he nestled into his chair. A while later he lowered the book to his lap.

'Fascinating,' he said aloud, tapping the cover with is index finger, 'my Chancellor's true nemesis.'

He floated high once more and replaced the hardback copy of 'The Odyssey of Daniel Bonner.'

Bengie Slink was in no mood to parlay. He was on the warpath with the Frenchman once more in sight and at his mercy, so to be recalled without finishing his destructive work was infuriating. However, Wothe was utterly insistent and, at last, his words began penetrating the veil of wild, violent hate in Slink's lost soul.

'They plan to cast your remains into the sea to join your brothers. Neither of us can let that happen. Do you understand what I'm saying, Mr Slink? If they succeed then you shall disappear from this place forever, consigned to a watery grave and timeless damnation.' Slink winced as Wothe's warning hit home. The idea of his bones being exhumed and thrown to the mercy of his vengeful brothers was inconceivable. Slink had grown to love his new calling in slowly destroying the Frenchman, but he also realised the absolute necessity to stop Bonner and his treacherous band; the alternative scenario was not even worth contemplating.

Under a bright moorland moon, Bengie Slink and Vincent Wothe headed south, and from an adjacent plateau, Tobacco, and what was left of Phillipe De Theiry made ready to follow. They had kept Slink occupied long enough. Now they must overtake their enemy and rejoin the league.

The Azura was a fine thirty-five foot recreational fishing vessel, with a stocky beam and proud bow, more than capable of sailing to the Bay of Biscay and back without re-fuelling and Bryony had soon struck a chartering deal with her skipper, Jim Roland. Due partly to the offer of a handsome fee, but equally for the sake of a beautiful lady who's reason for the trip was a birthday present for Daniel. She told the fictitious story of Daniel's loss of his grandfather, in the sinking of his destroyer in the second world war, and that Daniel's life long ambition was to lay a wreath over the war-grave's coordinates. To this, Roland had readily agreed, and Bryony had seen no real harm in the fib. She also noticed with an affectionate smile, how the captain tousled his bashful head with the palm of his hand whenever raising his peaked cap. Jim Roland, like most, was smitten by her presence, and for this she felt a little guilty at the deception.

On the floating pontoon, Daniel and Jesse found Bryony and their new captain loading enough provisions for a week's sailing. Bryony introduced them all and Daniel and Jesse took a liking to the grey-bearded, scruffy looking skipper. His humour was dryer than a cork on a desert sand-dune, and the droll flow of banter had them all laughing. The plastic rubble sack containing Bengie Slinks remains had been tightly sealed, and was stowed in the aft locker, as instructed by Roland thinking it to be the wreath.

'When do we sail?' asked Daniel.

'Tomorrow morning on the outgoing tide,' said Bryony, 'which means this evening we can 'give the town a glancing blow'.....another Roland quote,' she said with a chuckle.

'Sounds like Captain Jim's sayings are a little infectious,' laughed Daniel, but the idea of spending prime time with Bryony was hugely appealing in their wait for De Theiry's arrival.

The Ship Inn was a relatively small low-ceilinged atmospheric and comfortable public house, set back from the town quay along the narrow and winding Fore Street. It had been built in 1570 by John Rashleigh, a famous privateer of the time, and from that time to this the pub had altered little. The master bedroom boasted original hand-carved oak panelling, beams and architectural features, along with the usual history of ghostly sightings. It was this room that Bryony had booked for her and Daniel. Six weeks had elapsed since the episode at the drowning pool, and although her first terrifying experience with the Underworld was no less vivid in her mind, she had come to terms with its reality, with a far greater acceptance than Daniel could have hoped for. He had kept his side of the bargain, and in their private moments had explained in the best way possible, his fateful interface with the Devil's Chancellor and his followers. Had Bryony not been at the pool to see that certain episode for herself, she would quite naturally have doubted Daniel's sanity. She had not put the talisman around her neck precisely because of what he had told her, much to Millington's annoyance. It had also been her idea to return home, and to allow Charles Millington to believe nothing of any note had taken place during her visit to the moor. She had sensed his deep distrust of her account of her rather non-eventful sketching trip, she was lying, but he couldn't say a single word without exposing himself to his true calling, and the deal he had made with the Chancellor. Her continuing level of disinterest in him, was the thing that irked him the most, and he had to keep reminding himself of the coming hundred years in which he was to have with her. It kept him from showing his hand, and one day she would indeed wear the Talisman again, even if he had to force it on her. But Bryony knew Millington's secret, and he would have done well to pay better attention to her marked change in attitude towards him. It was almost all she could do, to prevent actual-bodily harming the man who threatened Daniel. Thankfully his visits to her had become less frequent, and he had given up his once tireless proposals of matrimony. He was going away for a short while to work on a project in the city, and Bryony's heart had risen with the news. She was suddenly able to spend the time she yearned for with Daniel, without having to justify it all to Millington, and without the slightest regret afforded to him, she pursued her greatest wish. It seemed that Millington had inadvertently set her free. That night, Bryony was going to hold Daniel to every lascivious word that had made her blush so deeply. She was in love with him, with every fibre of her being, to the point of aching.

Jim Roland flirted outrageously with Bryony, as they sat in a happy row at the bar, his mop of grey hair becoming more tousled, as copious quantities of Doombar ale disappeared down a seemingly un-slake-able throat. It was an evening of fun with expansive moments of laughter. For a wonderful moment in their lives, none of them cared about the reason for them being there, especially Roland, who had absolutely no idea of what was coming up to bite his arse.

It was arranged that Jesse would sleep aboard the Azura, and when the time eventually arrived, he and Jim wobbled merrily along Fore-Street to the boat and the comfort of much sought-after bunks. Conversely, Daniel and Bryony slipped quietly upstairs, and as the bedroom door closed behind them, the outside world no longer existed. The room was softly lit, with fat wax candles burning on period oak tables either side of the bed at the end of which, Daniel and Bryony stood face to face. This was their time, they had reached this point on several occasions, and it was then that Bryony realised Daniel had never journeyed further. She touched the contours of his handsome face and he the beauty of hers. She stared into his face with a hypnotic gaze, her blue eyes so penetrating that they seemed to reach effortlessly into the secret places of his mind. Then with consummately loving hands she undressed her man.

Daniel stepped unabashed from the shackles of unwanted clothing and she slipped from hers. They were unabashed, naked as new-borns and utterly in love. That ancient room was their universe with the glow of candlelight highlighting the intimate contours of their gender. He was hard, proud and driven as she climbed his body to lower herself onto him, and without restraint they made love, in ways that neither could have imagined with any other.

Early morning found the Azura testing her fenders on the pontoon, beneath the influence of an increasing easterly that had blown in from the open waters of the English Channel.

Roland stood bent over the plotting table in the wheelhouse as Daniel stepped aboard, and he couldn't help noticing an aura of contentment surrounding the big man. Something had happened to Daniel in his time ashore, and clearly for the good. Jim smiled. 'What have you done with the lovely Bryony this morning?' he said, flashing a set of false teeth through a bearded grin.

If only you knew, thought Daniel. He cleared his throat and although a novice to the skills of plotting and navigation, changed the subject with his sudden interest in Jim's calculations of wind, tide and current, laid open on the plotting table. Jim Roland, with due seriousness, reckoned, weather permitting, they would be half way across the Bay of Biscay in less than two days.

'We can sail any time Mr Bonner, just say the word.'

'Just waiting for Bryony and one other party,' said Daniel. 'When they arrive, we can go.'

Daniel knew he was taking a calculated risk. The whole escapade depended on De Theiry making the appointed rendezvous. But what if Slink had managed to destroy the Parisian? The very idea filled Daniel with dread, and if it were so, they would have little choice but to sail on to the inconclusive co-ordinates given in 'Myths and Legends,' and take pot luck. They really needed De Theiry to guide them in, as he had done over Slink's ancient grave, and he prayed silently for the Frenchman's safety.

Jim opened one of the wheelhouse windows, and looked up at the moody gathering of clouds already threatening to blot out the sun. As he did so the blur of Tobacco's rust coloured body leaped through the open frame, passing his startled face by inches.

'What the flying spinnaker was that?' he shouted, stumbling backwards against the plotting table, dragging several charts with him, as he struggled to regain balance. Finding his feet, he looked up to see Tobacco bouncing high with elation against Daniel's thigh. But who in the name of rancid galley slops was the big man talking to?

'We have to leave right now, my English friend,' pleaded De Theiry. And for the first time, Daniel was fully in tune with the limbo spirit and could see him without the convolution of steam and smoke. 'Wothe and Slink are not far behind,' said De Theiry, 'and if we wait too long they will be on us. It was all we could do to get ahead. We must leave immediately or, Daniel, believe me, all is lost!'

Daniel's immediate thought was for Bryony, but the look of terror in what was left of the Frenchman's face, was more than enough reason for drastic reconsideration.

'Jim, we must go…right now if possible.' The urgency in his voice apparent.

'It's like I said, the Azura's ready to leave anytime,' said Roland, puzzled at why laying a wreath should carry such an urgent time scale, not to mention thinking Daniel strange in the least, at talking to himself. But he had been paid handsomely and was prepared to do all that was asked.

The twin Volvo Penta engines had been flashed up and had been ticking over, half an hour before Daniel had stepped onboard. They were warm and willing. Jesse appeared from the lower decks, yawning, yet inquisitive to the commotion. He understood instantly the look in Daniel's expression.

'Jump the pontoon and let go fore and aft if you would,' instructed Jim to the emerging, would-be deckhand, and Jesse frowned. 'That means front and back….blunt and sharp end,' Jim explained.

'That much I do know,' said Jesse, in waspish retort. 'I've watched the repeats of Captain Pugwash you know.'

The laughter was shared only between Jim and Jesse, unaware of De Theiry's presence.

Jesse lifted the mooring lines over the pontoon bollards, and the gap quickly widened between the Azura's side.

'Best jump aboard if you want to come along my friend,' said Jim, his words galvanising Jesse into action. He leaped the increasing divide and clambered onto the deck, grinning inanely as though he had mastered the hurricane hawsers on an ocean-going liner.

'What about Bryony?' he asked. It was a spontaneous question and yet by the look on Daniel's face, Jesse knew there was no time for further delay.

'We're going right now,' and Daniel nodded to Jim, who replied with a regretful shrug of his shoulders as he eased open the twin throttles.

The Azura's screws churned the emerald waters into an effervescent broil, the stern thrust raising her displacement bow effortlessly through the rising swell like a butcher's knife. As her hull glided passed the ancient stone wall of the town quay, Daniel caught sight of Bryony standing aside from a crowd of tourists gathered behind the iron railings. Even from that distance her face was a picture of bewilderment and sadness. She stood motionless, her hand half raised as she watched the man she loved desert her again.

Daniel was about to instruct Jim to come about, but De Theiry was having none of it.

'It is our duty to protect her. Where we are going is no place for Bryony. She will be safer here. They are very close now.'

Daniel looked across the water and saw her walk away, his bellowed explanations lost on the rising wind, and a sadness he had never known swamped him.

The twin Volvo's pushed the Azura through the swell at a tireless twenty knots, but the sea state had risen and was running against them. The deterioration in the weather was nothing to test the Azura's capabilities. Jesse, however was not a happy man, and was soon laying his breakfast as ground bait over the rolling side. He was master in the ways of the moor, but certainly no seaman. Zip on the other hand loved the feel of the ocean beneath his feet. He stood square on the pitching foredeck facing the wind, enjoying every minute of the new experience.

'That dog makes a fine figurehead Mr Bonner,' said Roland, and Daniel chuckled, as they stared forward through the wiper radius of the sea-smattered glass.

In the far corner, De Theiry sat looking back along their co
urse feeling greatly troubled, and with good reason. He could feel the pursuing forces of evil growing stronger, but as the day lengthened it appeared they were still alone.

Captain John was a Fowey-based skipper with long experience at sea; an ex Royal Navy Chief Petty Officer who had served his full time, and was not given to suffer fools gladly. He was a big man with a reputation for speaking his mind, verbally or with his fists. Nor was he given to flights of fancy, or indeed believed in the fanciful. But what came aboard his vessel that day was to destroy all former beliefs.

From below the wheelhouse, he heard the steady beat of what he mistook as some idiot beating on the forward cabin deck, softly at first, but growing progressively louder. No one had permission to be aboard his boat and the sound warranted angry investigation. Descending the wheelhouse stairs, he crept along the cabin deck companionway, until reaching the third and last cabin. He pressed his ear to the door and the drumming stopped. Apart from the creaking fenders against the quay all was quiet, but as he reached for the brass handle it began turning by itself. He stood with fists clenched ready to manhandle any would-be stowaway off his boat with the point of his boot, and without ceremony. The door opened unaided, and in the middle of the cabin deck he saw a huddled form, shrouded by one of the blankets taken from the lower bunk.

Gripping the leading hem, Captain John yanked off the cover with bellowed expletives, designed to terrify whoever beneath. But it was he who received the greatest shock of his life.

Bengie Slink reared up and roared back, with the grave of Cranmere Mire on his breath. Face-to-face man and ghost bellowed, until Captain John's shout shrivelled to a mumble, before dying pitifully in his throat. Terrified, he backed slowly away but Slink followed him out, smashing his clubs into the deck beneath his retreating feet. Spinning on his heels,

John turned and ran. For a big man he made good his escape, racing up the companionway stairwell and into the bridge-house. He hardly noticed the thin loop of human hide thrown over his head from the unseen assailant, but as the strand encircled his neck he suddenly felt no fear. He turned to face the smiling figure of Vincent Wothe. The clairvoyant approached him in a casual manner to make final adjustments to the talisman, as an attentive mother would straighten a tie around her infant's collar on the first day of school.

'I need you to take me to the Bay of Biscay,' he said. 'And we need to go now.'

'Yes sir,' replied John, as if taking an order from a naval officer of the command watch. 'But first we have to take on enough fuel for the crossing.'

'Then get it done, our enemy already has a head start.'

The Sea Eagle glided into position against the fuel pontoon and a frustrating thirty minutes later, the thirty-foot sports cruiser was at last underway. Wothe had chosen wisely. Although smaller than the Azura, the twin engines of the Sea Eagle delivered more power, and with her bow parting the water like a cutlass, Vincent Wothe reckoned, despite the delay, they would be overhauling their quarry within a matter of hours.

Sitting deserted and angry at a table in the quayside bar, Bryony sat puzzled at what to do next when she heard the pulse of the Sea Eagle's engines passing the sea walls as it went to refuel. In a moment of extreme clarity she knew the vessel was somehow part of all that was happening, and she suddenly understood the reason for Azura's sudden departure and her being left behind. The Sea Eagle was Daniel's enemy, giving him good reason for such a hasty departure. And far away, Abdiel, the angel of light smiled upon her.

It was a startled gathering on the quay that witnessed Bryony's head long dive into the clear waters of the harbour. She swam strongly towards the pontooned Sea Eagle and, unseen by those on the foredeck busy with taking on fuel, she climbed the stern ladder and slipped silently on board.

The translucent wake of the Sea Eagle rocked the clusters of craft at their moorings, as she tore through the six-knot speed limit at three times the legal speed. She had exited the harbour and was out to sea before the authorities could react. Irrespective of the mounting swell, she rose and fell with ease under Captain John's competent helming, and Wothe peered constantly into the radar plotter in search of their quarry. Within the hour, the tell-tail blip of the Azura appeared on the far perimeter of the screen and they altered course to follow. The chase was on and they were already running the Azura down. The grotesque apparition of Bengie Slink was hunched low beneath the bow-rails, pointing his killing clubs at the horizon, but no matter how persistent, Vincent Wothe could not persuade the ghost to enter the turbulent water to cross the gap and seize the enemy. It was then he realised that Bengie Slink was petrified of the deep; a revelation he could understand given the legend, but one that had not crossed his mind nor had he counted on. In addition, the sea state had worsened in the open water of the channel, making it difficult for the Sea Eagle to further close the gap.

'They're coming,' said De Theiry over his shoulder, his face crumpled in dismay. 'We must go faster, for if they catch us……..'

Daniel understood they were no longer alone, but couldn't answer for fear of Jim Roland believing he had taken leave of his senses. He had spoken out once, but thought it wise not to push it. He nodded at De Theiry with the most reassuring expression he could muster.

'Any chance of increasing speed?' suggested Daniel, and Jim looked at Daniel as he juggled with the request, then over the pitching stern at the tiny white dot on the stern horizon.

'We are going as fast as safety dictates Mr Bonner.' He flicked his head sideways. 'That wouldn't be the law behind us, would it?'

'Certainly not Mr Roland, but it's bloody important we stay well ahead of that vessel if possible.'

'It's your money Mr Bonner,' he said, pushing the throttles obligingly as far forward as he dared, and the props responded, pushing the boat on with a reassuring surge. He then looked into the radar viewfinder, and the lone blip of the following boat winked at him through the cathode screen, like an emerald star. He turned the wheel five degrees to starboard and set a new course. For almost ten minutes the pursuing vessel appeared to stay on its original heading, but as Daniel gave De Theiry a secretive thumbs-up, Jim came back with bad news.

'She's turning onto our course, Mr Bonner,' and again he pressed his face to the viewfinder. Sure enough the radar confirmed the other's manoeuvre. Again he turned Azura, this time to port, and the shadow doggedly followed suit.

'Not only is she tailing us, but I'm afraid she's gaining. Hold the wheel on this course Mr Bonner; I need a free hand to make a few calculations.' Daniel did as he was told, as Roland lowered his face once more to the viewfinder. For twenty minutes he alternated between chart, radar and binoculars before scribbling in the charts margin.

'If the weather remains constant, our friends should be alongside by midnight tonight.'

From the far corner of the wheelhouse, De Theiry let out a moan of despair and for the first time, Roland heard the strange cry. 'What the fuckin' pitch and roll was that?' he asked scanning the wheelhouse. 'Mr Bonner, this is becoming weirder than when my aunt's bloomers were used as mainsails…care to enlighten?' His tone was deadpan as he ruffled his hair beneath a raised peaked cap, and if the situation weren't so serious, Daniel would have openly laughed. He had to think fast.

'It's a family matter, burial at sea for a set of ancient ancestral bones; last will and testament and all that sort of stuff.'

'So, that's not a wreath in the aft hold, it's a bag of old bones?'

'It is.'

'Then I shall turn about and invite your pursuing family to join us if that's what they so wish.'

Daniel rose to his full height, and then lowered his head, his face just inches from Jim's.

'That wouldn't be a very good idea,' he said.

The latent threat was clear and the Azura's skipper was in no doubt as to Daniel's sincerity.

'What's coming up behind us Mr Bonner?'

'Hell itself Mr Roland…Hell itself.'

'Anything to do with drugs?'

'Not at all, just a twisted son of a bitch who disagrees with burial at sea; bit of a spiritual nutter.'

'Well, why the fuck didn't you say so?' said Jim, though not sure he understood any of it. He pressed forward the throttles to the sea state's limit without breaking the gaze. The two hundred horsepower of marine diesel pushed the Azura forward, splitting the swell in a roll of white water, and astern, poor Jesse laid more solids into the broil.

As the Azura crashed into the oncoming rollers, Zip decided that being honouree figurehead was no longer that appealing. He trotted back to the wheelhouse, and ahead of Azura's starboard bow the western storm clouds darkened.

'We're in for a blow and no mistake,' said Jim. 'This might be what we've been looking for. A craft of comparable size, no matter how fast, is restricted by the swell. Gentlemen, we have a chance.'

Throughout the night the storm continued to hamper both vessels. Jim was tireless between helming his cherished craft, and plotting the other's progress, and the six-mile gap was maintained. He looked astern through a set of night-vision binoculars and stared for long moments at the translucent glare of the pursuing navigation lights. He then took the unprecedented step of extinguishing the Azura's lights, in the off chance they could disappear in the confusion of the storm. But it was soon apparent the pursuing boat was not to be thrown by the ruse. Jim reinstated the lights but reassuringly the distance between the two craft remained constant.

In the early morning of the second day the Brittany coast fell from Sea Eagle's port quarter. They were now sailing due south into the Bay of Biscay and frustratingly no closer to the Azura, but suddenly the Atlantic swell abated and Captain John seized the moment. With Wothe's enthusiastic prompting, he gunned his engines along the Azura's course. And at last the gap began to close.

According to historical maritime charts, the ships, War Piper and Drummer had gone down some one hundred and seventy miles west of La Rochelle, one hundred miles due south from the Azura's current position. Given the wind, tide and current it was a hundred and twenty nautical miles and Captain John knew the Azura had little chance of reaching those vital co-ordinates, before they would be able to board her.

Still the gap closed, until both boat crews could plainly see each others' faces across the ever decreasing range. The image of Bengie Slink gripping the bow-rail with one hand, the killing clubs in the other threw fits of panic into De Theiry, and for the first time Roland and Jesse could clearly see both apparitions through the increased spiritual energy they were expending. De Theiry and Bengie Slink appeared as grey-green transparencies, one cowering behind the chart table of the Azura, the other leading the headlong charge from the Sea Eagles bow.

'Jesus, Mr Bonner, I've seen most things but this takes the weevil-infested biscuit right out of my pudding chute,' and for the first time the metre of Roland's droll tone had gone west on the wind and was something of a high pitch.

'No time to explain,' said Daniel. 'Just keep going.'

'We're not going to make it?' De Theiry moaned.

'We have no option but to keep trying,' retorted Daniel angrily. 'Is there any more we can chivvy out of the engines, Mister Roland?'

'Afraid that's your lot, but the Azura's built like a brick shit-house and can turn on a sixpence if it comes to a battle of manoeuvres. Roland raised his glasses for another look at the pursuing craft, and he chuckled. 'Mr Bonner, no need to worry. I recognise the Sea Eagle and I know Captain John well. He wouldn't do anything to harm me, you, or the Azura. Panic over.'

'Sorry, but here's the bad news,' said Daniel. 'That's not the man you think at the helm. I'll wager a pound to a pinch of De Theiry's snuff, they've nobbled him.'

Roland was a perplexed man. Several days ago he had been happy with his lot. Now he was playing cat and mouse, with a long-standing friend, who apparently wasn't really himself. Forces from the supernatural world were chasing him down, and on board his own vessel stood a poacher going by the unlikely name of Jesse, and a giant called Daniel Bonner, whose immediate aim in life was to guard a wailing ghost, whose wish was to hurl an ancient bag of bones into the sea. If the fat wad of banknotes stuffed inside his shirt hadn't been so damn comforting, he would have taken greater heed of the chill in the pit of his stomach, and turned directly for home. But above all that, Roland was experiencing the ever increasing feeling that he was somehow there to help. No matter how bizarre the situation, action had to be taken. 'I have no idea who De Theiry and his snuff is, but I could do with a big pinch of it myself right now, and no mistake.'

His forebears had all been doughty seafaring men and Jim was no exception. With a set jaw he took the wheel and began the tactical task of outmanoeuvring their pursuers. In different circumstances the Sea Eagle would have been an inspiring sight. The gleaming white of her under-swept bow shining starkly against the backdrop of the storm laden sky, as she bore down on the Azura. Her bows threw out broad wings of spume either side of her hull, like a bird of prey coming in for the kill.

Bengie Slink was a terrifying spectre, and as the gap closed it seemed the Azura was at last at the cutthroat's mercy.

'If that thing comes aboard this boat, we're bloody finished,' Daniel told Roland, who in turn seemed not to have heard the warning. His eyes were fixed on the approaching vessel, his body unmoving as if frozen to the spot. Daniel wasn't prepared to wait. Moving forward he gripped the wheel to take over.

'Take your hand off the fucking wheel, Mr Bonner, just leave this to me,' and Daniel saw the look in the other's calculating eye. The skipper had a few tricks up is sleeve, and would use them with great effect before allowing that thing on the Eagle's bow to ruin his day. It wasn't fear in Jim Roland, but grim determination.

The Sea Eagle moved up on the Azura's stern quarter, and incredibly Roland throttled back to a crawl. Captain John cut his speed to match; the boarding would be easier than anticipated. Slink crouched low for the leap and with clubs at the ready, he very nearly took the leap. Then without warning, Roland pushed both throttles fully open, spinning the wheel simultaneously to starboard. The back thrust pushed Sea Eagle's bows away so violently it took everything Slink had to hang on, and for the first time all aboard the Azura saw fear in his rotten eyes.

'He's scared of the bloody water!' shouted Jesse, and De Theiry looked up with hope.

'We won't be so lucky next time,' shouted Roland, as the Eagle's bows rose in full pursuit. But each time she came close, Roland masterfully drew the other's bows into his churning wake, thinning the water with bubbles and robbing the Eagle of thrust. And all the while, Roland led them ever further south.

Aboard the Eagle, tempers were fraying. Vincent Wothe began ranting, and Captain John's eyes grew wild with frustration and misplaced hate. Beneath the influence of the talisman his mood was murderous. Slink pounded the fore deck with his clubs, and not for the first time looked nervously into the water as the legendary co-ordinates loomed. Captain John began another run, this time at full throttle. He came in on the Azura's port side at suicidal speed and this time Wothe believed contact was inevitable; the end would be brutally quick. But in the final rush, the Eagle hadn't realised what the Azura crew was up to, until it was too late. As she bore down, Daniel and Jesse threw coils of mooring line and fish netting over the stern, directly in line with the Eagle's flying bow and the convolution of strands disappeared miraculously under the keel. At first it seemed the intended entanglement had failed until Captain John's boat suddenly shuddered, before slewing uncontrollably away to port just several metres from the Azura side. The lines had fouled the port prop, and as the Azura cheered the Sea Eagle raged. Another piece of netting then found the sister propeller, and the Eagle's bow dug in low as the following wash lifted her stern high, and she settled dead in the water.

For the first time Phillipe De Theiry left the Azura's wheelhouse and joined the living world on the aft deck. Roland, still unnerved by his mutilated presence, re-took the Azura's wheel and without looking back took a heading south.

'Daniel, its me! And Bryony's voice travelled clear as a bell across the divide. All on board both vessels froze to the sound of her voice. She stood alone on the aft deck, seemingly utterly vulnerable. And Bengie Slink began moving aft, dragging his clubs as he came. Wothe instantly saw the chance. He had a hostage on board, a bargaining chip with which to halt the Azura in her trail, and he wasn't going to waste the opportunity. For a slight man he moved with surprising speed from the flying bridge, and had the girl in his grip seconds later. He dragged her brutally by the hair back to the lower bridge, and those aboard the Azura heard her scream in pain. Slink was almost there, and he was murderous. From across the water they watched Wothe, with all his persuasive powers, stop Slink from clubbing her right there and then. And for Daniel, that was the last straw. Jesse, Roland and De Theiry bore witness to his vengeful anger and before Jesse could react, Daniel had removed his coat and boots, climbed the rail and dived headlong into the water. His overarm strokes parted the water, and on board the Sea Eagle they watched as he powered his way towards them. Bryony saw her chance. Wothe had relaxed his grip on her hair and was watching with interest the events unfolding over the side. A squat CO2 fire extinguisher hung in its cradle just a foot from where she stood, and in a split second she had undone the clasp, yanked it free and swung the bottle directly into Wothe's lower torso. The breaking of his ribs was an audible thing and his shriek of pain and astonishment was heard by all. She was free, and as Daniel had done she sprang to the rail and launched herself over the side, just inches below one of Slink's swung clubs.

The gap between Daniel and Bryony was closing fast, when the sharp retort of a riffle smothered the sound of their splashing. The first bullet hissed over her head and a vicious kick of water appeared miraculously in front of Daniel's face, before the bullet passed harmlessly beneath him. The second hit Bryony's back with a meaty slap and she froze, gasped for air and sank in a swirl of crimson water. And Captain John whooped with triumph, as he pulled back the bolt of his riffle to press another round into the breach. As Daniel's legs disappeared below the surface in a dive, Roland now fully understood the transformation in his former friend. 'The murdering bastard,' he hissed, and from a small locker he took the Azura's flare gun. 'See if you can keep them busy with this,' he said, handing it over to Jesse, who took it willingly. 'I'll turn about for Daniel and Bryony. As if in answer, Captain John's third shot crashed into the woodwork above Jesse's ducking head, and that was enough for the man of the moor. There were no sights as such on the Vari Pistol, so Jesse just pointed and pulled the trigger. With a loud pop and a swoosh the red flare raced over the water in a lazy arc, and to Slink's astonishment, now back on the bows, it flew through his stomach, momentarily illuminating his form like a neon bulb. Surprised but untouched he watched it streak along the length of Sea Eagle's deck to smash through the lower bridge window. Captain John threw down the gun to save his beloved vessel from the resulting fire, as Wothe baled out on deck amidst belching red smoke.

Within a minute, Roland had come about and idled above the water where Daniel had made his dive and seconds later, and with much relief to all on board, Daniel surfaced with Bryony held firmly in his arm. As they were hauled out, blood ran copiously down her shoulder. They laid her on deck and Roland gunned the engines on his new heading, at last they were heading south again.

Daniel would not let go of the girl he loved, and cradled her head in his lap as Jesse studied the wound. 'Jesus, Danny, she was lucky. Looks like a flesh wound, bullet's gone clean through without much tissue damage.

Bryony looked up at Daniels face that couldn't stop smiling, deep relief etched on his face. 'What on earth were you doing on board that boat?' he asked. None of us were expecting that, what possessed you my love.'

'Do you honestly believe I was just going to sit by, and let you have all the fun,'

'But you could have been killed.'

'We all could have if I hadn't taken these.' She opened the palm of her right hand, and there with her index finger through the connecting ring were a small bunch of keys belonging to Sea Eagle's ignition system, snatched when on the bridge. 'But before that, while they were concentrating so hard on you, I remained hidden. Sneaked into the engine room and ruptured the fuel lines as well, I stank of diesel but it was worth it. They would have come to a halt soon enough.' Are you proud of me my gorgeous man?' She flinched at the dull pain in her shoulder as he pressed a bandage from the first aid kit to the bullet hole.

'Totally.' He lowered his face to her's and held the kiss.

'I think she'll live,' said Jesse with a chuckle and moved discreetly to one side. 'but don't keep her too long, Daniel, I need to dress that wound properly.'

It was now De Theiry's turn to be bow lookout. With the Eagle lost on the northern horizon his confidence returned, and at the strike of noon on the third day, the Azura continued at idling speed under De Theiry's enthusiastic direction. Roland turned his boat to the given headings translated by Daniel standing expectantly at the spectre's side. Finally he signalled Roland to cut the engines with a cutting action across his windpipe.

From the aft locker the sack containing Bengie Slink's remains was taken out and without a second thought for ceremony, Daniel hurled the macabre cargo over the side, and all aboard watched the bones sink quickly to the deep.

There then followed a shock wave below the Azura's keel, powerful enough to make them grip the rails, and Bryony held hard onto Daniel. Then a strange stillness descended until Roland broke the silence.

'What the bloody hell was that; a depth charge? I'm setting a course for blighty and a much needed pint or two of Doombar, if that's all the same to you good people...and others?' He side glanced a look at De Theiry.

It was music to their ears, especially for poor Jesse who had never quite lost that grey translucency around his sickly gills, even though the sea had turned to a flat calm.

Three hours later, Sea Eagle came into view, becalmed and seemingly without life. Even at a distance the damage to the superstructure was apparent. Sea slime clung to every surface from the waterline to the very top of her radar gantry and as the Azura idled half a cable to port, the salty vegetable whiff of the ocean and other organic decay crossed the open water.

Roland closed the gap and moved his boat cautiously alongside, nudging his fenders against the Sea Eagle's hull as Jesse looped mooring ropes over the stricken vessel's midway cleats. Once secured, Daniel stepped aboard, alert and wary. The boat appeared deserted as he peered through her shattered wheelhouse windows. The cabin door lay torn from its hinges on the aft deck in splinters. Algae and weed squelched underfoot as if the Sea Eagle had been consigned for years on the ocean floor, before being raised to the surface once more. Crustaceans colonised vast areas of the superstructure, and the twist of time unnerved Daniel.

It took great courage to step into the empty bridge, but Daniel was not alone. Jesse wasn't about to let him have all the fun and with a grateful smile, Daniel led the way through the shattered opening. Inside, the wheelhouse was a complete shambles. The ship-to-shore radio had been irretrievably smashed to pieces along with the navigational equipment, the echo-sounding consul and the radar screen. Every dial and gauge had sea water trapped behind the glass, supporting the evidence that the boat had somehow been dragged asunder. The plotting table was ripped from its fixings, sodden pieces of chart littered the deck, and the companionway leading to the lower quarters was now dark and ominous.

Armed with a torch Jesse had snatched from the Azura's cabin bulkhead, they began the descent, and in the bright beam more evidence of unbridled violence was revealed. Deep gouges scored the teak panelling, as if frenzied swordsmen had swung their killing blades in the confined companionway. Holes had been punched in the wood, made by the last desperate swings of Bengie Slink's clubs, as his vengeful brothers and crew had clambered aboard to drag him down, in the final chapter of the strange legend of the deep. The two men made their way along the corridor, searching every cubbyhole until they stood in the foremost, empty accommodation cabin.

'The boat's clear,' said Jesse with tangible relief. 'But what's with all this seaweed, slime and other stuff? It's just not natural.'

'Nothing we are experiencing here is natural, Jesse. It appears the War Piper and Drummer's ancient decay has somehow infested these decks, a distortion of time, and way beyond my comprehension.'

'Jesus,' hissed Jesse. 'Let's get out of here. What do you reckon, eh Danny?'

Daniel was ready to agree, when a small doorway leading to the cable locker caught his eye.

'Oh Christ, here we go again,' muttered Jesse under his breath.

Daniel placed his ear over the slime covered bulkhead and made a sign for silence. Jesse directed the torch beam onto the door with growing anxiety. The chill of the interior had crawled into his limbs, and he suddenly wanted out.

'What is it, Daniel? What can you hear? Bloody hell, this is giving me the friggin' jelly-wobbles.'

'Shut up Jesse! I can't hear a bloody thing with you rabbiting on.' And Jesse went silent, listening to his own agitated breathing.

'Put your ear against the door.'

'I can hear a sort of buzzing,' whispered Jesse, doing as asked.

'There's something behind here,' warned Daniel.

'Well let's whip the fuckin' door open and get it over with, for Christ sakes.'

Daniel rolled his hands around the slimy handle and on the count of three tore open the door.

The rotted remains of Captain John's body tumbled forward onto Jesse's chest, and with a bellow of revulsion, he threw a solid punch into the Captain's putrid face, knocking the skull backwards over the corpse's shoulders to hang at a grotesque angle on its back. 'Don't fuckin' touch me you bastard!!' The shrill in his voice betrayed his tattered nerves.

Captain John's carcass had been colonised by swarms of buzzing iridescent flies and their fat white offspring. Daniel fought hard not to wretch and swallowed hard.

He saw the talisman and without hesitation snapped the chord from around the captain's distorted neck with a soggy pop. Holding the silver in his hand he immediately felt the tingle of its power crawl up his arm, its magic hunting for his mind.

'Right, let's get out of here, right now, Jesse.'

Without prior knowledge to its power, Daniel would soon have been lost to its spell. He held the talisman dangling by its chord and led his friend out onto the aft deck and into the bright sunshine. With one stride to the rail he dropped the engraved silver over the side. As the talisman hit the water it began effervescing in a spiral of bright bubbles, until the depths took it from sight.

'Where's Captain John?' barked Roland, from the Azura's aft deck.

'You don't want to go down there…he's dead, along with a whole pile of spooky shit,' blurted Jesse, in his indomitably insensitive way.

'I'm afraid Captain John is dead,' said Daniel.

'The whole rotten mess fell on me,' continued Jesse. 'Knocked his fuckin' block off.' He was in mild shock.

Daniel leaped the gap between the boats as he saw the angry bewilderment mount in Roland's eyes. 'Don't misunderstand my friend, Jim. Jesse had a nasty experience down there.'

'I have to go and see for myself, Mr Bonner, you know that.'

'I know, but I warn you, it's not a pretty sight.'

Jim Roland stepped aboard the Sea Eagle and strode passed Jesse who was about to call him an idiot when the poacher noticed the sharp look on Daniel's face. He bit his tongue.

Captain Roland reappeared from the lower decks a few minutes later with a blank expression. His deep water tan faded to a pallor that matched his grey beard.

'Burn it,' he mumbled. 'Send it to the bottom.'

From the Azura they watched, as Roland lit a diesel soaked rag and threw it into the Sea Eagle's wheelhouse. At first there was little more than sooty ghosting on what was left of the already filthy windows, but slowly the flames took hold until the superstructure was an inferno of combusting fibreglass. Roland continued to stand on the aft deck, shielding his face from the intense heat until Daniel went aboard and led him firmly away.

They let go the lines and the Azura drifted from the pyre, and they watched the inexorable death throes of Captain John's boat with morbid fascination, until the last section of its bow slipped below the surface. Slick engine oil clung to the surface, the only evidence that the Sea Eagle had ever existed.

Without saying a word, Roland opened the Azura's throttles and rounded on a course for home, bitter that his friend had suffered such a terrible death under the forces of evil, and Daniel knew the league had another recruit.

As the Azura sailed away to the north, sixty fathoms down something stirred on the seabed. Cleaved and drowned, Vincent Wothe, butchered by the avenging captains, began to move. The talisman had landed on his chest, and not by mere coincidence. He was a cohort, and the Chancellor, recognising his worth had steered the devil's silver through the depths. He had need of him in the future.

Wothe stared unseeing into the impenetrable surroundings of the deep, his dreadful wounds already colonised by sea worms and oceanic bottom feeders. But under the power of the talisman, his misty eyes returned to life as orbs of polished jet. He rose to his feet and in the crushing darkness hung the talisman around his neck, and began the long journey north through the countless canyons, plains and abyss's that stretched away before him. The wreck of the Sea Eagle appeared before him. He floated through what was left of the deck hatch and using the power of the talisman, Captain John rose beside him as a member of the living dead. The Underworld had created a new and terrifying duo that one day would come ashore to seek revenge on the league.

Of Bengie Slink, his reign was over. The captains and crew of War Piper and Drummer had taken him down, fulfilling the curse and putting to an end an episode of family betrayal and murder that had begun centuries ago.

'Beaten yet again, brother Lucifer. What else can you possibly send against Daniel Bonner and his league of friends?'

'Ah! Brother Abdiel, I do not wish Master Bonner dead, in fact, on the contrary. He has become my Chancellor's true adversary, and for that he has escaped my interfering in the matter.'

'But surely, brother Lucifer, he cannot have two guardians from either side of the coin.'

'No, brother Abdiel, I am not his guardian, but the more he destroys that which dwells in my old world, then new and more terrible creations shall take their places. My kingdom is in need of a clearing out the old guard.

So be warned, there now comes a new breed that you have little idea of just how terrible...brother of mine.'

I the Scribe felt the cold hand of dread grip the hall of souls, and Abdiel's complacency, held by the familiarity of what he knew about Lucifer's world, was shaken. He was using Bonner as the hand of change. For those that think no evil, it was a worrying prelude of what was to come.

'Just for the record,' and Lucifer looked directly at me. 'My Chancellor sends forth the hound from hell. So let us see brother, is Bonner the one?'

'You tell me this, brother Lucifer. You divulge your current plan. Have you forgotten the code?

'No, brother. Just re-inventing it.'

It had taken several years of recovery, but Phillipe De Theiry was back, his apparition re-generated in stature and radiance. Slink's remains had long ago been cast down to his brothers, and now the Frenchman was back with his much-missed Parisian aplomb. Daniel was the first in the league to welcome him back, not only as a friend, but an invaluable weapon in their arsenal. The Underworld had left them mostly in peace as wars were raging across the globe, genocide, famine, flood and drought, not to mention a catastrophic collapse in the world's economy, had gainfully employed the multi-national emissaries from Hell. And during that welcome respite, Daniel and Bryony had created an unbreakable bond, so powerful that it surprised even the Chancellor.

Notwithstanding his growing frustration, Charles Millington had exercised uncommon restraint, obeying strict orders not to interfere. The Chancellor needed Daniel and Bryony's love complete, then he could watch the inevitability of its collapse, with Bryony retaining her youth, as Daniel Bonner grew old in the inevitable avalanche of advancing years. Then he would broker a deal, turn back time and give Daniel the same one hundred years he had offered Millington with the woman he loved; in exchange for his soul, naturally.

As for Millington, he was expendable. He already had that particular individual, to do with just what he liked. The plan was devious and foolproof. In the meantime he would further test the mortal, and should he succumb the Chancellor would triumph anyway. It was a no lose situation.

Tobacco sat beside Daniel as he hunkered crossed legged in front of the fire. De Theiry sat opposite.

'I bring you good and bad news my English friend,' said De Theiry, after much snuff taking. 'Bryony has allowed you into her heart. She loves you like no other, as I know you do her.'

'Ok Frenchy, that takes care of the bad news, now give me the good.'

For a moment, De Theiry looked puzzled. Daniel chuckled as the Frenchman remained serious.

‘The British humour hasn’t much improved throughout the ages,’ sighed De Theiry through a monstrous pinch of ground tobacco, and with a watery sniff and a monstrous flouncing of his handkerchief, he continued.

‘As I say, she loves you, but the ways of a woman are varied and often complex; though speaking as a Parisian of course, not so difficult to understand. You have wealth and yet she wants nothing of it. You have a lust for adventure of which she is willing to share, no matter how dangerous. But there remains one ingredient in your love, that so far you have not offered.’

Daniel looked up from the flames.

‘Stability my dear boy, good old-fashioned stability is what she needs. How can a woman feel secure with a man, who lives his life as a recluse out here on the moor? A man she has to track down each time she seeks comfort, a man who then leads her into danger with the Devil’s Underworld. She is a woman Daniel, a fine woman who carries the mark of the De Theiry’s. Therefore, it can be of no surprise that I am utterly biased.’

De Theiry applied yet another pinch to his nostrils with a gargantuan sniff, underlining the point most adequately.

‘I cannot tell you what to do. However, if you continue to leave things as they are you may lose her. Mark my words, Daniel, it is the truth. Create a more concrete future, convince her of your sincerity, and enjoy your lives together as you deserve.’

‘Consider your words marked my Parisian friend…thanks Frenchy.’

‘Perhaps! But when was the last time you told her you loved her?’

Daniel had to think about that one. ‘She knows I love her.’

‘Yes, but when did you say it?’

‘You know what? To my embarrassment, I can’t remember.’

With an accusing inclination of De Theiry’s head, Daniel watched the apparition fade. He had made a point, and made it well.

Daniel remained unmoving by the firelight. What could he possibly offer Bryony? The moor was his chosen way of life, shared only in part with the girl he loved. But due to the Frenchman's warning, he became suddenly aware that, that very love could fail. De Theiry was not one of the modern age, however, he was clearly no fool when it came to matters of the heart. Daniel would need to think long and hard.

As the sun rose the following morning, Daniel stretched his arms as if to embrace the eastern flow of light, and suddenly he hit on a solution. Jerry Green languished with his guardian sister Florence in Bristol, the poor man vowing never again to set foot on the moor, let alone in Delamere. Through no fault of his own, Artefacts of Ages lay untouched through years of neglect. Daniel had pondered the idea of securing the property some while ago, but had since done nothing about it. He would take it on, lock stock and barrel in a rental agreement, and in so doing, he and Bryony could enjoy an existence in both worlds. He would be on the doorstep of his beloved moor; Bryony could have her studio in what was once the shop, and together they could expedite forays onto the wild plains at their leisure. Given De Theiry's warning it was a matter that needed addressing sooner than later. The thought of losing Bryony was beyond imagination, and besides, the chill of last winter had crept into his bones deeper than ever before. It was time to come in from the cold.

Florence Green appeared considerably less hostile as she opened the door. It may have been in small part something to do with Danny's groomed appearance, but in reality, more so because of Bryony's presence.

'Come in my dear,' she said directly to her alone, and Bryony returned the invitation with a radiant smile. 'Jerry's been expecting you,' and she ushered them in, ignoring Daniel until he stood alongside. Daniel looked down and smiled at the roly-poly lady with severely scraped-back hair, ending in a tight bun perched on the top of her freckled head.

'You know my rules Mr Bonner,' she said quietly. 'He's never quite recovered from his ordeal.' She took him a little to one side. 'He's taken to muttering, as if someone's with him. He's OK but don't upset him! Clear?'

'Crystal,' said Daniel, with the same answer as his last visit. He bent down and gave her a kiss on an instantly blushed cheek.

'Inside with you, you big ox,' she said, with an ineffectual cuff to his broad shoulder. 'Just remember what I said.' And her smile momentarily beamed like a ray of sunshine. The idea that life had tainted her complexion, soured her disposition and sharpened her tongue, was a falsehood, and Daniel realigned his first impressions.

Jerry's face creased with delight as he greeted them in the hall, and after a brief backslapping embrace with Daniel, he rounded on Bryony, administering a huge hug.

'My God, you're a lucky devil Daniel. She hasn't aged a bit. I'm sure you don't deserve her. I think living in Bristol would suit her better,' he said, rapidly flicking his brows up and down, before ending the outrageous invitation with a grin.

He led them along the hall and into the kitchen. The smell of home-baked scones resting on top of the AGA, greeted them like an aroma from heaven. Jerry's sister's baking skills were legendary.

There followed an hour of easy talk and Florence realised just how much of a tonic the visit was for her brother. She busied herself around the kitchen while listening to their conversation, and for the first time, despite his visits over the years, felt embarrassed by the way she had so mistrusted Daniel. As for Bryony, she was and always had been a darling, from her very first time at the house. When she looked at her and Daniel there was no doubt they belonged together. Bryony needed a man that could give her love, mental stimulation and a sense of adventure. Tedium, Florence guessed, was something that neither could live with. These were two people who would forge their own life, without the constraints of conformity and routine, and when they laughed it was if the world laughed with them. It was a good match.

If she had begun to think well of Daniel, he suddenly became her absolute favourite as plans to rent the shop were voiced across the table. For a moment Jerry was dumbstruck until a lop-sided grin threatened to part his face. He drew a quick breath of excitement, and mopped the dribble from the corner of his mouth with an unnecessary apology. Then the smile was gone and he grew thoughtful.

'Could never go back there my old friend,' he began with a vacant expression. 'I still wake bathed in sweat, nightmares chasing me to consciousness, and even then I lie awake listening to every sound of the night.' Again he went silent. He closed his eyes and squeezed the lids tightly shut. Suddenly they opened with the rebirth of an accompanying smile. 'Now, thankfully, I shall never have to return, I can't express my gratitude enough old friend.'

Everyone around that table found themselves matching Jerry's jubilant grin, and Daniel slid a hefty cheque across the table in down payment of rent and the cost for the necessary legalities, along with fifty per cent of all 'Rags to Riches' royalties to date, less expenses.

Jerry rose slowly from his chair and with tears in his eyes, embraced Daniel. Eventually they broke the hug of mutual love and shook hands. Further words were redundant, but the joy in Jerry's face continued, reminding Daniel, that if used well, the power of money was certainly no bad thing at all.

Eventually, amid mild protestations, Daniel and Bryony made ready to leave and as Jerry said his fond farewells to Bryony, Florence pulled Daniel once more to one side. 'Daniel Bonner, I can't tell you what this means to Jerry. I still don't know what really happened down there in Delamere, nor do I really wish to know. But what you've done here today, is the best thing that's happened to my brother in these last distressing years. Words can't thank you enough. This house is and always will be, open to you both, so don't you dare let us down.' She reached up and cupped Daniel's face as a tear rolled from her eye. Again Daniel bent forward and kissed her cheek. Apart from the evocative aromas of home baking he realised his liking for this formidable battle-axe was completely genuine. Jerry couldn't be in better hands, and perhaps one day, when all had been restored, they might even brave a visit to Delamere. At least they could live in hope.

The Chancellor sat high on his dais, looking down at Charles Millington who appeared hugely unhappy. The mortal had asked for a meeting, and the Chancellor had begrudgingly granted audience. The unearthly cohorts appeared like phantoms along the causeways, and with demonic eyes, watched Millington as he made his plea. To ask favour in the underworld was tantamount to weakness. And the creatures were no friend to weakness.

'I want Daniel Bonner dead,' Millington whinged. 'You granted me one hundred years to be with her, but fifty of those may be wasted if she continues to stay with him. Even now they make a home for themselves in the old shop and it seems he now has a great deal to offer, including money. He has overcome his hate of wealth, won over the power of the Talisman, twice escaped the deadly Tarquills and destroyed the so-say invincible 'Bruinscrofa'; as for the dread Mr Slink, well, dare I say more? For two years now he has been left in peace, to create a bond of love that even after his death, may take many more years to unravel, if ever at all? Give me something to destroy him with my all powerful Chancellor. Let me oversee his destruction.'

For long moments the Chancellor stared down at Millington. His eyes were wide, his fists were clenched and he shook with rage. He rose from the throne and towered over the now shrinking human form. He became metamorphic, his body bulged, undulating like a sack of fat maggots and his lower jaw hung open, crowded with fangs and strands of flesh, his skin scabby and livid, redder than the heat in his very hell, and in the creases between the scabs, rivulets of yellow discharge flowed freely.

Millington sank to his knees like crumpled paper. Drool splattered his cowed head and the copious flow from his expunging bladder, steamed around his legs on the hot rock. The army enjoyed again the human trait of urination when petrified, but dared not be loud. The Chancellor's rage was complete.

'You dare remind me? You excuse for life!' his voice rumbling like a thousand watt base, and the detestable stench of his breath quickly reduced Millington to tears. His terrible jaws open in readiness to snatch the mortal's head from his cowering body, and would have done so had it not been for the fact that Millington, regrettably, still had his uses. Exercising the utmost restraint, the Chancellor returned to his mortal form and sat again on the throne.

With a clap of his hands, he summoned one of his pets from a dark opening at the end of a selected causeway, and the chamber held its breath. For minutes an expectant hush took precedent, until all those that dared look up saw eyes of fire coming at them along the avenue. Even Millington's curiosity got the better of him and he turned his fearful head, and then looked hurriedly away. He heard the beast draw close and truly believed his shocking end had been orchestrated. He listened to its final approach until it was so close that he could feel its hot breath on the back of his lowered head, and Millington wished, more than life itself, that it would end quickly. Millington had never truly understood the ramifications of selling his soul. In Hell, it was never over.

'Millington,' rumbled the Chancellor. 'Raise your snivelling head and feast your eyes on my little pet.'

Millington dared not disobey, and looked straight into the furnace eyes of the Demon Dog, an abominable vision, a hound the size of an adolescent bull-calf, with a dark shaggy mane surrounding a head the size of a bear, and six-inch canine teeth standing sentinel to a throat that could devour a horse in one sitting. It waited, ready for the command to feed, and the mocking army of freaks unilaterally shuffled and slithered below, with death on their minds.

'The hound is yours Millington, to be let lose upon your sworn enemy. Use it well for I shall give you no other. I also want revenge, but should you fail with this outrageous pet of mine then we can always revert to the original deal.' He leaned forward. 'See how charitable I can be, Mr Millington? You're quite right,' he continued, 'the longer he lives the less time you and your woman shall enjoy together. Now go and get this matter finished.'

With a dismissive wave, the Chancellor and the greatly-disappointed cavern watched the uneasy Millington and the Demon Dog pass through a portal set in the base of the dais, the fast highway to the upper world.

For the Chancellor it was clear. If the Demon Dog failed to kill Daniel Bonner then the original plan would take effect. The schedule of events may not be to Millington's liking, but then he was merely a pawn in the great game. Besides, the league had been left in peace for too long. It was time to remind them that the Underworld was still in command.

'Mark it so,' the Chancellor growled. And I the faithful Scribe, did his bidding.

The League stood as one facing the shop. Jesse made an appraisal with the eye of a skilled builder, his chosen profession before discovering his true calling as a poacher. De Theiry, showing off, floated back and forth through the window, and Bryony stood next to her man applauding the show. Her happiness seemed to radiate from her very core. It infected them all. Daniel had told her of his grand scheme and the very day she thought would never happen, had arrived.

‘Is this truly what you want, my sexy man?’ she whispered the question close to his ear. He looked down and his love showed in his smile. She looked exactly the same as when she had walked up the hill to his camp picking flowers that late summer’s evening ten years before. Saving her from the drowning pool had been one of the finest days in his life. This was another. As promised he was coming in from the cold, with the only woman that had ever taken his heart.

‘I can’t think of anything I would rather be doing,’ he whispered. She inhaled deeply. ‘I love you, Daniel Bonner, more than you could ever know. Now show me our new home.’

The door was unlocked and thrown open. Tobacco and Zip couldn’t restrain themselves and dashed inside, tearing around as if demented with Zip playing Bambi on ice, trying to get a grip on what was left of the polished floorboards. It was his piping squeal that had them running to find him gnashing at a splinter in his paw. The damage to the majority of the floor reminding them that there was plenty of work to do before any future dreams were fully realised. Fortunately for Zip the splinter was superficial.

With Daniel’s arm around Bryony’s shoulders, her’s around his waist, they paused for a moment and spared a thought for Jerry.

Within two days the shop was a different place. Not many curios or artefacts had survived the blunderbuss blast, and the waste skip outside was soon brimming. The few salvageable pieces had been taken to the vault and once cleared, Jesse had assessed the true damage. The ceiling needed numerous Acro props to support it as ‘Bruinscrofa’ had been close to causing catastrophic failure of the oak beams, some of which remained near to collapse. Little wonder the insurance company had been so evasive. Most of the damage could never have been orchestrated by the gun alone. Whatever carried a question mark with the underwriters was not necessarily payable, despite the exorbitant premiums.

One by one the broken beams were removed, with Daniel and Jesse heaving replacements into position. It was hot and dirty work made humorous by De Theiry’s ineffectual help. He went through all the motions. He even broke into a sweat, and yet had no bodily effect whatsoever. It was all Daniel and Jesse could do to prevent outwardly laughing.

'Nice one, Frenchy, you're doing fine,' prompted Daniel, assuming an appropriate expression of encouragement. Jesse managed a hard-won, stoic silence, and when Daniel's eyes were on him, he pointed with his chin at the next task to hurriedly change the subject.

The splintered floorboards were carefully lifted and turned over creating a floor as good as new. Bryony had volunteered to scrub the office walls and ceilings and painstakingly laboured at the task with buckets of disinfectant and bleach, removing all traces of blood from the walls, stone stairs, and vault. It was in the vault that Daniel found her beavering away undaunted, and his heart reached out to her. Despite the arduous nature of the task, she remained the most captivating thing he had ever seen. Lovingly he removed her protective shower cap, rubber gloves and a workshop coat many sizes too big for her slender frame. He then led her back up into the shop.

Together they stood at the bottom of the stairs leading to the two bedrooms which, until that point, had been strictly out of bounds until the repair of the beams and ceiling had been completed. Taking her by the hand he led her to the master bedroom. They stepped in and Daniel closed the door. Fresh linen covered the large bed and a vase of flowers stood on the central table. Bryony smiled kindly at the clumsy display, fully guessing it was Daniel's work and amorous motives.

'What about Jesse?' she asked, her voice suddenly taking on an uncontrollably husky tone.

'I sent him to the Pink Pig. Gave him the afternoon off, and that my darling just leaves you and me holding the fort, and hopefully a great many other things.'

'Hmm, you randy ruffian, and what else indeed would you like to hold?' And within moments she had her answer. Daniel led them naked into the existing En Suite, the tiles and fittings sparkling as a result of his fervent labours. The walk-in shower, apart from Daniel, was the most inviting thing Bryony had seen that day, and together they stepped into the steaming torrent. They washed each other's bodies with loving and exploratory intimacy and when they eventually stepped out Daniel lifted her warm wet body in his arms and carried her to the bed. He sat on the edge as Bryony knelt astride him. She lowered herself wholly and deeply onto him and they groaned in tandem for that moment where they gave each other all and everything. He then stood. She pressed her heels into the small of his back moving skilfully to the rhythm of his body as he strode wantonly around the room. Erotic senses pulsed throughout her lower body until she felt she might explode. She held his hunting mouth to the erect nipples of her breasts, her moans loud in his ears as he laid her on the bed without breaking the union. They were adrift in the heaven they were creating and together they felt the sudden flood of his seed deep within. They looked into one another's eyes and laughed through sweet, ragged breath. And as they lay together in each others arms, the fertility of her womb and the strength of his count joined as one in the creation of new life.

The Pink Pig was exactly as Daniel remembered. Nothing had changed from his days as a hedge fund speculator. He showed Bryony where he and Tony Windrow used to sit and celebrate, and Bryony noticed a distinct shift in Daniel's eyes at the mention of the other's name. It saddened her that his life should suffer under the burden of hatred and yet fully understood the reasons why. He had travelled a long journey as an honourable man, but would gladly relinquish that title each time Windrow was concerned. However, he had come full circle, and arrived back, now with Bryony at his side, in unbreakable companionship.

Jesse, with Zip at his feet and Tobacco sitting likewise made room for Daniel and Bryony's arrival at the bar. Conrad Sweet, who had ministered Tobacco's injuries long ago, felt inclined to invite himself to join the group, to which he was made most welcome. Even Mrs Tucker, owner of the Out Of Town Store, muscled in and flirted unabashed with Daniel, despite Bryony's presence. Twice Daniel and Bryony caught each other's eye and grinned discreetly at the plump lady's advances, as the unseen De Theiry made faces of unfair revulsion behind her back.

'That Frenchman can be a bugger at times,' laughed Daniel in Bryony's ear.

'What Frenchman?' interrupted Mrs Tucker, looking salaciously about after hearing the remark…a Frenchman in her midst, how wonderful? Which one was he?

For the following week the group slipped seamlessly into village life with acceptance and acquaintances being reaffirmed, and Daniel wondered at the social somersault he had willingly allowed himself to take.

The Pink Pig offered comfortable accommodation for Jesse who greatly enjoyed a private room with hot and cold running water, visited none too discreetly by Mrs Tucker, who couldn't quite understand why Jesse's accent wasn't quite that of the Parisian he had professed to be. As for Daniel and Bryony the deserted shop was Utopia.

Within two weeks they had all been welcomed by Delamere, until on one blustery afternoon Jesse, having taken much sought after refuge in the Pink Pig snug, overheard a murmured conversation between a couple of local hill farmers talking in the main bar. After ensconcing himself to enjoy a quiet moment with a daily newspaper, not to mention the odd pint, he had remained within earshot.

'Ever since that lot have come to town old man Jenner has lost three sheep out on the moor. All he found were a few bones and a bloody patch where something had eaten its fill and more. It's too much of a coincidence if you ask me; and let's not forget what happened to poor old Jerry Green. That Bonner bloke was involved then, and you know what? I reckon he could be now. I don't like the smell of it.'

'Aw! Shut up Dave,' replied his drinking partner, 'you've been reading too many horror stories.'

'Perhaps, but we shall see.'

The conversation was enough for Jesse to take it to Daniel who listened with interest. Had the Chancellor and his demons returned, or was it merely a rogue dog? It was time once again to consult the French oracle.

The following day, Bryony announced that she was going back to fetch the first of three loads from her old studio. She had the air of a young and excited schoolgirl, and for good reason. The glass in the windows of the shop had been replaced, the interior walls had been first coat whitewashed and the floorboards stained with a rosewood varnish. Although the repair bill was high, it was Daniel's deepest pleasure being able to pamper Bryony's every design and architectural wish. The shop had been transformed into the finest studio and gallery she could ever have wished for. Apart from the installation of four rows of ceiling mounted designer lighting, the gallery itself was achieved with very little further modification.

However, despite their jubilant mood, Daniel felt a little guilty for not volunteering to help transport the vital studio equipment. But he had his motives. Firstly he needed to re-organise the machine workshop in the vault, remove the dust-covers and boot-start the machinery. It would be a wonderful surprise for Bryony; after all, a workshop was vital for the construction of armatures, picture frames and all matter of what have you, that an artist may need.

It was agreed that she would go alone, and that her brother Peter would help her on arrival, and follow her down in another loaded vehicle.

Like the loss of sunlight she had gone with a loving kiss, and for a short while Daniel felt empty along with that persistent feeling of guilt tugging at his thoughts. He hadn't mentioned the second and more serious reason for staying behind with the plan of investigating the sheep killings during her three-day absence. It was probably nothing of concern, and therefore there was little reason to worry Bryony unduly, but he had to find out for his own peace of mind. It had been arranged with Jesse, always the willing conspirator, and early the following morning they set out.

In less than a day's hike from Delamere, they were alerted to Zip and Tobacco's distant barking. As normal the two dogs had led the way and raised the alarm. What the two men found was as the hill farmers had described in the Pink Pig. A bloody patch dark with age covered the ground. A severed hoof and the sporadic tufts of wool were all that remained of the animal. All else had been taken. The two men dropped to one knee and studied the ground.

'Could be poachers, Jesse, doing the butchery out here to save having to do it elsewhere?'

'This is the work of no poacher, Daniel. This has all the hallmarks of a wild animal and no mistake. Look at the random area of the kill. Whatever took this sheep, tore it to pieces, scattering the body parts over a wide radius.'

To anyone else, Jesse's analogy would have sounded dramatic, but in his heart, Daniel knew it was an accurate assessment.

'Any ideas?' he asked.

'Not yet matey, but I have a feeling we're going to have to treat this one with the respect it deserves. A very big animal did this.'

'Just one? Perhaps there's a pack.'

'No Daniel, my guess this is the work of a big loner.' He studied the surrounding area with a discerning eye. 'If it were a pack there would be opposing scrape marks in the ground as they tugged the carcass in different directions. Look for some soft ground without grass,' said Jesse. 'We need a print.'

The two men separated to make a larger sweep and before long, Jesse had found what he'd been looking for. He called Daniel to his side.

Look here. 'Look at the size of this fucker.'

Daniel stooped beside his friend who had spanned his big hand over the mark which barely covered the impression.

'Bugger, Jesse! What the Hell made that?'

'Like I said, Daniel, it's something big that deserves respect.'

'Is it a cat?'

'Canine, and carrying a lot of weight with the biggest paws I've ever seen. It's not natural.'

'You know what I'm thinking, Jesse.'

'I know exactly what you're thinking. I think our nasty little friends are back.'

The warmth of their evening fire was familiar and comforting, surrounded by the much-missed open space after being cooped up in Delamere town. It reminded Daniel that living on the edge of the moor was essential to his sanity, a key factor in his and Bryony's future. And yet on the very moor he so loved, something bad was brewing. They both sensed it. It was time to summon the snuff-addicted Parisian.

Since the run in with Bengie Slink, Jesse had thankfully been able to see De Theiry's apparition, and Daniel was now able to communicate his wish for their meetings by power of thought alone. He shut his eyes as he mumbled the Frenchman's name, and the ghostly form appeared before them. This was something Jesse had not experienced, and he sat quietly, in awe of his friend.

'Welcome Phillipe,' said Daniel, as his eyes re-focused, and De Theiry raised a nonchalant eyebrow, followed, naturally, by a large pinch of dust to the tip of his nose. This would have normally taken forever. But that night, De Theiry appeared to be in something of a hurry.

'Mortal friends, you have company,' he told them snapping the lid shut. 'Its bad company I'm afraid, and it's out here on the moor with us now.'

Suddenly, De Theiry's eyes rolled away to the back of his sockets showing only the whites, and Daniel realised he was in the struggles of supernatural divination.

Jesse looked sideways at Daniel, who in turn never once removed his gaze from De Theiry's face. Slowly De Theiry came back to them.

'The Demon Dog is here, and nothing is safe. It hunts as we speak, led by Millington, and it is you they seek, Daniel. Normally its hunts alone, but this time it's different. This human cohort controls its every move and has drawn you out to investigate the killing of livestock.'

'Millington!' hissed Daniel. His fist tightened and blood drained from his knuckles into luminescent peaks.

'Is that the fuckin' tosser you told me about who tried to win Bryony over?' asked Jesse.

'The very same.'

'Indeed,' De Theiry confirmed, 'though why Jesse refers to him as one, who, whilst in the throes of procreation throws things about the place, utterly eludes me.'

Daniel and Jesse exchanged glances, just managing to catch the laughter that threatened to disrupt the severity of the moment.

'Any advice Frenchy?' asked Daniel, giving Jesse a severe jab in the ribs, and making his eyes glisten with tears. Jesse checked himself.

De Theiry looked at Daniel in a manner as never before, his expression etched with lines of sadness.

'Sharpen the Devil's Dagger, Mr Bonner. Hone it to a stiletto. The carved splinters I want you to give to Jesse. He will know what to do.'

'Bloody hell Frenchy! That little riddle sounds serious.'

'It is, Daniel; save your English humour for another day and listen.'

'OK, Phillipe…go on, and I promise to listen.'

De Theiry noticed Daniel's face now held the appropriate expression of sincerity and continued.

'You must leave this place right now. Do not linger, just go.' All De Theiry's pomposity had been replaced with genuine concern, perhaps even fear, but not for himself. 'From now on do not venture onto the moor alone. Work as the League; remain most diligent and live to fight another day. Now go!'

'What do you see, Frenchy?'

'Death, Daniel. I see death.'

'Hmm, well you've seen that before, eh!'

'Your death, Daniel…it's yours,' and the look of sadness returned to crowd his eyes. Normally De Theiry would part with some sort of civil nicety, but that evening was different. Suddenly he was gone.

'Blimey!' exclaimed Daniel, 'Never seen him like that before.'

'Look, Danny, I don't want to be an alarmist, but I found that warning a bit fuckin' dire.'

‘Don’t worry; he’s said things like that before.’

‘Yeah…but did you see the look on his face?’

‘Don’t worry, Jesse. It’ll be OK, trust me.’

Preoccupied with their discussion, neither had noticed how skittish Tobacco and Zip had become. Constantly they stared, growling into the darkness until suddenly the humans got the hint. As one they stood, dampened the fire and began the long trek home. Hardly an hour had elapsed before they heard the first howl from hells hound, faint with distance, but the second was decidedly nearer.

‘I don’t suppose you’re somehow related to the Baskerville family by any chance matey- boy?’ snorted Jesse, and as one they increased pace, and side by side, led by the animals, they began to run.

The lights of Delamere winked invitingly across the last tortuous mile, and behind them Charles Millington raced down their trail, struggling to keep up with Demon Dog’s ground-eating gait.

By the time Daniel and Jesse had entered the high street, they had no idea how close a call it had been. With the animals inside, the shop door firmly shut, they slumped to the floor, firmly on their backsides, with tired legs straight out in front, as they drew heavily for breath.

‘Well, at least we know what we’re up against, Jesse. Did you see it?’

‘No, but I sensed it was fucking close.’

‘Are you with me on this one Jesse, or do you want to step away? I’d fully understand if you do.’

It was only the second time Daniel had seen anger towards him in his friend. The first was in the pillbox. He could see the affront in Jesse’s eyes. He was without question staying for the fight. They rose to their feet and looked through the window for any sign of life. Satisfied the coast was clear they moved deeper into the interior.

After several oversized slugs of Scotch the two men, with double recharged glasses in hand, descended into the vault and Daniel set the ‘Bruinscrofa’ tusk on the workbench. He began marking out a design for the handle and blade, and once satisfied with the overall proportions he threw the light switch, and after another monumental nightcap, they retired to their rooms.

The spare bedroom resonated to Jesse's snoring, not that Daniel noticed as the effects of fatigue and whisky made a lullaby marriage. However, below in the shop, Tobacco and Zip were alert and on guard. The hours of darkness passed without incident until Tobacco froze in her basket. Something was looking in at them through the glass. With an impressive ridge of hackles she walked stiff legged and growling towards the window, and once on the plinth, she and the Demon Dog locked eyes. Acrid smoke curled from its eyelids like expensive cigars and Tobacco sat mesmerised. Zip, however, forever the ball of fighting canine muscle, slammed into the pane. It shook Tobacco from her trance and kick-started a cacophony of excited barking. Outside, Demon Dog curled back its top lip. Zip and Tobacco did likewise in an attempt to match the intruder's deadly row of killing teeth. It was a valiant but woefully inept attempt, and yet a second later Demon Dog had gone. Believing they had won, Zip and Tobacco stood as heroic guardians for the remainder of the night with their masters snoring loudly above.

The following morning, Daniel brewed a large jug of coffee and shouted upstairs for Jesse to get his fat, lazy arse out of bed. He then descended into the vault. Despite the whisky he was pleased with the pencilled design he had drafted on the tusk, and with a buzz of machinery he began crafting. The material was a great deal tougher than he had expected and soon the bandsaw blade needed changing, as wisps of acrid smoke from the blunted teeth snaked into his nostrils.

An hour later, Jesse joined him, and, despite a set of bloodshot eyes, a furry tongue and dehydrated brain, he was duly impressed with the initial craftsmanship. Daniel was fashioning the tusk as an exhibition piece, and the attention to detail showed.

'Zip and Tobacco are acting a little strange,' said Jesse, after swallowing another mouthful of coffee. 'They're just sitting on the sill, staring out the window as if expecting something to happen. Called them away but they took no notice.'

Daniel stopped carving. 'Come to mention it I noticed they hadn't eaten their supper last night; it was still in their bowls this morning. Perhaps we had a little visit when we were deep in the land of nod. Let's take a look.'

Both animals, although glad to see their respective masters, were reluctant to break their gaze from the window but quickly followed the men outside. It was Zip who found the single strand of coarse hair lying on the pavement. It would have gone unnoticed, but through his dog's direction, Jesse spotted it immediately. After a brief examination he handed it to Daniel, who rolled the resilient strand between his thumb and forefinger.

'Reckon we had a prowler last night, Jesse. No wonder the animals are acting up.'

'I think you should get on and finish that little toothpick of yours, and the sooner the better, chummy boy. Don't know why, but I suddenly feel very uneasy.'

Together they ushered the animals back inside, closed the door and went back down to the vault.

It was late in the afternoon when Daniel emerged from the workshop clutching the fruits of his labour, and Jesse was highly impressed. The handle had a solid ergonomic feel and a sure grip, the twelve inch blade perfectly balanced, heavy at the hilt for strength and tapered to a stiletto for effortless penetration.

'Nice bloody work,' Jesse kept saying, as he made a thoroughly critical inspection. 'I reckon this could pierce a sheet of mild steel,'

'De Theiry told me that you would know what to do with the off-cuts. I've left them in a pile on the workbench. They're all yours Jesse.'

'Nice one.'

'Go on then you old bugger, spill the beans. What's the big secret?'

'Patience big man, you'll see soon enough.'

From a rocky crag overlooking Delamere, Charles Millington watched and waited. On the face of it he appeared nothing more than the quintessential naturalist, observing the moorland fauna. No one would guess his sinister secret, nor question the direction of his tripod-mounted binoculars covering the open mile to the village.

Through the lenses he had watched Daniel and Jesse step outside with the poacher stooping to retrieve something from the floor and then give it to Daniel. A minute later they had disappeared back inside.

He had sent Demon Dog into the town the night before to familiarise itself with the scent its intended victim. It had later returned to the moor, answering the call of the Chancellor's whistle made from human bone. Despite the hound's great size it appeared from nowhere, and likewise vanished like a shadow, but never appeared before dusk. Daniel Bonner would have to be lured onto the moor at night which could prove difficult, and for that, Millington would require help.

Jesse had disappeared into the vault and was not seen again for several hours. Daniel placed an ear to the stairwell and heard the pillar drill at work but left Jesse to his own devices. Another hour elapsed before the stocky little poacher emerged with a satisfied grin. Daniel had all but completed the second and last coat of whitewash and was glad of the interruption, intrigued as to what his friend was holding.

'Well are you going to show me now, or is it still top secret?' And Jesse opened his hand. His palm cradled six small balls of lead shot no more than ten millimetres in diameter, and Daniel was puzzled.

'A bit of ammo for Viv,' said Jesse.

'And who the hell is Viv?'

Jesse went to the rack of hooks by the door and from his ankle-length bush coat, extracted a fold-away 4.10 shotgun from its designed pocket holster. It was such a neat packet that at first Daniel was unsure of what he was actually looking at. Then Jesse unfolded the barrel from its equally short stock, until the breach and block met with a sharp metallic click of oiled gunmetal.

'I give you, Viv.' he announced. 'Named after a certain barmaid I once knew; small in stature, but who could pack a real punch. When the weather was cold she used to warm her hands down the front of my shirt before starting her shift.' Jesse grinned wolfishly as he reminisced. 'We never stood a chance; jealous boyfriend and all that sort of annoying stuff.'

Daniel chuckled; it was good to hear things from the past when Jesse's life had once been normal. He looked fondly at his ruffian friend.

'Jesse, I hate to say this, but this creature is obviously something to do with the Chancellor, mere lumps of lead will be no match against it. Jerry found that out to his cost. I mean what have we been doing here for the last three weeks? Repairing the damage caused by a full load of assorted shot, that didn't even scratch bad-boy 'Bruinscrofa', let alone destroy it. And now you present six small balls of soft lead. We'll require much more than this old friend!'

'Look again, ugly brother.'

Daniel held out his hand and Jesse tipped the shot into his palm.

On the face of it they were nothing more than small musket balls, hardly enough to create overriding confidence.

'Look hard Danny, rub away the film of lead dust and tell me what you see.'

With the pad of his thumb, Daniel did as his friend suggested and exposed the eye of an alien material drilled through the ball like a pimento in a stuffed olive.

'Tusk?'

'Tusk.'

'You cunning bugger! What made you think to do that?'

'Spent time chatting with De Theiry on board the Azura, and after telling him of my gross worldly possessions, including Viv, he told me about fighting like for like, fire with fire, using the tusk against the Chancellor's emissaries. After all it worked against 'Bruinscrofa'. I've just invented a new round of cohort-killing ammunition, and with that toothpick of yours, perhaps we now stand some sort of a chance.'

With the dagger in one hand and Jesse's crafty ordinance in the other, Daniel nodded with a cunning smile.

That night the two friends sat in the shadows facing the shop window, Tobacco and Zip at their feet. On the window ledge sat 'Myths and Legends', and Daniel looked down at the book from where he sat. 'Certainly have come full circle,' he told himself quietly. He reached across to pick it up and Jesse watched with interest as he opened the pages.

'Let's just see if our little killing pooch has its own feature in the canine column.'

'That wouldn't surprise me in the foggiest,' said Jesse with a snort.

It wasn't long before Daniel had found what he was looking for. 'Blimey! I wasn't sure it would even be in here. But, Jesse, I've found it.'

'Read it out then.'

Daniel squinted down the half-page column, speed reading the highlights of the legend as he went.

'Come on Matey, don't keep me waiting.'

'It's pretty much as De Theiry said. The hound normally hunts alone, appearing from nowhere, and it is said its sense of smell is so acute, it can track its victim from ten miles away.'

'That's a sniffer all right,' chuckled Jesse. 'Perhaps I should blow one of my specials down its snot locker,'

'It is also said that throughout the ages, none of its victims have ever survived nor borne witness to its existence. Apparently, once the Hound from Hell is unleashed there is no escape.'

'Well that doesn't make any sense,' said Jesse. 'If there's never been a survivor or witnesses, how the flying shite does the author know this? Who wrote that book, Daniel?'

Daniel acknowledged it as a valid point. Turning to the front cover he looked for a name. In the flysheet he found Drew Theodor Llundorf. Ferry Coin Press.

'Well that's weird…never noticed that before. These are the same people who published my book.'

'It's all bloody weird, Daniel. Now if we're going to stand any chance of nailing this brute tonight, I suggest we shut up.'

Daniel replaced the book on the sill as softly as a landing moth, picked up the Devil's Dagger and reclined into his chair.

Neither of them said another word nor moved a muscle. They were natural hunters, and if they were going to get a shot or stab at the beast, they must remain quieter than the night itself. They took it in turns to power nap throughout the otherwise uneventful hours of darkness.

Eventually the light of dawn seeped through the window, and within an hour the sun had spread into the shop. Daniel stood from his seat and massaged blood back into his legs, and Jesse propped Viv against the wall.

'Typical! A bloody 'no show'!'

'It's a real bugger all right,' said Daniel with a much needed stretch of his limbs. 'Bryony gets back this afternoon…would have been perfect if we'd nailed the mangy mutt before she arrived. I really don't want her coming back to this. The Underworld leaves us alone for almost two years, and the moment we settle down the bastards send along another bad boy…and you know what Jesse? The more I think about De Theiry's warning, the less I like it.'

'Aw! For crap sakes, don't start giving me the fuckin' jitters now,' retorted, Jesse. 'I don't like it any more than you do.' He followed Daniel's gaze through the window with matching uncertainty.

'Coffee?' And Daniel nodded.

Charles Millington and Demon Dog had travelled the secret highway to the Chancellor's exchequer. The Chancellor was a busy man these days and detested the interruption, especially from Millington who had begun to irk him at the best of times. However it was in connection with Daniel

Bonner, and he was therefore willing to forego his pet hate and aid the project, as he felt he should.

'My Lord,' Millington began, standing at the foot of the steps to the dais, hoping for an invitation to ascend. 'It seems that Bonner is content with staying at home. We hunted him down on the moor, but he ran like the Devil himself...if you'll pardon the expression. Since then he hasn't ventured out. We need him in a place of our choosing, where there can be no escape.'

There was a whinging in his voice, and the Chancellor noted Millington's sandy hair was ruffled, his eyes round with uncertainty, chin unshaven and showing a distinct lack of confidence; a man who would much prefer not to be there, an habitual coward to confrontation whenever the Chancellor was concerned.

'Let us hope my boss didn't hear that analogy concerning his name, Mr Millington, or I might allow my darlings a little sport!'

The army had gathered in rows behind Demon Dog, and stood like a cocked avalanche behind Millington which did nothing for the mortal's nerves.

The Chancellor, with thumb tucked under his chin and index finger tapping his puckered lips came to a thoughtful conclusion. He changed his hand to the universal sign of a telephone receiver, and the crowded cavern heard a loud ringing tone, the sound so out of place it startled both human and beast alike.

'Hello, Bonner here.' Daniel's voice echoed around the chamber for all to hear.

'Hi honey,' replied the Chancellor, perfectly mimicking Bryony's voice, fooling the entire gathering, most of all Millington.

'Darling I'll be home this evening and I thought it's such a lovely day we ought to spend a night together under the stars at the Devil's Umbrella. I shall meet you there with a picnic and several bottles of our favourite wine. It'll be such fun. What do you think, baby?'

'Bryony, sweetheart I want you to come straight here to Delamere.'

'Aw don't be such a stick in the mud, the weather forecast is fab. We can lie alone under the night sky, my darling, and who knows we might even see our shooting star.'

'Bryony, listen to me…

'That's settled then my gorgeous man, I'll see you there, can't wait to be in your arms…I love you.' And finishing with a laugh, bright with love, the Chancellor clicked his fingers and the line went dead. He looked down at Millington who wore not only the look of surprise, but also the unmistakable edge of jealousy.

'You are not happy with my devious plan, my friend?' quizzed the Chancellor. 'Have I not delivered Bonner to the place of our choosing? Even as we speak he plans to journey out.'

'Sorry my Lord, it all just seemed a little bit real, you know, the 'darling' and 'I love you' stuff. Pisses me off. Besides what if Bryony arrives back early?'

'I have contrived a lorry to shed its load on the southbound carriageway of the M5. Bryony, although safe, will be stuck in a tailback for many hours.'

With his hand he beckoned Millington to join him on the dais. He leaned forward from the hot rock throne, until his face was just inches from the whinging human.

'So Mr Millington, if all that Daniel Bonner and Bryony Carter are building together pisses you off, then my advice to you, is to cease this infernal bleating and get the job done! Now fuck off.'

'Yes my Lord…sorry my Lord.'

'Mark it so,' said the Chancellor, and I the Scribe, did as was ordered.

'What's up matey?' Jesse asked, as Daniel returned from answering the landline. 'I don't like that worried look.'

'That was Bryony. She wants to meet at the Devil's Umbrella tonight, wouldn't take no for an answer. Christ, Jesse we've got to get out there. She has no idea about the hound. Are you with me?'

Within the hour, the two were on their way, with Zip and Tobacco blazing the trail. Danny held the Devil's Dagger as he marched, with his heavy arms swinging, the stabbing blade like a pendulum in his fist, his anger rising.

At his side trotted Jesse with Viv at high port across his chest. Not once did they let up. They couldn't afford to. They had to find Bryony and lead her out of danger, and the miles bled away beneath their troubled feet. Intelligently, Daniel swung onto a heading that would intercept the most probable course she would have to take, from the A30, to cross the moor. But the further they marched there remained no sign of her. If by chance she had taken another unlikely route there was only one place to find her.

Eventually, in the dying light, the Devil's Umbrella loomed large, and it was only then that Daniel stopped dead in his tracks.

'Hang on Jesse,' he said with slow deliberation. His League brother halted, drawing in breath.

'Aw shit, Daniel, I've seen that look before. What's up mate?'

'Where the fuck is Peter in all this? He's supposed to be with her!'

'So what's your point?'

'I've just remembered that Bryony ordered the telephone to be re-connected, but that isn't due to happen until the middle of next week. It's a trap Jesse, and we're the fuckin' bait.'

'Aw shit!'

'Right, Jesse, we have no choice but to get to the Umbrella, light a bloody big fire and place our fat backsides against the fuckin' wall.'

'You're swearing rather a lot Daniel…something fuckin' bugging you?'

As the men began the dash, their snorts of somewhat juvenile laughter could be heard from a distance. Demon Dog took in the scent and sounds of the running humans through its ears and wet snout, homed in and took up the pursuit.

Jesse had no sooner lit a fire when Tobacco and Zip began throwing out their long-trusted warnings. Daniel was caught out in the open collecting wood as Demon Dog charged in. He stood little chance of avoiding the brute; it had caught him completely unawares. A lesser man would have crumpled beneath the weight, but somehow, Daniel remained standing. The beast had attacked from behind and had embedded its fangs half-way through his left shoulder. Mercifully, his right arm was free to snatch the dagger tucked into his belt. As his hand locked around the handle, he felt muscle and tissue tearing in his shoulder followed by a sudden numbness in his arm. Blood flowed in rivulets from his fingertips and down his torso as the hound attempted to drag him off his feet. Pound for pound, Daniel was outmatched, and in his fight for life, he felt his body being torn apart.

'Jesse!! Get in here and shoot the fuckin' thing…Jesse!!

'I'm coming Danny…I'll blow the bastard's fuckin' nuts off,' and as he ran he heard Daniel call again, with terrible urgency.

It was Zip who arrived on the scene first and without checking his courageous charge, latched into the Demon Dog's hindquarter and hung on for dear life. Tobacco, not to be outdone, went for the jugular as best she could, and Hell's Hound seemed not to notice. Each time Daniel swung the dagger the beast was ready, spinning its body away with a supernatural sixth sense, and Daniel knew that this time, he had met his match.

'I see death, Daniel. Your death.' De Theiry's words entered Daniel's thoughts as always, and his foolishness in refusing to heed the Frenchman's warning fuelled his anger, and gave him strength. He raged from the core of his being and bunched his legs, stomach and torso for the next lunge.

For Jesse it was a horrific spectacle. The beast was a monstrous wall of death, tearing relentlessly at his friend, who was fighting for his life in the dusk. The sounds of the beast, the animals and Daniel's grunts of fury and pain, were the ingredients of nightmares.

With trembling hands, Jesse dropped a cartridge into Viv's breach, and ran forward. He had to get in close for fear of hitting the struggling animals, and with little regard for his own safety, he lunged in. He slammed the muzzle into the beast's flank and pulled the trigger. Above all other sounds the deafening report seemed to still the night. Viv danced willingly in his hands and Demon Dog released Daniel with a bellow, and a pain it had never experienced before. Daniel, at last, saw his chance and swung the Devil's Dagger with all his reserve. The chiselled stiletto punctured the hound's colossal shoulder blade, and passed unhindered into its cavernous chest. For an instant the conflict froze, as if suspended in a still of flash photography, until the hound reared sideways to escape another thrust. It travelled twenty paces, suddenly aware that Zip was still hanging valiantly from its back quarter. In a single fluid moment it had the plucky dog in its huge jaws and without effort, Zips spine was crushed with an audible pop before being tossed high into the air. With an open mouth Demon Dog caught and swallowed Zip whole, as his lifeless body fell back to earth.

For Jesse the horror of the event was enough, but the loss of his dog was incalculable. His beloved Zip had died without a yelp. He was going to kill this monster or go the same way in the attempt. Utterly fearless, he loaded the dainty Viv and walked straight into the jaws of Hell.

Demon Dog turned to face the king of poachers, its eyes burning like blacksmith's forges. Undaunted Jesse advanced. The beast hunched its monstrous shoulders and lunged with open mouth, and in that instant Jesse thrust Viv against the roof of its mouth and pulled the trigger. Burning coals blew from Demon Dog's eyes as the shard of 'Bruinscrofa' tusk found the very engine of its being, and the beast crumpled to the ground.

Jesse stood over the carcass, panting with rage as he loaded another round. But before Viv could jump again, the mound began disintegrating until all that remained was a thick blanket of dust in the centre of which, lay a pathetic little bundle. Jesse picked Zip's broken body from the ash and with it cradled in his arms, Daniel watched him walk slowly and silently onto the moor, to place his dog into a grave.

Tobacco wouldn't leave Daniel's side and with legs limper than overcooked pasta, Daniel collapsed to the ground bleeding heavily. With a trembling hand he stuffed his fingers into the wounds to staunch the flow, and with a moan coming from the core, his world went out like a light.

From high on the ridge above the Umbrella, Charles Millington stared incredulously onto the battle ground. This most definitely was not the intended ending, and for the very first time he understood the power of the evolving League. Without a sound he slunk bitterly away from the carnage.

Both attending plastic and orthopaedic surgeons agreed with the trauma therapist, that Daniel's power of recovery was more than remarkable. Within three weeks of hospitalisation, his wounds had healed sufficiently to enable a voluntary discharge. He was going home.

With all the love she could give, Bryony continued to nurse him back to full health, fending off the media's insistence of running a story of the man who had come in from the cold; the same man who had then gone back out to rid the moor of some wild animal, most probably the very thing that had so very nearly killed his friend, Jerry Green. Although no carcass was ever found the sheep mutilations ceased, and eventually, in the drought of further information, the press reluctantly faded from the scene and a degree of normality returned to Delamere.

Three weeks after the hacks departure, a bundle of young ungainly legs and oversized paws tumbled eagerly through the shop doorway followed closely by Jesse. 'Zip the second,' a present from Daniel and Bryony, galloped across the floor to greet them. It had taken Jesse almost a full minute to wholeheartedly accept the troublesome gift. When presented, a tear had appeared in the hard man's eye that no one had seemed to notice. Tobacco sat with a regal air as the puppy scooted round her, and yet when Zip finally lost interest and trundled off, Tobacco protectively followed.
Bryony had laid out a banquet in the shop on sheets of fresh white linen covering several workshop trestles. The League had assembled and for once was complete. They talked and laughed with wine and beer flowing under Jesse's rather heavy bartenders hand. Phillipe De Theiry sat at Bryony's side as they compared birthmarks. Daniel, on her other side, laughingly pointed out that she was perhaps showing a little too much naked shoulder, and that De Theiry, being a relative of incalculable title and age, should lead by example with some old fashioned modesty. Jesse, and a much welcomed guest, Jim Roland, booed when she did so with open laughter. Even Conrad Sweet joined in, as Florence Green sat prim and proper beside Jerry, who had at last found the commendable courage to visit.

Beneath the table cloth, Daniel held Bryony's hand, as he remembered another very special visit several days previously, which had allowed the League to gather free from threat.

Bryony had been absorbed in her latest studio work, as Daniel had pottered about in the vault as best he could, with the use of his one good arm. Light duties had been Bryony's firm order, but he was feeling stronger by the day, and the more he went about the normality of living, the speedier his recovery. But something most unexpected was to happen. As he wrestled with a large screwdriver in the execution of removing a hanging bracket, and with his back to the main interior of the vault, the Chancellor had suddenly appeared sitting on the end of the workbench. Daniel sensed his presence and with hair on his neck erect, turned to face his arch enemy. The Chancellor's arms were folded, with legs dangling nonchalantly over the edge, as if he hadn't a care in the world. His swarthy, dangerous appearance hadn't altered one bit since introducing himself as Tony Windrow fifteen years before, and not a single wrinkle marked his well-structured features. However, the way he had maintained his looks was hardly Daniel's concern. The Chancellor had obviously come to seek revenge, to exercise his power, to dish out his own style of grotesque retribution for the destruction of his demonic beasts? Daniel could think of no other possible reason, and that was good enough for him to search for the rage that had held him in good stead in the past.

'Good afternoon Mr Bonner. I see my hound did its work…in part at least.'

'Chancellor!' Daniel acknowledged his sworn enemy with a curt nod. 'You won't mind if I don't shake hands.'

'Not in the least.'

'I suppose you've come to finish what your dog started, to change into a fat bag of maggots with all that puss bullshit and teeth, to chew off my head under that foul smelling breath of yours. Well! Have I got it right?'

'You are not scared by that very real possibility?'

'Not anymore, no.' And within a blink of an eye, Daniel had crossed the ten feet that separated them and with a deadly thrust to the Chancellor's forehead, the screwdriver sank to the hilt between Windrow's eyes. It was a thrust from the soul, and deadly accurate. It was for the betrayal as friends, for Stephen Bonner, for Jerry Green, for Zip, and all that this vile-minded being from the Underworld had instigated. It was delivered with an overwhelming hate that de-sensitised what was otherwise a brutal act. Daniel gave it one last thrust to complete the kill and stood back. The Chancellor's eyes turned inward and upward to look at the red plastic handle between his eyes as if he hadn't understood the murderous drive. Then he began to laugh.

'Do you honestly believe you can destroy me, Mr Bonner?' With a smile he gripped the handle and slowly extracted the blade with a sickening squelch. The entry hole closed, faded then disappeared as if it had never happened.

'It might be a surprise to learn that I'm here to congratulate you,' said the Chancellor, gently rubbing the ticklish spot between his trim eyebrows. 'Had a chat with the big boss, and believe it or not he's rather impressed with you and your merry little band. He has granted your freedom. There shall be no further dealings with my office. You are free to live your life as you see fit. If I didn't know better, I would believe the Devil actually likes you. Personally, I find it all terribly irksome.'

Daniel's jaw moved a fraction, the only indication of his startled emotions. This was not what he expected and it rendered him momentarily speechless. He found his voice.

'Is this a trick, all part of the great game?' he accused.

'Not in the least Mr Bonner. It's like I told you, you're free. Thought I'd come and tell you in person. You shall soon come to realise it's the truth. Once again congratulations.' His tone was relaxed, almost convivial.

For a split second, Daniel remembered the good old days when Tony Windrow had been Daniel's friend and mentor, and a flash of regret momentarily entered his thoughts. He slumped against the workbench, looked heavenward and closed his eyes. When he returned his gaze, the Chancellor had vanished.

With a clenched fist on his good arm, Daniel punched the air in triumph. He raced up the stone steps and taking Bryony in his arm, they climbed the stairs and kicked the bedroom door shut behind them.

Back on his dais the Chancellor instructed his scribe to write, and with a flowing quill it was written, that indeed there would be no more interference. Daniel Bonner would grow old as would Bryony stay young. She would watch him grow frail and weak as his skin turned to parchment, the bright fire of life wither, until neither could bear the agony any longer. With use of a talisman, Charles Millington would step in to claim his promised prize. It would be utterly unbearable for Bonner, and then, and only then, would the Chancellor return offering Daniel youth and one hundred years of happiness, with the woman he loved. All this he would give for the bargain price of Daniel's soul, an offer not even the founder of the League could refuse. The mortal had outwitted the Servant of Mammon, many of the Tarquill numbers, the thief of hearts, Charles Millington, the supposedly-indestructible 'Bruinscrofa', Vile Bird, the Buzzards and had slain the Demon Dog. The Chancellor would have his revenge; and Daniel Bonner would serve everlasting days in Hell.

And as instructed, I the Scribe marked it so.

Daniel looked on Bryony's youthful beauty as they cleared the party debris.

The others had adjourned on Bryony's instruction, to the Pink Pig. She had noticed Jesse's highly buoyant mood.

'You told him didn't you, darling? You told him we're free?'

'I told them all. It was if a great weight had been removed from their faithful shoulders, and you know what, little one, I have come to believe every word the Chancellor said.'

'Then take me to the pub to join them, vagabond man. I feel like getting drunk.'

'Not before taking you to bed,' Daniel told her with a highly lascivious look in the rakish slant of his eye.

'What about the others?'

‘Trust me, fuzzy butt, those buggers are well ensconced. And we are wasting time.’

‘Daniel?’

‘Yes.’

‘I’ve missed my cycle…I think I’m pregnant!’

Like a figure in quick-set concrete, Daniel was that man. He froze for long moments, before a smile capable of encompassing the entire world, broke across his face.

‘Oh my darling…words…I have no words that can describe…sit down. How do you feel?’

‘I feel like making love! And don’t spare the horses, my handsome man.’

As they entered the bedroom, the scent of honeysuckle wafted in through the open window, the evening sun warm and seductive across the bed.

As one, they sank naked onto the duvet, and with utmost trust of two people in love, they joined in every way two people can, wrapped in the balmy warmth and scent of a moorland summer.

‘What do you think’s happened? Why aren’t they here?’ said Jesse, propping up the bar, as he ordered a new round of drinks, with a crisp twenty pound note.

‘Leave them be,’ said Roland, through a telltale hiccup, ‘and allow me to take you up on that thoroughly fulsome offer of another drink.’

‘All right, one more before I break down their door, and drag them kicking and screaming to the party.’ And with a mighty belch as if to punctuate the remark, it was agreed.

An hour later, and with several more beverages awash, Jesse made good his threat.

'It's not the same without my friend and his utterly delightful damsel. I'm going to get them.'

Behind a chorus of cheers, Jesse left the Pink Pig and wobbled down the high street to rescue his two most favourite people before they were lost forever in their own private world. There would be plenty of opportunity for all that sort of foolishness later. But right now it was party time.

Daniel and Bryony lay in each other's arms without a word. With their union complete, nothing needed saying, and if ever there were two people more in love, they didn't exist in this century. They drifted into an induced sleep of lovemaking, until the tinkle of the bell above the door, brought Daniel to his senses.

'Told you they'd come back,' said Bryony dreamily.

'Bugger!' said Daniel, climbing into his towelling robe. A moment later he descended the stairs to fend off the friendly intrusion.

Charles Millington was beside himself with rage. Bryony had become his everything, his very reason for existing and with one hundred years at his disposal the idea of losing anything up to half that time, drove him beyond reason. Demon Dog was gone, and as the Chancellor had pointed out, it had been Millington's last chance to rid the world of Daniel Bonner.

Surprisingly the shop door was unlocked as he tried the handle, but he had forgotten the little bell above his head, as it sprinkled its bright tune into the room. However, the unfolding circumstance couldn't have offered him a better opportunity to carry out his intention. He was there to kill Daniel Bonner and coming down the stairs was the very man himself, unarmed, and dressed only in a towelling robe. Bonner's murder was going to be easier than expected.

Millington's very name died on Danny's lips as the .38 snub-nosed special roared in the intruder's hand. The soft hollow-point bullet smashed into Daniel's sternum with an audible slap, like the noise of a wooden mallet on heavy meat. The big man staggered then fell backwards onto the lower treads. But to Millington's superstitious astonishment, Daniel clutched the handrail and hauled himself to his feet, made the last few steps onto the shop floor and advanced. The .38

jumped again in Millington's hand, and the second bullet hit Daniel through the heart. And Daniel Bonner died before hitting the ground.

The first shot, Bryony thought, although startling, was nothing more than Daniel tipping something heavy onto the floorboards. With the second she recognised the chilling call of death. Dragging on her robe she fled from the bedroom, and tore down the stairs to find the only man she had ever loved, lying in a spreading puddle of blood. Without a moments hesitation she dropped to her knees, cradling Daniel's head in her lap. She tried to dam the crimson tide with her hands, scooping it back into the horrendous wounds, in a pathetic attempt to save him.

'I did it for you Bryony…I did it for you,' said Millington, but his words were lost, as Bryony felt the final shudder of Daniel's precious life force leave his body. Her stricken eyes looked heavenward, and the sound of anguish filled the room; the appalling sound of utter grief, in a sea of tears.

Millington, shocked at the outpouring from the one he loved, came to his senses, suddenly realising the ramifications of his actions. He dropped the gun and staggered backwards before turning to run. But he hadn't counted on Jesse's return or the single punch that dropped him unconscious to the floor, and swaying slightly, Jesse realised Millington's murderous act. With his hand clamped over his mouth, he stifled the uproar of sudden grief from his soul.

High on the plateaux where first they had kissed, Bryony laid the ashes of Daniel Bonner, into a pit dug by the attending League. They stood silently at a discreet distance as Bryony laid a posy of wild flowers into the grave, and whispered her final farewells.

'When first we kissed, I was born. When you died a part of me died also, but my darling Daniel, when we were together…I truly lived.' Fat tears fell from her cheek, splashing the posy. 'I vow to you now, my handsome man, that your child shall grow to walk this earth, tall and strong as you have done; forever a part of you. If you can hear me darling, then hear this oath.'

With spade in hand, Bryony filled the tiny grave unaided, and when done descended from the plateaux, without another word. She appeared resolute and strong, and high above the covering emulsion of clouds, a shooting star streaked across the heavens unseen. But Bryony sensed its fleeting presence, and with a tear remembered their time together under the stars.

She left the brotherhood to make their own silent farewells, but try as they might, they could not coax Tobacco to leave the grave. Twice Jesse picked her up and carried her a few feet, before she wriggled from his grip to lie like a scruffy tea-cosy, on the small mound of freshly dug earth. They left her there, and despite numerous efforts to later find her, she never returned.

The cell in which Millington had been placed was a Spartan affair, with a single blanket cot-bed being the only furnishing. Millington had been refused bail, with his case being automatically referred to the Crown Court. He had been advised by his defence lawyer to plead guilty which, in turn, would reduce the otherwise unavoidable sentence, especially as his defence hinged on the grounds of diminished responsibility. With psychiatric treatment and assessments, along with good behaviour he would probably serve just eight years or less. When released, Bryony would be his at long last.

As he sat at the end of the bed facing the door, contemplating his options, the Chancellor appeared silently behind him, sitting cross-legged at the other end.

‘Think yourself fucking clever? Eh! Mr Millington?’

‘Bloody hell you scared the shit out of me,’ shouted Millington, as he stood to face his supernatural master.

The Chancellor waved airily. ‘No need to raise your voice to me, dear boy, besides it is me who shall be doing the talking.’

‘Yeah but I got the bastard in the end didn’t I? Eh? Avenged your little beauties and all that. And when I get out we can complete our bargain,’ said Millington.

Then a thought suddenly occurred to him. ‘You’re here to spring me? You’re proud that I got him and you’ve come to get me out. That’s it. Well I’m ready when you are.’

‘

You're an imbecile, Millington, an utter fool? You assassinated Daniel Bonner when at his most powerful, when their love was at its highest level, unbreakable, unshakeable, undeniable. Even though you've put him in his grave, the love that Bryony holds for him grows stronger with each passing day, and I am powerless to change it. Had his death been through my little pet, you may have stood a chance with our deal.'

'But…' the whinging note in Millington's voice had returned.

'Shut up Millington, and listen! There exists a counterbalance to our calling; the spirit of humanity, of good, of kindness and spiritual belief with places of worship across the globe, to remind you mortals of that fact. Although done in different ways, they all carry pretty much the same doctrine which naturally I personally loath. However, it keeps me busy. If they didn't exist, and we held complete spiritual autonomy, there would be nothing to compare. Good could not exist without evil. We are matched equally. Admittedly the balance swings in my favour from time to time, when you mortals fuck up, but in the grand scheme of things the status quo remains intact. You have immortalised Daniel Bonner in Bryony's and the League's heart and because of that very reason she can never be yours.'

'The talisman! Give her the fucking talisman!'

'You still don't get it do you? Against such power the talisman is no more potent than a cheap bauble. You alone have masterfully seen to that.'

'Our deal!' choked Millington. 'What about our deal?'

'Ah the deal…you reneged and therefore must accept the consequences.'

'Oh God, get me out of here. I must find Bryony. I have to try.' And the micro-spasm in the Chancellor's eye flickered.

'I shall ignore that plea, and to whom it was addressed. However, the good news is, that I am indeed here to get you out.'

Millington looked into the Chancellor's eyes with renewed hope. It was then he saw the kindly look as given to a failed pupil, by a head teacher in a forgiving mood, an avuncular look, the expression of impossible kindness, that kindly terrifying smile; the smile of death.

Millington's attempt at a reply was instantly stifled by the Chancellor's extended tongue ramming into his open mouth, with any forthcoming words dying on the vocal vine. With bulging eyes, Millington watched the Chancellor's body disfigure into his true monstrous form. His jaws were open wide as his tongue pulled the hapless mortal ever closer, and the Chancellor swallowed Millington's entire body, as would a giant toad devour its victim alive, the distorted shadows on the walls enhancing the grotesque spectacle.

The Devil stood motionless, as the doors to the Library of Time swung on their colossal hinges, shutting the Chancellor out on the other side. He had listened to his report but said nothing; there was no need, for he already knew. It was all as written in the books from the past, present and future until the end of days.

He walked slowly down the never-ending path between the countless shelves, until he reached the barrier marking the present time of man. Stepping through, he continued a short way, before drifting up two hundred feet to extract the hard copy of his choice.

When sitting comfortably in the wingback chair, he tested the binding on the first page. He kicked off his shoes and tucked his chin into the neckline of his pullover. Not once did he look up, until he had read the copy from cover to cover.

'So, this particular game is far from over,' he said thoughtfully. 'It pleases me greatly for I need worthy opponents for my idle children!'

A minute later, he reshelved the volume with gold lettering on the spine, that read, 'Kennan Bonner, Son of the League.' And the Devil grinned.

Daniel Bonner stepped from the shadows and into a pool of light, in which a figure sat writing at an ornate, red, leather-topped desk. As he approached, his footfalls were soundless on the polished white marble floor, enabling him to close in unnoticed. Looking over the writer's shoulder, he saw the orderly handwriting laid by the nib of a gold quill on the heavy parchment. He began to read.

'The Odyssey of Daniel Bonner', eight chronicles, stranger than fiction, belonging to the age-old struggle between mortal man, and the powers of the lower world.

It was the strangest thing for Daniel, reading what appeared to be a concluding chapter on his life. He read on.

'As mentioned in the beginning, I hope to have done justice to these small but important chapters of incredulous tales, because for me they represent a time of great personal importance.

'The reader, whosoever it may be, may wonder how I am privy to all here written in the physical, spiritual and lower worlds. I am a servant of low cast in the great order of the Underworld. I am the Chancellor's scribe…Jerry Green.

As Daniel read the words he suddenly recognised his friend. 'Jerry!! It's me, Daniel…Daniel Bonner.' He rushed to his front to be seen. 'Jesus, Jerry, why can't you see me? Why can't you hear me?'

Jerry continued his work, oblivious to his once-living friend, ink from the busy quill concluding the final entry.

'No one had ever previously survived the 'Bruinscrofa'. Daniel Bonner was the only mortal, not only to live, but also to slay Hell's creation and do so much more. As for me, Jerry Green, the solution was simple. I was about to die, just another number on the butcher's bill. I had little option but to sell my soul in order to survive. However, the Devil is not the being that most perceive him to be. Often I sit with him in the Library of Time, an invitation of which even the Chancellor remains ignorant, and for good reason.'

'Like any employer, the Devil must keep his workforce occupied, lest they grow idle. He guided Daniel Bonner to the book 'Myths and Legends', of which my master is the author. It gave Daniel vital insight into what the Chancellor was about to unleash. It saved him on many occasion under Lucifer and Abdiel's varied protection, and for their different reasons, the story has yet to run a long and varied course.'

'So, with that revelation, I have almost reached the conclusion of this entry. But before I do, I wish to spare thought and love for my once dearest and closest friend, who sold his soul and won. Let him now find his brother Stephen, united forever in death.'

‘Jerry, for God’s sake, why can’t you hear me?’ shouted Daniel. ‘Speak to me my friend. Please don’t ignore me. I am lost and scared. Everything is fading to dark around me.’

The light around Jerry began dimming, like the final scene in a stage production, until all that remained was a terrifying darkness and an ominous silence that enveloped Daniel like a shroud, his final curtain call of life.

The Hall of Souls had fallen strangely morbid, as if in mourning for a fallen brother. Each end of the table was quiet and respectful. Both Abdiel and Lucifer had read ‘The Odessy of Daniel Bonner’ and knew of its outcome, and although expected, no one is ever really prepared

'So brother Abdiel, he was not the one!!'

'No, brother Lucifer. He was the forerunner. The one of whom you speak is coming, and when he or she does, I have a feeling, Daniel Bonner shall live again.'

Proof

Made in the USA
Charleston, SC
19 November 2013